THE
RAHAB
CHRONICLES

Life on the frontier of the Promised Land

A NOVEL

By Bill McClure

Comfort PUBLISHING

Contents

PART 1

PART II

PART III

Epilog

1400 years before Christ was born ...

1

Visit of the Spies

Two men burst into Rahab's apartment like a gust of desert wind.

The taller man grabbed the young woman with one hand going for her jaw, practically squeezing out her back teeth; while his other hand wrenched her right arm behind her back. In this split second, she could neither make a sound or a move. All she could see were those strong, penetrating, gray eyes three inches from her face. He was looking around, nodding instructions to the other man. The men said nothing, and made no sound.

The other intruder quickly searched her rooms for other people. Then he went back to the front window and, without disturbing the draperies, checked the courtyard beyond. No one had seen them enter the inn.

"Jasmine."

"What did you say?"

"Jasmine. This woman is either rich or has a good business. Smell that expensive perfume."

"Prostitutes sometimes have good business," the captor whispered. He was studying Rahab's face. She was registering fear with the little wrinkles between those beautiful eyes.

Rahab feared she was about to be raped by the two strangers because they were big enough and strong enough to do whatever they wanted. His grip on her face and arm was hurting her but she did not resist. Instead, she must watch for options.

"We're not here to hurt you," the captor whispered. "We only want to talk with you. I'm going to release the pressure on you, but if you scream or let anyone know we're here, you're dead. Do you understand?" He was studying her eyes and watching her little fright wrinkles. "Let me make this very clear: If you make a single noise, I'll kill you." He shoved her arm up her back a little more causing her further pain. "Do you understand?"

The 23-year-old woman was paralyzed in his grip. She could only blink her eyelids while trying to nod her head. Tears ran down her cheek. Rahab had never been so scared in her life. Cautiously, the iron grip relaxed a little on a trial basis. Then, when he was satisfied, he released her altogether but he hovered within an inch or two of her body. She could still smell the garlic on his breath and the sweat on his neck.

"Anyone else here?"

"No...No, I'm the only one here." Rahab rubbed her arm. He left white imprints on her smooth, tan skin. She touched her jaws with both hands — checking to see if she still had teeth. Her whole face was so numb she could hardly speak, but her mind was racing with questions: *Why would they break into my apartment and hold me captive if they just wanted to ask me questions? People come and go from my inn all the time, but they respect the customs of Canaan. What do these men really want?*

The intruders were young, rugged, outdoor people. They could have killed her instantly, but they didn't. There was something strange about them. They were not like the nomads who often visited.

"W-w-what do you want to k-know?" Her jaw could hardly move. Her mouth was dry from fright. Her lip color hardly showed.

"Just some basic information," the taller one said. "For instance, how many people live in this town?" Their travel robes were open, showing white tunics with ornate, Egyptian style stitching around the neck.

"I - I think the last census said we had about 10,000 people in Jericho. There are some farmers who tend to orchards outside. They're fruit growers and don't depend on us for anything, so they're not counted," she said.

This time the shorter one asked, "And how about your water supply. If the city is shut down, how do you get your water inside the walls?"

"It — I don't know. We have the courtyard well that serves the city. The King may have another source but I'm not sure. This is a 2,000 year old city and I've never heard of ever running out of water." Rahab sensed her first opportunity of defense. "The natural springs around here have always served our needs," she continued. "Let me get you a drink of the water and you can see how good it tastes." She looked into the tall man's eyes for permission. He nodded his approval but followed her closely into the cooking area. She must figure this out.

While she poured two mugs of water, she moved into her element. "This is what makes Jericho such a nice place and keeps the area green. We have no water problems. If there is an underground stream, I don't think it has been used in many years. We're a peaceful people. We mean no one harm."

The men gulped down their first mug of water and she poured them another. She had never seen such clothes or mannerisms as these two strangers. She could tell they were civilized and wealthy. They wore a dark blue border was at the bottom of the tunics. Only the rich could afford such a color.

"Why are you starring at us? I told you we were not here to hurt you." The taller one was all business. "We only had to make sure this was a safe place. We thought the guards in the courtyard wouldn't notice strangers coming into an inn. That's why we chose this place. We must talk safely." The intruder seemed to relax a little. "Woman, where are your government facilities? Where are the King's residence and his council rooms?"

"I've never been asked that before. But they're straight back opposite the big gate. On the second level. Anyone can see." Rahab noticed a nagging feeling welling up inside her. She was overcome by the feeling. Was it related to her fear or something entirely new? She only knew that she needed to answer the questions being asked. She didn't understand, but she was compelled to answer their questions.

"And where is your treasury? Where does the King keep his treasure?"

"I don't know. Close to his chambers, I guess. I've never seen any. No one talks about it. There's very little need for much treasure because the whole countryside is at peace. There are no warring parties. The King doesn't have to buy protection with these heavy walls and gate. The city has withstood all enemies for more than 2000 years. It's a very strong city." However, the city's strength was of no interest to them. "How did you get here?" Rahab posed the question of her own. "The Jordan is too wide and dangerous to cross this time of year."

"Look, woman, we'll ask the questions. We're here for just a short time and then we will be out of your life. Just answer our questions." The two foreigners were no longer threatening. The tall one left her side and stepped over to the window to peer into the courtyard beyond. "Tell us where you go to worship."

"Our gods are all around the courtyard. At anytime during the day you can stop and say a prayer or offer a food sacrifice to any of them. They are very convenient gods." She picked up her water pitcher and started to pour more water into their mugs. "The moon god is in the center of the courtyard on a pedestal to show her importance. Why do you ask?" She said.

The intruders ignored her question by asking another of their own. "How do the soldiers mount the walls to get to their battle stations?"

"Are you fighters?" There was no reply. "Are you blind? You can see there are steps and ladders between each group of apartments and a set on each side of the main gate. You can plainly see them. There may be others but I don't know about them," Rahab answered trying to cover her fright. These two did not act like robbers. They didn't act like fighters. With rich clothes like they wore, they certainly didn't need money.

"When is the gate closed? How many people operate the gate?" It was the taller one again.

"It's usually open during the daytime unless there's some threat to the city. It's so heavy it takes four men to open and close it. Once it's closed, it's generally shut for the night."

"Where are your stores?"

"I don't understand why you ask such questions. But the granary is on the north side almost straight across from my apartment. The stores are used only for poor harvest times and to trade with the caravans when they come along."

"And where is the nursery for your little ones?"

"Most of the babies are in their mother's care in their own rooms. The older children stay in the courtyard. Why do you ask?"

"We just need to know." He was interrupted by a rumbling sound. "What's that noise?" The men reached for their daggers. The tall one rushed to Rahab's side with a dagger in one hand and his other hand ready to go for her jaws again.

"That's the gate coming down. Strange. It's not yet dark. Something must be wrong for them to close it so early." Rahab was thinking: *What's going on here? Is it because of these two men standing before me? Or something else? What's that strange feeling running through me again? These men had the power to kill me or rape me, but they didn't. They have gentle faces. They're not savages, but they're certainly mysterious. They seem to be verifying information they already have. They must have been in the city for sometime. They might be spotters. Now, they're as nervous as I am. They're afraid of something. There's more going on here than I understand. I must watch for a chance to bargain with them.*

There was a surprise knock at Rahab's door that shocked everyone for an instant decision. Perhaps this may be her bargaining time. She quickly took charge by pointing to her back room and stairway. There was a second knock, a little impatient this time. As the men vanished behind the beaded curtain, she turned to the front and opened the door. As a gracious hostess, she politely asked, "Y-e-s?" There was a lilt in her voice.

Guards Arrive

Several guards stood peering past her into the house, but in true Eastern custom, the men would not enter a woman's house without being invited. They said, "Rahab, are you all right?"

"Why, yes, of course," she replied. "Nice of you to ask." The guards were watching the beaded curtain move. "I -I was just in the back." Then she turned and pointed to the moving curtain.

"Rahab, those two men who came to see you are spies. They're armed and dangerous. We've been ordered to arrest them and take them to the King."

She gasped and placed her right hand over her mouth. "Spies? Who are they spying for?"

"We're not sure yet, but most likely for that group of escaped slaves across the Jordan. The ones that killed everybody two years ago when they took over Moab. The King thinks these men may be gathering information so they can come capture Jericho. Maybe burn it down. Now, where are the spies, Rahab?"

Capturing Jericho would be different than the cities in Moab. Jericho had defenses that no other city had. No one could ever capture Jericho. On the other hand, if the band of strangers actually had that mysterious power to take the city, what difference would two men make? Of what consequence would be her answers?

"I'm sorry. Your news is shocking. I was lost in thought."

"Rahab, we must ask you to bring out the strangers, or let us come in and get them," they said firmly.

That strange feeling she had earlier now surged through

Rahab's entire body. *Should I expose the strangers and get it over with or should I protect them? Should I help them or have them killed? The men could have killed me instantly but they didn't. They already had some answers to their questions. They were only using me to confirm what they had gathered. My answers were of no consequence to them. They didn't come here to get my answers. They must have come for some other reason. Perhaps to give me a message. I don't understand this. These are not mad men. They have gentleness about them. There is more to their visit than I understand right now. There is more to this than just two spies coming to my door. I feel so strange .... I know what I must do.*

"The ... the men are not here," she lied. "They just came in, asked for a drink of water and left. I don't know where they went."

"Rahab, are you sure about this? These men are dangerous. They could be from that murderous group across the river," one of the guards said.

"I don't know if the men just here are spies or not. I have many visitors who come to stay here. I'm not in a habit of asking guests where they come from or where they're going. In my business you can understand that. I didn't ask these two men either. They just came to the door, I gave them a drink of water and they left. See, here are their mugs." And she pointed to the water mugs in the cooking area. One of the guards leaned in to see into her cooking area.

"I think one of them mentioned something about Gilgal, but I don't know if that's where they went or not. I don't know which way they went but they couldn't be far. If your guards left now, they could probably catch them."

The two guards in front who had been questioning her turned to each other. "She seems to be safe enough."

"She has always been helpful before."

"Her story seems reasonable. After all this is an inn and the water mugs verify her story."

"Thank you, Rahab. You've been helpful. We'll be on our way. But if you need any help be sure to call out."

"Oh, you can count on that. Let me know what you find out there. Please come back and visit with me soon" she said.

From her doorway, she could hear them rushing the gate keepers to open up so they could go after the spies. She could see some of the neighbors in the courtyard excited about why the guards were going from house to house looking for somebody. She heard the guards say they were going to search the road that leads to the fords of the Jordan; others in the group would continue to search the city. As soon as the guards passed through the gate, it was shut with a bang and locked for the night.

The late afternoon light had turned into early evening dusk with the beginnings of sunset. The guards would have to search quickly to be able to see any fugitives tonight. Rahab closed her door. She fell back against it and let out a deep sigh. She was trying to gather her wits and figure out what to do now. She took a moment, breathing deeply. Then gathering up her strength, she went to the roof.

Like most of the living quarters in Jericho, her place was built with a flat roof where people could sit in the evening and enjoy the night air; even sleep there when a breeze was blowing. Everyone stored things on their roofs. Rahab had bundles of flax as well as fresh peaches, which she had just gathered.

"You can come out now. The guards are gone. You're safe for now." She called to them and the men came out from behind some bundles of flax with daggers in their hands. They were ready to fight if the guards had approached.

Now Rahab was facing two armed spies. Her chief advantage was that they must be on a mission and must report back to their command. They were now locked inside the 30-foot walls of Jericho. She had the key to their escape, but they didn't know it. Rahab was now suddenly in charge. In a sense, she now held the spies captive. What should she do? Rahab decided to attack.

"I know who you are," she began; her voice level, confident and flat. She covered her fear by pulling her long hair over her shoulder and stroking it a little. The big collar on her thin robe covered her fast beating heart. Rahab had some experience in dealing with rowdy people. She got them sometimes as customers. She knew that the best way to hide fear was to look the opponents directly in the eye. So she laid out her case.

"I get the news from the caravans. I keep up with what's going on. I'm not dumb. You're the Israelites who roam the desert." She pointed her finger at them. "I'll bet you intend to come in here and somehow destroy our city. You want to kill us like you did the people across the Jordan. You want to take away our land. You want to take away our homes. You want to take away our lives. You want to take away our heritage. Why do you want to do such awful things? Why do you want to destroy us? What have we done to you?"

The taller man shoved his dagger into its holster and took a step closer. "You've done nothing to offend us, personally. You've offended the Lord God Almighty. You have idols in your city. Your people have idols in the land that God gave to our ancestors and they must come down. The Lord God said 'You shall have no other gods before me. I am the Lord your God.'"

"But these are our gods! You have your God. We have our gods. Why do we have to give in to you? A god is a god. Just look at them in the courtyard. See how strong they are. See how tall they are. And you can't even see your God. You're telling me to give up all of our pretty gods for one that I can't see, or touch? What kind of people are you?" Rahab had her hands on her hips; staring at them for an immediate answer.

"The God of all creation declares that He is the only God," the shorter man was speaking. "He proved that in Egypt by defeating every single false god that existed there. And He will do it again throughout the land of Canaan."

"We're not dumb people," Rahab countered. "We have heard how your God dried up the water in the Red Sea when you came out of Egypt. We know what you did to the Amorite kings just across the river. You're murderers! You're escaped slaves who murder people!"

She was beginning to raise her voice. The big veins on her neck stood out. She was turning angry. "I've heard how you destroyed their cities. You showed no mercy at all to those poor people. There was nothing reasonable about your madness. Nothing at all! Some of those people were my friends, my customers, and you killed them! You killed my friends!"

Her anger was full blown. She was ready to go after them like desert wolves. Yet the men did not defend their actions. They listened to her. These big, strong soldiers stood like little boys getting a lecture from their mother.

Rahab took a deep breath and stepped back. She glanced across the roof to the courtyard beyond. Then she turned back to them and in a calmer voice said, "When we heard what your people did to the Amorites — how you raced into their land and slaughtered them, even the little babies, how you killed their animals — our hearts melted and everybody lost their courage." Her heart was racing, but she had to let everything out.

The spies both started to speak and then withdrew. "You just moved into the land and took over the entire plains across the Jordan." Her thoughts wouldn't come fast enough for her. Rahab's heart was pounding. Her lungs were burning as if she had been running a long ways. "How could you do a thing like that? Who would have the strength to do something like that? Is it your strange powers?"

"We have no power of our own. It is the power of God that gives us victories. God gave us the land of Moab to rid it of idols and sinful practices. God doesn't want people to be sacrificing babies to false gods. God has overcome the false gods." The taller one was looking directly at Rahab. "We are strong because God is strong. That's the sum of it all."

"Your God must be the God of everything! Heaven, earth; everything," said Rahab.

"And the God of everyone," said the shorter spy. "God hears everyone who calls on His name. Remember that. God hears everyone who calls on His name."

Rahab began her plea. "I've got to confess, our people are all so afraid of your people. It's because of your power – your God. All the people of this country are melting in fear of you. We hear how strong your army is." She was nervous and as she tried reasoning out what to do, she started pacing. First, looking at the floor and then at the sky, but mostly directly into their faces. Eye to eye.

The shorter spy used his outer robe to polish the handle of his dagger. Then he placed it in the holster at his waist. "We serve God. We are God's army. We do what God says to do. We are on His mission. That's why we came to you. God showed us the way to your door. We give Him glory and honor for the blessings He extends to us."

She was reasoning to herself. Her voice grew quiet. "Me? I don't understand. Why would your God have anything to do with me? Our gods never give directions. They never help us win battles even when little babies are sacrificed to them. I don't know why or how, but your God is far stronger than our gods."

The thoughts were spilling out of her like water from a jug. "I've been wondering how to learn more about your God," her voice trailing off; now almost a whisper. "But no one here knows anything about an invisible God. All I learn is from the caravans. Oh, that we had a god like your God."

In a sudden surge of adrenaline, her fist came down hard on

the table, rattling the dishes. It shocked both of the strangers. There was fire in her eyes again. "Oh, that we had a god like your God!" She repeated the phrase to all of heaven.

She turned away from them. Tears were coming to her eyes. Her hands were shaking. She didn't like to be seen like this. She felt like her body was filled with ice. She was shivering from the inside out. She was carrying the burden of fright and anger as if they were burning coals in her mind, but at the same time, freezing her tongue. She was pleading without thinking. Something else was directing her words. The strange feeling had encompassed her body again. Then she turned back to them, pouring out her soul.

"Please, please. Swear to me," Rahab was begging them with crying eyes and heart. "By your Lord, please don't kill my family!" She was holding her nervous hands against her cheek bones. Sobbing between her fingers. "Just as I have spared your lives just now, please spare our lives. I pray you to give me a sign that you will spare the lives of my father and mother, my brother and sisters and their servants. Save us from death." She pleaded with them; her cheeks covered with tears of desperation. She was on her knees before them, looking up into their eyes, releasing her last ounce of persuasion. She was pleading with them, crying out to them with all her barren soul.

The two young men looked at each other and then back to her and both reached down to help Rahab back to her feet. Now it was their turn. They held her life in their hands once again.

"Very well," the tall one began slowly and quietly. "You have done a good thing here." He paused, looking at her before making his decision. Then he said, "Our lives for your lives. If you don't tell what we're doing, we'll treat you kindly and faithfully when the Lord gives us the land."

A measure of new life began to creep into her veins. She held her cheeks and chin in both of her trembling hands. She was so weak she had to sit down. She didn't have enough strength to stand. Her body was so nervous she was shaking all over. There was a space of silence for her to recover.

"But first," the shorter one said, "we must be able to leave Jericho."

The men, too, were nervous because guards were now looking for them both outside and inside the walls of the city. The heavy gates were shut. They began searching for a way to escape. Was there another gate? Could they find some rope to repel off the high wall? Was there a tunnel, a secret passage? They were talking among themselves about different possibilities.

"I have an idea," Rahab offered. She dried her face with her hands. She was not finished with her plea — her proposition.

"What's that? They both asked at the same time.

In measured tones, she made them an offer. "By your word that you will save me and my family, I think I know of a way you can get out of here."

The two strangers looked at her in silent agreement.

Plan of Escape

"As you can see, my apartment is built into the wall. There is a back window in my sleeping room. It's your best chance." Rahab got a long rope she had woven from dried palm leaves. She gave it to one of the spies and the three of them went down to her sleeping room. On the way down, the shorter man kept pulling on the rope, testing it for strength.

Rahab lit her oil lamp and placed it on the bedside table like she always did. However, one of the men quickly moved it to the floor behind a storage box so there was no direct light in the room. Only then did the two open the shutters and look outside. The sunset was gone and darkness was settling in. There were stars shining in the clear night, but the moon had not yet made its debut. The men could see no one moving among the palm trees. They watched for several minutes and then agreed it was safe. They would chance it.

"See that beam along the ceiling? Throw this end of the rope over the beam and then tie it off. Throw the other end out the window. It should almost reach to the ground." Rahab gave the orders.

The taller man threw it over the beam and quickly tied a knot and threw the other end out the window. The window was small: Taller than wide, typical of fortress construction.

"Hurry, go to the hills northeast of here, so the guards won't find you. They will be looking towards the river for you. Hide yourselves in the caves for three days until the guards return. Then go on your way. You'll find fruit in the trees and vegetables in the ground. You won't starve," she was whispering.

The taller man took a wide scarlet cord from his inside pocket and placed it into Rahab's quivering hand. "Here, take this cord and tie it to the shutters of your window. The oath we have sworn won't be binding unless we can see this cord when we return to take the land. When you see our army, bring all of your family and servants into your house. Everyone in the courtyard will be killed. Do you understand?"

She nodded; tears still on her cheeks.

"When the Lord gives us the city, we will pass over your house and then save your family." He was looking at her with great measures of confidence. "But, if you tell anyone what we're doing, we'll be released from this oath. Is that clear?"

Rahab nodded her head in understanding.

The man with the broad shoulders looked at the window and stepped up on a little bench. He tried to squeeze through, but he couldn't make it. He tried first one shoulder and then the other, but couldn't get through the window. He tried placing his head first and then his feet first, but he couldn't get through the opening that way either. Desperation was welling up inside him. His friend might have to go alone.

His friend was watching. If the time had not been so desperate the situation would have been humorous. "Let's try one more thing. Take off your robe and your holster. Let's place some grease on the sides of the window and you try it one more time."

Rahab had some face cream that she secretly used at night. She reached for the jar and rubbed some on the stones in the opening. The tall man dropped his robe and holster to the floor. He did look thinner in just his tunic.

This time he stuck one arm out to catch the rope and the other hand on the stone sides to guide him. He turned on his side. His head and one shoulder were through the window and he carefully wiggled the rest of his body. He was squirming and gritting his teeth. He was hurting, but he didn't complain. He began to bleed as he scrapped his right side on the ledge. But he kept inching out the narrow opening, making his body fit. Finally, he could slowly squeeze his hips out the window. He was in great pain but he remained silent and determined. At last he was hanging onto the rope and standing on the window ledge. He took a deep breath. He was free of the window. With his feet, he pushed away from the great wall of Jericho and repelled down into the darkness. His friend carefully wrapped the dagger and holster in his robe and dropped them into the outside blackness. There was no sound.

Then the second man easily slid through the window. He held the rope in his hands, with his feet against the mighty Jericho wall. With his face close to the window, he looked at Rahab one more time. "Tell me your name," he gently asked.

"Rahab," she answered in a single word.

"My name is Salmon." He seemed about to say something else, but didn't. He only pushed away from the wall with his feet and slid down the rope. She watched as the rope tightened and strained as he pulled against it and then relaxed with each repelling action. One, two and three times the rope strained and then it fell loose. It was swinging freely in the night air.

The evening was quiet. It was as though nothing had happened. Methodically and thoughtfully Rahab pulled the rope back through the window. She closed the shutters, untied the knot and took the rope back to the roof.

A Realization

Halfway down the steps to her sleeping room, Rahab lost her balance and almost fell. She was tired. She was suddenly exhausted. She was drained emotionally. She was so weak in her knees and lower back she had to stop. Her hands began to shake. Carefully, she crept down the stairs like a very old woman.

Then it hit her. "Oh, my God, what have I done? What's the matter with me? What have I done?" She opened her fist that carried the scarlet cord. She stared at it for the first time. She stared at it through glassy, misty eyes. She shook her head trying to clear her mind. She squeezed the blood red cord again, testing to see if it were real.

"What have I done?" She cried. "What have I done? Oh, God, what's wrong with me?" She had discovered a monster. The monster was inside her. "I'm a traitor! I've committed treason!"

She clamped her face between her two sweaty palms. She must reason this out. "I've committed treason against my King! I've done a horrible thing. I've lied. I hid two men I don't even know. I don't know how they got here. I don't know where they're going. I know nothing about them. I only know that I lied and the two men I lied about are going to get their soldiers. They're going to crush my city. My city, my friends, everybody is going to die because of what I've done! I've done a horrible thing! I'm a traitor! Oh, God, what have I done? This morning I was a happy person. Tonight, I sit here a traitor about to die!"

She sat there a long time, sobbing into her hands. All evening she has been tied up in fear she couldn't show. Now it was erupting from inside her like a volcano. She had seen herself as coy; a negotiator; a bargainer, but now the oath was a millstone around her neck. A terrible pestilence on her shoulders. A plague that she spreads with every breath. A plague that will destroy the city, and she is forbidden to warn anyone.

What could she do? What should she do? All her friends were about to be murdered and she can't tell them because she had sworn that selfish oath! Oh, the tragedy of knowing the future!

If the King found out Rahab had lied to protect the strangers, he would kill her. If the strangers didn't keep their word, she would die at the hands of the invaders like everyone else. There was nothing in writing. She didn't even know if they would make it back to their commander. Would the spies be able to cross the stormy river? Would their commander honor their oath? Questions were tearing at her insides. She was filled with doubt.

She felt so tiny, sitting on the steps. She sat like a statue, frozen in one position. Slowly, calm began to seep back into her body. The mix of arrogance and fright evaporated. Reasoning returned.

In a quiet moment, her soul reasoned there was still a possibility of salvation. If the King doesn't find out, and if the spies make it back and if the commanders accept the unwritten oath, her family might be spared from the slaughter that was sure to come. Rahab's life was suddenly one big IF.

Her heart began to plead, "Oh my Lord, if I could just die and save my family and the city!" She held her face in her trembling hands. Her heart was exploding in anguish. Her face was drained of its tears.

The Lord heard her cry, but Rahab was not ready for his answer. There was a better solution available; a better blessing for the woman with the scarlet cord.

2

Search for the Spies

Rahab was still creeping down the stairs with the lamp in her hands, when there was a knock on her front door. It was her mother's knock. She had too much to sort out in her mind for company. Especially Mother. After her knock, Mother walked right into the main room and said, "I thought we were going to have tea today."

"I'm sorry Mother; I just don't feel well today. I'm not good company."

"What's wrong, dear? You look like something has happened to you. You're so pale — like you have been frightened out of your skin. Dear, what has happened?

"You sound just like a mother," Rahab snapped back. They were use to trading barbs. Then she smiled and her mother smiled and they were on even footing. Rahab sank into the cushions and pulled her feet up under her. "I don't know. Just run down. A little depressed. It must be the weather. My arms and legs are just not connected to my brain today."

"Well, I don't think even my herbal tea will fix that. You do look pale. Have you been eating any strange food?" And mother eased herself onto a bench opposite her daughter.

"No."

"Have an upset stomach?"

"No."

"Are you close to your period?"

"No."

"Are you in love?" And she smiled a little. It was that sheepish little grin that was distinctively Mother.

"No. I haven't seen anyone to fall in love with. Where am I going to find a handsome prince in Jericho? And you don't want me to ride off with some camel jockey in a caravan."

"I think what you really need is a good boy friend. I'm going to tell your brother to find one for you. There is probably at least one handsome prince in all these young men in Jericho. You just need a tonic and then to be out among some fun loving young people. You work too much."

"Now you *are* sounding like a mother." Rahab reached over and hugged her. "But I don't want Olmad finding me boy friends. I'll do my own looking."

"Your brother is three years older than you and has been married long enough to give me two wonderful grandchildren. So, I imagine he has some tips to share with you. Dear — oh, how does a mother say things like this?"

"You have never had a problem in speaking your mind before. So, Mother, just give your advice like you always do." Rahab smiled.

"Dear, there is a difference — a big difference — in serving men and loving them. When you are working here, you only see their wants and their satisfaction. When you love a man, you see all of him: his wants, his charm, his frailties, his faults, his attempts to make good, his need for forgiveness, his hard work, his energy, his tiredness, his grief — you have never seen your father cry, but I have. It is a heart wrenching experience to see such a strong man to suddenly appear so humble. That is why I love him so much."

"Mother, when did Daddy cry?"

"The first time I remember was when his mother passed away and we buried her in the desert. We were both crying because we lost her when we were both quiet young. Our friends had to help both of us back to our rooms. Understand his crying was not out of weakness, but of love. Your father is filled with love for you and all the rest of the family. He is proud of your being able to take up a business and manage the inn here in Jericho. We are all proud of you." Her mother paused, and then continued. "But, you need more than work. You need the touch of a man who cares for you. Someone who has respect for you. Someone who will take care of you and give you sons and daughters. Someone to comfort you and hold you when all you can do is cry. That is what is missing in your life now. — Take it from an old married woman."

They both smiled and Rahab touched her mother's fingers.

"Can he be a camel jockey?"

"No! Absolutely not. He must be so tall, have dark wavy hair, be rich, and love mothers-in-law. I have to approve everything about him." She smiled.

"Mother!" Rahab hugged her mother.

"Oh, did you hear?" Her mother changed the subject. "The courtyard is filled with rumors about spies being inside Jericho and then disappearing. Have you heard?"

"Spies? I have been inside all afternoon. I haven't talked with any neighbors. Where would spies come from?"

"They are saying that the King is concerned that the spies might be from that big group across the river. You know the ones that took over Moab by killing every one. He thinks that now they might be coming here."

"Mother, if that were true they would have some awfully big obstacles to overcome. I think the first thing they would have to do is to figure out a way to get their army across the river. The Jordan is dangerous this time of year. How are they going to get their men through all those swift currents? I don't see how anything could happen until after the spring floods."

"You have a point, dear. But the rumors are still unsettling."

"I think that it will take time to find out if the rumors are true or not. Remember the time they were telling stories about a wild man coming through and spreading disease in the fields and we were all going to be poisoned? Most of the time, they're just gossip. I wouldn't worry about it now." She paused and then hesitantly said, "I hate to say this Mother, but I really am tired."

"Of course you are, dear." And she smiled her biggest smile. "I understand and I need to go anyway. But I do hope you get to feeling better. Remember the tonic. I'll check with you in the morning." And she stood up, pulled her gray shawl over her head and walked out into the torch light of the courtyard. The torches were flickering against the darkness, dancing like little stars on Mother's shawl.

With the door open, Rahab could hear someone playing the lute in the grand courtyard and a few people were singing. Children were playing and laughing. The courtyard was a happy place tonight, but Rahab was sad. She went back up to the roof and fell on her big thick sleeping pallet — her favorite spot for solving problems. No one could see her cry up here. It was private, but she could hear the sounds in the courtyard below. The music and the children's playing faded away and only the adult conversations remained. Everyone seemed to have an opinion about the spies.

Rahab was playing the events of the evening over and over in her mind. *Why would two spies choose me to get information? I don't know anything about war, or killing people. I don't know anything about murder. I think they already had their answers. Was there another purpose of their coming to me other than the questions? I wonder if I did the right thing or not. Have I set a storm in motion or was it already in motion? When I let the two men out my window, did I do right or wrong? Maybe things will be more reasonable in the morning.*

God was listening to Rahab. But she was neither asking the right questions nor was she ready for the answers. Her disjointed thoughts ran through her mind over and over until her consciousness left her and she dozed off.

The next morning Mother awakened her by walking into the apartment and singing out her cheerful good morning chant. Somehow Rahab had wandered back to her sleeping room during the night. She threw the covers back and sat up, trying to get her gown untwisted. Her hair felt like a bird's nest. She was searching for daylight. By that time Mother was up the stairs and at her side. "Oh dear, I think I should have brought you black roses instead of breakfast."

"Thanks, Mom, you know just how to encourage people. Just give me a minute. I was still asleep. What are you doing up so early?"

"Dear, it's not early. The sun will be shining soon. Besides, I wanted to make sure you were all right. I'm worried about you. Are you better?"

"Yes, I think so. Just hungry."

"Here, baby, I brought you some date loaf fresh from the oven and some honey. It's your father's favorite."

"Thank you, I appreciate your offer. I'm just not in the mood to cook. In fact, I am not a mood to do anything. I think I'm going to stay here. I planned to go help Rebecca with the flax weaving today, but I'm going to stay home. Sorry to be such bad company, Mother."

"Dear, that's all right. Just let me know if you want anything. I'm just down the way and I had better get back there, before your father takes off for the sheep pastures. Remember the tonic."

"Thanks for breakfast. I'm sure I will feel better later on."

Her mother let herself out and Rahab remained sitting on her pallet. She saw the bright red cord on the table nearby and remembered yesterday. Automatically, her fingers touched her jaws to check for teeth and she looked at her arm but there were no signs of white splotches. Her body flinched as she thought of how frightening it was to suddenly be grabbed by that big man and how close he came to actually breaking her arm. How strong he was! How focused they were on getting their job done. Yet, how scared they were when the gate closed and they were locked inside the city. She tried to recall what was said but nothing came to her tired mind. She could only remember how funny it was to see the tall man trying to get through that narrow window where now the light was shining in. Rahab got up and walked over to the window and touched the stones on the side of the opening. They were still a little greasy.

Over and over, she wondered if she had done the right thing, would the men be able to get back to their camp and would their commanders accept the oath. Days of doom were on their way and Rahab could feel it across her shoulders. Was it right for her to keep the secret of the spies and hopefully save her family while the rest of Jericho was destroyed? Would this strange God of the Hebrews accept a person like her — just an innkeeper; just a prostitute? Why did the spies choose her out of 10,000 people in Jericho to visit and then make a way for some merit of salvation? Did they come to spy out the city, or did they come to bring her a message? Rahab couldn't figure out the answer to one question, much less all that were flooding her mind.

The King's Response

Needless to say, the King of Jericho was very concerned about the report of spies in his city. How they could appear and then disappear was a real mystery. A mystery he wanted solved at once.

His concern was that the spies could be from the Israelites who had settled across the Jordan River in Moab. For two years they had been building new cities — some with walls. But none of them were as strong as Jericho. But their great number was a concern to all nearby cities. They outnumbered the entire current population of Canaan.

The King called his counsel and gave three direct orders: First, post 24-hour guards in all the turrets. Second, send out spotters to key points within a five-mile radius around the fortress to see if the spies were still in the area. And third, interview everyone who may have seen the spies.

The Captain of the Guard activated a basic cadre of guards to mount the turrets and maintain watch 24 hours a day to protect the oldest city in Canaan. Atop the 30-foot walls the guards in the turrets could see for a very long ways. The turrets had convenient places to store fighting tools such as catapults, spears, hurling knives, and pots for boiling water to pour on the advancing enemy.

The captain dispatched 100 spotters with runners to selected points within the five-mile defense radius of the city wall. They were to report back late afternoon if they had nothing to report before then. They were looking for the spies and anything suspicious. They were investigating any clues from campsites, any people with them, and perhaps, determine where they may have gone.

The guards selected to interrogate the residents were sent in teams of two. In the interviews some residents told how tall the strangers were. Some reported they were short and fat. Some said they had long beards. Others said they were clean shaven. They were cute said some and others said they were ugly and carried big swords. There was such a divergence of descriptions, the guards were about to give up when they remembered Rahab.

When the two guards knocked on Rahab's door, she was still in her nightgown and barefooted. On her way to the door, in one sweeping motion, she pulled on a light green robe, slipped into some sandals, hooked two gold earrings into her ears as she opened the door and asked "Y-e-s?"

"Rahab, the King has asked us to talk to everyone who may have seen the spies yesterday. We need to talk to you for a few minutes."

"Of course, come in. Have a seat. May I get you some tea?" Rahab's auto defense system clicked in. By being gracious for a few minutes, she could find out what they wanted and find a way to get out of it without being suspicious.

"No, thank you. Just tell us what you remember about the spies." And the two guards sat down on the big cushions. Rahab chose the light colored bench because it went well with her robe.

"I am not sure I remember very much. I am not even sure if the visitors were spies. They were not here very long." Rahab was looking around the room. "You will have to excuse the mess here. I was not feeling well last night and I didn't clean up. See their mugs are still on the table."

"Don't worry about it. Just tell us about the men."

"There were two of them. One was taller than the other. They seem friendly enough. They were polite. They looked like travelers."

"Were they old or young?" One of the guards asked.

"I would say 23 or 24 years old. Both were about the same age. Good looking. The taller one was four or five inches taller than me. They had short trimmed beards. Oh, I remember now. The most impressive thing about them was their neatness. They had trimmed hair and beards. They wore clean clothes. Even their travel robes were rather fresh. They didn't smell so much, — you know, like people who have lived in them for weeks at a time. Their travel robes were unbelted and I saw their white tunics underneath. The tunics looked like they had just been washed and dried."

"Were there any identifying marks. Anything that would hint of their background?"

"Ummm, I don't think of anything. Oh, I can too. Their tunics were white and had an Egyptian-like design embroidered around the collar and there was a blue border around the bottom. I was attracted to it because that is such an expensive color." Rahab was looking at the ceiling in after thought and then became frightened that she might be telling too much. So she cut off her description. "They just came in and I gave them some water and they thanked me and left. I guess those are the people you are asking about."

"Thank you, Rahab, you have been the most helpful person so far. If you think of any thing else, please let us know," said the guard.

The guards reported to their captain and then the captain reported to the King and his counselors. Around the table in the royal chambers, the captain told those present that there were two strange men but he couldn't determine if they were spying or not. No one remembered them asking unusual questions. They just seemed to have come in, stayed for a short time, and then left. They were 23 or 24 years old, tall, clean, and well dressed. Then the captain said one important thing. "The two men were wearing tunics with Egyptian designs around the neck. And they had expensive blue borders on the bottom of their tunics."

"That's it!" Exclaimed the historian. "We have just been spied on by the Israelites across the river. They spent many years in Egypt. Egyptian slaves, in fact. And they made many of the clothes, pottery, even built many of the Egyptian buildings. I don't know if they are Egyptian or if Egypt is Hebrew. But the Egyptian influence dominates the Hebrew culture. So, if the men were wearing their own clothes — that is, they didn't steal them from someone — then they came from the group across the Jordan!"

Only then did the King speak. "Men, it seems that its time to begin preparing for battle. All these years of peace are about to come to an end. Let's gather the facts as we can. Let's secure the gate and not let any more spies in here." And with that, the meeting was over.

Fear and Depression

Rahab slumped around her apartment all day after the guards questioned her. Her mother's dish was still by the sleeping pallet where she had eaten her breakfast. The dirty dishes stayed on the table. She didn't brush her hair. She didn't wash her face. She was sloppy in her gown and that light green robe — one which she never really liked. And that's how she felt. She was carrying a big secret. She was worried that she had said too much to the guards. Rahab had a problem she did not know how to handle.

She didn't know what to do. Will the guards come back, asking her more questions? Are they suspicious of her? What if she accidentally exposed her secret? What if one of her guard friends heard her? She could see herself being dragged before the King and executed in the central court. As she would draw her last breath, everyone would be cheering because they had found — and gotten rid of — a traitor! Even her family would be killed; if not right then, because they had raised a criminal, then, surely, when the Hebrews came to take the city.

So, she decided not to see anyone. She just stayed inside with the draperies drawn and shutters closed and her hair a mess. She tried to reason with herself that the event had not yet happened. That Jericho's walls had resisted every enemy for more than 2000 years. There had yet to be an army that could force its way inside. The citizens were perfectly safe, as they had always been. Who could possibly change the course of history that had stood for 2000 years?

But the nagging thought that overrode all her positive self-talk was the fact that Jericho had never been attacked by an enemy with a secret power. There was little resistance by the Amorites across the Jordan. And they were giants who were strong enough to keep their cities and land from every enemy for many years. Is that the way it was going to be in Jericho? The spies were just men like every other man in Jericho. What was so special about them? How could the invaders be stronger than the men of Jericho? How could they possibly mount these tall walls and fend off the knives, spears and dodge the boiling water that would be ready for them?

The difference seemed to lie in that unusual, invisible God

they claimed for their strength. If Rahab was going to be able to handle this secret, then she must learn more about the Israelite God. But how could she do that when there was no one to teach her? Had the spies heard her plea? Could they send their God to her? She was still a basket of questions.

So, she washed her hair. This is always a sure way to solve problems and cure the blues at the same time. But it didn't help this time. Rahab kept a low profile and stayed inside.

In the late afternoon sun, the spotters began to come back from the safety net that the King had set up around the city. They told of no suspicious characters. They found no spies in the area around Jericho. It was all quiet.

"What do you mean no one is out there?" The King growled.

"There was no one threatening, your Majesty," one of the spotters was summing up their reports. "We saw a man and his woman crossing the plains with a sick donkey and they rested under one of the palm trees and watered the donkey. Then they moved on. We saw a three-camel caravan on the very edge of the watch area but they didn't come close to us. So we didn't expose our position. They were moving away from the plains into the mountains. But I don't believe there was anyone else all day. The area is very quiet out there. There were no signs of people camping, or of groups of people traveling."

"Then let's get the new guards out there and be cautious of everything through the night. Send your runner back here if ANYTHING moves out there that might be suspicious. I want to talk to those spies. I want to know how many men they have with them; how many soldiers are out there. They've got to have campfires. They've got to have horses or camels or something to ride. They've got to leave signs of some kind. Spotters don't just travel alone with no purpose."

"Yes, your Majesty."

The Second Day

Again, on the second day after the spies, the King kept the city shut down. He added more soldiers to the top of the walls. He sent spotters out to the mountain tops near the Jordan and placed more in a wide perimeter around the city. The spotters would be rotated day and night, so there was a constant vigil over a safety zone around the city. The search for the spies was intensified, but the spotters found no evidence they had ever been there. There were no campfires. No trails. No animal signs. Day and night, spotters had been watching the fords near Gilgal and no one had crossed the river.

In addition to searching for the spies, Jericho's mountain top spotters watched the Israeli encampment more intently for any signs of movement. They would not likely attempt crossing the Jordan until after the dangerous flood season. Every spring, when warmer temperatures melted the snows up stream in the Lebanon area, and especially Mount Herman, the river rose quickly and ran fast and cold. The flood lasted until well past first harvest. The Jordan was a collection of hundreds of rapids, waterfalls, very swift white water, undertows, and nasty currents this time of year. Anyone would be foolish to try to cross the river with an army, but the King was a wise man, and he took no chances.

The Third Day

On the third day, a 10-camel caravan approached the area without advanced notice. Normally, the caravans have at least one or two people who ride ahead and notify the cities and villages that they are coming, so the cities could prepare for their arrival. The advance people helped separate their caravans from the robbers that sometime masqueraded as traders.

Two of the Jericho guards rode out in front of the lead camel driver. "Stop by order of the King of Jericho. You're entering our protective zone. No one is permitted to approach the fortress without first getting our assurance," said the lead guard.

"What's the matter? We're just traveling through in hope of making a trade or two. We have some nice trinkets from the Nile, some spices from the coast of the Great Sea and perfumes from distant lands. We have many other things. Why do you stop us?" The lead driver was curious.

"The King of Jericho believes some people plotting to attack the city and he is having everyone questioned before approaching. That's all. We need assurances that anyone coming near the walls doesn't mean us harm. Why do you have so many men with you?"

"We, too, have met trouble. Three days ago we were attacked by a band of robbers and they killed two of our donkeys and stole two of our camels with cargo. All of us were able to escape with our lives. We need to do business in order to recover." The leader was almost pleading for an opportunity to stop at Jericho.

"You can't stop here at this time. But I suggest you go just over that ridge to a town called Ai. They are a little larger than Jericho and can get you more business. Then when you have finished there send one of your men back to Jericho and see if our condition has improved. Perhaps the King will allow you to stop then," said the guard. And so the caravan was turned away for fear they might be harboring soldiers who could attack the city.

The caravan was reported that evening to the council of the King. And there was some discussion that perhaps the spies were among the robbers who had hit the caravan. That could explain the Egyptian style clothing - for the drivers had bragged about having items from the Nile. It could also explain their sudden disappearance. But the nagging question was why would they just come into the walls, get a drink of water and then leave? It just didn't make sense. There was something else going on.

Otherwise, on the third day after the spies' visit, there no important news. No spies were found anywhere within the safety zone, including near the fords of the Jordan, but the King was not satisfied. He continued the lock down and the search continued for anything suspicious.

Since her apartment was near the front gate, Rahab could see the men go out to watch for intruders and overhear them as they reported to the gate keepers. Still, there were no reports of spies. No reports of active intruders. The silence was paralyzing. The fear continued to grip Rahab's back bone. She felt sluggish with her secret.

That evening she pulled a black shawl over her head and went out of the house. She walked around the courtyard a little just to get some fresh air. There were not many people out walking. Most had already bedded down the animals in the courtyard and went home to be with their families. Rahab could smell the new hay and watch the baby animals, especially the lambs.

She looked up to the torches that were burning to light the courtyard. The torches had long flames that rose more than a foot above the holder. They would dance in the breeze protected by the great wall, bending and swaying in all directions. She watched the contrasts of shadow and light flit from here to there as the flames danced overhead.

She walked slowly around the entire courtyard wondering if the torch flames would be anything like the flames of a burning city when the invaders came. As hard as she tried, she could not get the bad feelings from her mind. Everything seemed to remind her of the coming doom. The secret doom had become a jagged rock in her heart. Tonight, the secret had moved to her throat making it hard for her to breathe and it silenced her crying. She headed back to her apartment. She didn't see the lovers holding hands, or the lute player trying to play a new song. She even forgot about the little lambs, as she took her secret burden home with her.

Just as she was opening her door, someone cried out, "Rahab! Rahab!" It was Jebuk, the town drunk. "Rahab, I've got to stay with you tonight. I have no place to go."

"Has your wife locked you out again?"

"Yes, she is a tough woman. She won't let me in. I have to stay with you."

"Come on in. I'll see what I can do. I have a headache tonight. You will have to sleep alone on the far pallet, and then leave first thing in the morning. No food tonight and no breakfast. Do you understand?"

He nodded his head. Anything was better than what he had at the moment. He was still swaying a little, trying to stand on his feet.

"What do you have?" She asked.

"I got out with these earrings. Is that enough"

"They'll do. Go wash your face and take the far pallet next to the wall. No one else is here. And be quiet tonight."

"I will. I will," he was muttering as he headed upstairs.

The next morning he left her inn at daylight.

After several days there was still no explanation for the spies. The King was taking no chances. They considered the possibilities of the enemy masquerading in small groups as travelers and slowly assembling around Jericho and attempt to take the city by surprise, but they found no suspicious people. Despite the harvest, everyone remained within the walls.

The following days were long. The nights were stuffy. Fear hung thick in the air, but no one talked of it. Like their invisible God, the mysterious enemy could be felt but not seen. Rahab sensed a big storm was coming and she couldn't do anything about it. Even the little children sensed something was about to happen, but no one knew when.

Everyone just waited.

And waited.

And waited.

3

Rahab's Prayer

The weeks moved on and yet there was no indication of any movement across the river. The massive enemy just stayed there, biding its time. The spotters on the top of the mountains reported how the enemy went about normal business of grazing their herds, harvesting their fields and continuing to build cities. There was no hint of invading the Jericho Plains.

Each day that passed was a day adding to the confusion for Rahab. Despite the long waiting time she knew that the city would someday be destroyed and she felt guilty that she had to keep it secret. She could never forget that she was a traitor. She had protected the spies. *Are the Hebrews actually going to cross the madding river, or were the spies a decoy?*

Rahab went back to her sleeping room to consider the events. She searched around the room, until she found the red cord and held it in her hand. Two men did swear an oath that if she didn't tell anyone, they would save her and her family. She couldn't think about being saved. She only worried about the band of soldiers coming to Jericho, ripping open the big gate, rushing in stabbing everyone, and then setting everything on fire. Because that is what she heard that they did to the towns across the Jordan.

Every night she dreamed about how the horrible day would come. Every night was one long nightmare. Every time she closed her eyes she could see men with spears jumping at her. She would close her eyes and see swords jabbing at people. She could hear the thrust of steel into flesh and hear the blood gush out. On other nights, she would see soldiers reaching into her chest and pulling out her heart. There was no sleep for Rahab. She spent the nights turning and twisting and beating her pallet with her fists.

How can you breathe, knowing that your city is about to be destroyed? These dark secrets inside you get heavier every day. It's a dull pain that begins in your heart, pulling you down, and then pierces through you to your back bone right between your shoulder blades. It's a twisting, thorny vine that wraps around you, strangling you with every breath you take. You go to bed afraid of the dark, for wherein lie the men and swords and daggers. If you do go to sleep, you awaken wondering if this is the day. Lord, where has my life gone?

Rahab broke out in cold sweats. She dreamed of the invaders spending their time sharpening swords. She could hear them in a contest of who could get the sharpest edge so they could kill more people in Jericho. She reasoned that the prostitutes would die first.

She lost her appetite. She became weak. She became pale. And since she couldn't sleep, she became irritable. Very irritable. The secret burden drove her to vomiting.

Mother came to rescue her from her sickness, but with all her guessing of what was wrong with her daughter, Rahab yelled at her. "Mother, I just can't take any more of this! Go home. Never come back here again! I don't want you around any more!" She was yelling at her mother. "Get out! I don't want your tonics. I don't want your advice. I don't want anyone here. I want to be alone! I want to be alone! Don't you understand? I want to be alone!" And with that she picked up a ceramic bowl and threw it against the wall and broke it.

Mother was frightened at Rahab's fit of rage. She rushed out before Rahab could throw another bowl. She had never seen her daughter so upset.

That night when the men came in from the pastures, Rahab's mother took the matter up with her husband and her son, Olmad. Rahab was in a bad way. She needed attention before she would hurt herself. Olmad promised to go see her. They had a good relationship and she had always listened to him. However, when Olmad knocked on Rahab's door, she only yelled back, "Go away. I don't want to see anyone!"

"But this is Olmad. Please, let me in."

"Never! Go away! I don't want to see anyone. Leave me alone. Can't you people understand? I want to be alone!" Then there was a crashing sound of something breaking against the door. She was not a good relative. She did not feel like a good person. Naked fear had conquered her soul and petrified her veins. There was not an ounce of goodness flowing in her entire body.

She went up to the roof and flung herself on the pallet and lay there looking at the sky. She watched the clouds change shape and move from side to side. She watched the bright sunny sky begin to turn darker and in the haze of sunset saw the first stars come out. She was just so torn up inside. She felt sorry for having been so rude to her family. They all mean well, but she must bear her burden alone.

So Rahab lay there looking at the stars in the twilight of the day. She was thinking this may be the twilight of the city or of her friends, or even her family because she never knew if the spies made it back to their camp. She didn't even know if their commander would accept the bargain they had made.

How can I tell you how gut wrenching this awful feeling of guilt and sadness, and anger, and everything else bad can eat away your heart and soul? It's like its raining inside you. And the cold, gritty, rushing water is tearing at your insides. And when you feel like you can't take any more of the turbulent abuse, then it begins to thunder in your head and the pounding headaches lead to lightning striking at your soul. No one can live in such internal pain. I must have died and they forgot to bury me.

Oh, Lord, I wish I could understand what is going on. Where is that invisible God? How do I reach something that I cannot see?

God heard her pain. He dispatched someone to help her.

The Servant Girl

There was a soft knock on her front door. It was a polite knock. Rather timid. So quiet, so patient, so kind, that it was irresistible. And against her feelings, Rahab went down and opened the door to see Olmad's servant girl standing there. The servant said nothing, but only looked up at Rahab and with the expression in her eyes was asking for permission to come in.

Rahab surprised herself by stepping back and with a motion of her hand invited the girl into her apartment.

"I've come to see how you are," began the servant. "Is there something I can do for you?"

"Thank you for asking. But no, no one can help me."

"Then you won't mind if I brush your hair. Sometimes that makes a woman feel better." This time without permission, the servant found a hairbrush that had been thrown to the floor. She picked it up and stood behind the bench until Rahab came and sat there. As soon as Rahab sat down, the thin girl began to softly brush the long black hair that Rahab treasured so much. The long, gentle strokes felt good to her. They were calming.

The servant began humming and then singing softly as though it were to herself rather than to anyone else in the room. It was a pretty voice – gentle as a breeze lost in the leaves. No words were spoken. Only the soft notes of a strange song surrounded Rahab. Gentle. Loving. Reassuring. Comforting.

The servant girl's touch of Rahab's hair was an admiring touch. She pulled the long strands from the shoulders and grouped them together and pulled them straight out from her neck and shoulders. Then the girl carefully brushed the underside of the long strains of black gold. Gently tugging against Rahab's scalp to revitalize it. "You have such pretty hair," the servant said at last.

"I don't feel pretty today. And I haven't in a long time. Olmad must have sent you."

"Yes. He is worried about you. He thought you might be ready for a gentle touch."

"Olmad is quite perceptive. He is a gentle person himself and always means well. But these days I am beyond help. But I am enjoying your brushing my hair. It's been a long time since someone gave me this kind of attention." Rahab was trying to remember when someone had been so kind to her. There was a space of silence.

As the long brush strokes continued, the girl began quietly and hesitantly to speak. "I will tell you a story. One my mother learned when we lived with our previous owners across the river. Before I was bought by Mr. Olmad.

"There was a person once who had a problem," she began. "A big problem. He couldn't tell anyone about it. He thought that the problem was his alone and he alone should solve it. Part of the feeling was that he was never good enough to fix whatever was wrong. When he was a child, he wasn't good enough to win at the games. He wasn't good enough in the classes he took. He felt he wasn't good enough at work. He was afraid to get married because he wasn't good enough to find just the right woman. He went through most of his life not being good enough. Now, he had this big problem that he must solve alone, but he was still afraid that he was not good enough.

"He needed help. He needed a lot of help. But he couldn't go to anyone and still be the only one to solve his problem. He tried going to the gods about it. He started with Baal. But Baal paid him no attention. He wasn't important enough for Baal. He took his problem to the moon god but she had no interest in him. He took it to the other gods but no one paid any attention to his needs. He felt he was not important enough for these gods.

"Where else could he go? The only other god he had heard about was the God of the Hebrews. But he knew nothing about an invisible God. All he could do was go to a private place. Somewhere where no one knew what he was doing. There he would talk out loud, so the invisible God could hear him.

"The man went into the back of his house and all night long, he kept telling his problem over and over to this invisible God. He talked while he was looking for a solution. At first he was afraid that someone might hear him, or see him, and think he was talking to himself. But later, he didn't care. He was looking for answers. Soon he began to feel better about himself. Perhaps it was just the still of the night, or that he had been concentrating so long on his problem and its solution. But he began to feel better. Soon he grew tired and sleepy. He lay down on his mat and fell asleep.

"In his sleep he heard the voice of the great God of the Hebrews. 'You are worthy of the tasks I give you,' said the voice. 'I am the one who formed you in your mother's womb. I protected you and caused your mother's body to provide nourishment for you to grow and have arms and legs and fingers and toes. I was the one who decided whether you would be a boy or a girl. I was the one who determined when you were strong enough to take your first breath of air. I am the one who this day gives you tasks so you will learn and grow even more. I challenge you to reach higher and stretch yourself, but I never give you a task you cannot handle. When you come to a closed pathway, I show you an open one. I am your God. I am love. I am the way. Follow me in love for other people. You are always worthy of the tasks I give you. Walk with me. I am your God.'

"The next morning, when he awoke, he felt stronger about himself. At least now he thought he could begin solving his problem. And once he began, he solved it. He gave the credit to the Hebrew God." Silence filled the room. The story was finished. The girl patted the perfect strains of coal black hair and then Rahab's shoulders. Then, without a word, she left.

In the quietness, in the peace that was left by the girl, Rahab sat for a while. Could the solution to her problem secret be as simple as the servant girl suggested? Rahab was as still as a statue. She did not want to disturb the peace that filled the room. Ever so slowly, she moved to the couch, curled up and promptly went to sleep.

Voices in the Wind

When she awoke, she felt so peaceful inside. She slowly made it up to her favorite place on the roof. She began to reason. These strangers across the river were said to have a mysterious power. Rahab had always wanted to understand it, but she never knew how. Now, she began adding things up. The camel drivers said the Israelites' strength lay in their invisible God, but how do you understand something that is invisible? How can you bow down before a God you can't see or touch? How do you make sacrifices to something you cannot understand? Yet, she sensed that is why she needed a god much bigger than anything they had in Jericho. She needed to share this secret with a power much greater than the whole city of Jericho. She must find relief somewhere for this terrible secret that had conquered her soul.

She began to try to recall the words the spies offered while standing on the roof, just a couple of feet from where she now lay. Besides the caravans, her only teaching about the invisible God came from the spies. They were in a hurry to make their escape. She remembered saying a lot of things. She accused them of a lot of things. She remembered how long their daggers were. How tall they were. How strong they were. How they were dressed. How determined, but the words were still a blank.

Finaly, a few words began coming to her again. "We have no power of our own." Yes, that is what they said. "We have no power of our own. It's the power of God that gives us victories. We are strong because God is strong."

How Rahab needed such strength right now! But she didn't know how to approach a God she could not see. How do you ask for strength? Is it just right out and ask or is there some protocol? Some fancy words? Some procedure? Do you have to bow down like a person does to Baal? She lay quietly watching the sky. She thought that the Israelites had to have abnormal strength to live in the desert all that time. They must have had some driving determination, some unusual ability to have been freed from the Egyptian slavery. The cities in Moab were big cities with strong fighters. Those cities would require great strength to be overcome. *The power of God gives us victories because He is strong.* But how can a prostitute in Jericho approach such power?

Another quiet voice returned to the roof. "Very well. You have done a good thing here. Our lives for your lives. We will treat you kindly when the Lord gives us the land." She remembered the words so clearly now. It was as though they were being said for the first time. She kept saying over and over, "We will treat you kindly when the Lord gives us the land."

The men did not mind that she was a prostitute. They didn't separate men from women. This was not a God for men or Israel. This was a God, they said, that would give them the land and they would treat her kindly. They would treat Rahab kindly. This was a new kind of power and strength to her.

She felt better in her soul. Her heart rate had slowed. She was coming to a new level of peace with herself. *You have done a good thing. We will treat you kindly. We will treat you kindly when the Lord gives us the land. The power of God gives victories.* Such strange words for her to hear again and again. She didn't know how important it was to save these two men of the Israelites. She didn't expect such a reward to be treated kindly. No one treated a prostitute kindly, but that was their promise. A fleeting thought raced across her mind: Could these two men have been from the Almighty God himself? Was their visit a message for her? *A message to treat her kindly?*

A tiny, soft breeze brushed through Rahab's hair and across her face. It seemed to blow words into her ears. Words that had a voice. *You have done nothing to offend us. You have offended the Lord God Almighty. You have idols in your city.* The Lord God said, "You shall have no other gods before me. I am the Lord your God." The Hebrews were not against the people. They were against the gods of the land. They were out to destroy the idols and the idol worshipers.

If she took the idols out of her life, would the Lord God be her God too? And then she remembered again, *God hears everyone who calls on him.* She repeated it just as the man did. *God hears everyone who calls on him. God gives victories. We will treat you kindly. You have done a good thing.*

Tears were in her eyes as she looked up at the stars. They were so far away. She was so alone. She felt so little. She turned over to her left side and pulled her knees up against her chest. She felt so helpless, so worthless. A little breeze swept over her, bringing a chill in the air. She pulled her robe closer, and she was not so alone. She had never felt so small in all her life.

Thoughts were racing through her mind like raindrops in a desert storm. Some of the thoughts were for reasoning. The Hebrew's power was a gift from their God. It was as simple as that. Obey God's wishes and you get power. The Hebrew God was able to change things and bring about good things to people, but Rahab was different and she wondered if He would do the same for her. Wasn't that the point of the servant girl's story? *You are worthy of the tasks I give you.* Why couldn't it work for her? Would God hear her if she cried out to Him? The spy said that God would. The girl's story indicated God would. This could be the hope she had been searching for.

Rahab turned back to the far away stars and words begin to slip from her soul. "If there is a God out there that is the power of the Israelites, will you hear me? Will you listen to my cry? If there is a God that can change things and bring victory in war, and safety to people, will you hear me?

"I can't see you. I can't touch you. I don't know where you are. But if you can hear me, remember me, O Lord, when you feel merciful.

"I may not be much of a person; — who could love a prostitute? We are just bodies to be used by men. But I am all I am. I am a person. I want to be your person. The news from the caravans tell us that the God of Israel was the One who created the stars up there and the earth down here and the people who live here. So, if you made people, and I am a person, perhaps you had something to do with my being here. Maybe you had something to do with those strange feelings that guided me when the spies were here.

"I don't understand. All I know is that I have committed treason against the people I love. I have bargained with strangers I don't know. I am fearful of an enemy attack that could destroy my city. And I don't know what to do.

"I don't even know what to say. I'm so frightened. On one hand, I feel so empty because there isn't much of the old me left. No joy, no smiles, no future, no friends. Nothing. On the other hand, I am filled with this big rock inside me that I must carry around in secret. A big, heavy rock with jagged edges. A rock that pushes against my rib cage, and against my backbone; that petrifies my legs and arms, that dulls my brain. A rock filled with a secret that grows heavier day by day.

"Lord, what do I say? What do I do? If the people come across the river and destroy the city, will they honor the agreement and save my family and me? How do I know that the bargain even got through and that the commander will honor it when they get here? Why must all be destroyed? Why do so many people have to die? How will it happen? What happens to us after they destroy the city? Is there something I should be doing to save the people here?

"Lord, how do I know if things will work out? How do I know that my family and I will live? I am so worried. I am so very worried. Lord, where do I find a little relief for my troubled soul? O Lord, I am so frightened, will you grant me mercy and save me?"

The Night Visitor

Rahab's lips stopped moving as she wiped the tears from her eyes and cheeks. It seemed the world was frozen. She lay there on her back with tears on her face, looking at the stars. The world was quiet. Not a leaf fluttered. Not a star twinkled. Not a cloud moved. Something was about to happen.

A little bird attracted Rahab's attention. Out of the orange-pink of the sunset came a white bird. A white dove. It flew across the courtyard and landed on one of the pillars that supported her rooftop. She had never heard of a bird flying at sunset. The dove was only a couple of feet away from her. He just stood on the pillar and looked at her. He was perfectly still. He seemed to be in no hurry to go anywhere. In his beak was a small twig of grain. There was something very peaceful about the bird. No one has ever seen a dove so white, so peaceful, so assured of himself, so unafraid. Then, it seemed, with determination, the bird placed the twig of grain on the pillar and flew off into the gathering darkness. He had brought her a gift.

Slowly Rahab got up, mystified by the encounter, and stepped over to the pillar and picked up the little twig of grain. It was wheat, the bread of life. Was this a sign? She didn't know, but for the second time in as many nights Rahab slept well. There were no nightmares. And the next morning she awoke to a sunshiny day. In the peace of the new morning, she looked at the sky and touched her fingertips together and said, "I want to worship you, Almighty God. In your great power and your great love I submit all of myself, body and soul. Please find mercy for my misbehavior and my little faith.

"Lord, help me to grow in your great love and be more like you want me to be. God, please give me strength to accept your will in my life. I pray for faith to remain loyal to your cause. Lord, please give me patience to await your answers and please forgive me for asking so many questions."

She bounced off her sleeping pallet, feeling like the sun itself. She felt so good, Rahab actually smiled while she pulled on one of her favorite robes, the one with the big collar of soft, pale purple. She added two ropes of gold chain and a gold comb in her midnight hair. Then she went over to greet her family with all the apology and love that she could gather. After all these days of worry and agitation, she felt like her old self. It was time to apologize and see if they would take her back into the family.

Mother was first to notice the change and early in their conversation said, "See, I told you a tonic would make you well."

"Mother, there is more to life than a tonic."

"Then you found a new boy friend last night."

"Not exactly. But I did find a friend. And I'll tell you about him some time. But right now, where is the tea and where are my date cakes you promised me? I've got some catching up to do." And mother and daughter had a good visit. It was old times again.

"Mother, I must apologize for the other day when you came over and I was rude to you. I didn't intend to be, but I was feeling badly. I was distraught. I was frustrated with myself. I wasn't throwing things at you. I would never want to do that. I was throwing things at myself for being so depressed. I was mean to you and I never want to be that way again. I love you and I hope you will accept my apology."

"My dear, that is all right. I just hope you're better now."

Rahab had barely tasted of the second date cake when Olmad dropped in and said hello cautiously. Rahab responded by bouncing into his arms, hugging the life out of him and saying "Hi."

His response was only that he was glad the Jebusite aliens had brought her back in exchange for that witch of an old woman they had left in her place. And they all had a good visit.

All the following days Rahab felt better. She still couldn't explain the white dove and the gift of wheat, but somehow she believed that the invisible God was going to take care of them.

4

Preparation for a Miracle

About two weeks later, Rahab arose early one morning to a stuffy house. There was no air in the room. She quickly washed her face and pulled on her sheer, light-blue linen robe. It was one she had woven herself. She headed straight for the roof. Even the outside air was thick and heavy. It was so warm and sticky that it hung onto the palm leaves keeping them as still as the walls that surrounded her. Generally, Jericho had very little humidity. It was a dry, arid land, especially in late spring, but this day was sticky and muggy and overcast: A very strange day. There was hardly enough air to breathe.

She was in a daze with her brain hardly reliable. She just dropped into the chair and leaned back, her frizzy hair spreading over the pillow on the back. Surely a breeze would find her here. She instantly dozed off, then jerked awake with someone banging on the door below calling out "Rahab, Rahab!"

She thought: *Don't they know this is a bad day?* It was her brother. From the roof she waved to him and called "I'll be right down."

They made some tea and went back to the roof in search of that elusive breeze. She just told him she was not feeling well. "I feel like I'm tied up like an Egyptian mummy."

Always an encourager, Olmad said, "Oh, now Sister. I think you look a little better than a mummy. You probably could shake off the mood if you got up and did some exercise - like cleaning house or better yet, cleaning my place." Then he flashed that mischievous smile of his and Rahab did feel a little better.

"Olmad, you can go clean your own house. But, while you are here, why don't you grab a broom and we can start on this one?"

Olmad didn't move an inch. He only smiled, and looked

concerned about her and her strange feeling. "I just wanted to come by before I get to work."

They sat there making small talk, expressing their feelings about their parents and siblings. Olmad and Rahab always got along well and enjoyed each other's company. They were closer than any of the other siblings.

"I want to ask you something," Olmad was studying her face.

"What's that?" She looked back at him.

"A few weeks ago you went through some sort of spell. I don't know how to describe it, but you were sick a lot. Mother told me you were even vomiting at one point. You were so bothered. So worried. You had all of us worried about you, but you resisted any help. And then one day it was all over. Is there anything about that you can tell me?"

"Well, can you keep a secret?"

"Sure. Whatever you say is confidential."

"My secret is that I do have a secret, but I can't tell you now. Perhaps one day not too far away I can tell you. I hope I can. In fact, I pray that I can tell you and the rest of the family, but for now I can't. I have given my word," She was speaking softly, holding his hand in hers.

"That's all I needed to hear," Olmad said, patting her hand. "But you know that you can always talk to me."

"I know, and I will. Believe me. Now, I have a question for you."

"What's that?"

"What do you know about the Hebrew God? Their invisible God has been on my mind a lot lately."

Olmad took a moment to gather his thoughts and then said, "Very little, really. A few of the traders have been in the Hebrew desert camps before they moved into Moab over there. They've done some business with them. Most of their goods have a strong Egyptian influence. You know, their pottery, jewelry and clothing. They looked as Egyptian as similar items from the Nile region. But they said little about their God."

"I have been told about how their God helped them escape through the Red Sea. He was supposed to provide food for them while they are crossing the desert. Our gods could never do that. Not even Baal," Rahab said.

"I wonder if he is still providing their food while they are camped over in Moab." It was a wandering thought from her brother's mind.

"That would be interesting to know. But more importantly, I would like to know how and why they worship their God. I am not sure about the advantages of having an invisible god as opposed to these we have in the courtyard."

Rahab was lost in thought and asked, "Can I share with you one experience?"

"Sure."

Rahab took a deep breath and then let it all out. "A few weeks ago when I was so worried and depressed, I was up here and was just filled with tears inside. I didn't know what to do. I felt so badly I started to pray to the Israelites' God. I didn't know what to do or what to say or anything. I just started talking and asked for His mercy on me and to help me. It was right at sundown. A white dove flew in and landed right over there on that support beam and brought me a little stalk of wheat. I feel like it was a sign from their God, because right after that I started getting better. An awful burden was lifted from me. It just melted away. That was the first night of good sleep I had had in weeks."

Olmad reached for her hand again. "That is when you came over to Mother's place and we had such a good time. I remember it well. I was so glad to see you feeling better."

"Olmad, I don't want to have anything to do with idols any more. I want to worship the God of the Israelites. I'm discovering that the power of their God is more than conquering, it's also love. Very great love. This is a whole new chapter for me but when I learn more, I want to share it with you."

"Of course. That's how we learn the most. I always enjoy our time together," and he smiled his big brother smile; the one where his eyes turn up a little on the outside of his face. He patted her hand. "I'm just so happy that you're feeling better now. I had better get to work, or I'll have starving children over there; and I might have to send them over here all the time." And he grinned, mischievously.

"In that case, I think you should get to work. I'll even open the door for you." The brother and sister stood up and started to make their way downstairs.

"Oh, by the way, there's a small caravan coming by later today. We're going to meet them outside the gate. Do you want anything? I can look for some Hebrew religious material." Olmad said.

"Thanks. That would be great." Rahab opened the door for her brother and he walked past the idols in the courtyard to go to work. She watched a woman with a big water jug on her hip. She was coming back from the courtyard well. Olmad greeted her as he hurried to his apartment.

Rahab went back to the roof where she could see the palm trees moving a little in a breeze. It was a comforting sound. A sound of movement and dance as one frond communicated with another. She picked up the little box where she had placed the wheat straw from the white dove. She looked at the sky.

Quietly and very hesitantly, she said, "O Lord, I don't know where you are or if you can hear me, or even if you care to hear me, a prostitute, but I cry out to you to save my family. When your army comes to destroy the city, have mercy and please save my family.

"Lord, please hear my voice. Let your ears hear my cry for mercy. Lord, forgive me of my sins and help me to grow to be a good person for you.

"Remember me, Lord, in all my distress. My enemy is your army. They are a large army. They are coming to destroy our city. Only you can save my family, because your army is so large.

"Into your hands I place the lives of my family and their servants. Have mercy on us, O Lord."

She stood silently for several moments and then placed the little box back on the table. God was smiling. She could feel it in her bones and in her face. It was like an extra measure of sunshine on a beautiful day.

Runner's Report

About mid-morning, a runner shouted for the city gate to open. He had news for the King. The guards in the turrets verified that he was alone and was one of Jericho's runners. The big gate rumbled open as the four men pulled at its ropes and the runner quickly crossed under by ducking his head. Breathlessly, he ran directly through the central courtyard with his sweaty tunic pasted to his body. He ran directly to the apartments in the back wall, and up to the second level to the royal chambers. The guard opened the door to the King's reception room.

"There is movement in the camp across the river!" reported the runner. "One of the spotters has come down from the mountain top saying the strangers have begun leaving their camps and are moving everything toward the river. Big groups of them are moving from the plains of Moab through the mountains to the edge of the mad river. None of us can figure out why they were moving now. No one could cross such a dangerous stream."

The King accepted the message. Then he ordered the Captain of the Guard, "Better double the number of spotters on the mountain tops along the west bank. Reinforce those stations to be manned day and night. Get me at least daily reports and more often when anything happens over there. After two years of living in Moab, it looks like they may be getting ready to make their move. I want to be informed day or night. Understand?"

"Yes, your Majesty. I'll get right on it," said the Captain of the Guard.

When Rahab heard the news, ice-cold fear swelled up inside her. She turned sick at her stomach again. She began to shake a little. The enemy was coming. She didn't know how they could cross the river, but somehow she felt they would and it would be the end of the world for all of Jericho. She knew what was going to happen, but she was sworn to tell no one, not even her family. She hurt inside. She had pains in her chest. Her heart felt like a rock again.

This was the beginning of the end. What she had feared most was beginning to come true. She ran back inside her house and slammed the door. She ran up to her bedroom window to check the red cord. She shoved open the shutters and they banged against the fortress wall. The scarlet cord was still floating out her window. It was moving in the slight breeze. She held it in her hand and looked to the hazy sky.

"Oh, God of Israel, please hear my prayer. With all my heart I cry out to you. I cry out that the Hebrew spies made it back to their camp and that their commanders will honor their oath with me. I know you have control, O Lord, please see to it that the commanders remember the oath to save my family when they come to take the city. Please have mercy on us, Lord. Please show us your mercy." Her voice trailed away. She slowly let go of the cord. A beam of sunshine broke through the haze and fell across her floor.

She had a measure of comfort and turned to go down the stairs on her tiptoes as she sometimes did. It was her private, secret activity to keep the muscles in her feet and legs strong. Of course, she would never admit such practice to anyone. Her mind went into neutral and for no reason at all opened the front door and walked out into the courtyard. She didn't notice the people, or the animals, or any activity at all. Rahab almost bumped into a woman at the courtyard well. The woman barely was able to keep the big jar balanced on her head. "Oh, I'm so sorry," said Rahab as they walked on. She seemed to be in a trance. She was totally removed from this civilized world. A little lamb ran up to her and stuck his wet nose against Rahab's hand. She smiled a little and walked on.

Around the corner and down a ways from her house she realized that she had left without her shawl, something no woman would ever do in Jericho. So she turned to rush back, guilty of being so undressed. When she returned to the front of her apartment something snapped inside. Maybe it was the guilt of not being properly dressed. Maybe it was because she was accusing herself of being forgetful. Maybe it was the reaction of the secret she was carrying. But something mean snapped inside her.

She saw the little four-foot god of fertility at her front door. It told everyone that this was an inn. It was a custom for the men to improve their manliness by rubbing its head before entering the door. Sometimes the local men would come by and rub its head before they headed home for a romantic evening with their wives; thus the shiny spot on its bald head.

This time the statue made Rahab angry. She became furious at it. She picked up a big rock in the flower bed and threw it at the idol, smashing the clay figure down the middle. *No more idols!* In her rage, she threw the rock again and further smashed the pieces so that she could smell the musty, red dirt and the stale, pungent air that the idol had imprisoned for so many years. *No more idols!* It lay in a hundred pieces by her doorstep. She was sobbing as she went inside, slammed the door and locked it.

Joshua

Meanwhile, across the river the Israelites were busy. Two million people were packing up their things and preparing to move in accordance of the commands from Joshua, the leader. Joshua was an old man, thin, with long flowing white hair. The eighty-year-old leader had succeeded Moses. His appointment was to take the people across the river and possess the Promised Land. This was to fulfill the promise God made to Abraham more than 400 years ago.

Joshua had been born into slavery in Egypt and had served Moses as he liberated the Hebrews from the iron clutches of Pharaoh. He had seen the ten plagues where God had conquered all of the Egyptian gods to prove that the God of Abraham was the one true God. Joshua was with Moses and Aaron when they led the people across the Red Sea on dry ground. He walked part way up Mt. Sinai when God gave Moses the Ten Commandments. Joshua was one of the 12 men who first went into Canaan to spy out the land 40 years ago. He and his friend, Caleb, told Moses that the land was ready to be taken. But, others in the group feared the giants in the land and convinced the elders that it was dangerous to try to enter such a land. Such doubt and failing faith angered God and caused the group to wander the desert until the timid people died. A new generation would inherit the Promised Land.

So now, the new generation had arrived to the crossing point. Moses had climbed the mountain to see the land of milk and honey and placed Joshua in charge of the entire nation. Then Moses was taken up by God. With this heritage, Joshua saw this time as a momentous event and he was ready. Joshua was about to move on his greatest accomplishment. Dramatic history was about to be made.

The next day another message came to Jericho. More people had moved their belongings through the mountains to the river's edge. The line was as far as one could see from left to right.

The mountain top spotters were watching the movement by day and the campfires by night. They would send messages down to runners who would collect the news and then have it run over to Jericho. None of the news was good. The massive Israelite encampment grew larger and larger. It was the largest group of people they had ever seen in one place. It was more people than now lived in all of Canaan. There were so many Hebrews they could make up more than a 1000 Jerichos. But they were still on the other side of the Jordan. No one could manage such turbulent water.

While others had suspicions, inside the walls of Jericho only Rahab knew what was coming. The guilt and weight of the secret inside her broke open and its poison flooded through her body like a giant tidal wave. Her arms and legs were weak. She had a red rash across her chest and stomach. Her heart was pounding. Her head felt like someone with a hammer was pounding and pounding on it. She couldn't eat. She couldn't sleep. She couldn't sit or stand or lie down. Everyone was going to be killed and Rahab couldn't tell them about it.

"Why me? Why should I be entrusted with this terrible, awful secret? Why me, God? Please, Lord, never tell me the future again!"

She pounded the covers on her pallet and kicked her feet as tears welled up. She was crying from her toes to her eyes until she could no longer cry. She lay there exhausted, ready to die. The Lord was listening to her cry, but she was not yet prepared for His blessings.

The Scroll

A soft knock came tapped her door. The soft, friendly knocking code of her brother. She really didn't want to see anyone, but she couldn't refuse her one true friend. So she wiped her face, straightened her robe, trying to brush out the winkles and then opened the door.

Olmad was smiling. He was holding a scroll in his hand. Then his smile fell and his first words were, "My god, what has happened to you?"

He helped his sister to the pale green cushions and they both sat down, his arm still around her.

"I don't know," she said. Her voice was shaking. "I'm having another one of those spells like I had several weeks ago. Olmad, I am just so afraid."

"Just sit still. You are safe here in my arms. I won't let anyone hurt you. When you are ready, you can tell me about it. That will help you get hold of yourself. I promise you there is nothing to be afraid of."

"Thank you, Olmad. I wish what you said were true, but ... I do feel better with your being here. What was it you had in your hand?"

"Did someone try to break into your apartment?"

"No."

"Is someone threatening you? Does someone want to harm you? Beat you up or something?"

"No. No. Nothing like that," she told him. She wiped her eyes with her sleeve. Olmad was silent as he held her close.

When she had settled down some, Olmad turned her loose long enough to pick up the scroll he had dropped and began to unroll it. "I told you I was going to meet with other traders when a little caravan stopped outside the gate. Well, there wasn't much to trade on the caravan. But I mentioned your interest in Hebrew religion and one of my friends had come upon this scroll. This is a section of the instructions their leader Moses had given to the people. I thought you might like to see it."

"Oh, thank you, Olmad, but you didn't have to go to all that trouble." He handed her the short scroll. It was their first written insight into the Hebrew God. Rahab began reading the first words, "The Lord said to Moses, speak to the entire assembly of Israel and say to them: Be holy, because I, the Lord your God, am holy."

"Oh, Olmad, this is so exciting," said Rahab. Her eyes were gleaming. Rahab was one of a very few women in all of Jericho who was able to read. The boys went to class and learned reading and writing and other things, but girls did not. From the first day of school when Olmad would come in from class, he would teach his little sister what he had learned that day. They did their practice reading together. Their mother listened and learned to read some, but Rahab was as good a reader as Olmad.

"Look it says, 'Each one of you must respect your mother and father and respect my Sabbaths. I am the Lord your God.' Can you imagine a god that tells you to respect your parents? But I don't know what a Sabbath is. Do you?"

"No," said Olmad. "Maybe it's some sort of special day or a celebration. We'll have to find out."

"Then the next saying is, 'Do not turn to idols or make gods of cast metal for yourselves.' Most of our gods are made of stone and wood. I wonder if that counts?"

"I don't know. What else is there?"

Rahab began reading again, "When you reap the harvest of your land, do not reap to the very edges of your grain field or pick up grapes that have fallen. Leave them for the poor and the alien. I am the Lord your God.' Isn't that wonderful. The God of Israel shows concern for the poor. Our gods have no such blessings. Then it goes on, 'Do not steal. Do not lie. Do not deceive one another. Do not swear falsely by my name and so profane the name of your God.'"

"I heard that He is a God of love, but I never knew what that really meant. And these rules or sayings — whatever they are — are the opposite of love. Look at this: Do not steal, lie, deceive or swear falsely by His name, seem to be encouragement to be true, honest and loving. This is very different than what we have been taught," said Olmad.

"Look how someone has underlined some of the words, 'Love him as yourself for you were aliens in Egypt.' Imagine what a different world this would be if everyone loved their neighbors in respect to themselves."

"A very different world. Look, someone has written across the bottom, 'Love the Lord with all your heart and soul.' This whole message is about loving God and loving everyone around you. Oh, Olmad, I'm so proud of this. Thank you again and again."

"I am glad you like it and I hope you're able to learn from it."

"Oh, I am going to study this. It's so very helpful. Thank you again,

Olmad. I feel better already." She reached over and hugged him.

Just then there was a polite knock on the door, the latch opened and in came Mother. "You two seem cozy," she said.

"Hello, Mother. How are you today?" Rahab greeted her.

"Just out seeing what's going on. What happened to your god out front? Did you have an incident here?"

"No, I just decided I don't want idols around me any more."

"Oh, my dear! What has happened to you? How will the men know to come to see you? How will they be able to improve their manhood? What if you made the god angry? What have you done?" Her mother was suddenly as full of questions as a pot of tea.

"Mother, it's all right. I promise you, it's all right. Just calm down and have a seat." Olmad got up to move a bench closer to where they were sitting. "I broke the statue because I don't believe it has any powers. Instead, I am turning to the Hebrew God that has a lot of powers. He takes care of people. He loves His followers."

"I've never heard of such things," Mother said as she sat wringing her hands in her apron. "Have you gone mad?"

"I don't think so. Olmad just brought me a scroll from the Hebrew camp that he has traded for. It gives us a little insight into their God. It says to love everyone as you love yourself. See?"

"Dear, that is so simple, everyone knows that." Mother couldn't see the point. "I've taught you that all of your life."

"Yes, you have. And I appreciate it. I wish everyone else had been taught as well as you have taught me." She reached for her mother's hand.

"I'm just going to have to go tell your father about this. I don't know what else to do. My daughter is out destroying gods and doing something foreign and strange," she began to cry. "Where have I gone wrong?" She stood up and walked to the door, saying nothing more.

"Mother, ..." Rahab tried to reach her but she was out the door. It was troubling to Rahab. A person never likes to disappoint their mother.

Olmad was on his feet as well. "Sis, I'll go talk with her. Don't worry." He gave his sister a quick hug and was out the door chasing down Mother.

Rahab must have read the scroll a hundred times that day. The laws were simple and practical. But the nagging question remained that this God who wanted love was about to strike their city. What had they done to warrant such awful actions from the Hebrews? She was filled with questions.

5

The Crossing

By the third day most of the Hebrews had moved to the river's edge. Some of the people remained in Moab to continue building cities and occupy the land. The guards of Jericho watched from their perches atop the mountains along the Jordan and from the turrets of the fortress. They could see the massive number of people lined up on the Jordan's eastern shoreline. The thick heavy line was more than 50 miles long.

The King's counselors all agreed that the Hebrews were preparing for something, but they were not sure what it was. The river remained the strong line of defense and would be so for months to come.

Across the Jordan, the Hebrews could see the little open town of Gilgal, then a few miles further stood the fortress of Jericho. Joshua called his people together. He was going to address all the tribal leaders, elders, judges, and priests.

The old man in a colorless robe, pushed back his hair from his long, thin face and cleared his throat. He looked at his audience. He looked at the sky as though gathering new inspiration. His skinny legs began to pace while he held his bony hands together in front of him. Now he was ready.

"This is the time," the old man began. His voice crackled and was raspy. "For forty years we have prepared for this moment. When God saved us from the Egyptian whips and tyranny, He saved us to the desert. Now from the desert He saves us to the Promised Land!" A cheer went up from the crowd.

"Tonight, we end one life and tomorrow we begin another. We have followed the Almighty's commands and He has brought us to the edge of the Promised Land. Once before, Israel was prepared to enter this land, but the nation refused to go and the Lord sent us back into the desert until those people died. Now we have the opportunity again. Let us go possess the land as the Lord has commanded."

A great shout of agreement rose from the masses.

"You are the people chosen to fulfill the promise that the Lord made to our father Abraham so many years ago. This is our land, says the Lord. God will go before us and show us the way. We must possess the land according to His will and His way and for His glory. This is the promised task. This is not a job for weak people. This is a task for strong people, who know and understand and obey the will of the Almighty. This will be a test of your faith. It is a test of your endurance. It is a test of your abilities, your talents, and your courage. You are likely to be called on to do things you have never considered before. You are to be strong and faithful. You are to obey God's commands without hesitation. You are God's army. Remember that: You are God's army. You are to do His will."

The audience interrupted him again with cheers and applause. Joshua spread out his long arms to encircle the cheering crowd and eventually to signal, he had more to say.

"Tonight, we are desert people roaming the sands." Joshua raised his old arm and pointed the same crooked finger at his audience. "Tomorrow, we will be Israel at home." Another cheer went up from the crowd. Joshua smiled. He had waited so long to say that.

"Tomorrow will be a day to be remembered by everyone for the rest of your lives. You will tell your children about it. And their children will tell their grandchildren about it. But you are the ones to live it.

"Tomorrow morning early, The Lord our God will lead you into the Promised Land. Look for the Ark of the Covenant. When you see the Ark of the Lord your God, and the priests carrying it, you are to move out from your position and follow the Ark. Then you will know which way to go. But keep a distance of about a thousand feet between you and the Ark. Don't go near it.

"Tonight, we must rid our nation of any sin that may be amongst us. We must enter the land of New Beginnings as purified people. So consecrate yourselves. For tomorrow the Lord will do amazing things among you. Go through out the camp and tell your people what you have heard. Draw near to God. Consecrate yourselves by washing your clothes. Wash your bodies. Abstain from sexual intercourse tonight. Make yourselves pure for tomorrow."

The commanders, leaders, judges, and all who were there,

together shouted back to Joshua "We will obey."

And so, more than 600,000 men drew buckets of water from the mighty Jordan and washed their clothes and bathed and that night slept by themselves. When getting their water, every one of them looked at the river and saw how wide it was; how fast, how furious, how deep, and how mad it was. And every one of them had a silent question in his mind, "How are we going to get across?"

Happy Times in Jericho

Inside Jericho that evening, the torches burned brightly and there was a group of children dancing in a big circle, singing songs for the adults. Rahab had heard the singing and also joined the group. She was petting the wet nose of a little lamb as she watched the leaping and running of the circle of mostly girls. There was more giggling by the youngsters than singing, but that was enjoyable for the elderly as well. Everyone was laughing and having a good time in Jericho. They knew nothing of the Joshua speech or of so many buckets of cold water being drawn from the Jordan. The Jericho walls amplified the joyous sounds of children playing. There were smells of food cooking. There was music and a party in progress. A few young adults were dancing with the children. Everyone was happy in Jericho.

Just after dark, when the moon began to shine into the grand courtyard, Rahab had a little tingling sensation in her back bone. It was a surprise, a little nervous, a little fearsome. She brushed off the first incident, but when it happened a second time, she took notice. She returned to her apartment. When she got to her doorway, the feeling struck again, something like a pain, but not really a pain. Almost like something was calling her. She got herself a cup of tea and then went up to the roof, so she could hear some more of the children at play.

Again, as she got to the chair where she could relax, the tingling sensation called her once more. It was an odd feeling. She spread out in the chair, very unladylike. Her feet apart, her robe up to her mid-calves, her head leaning against the back of the chair with her hair frizzed out in all directions. She took off her earrings and necklace and closed her eyes. And when she did, she saw the time when Olmad came over with the scroll containing the instructions from God Almighty. Her vision was of Olmad tugging at the scroll and she would not let go until she had read an inscription someone had written across the bottom of it. "Someone has written, 'Love the Lord your God with all your heart, mind, and soul. Love your neighbor as yourself.'"

The message was repeating itself over and over in her mind. Again and again, she heard 'Love the Lord your God with all your heart, mind, soul and strength.' She reached for the little box with her grain of wheat that the white dove had left her months before. It was a comforting feeling. Almost automatically —as without thinking — words began to fall from her mouth. "Lord, I believe that you are the Creator of the whole world. I believe that you made the hills and the sand and the Jordan. I believe that you made all people, including all those across the river. Lord, I believe you made the Jordan to keep the Israelites from destroying us. I am not sure how to love you, God, because this is a new experience for me. I love my family. I love my friends. I don't hate the spies who came here. Perhaps, you sent them to me.

"I love you for the warning they gave me. I love you for the oath we swore that could save my family when your soldiers come to take the land.

"I have tried to remove the idols from my life. I still get frightened. I still have nightmares, but I do feel better now. I feel that you are with me. And whatever happens in the coming months, you will protect me and my family. Because, I know that you made us all.

"Thank you, Lord, for loving us, for providing for us, and for taking care of us. Open our hearts, Lord, so we may learn to love you more. I know that our lives are in your hands. Give us your mercy."

She was almost whispering, so silently, so peacefully, so freely. She had connected to a higher power. A warmness was flowing back into her. For the first time, she felt that God was listening to her.

Rahab closed the little box and slowly returned it to its place on a low shelf by the support beam. She closed her eyes and dozed in peace.

The Big Day

The nation of Israel was awakened early the next morning and after a hurried breakfast, groups begin to form. The army took position on the banks of the roaring Jordan. They fanned out from where the Jordan empties into the Dead Sea to more than 50 miles north. The Ark of the Covenant and the priests carrying it were almost directly across the river from Gilgal. They would be the point men. As the sun's rays reached over the mountain tops and lighted the way, they could see what lay before them.

Nothing had changed. The river was still there. It was still a mile wide. It sounded very deep. The currents ran wildly. Debris floated and swirled in the whirlpools. The water was swift with whitecaps on surging waves. The river was still as dangerous that morning as it was when they went to bed.

Then, the order came: Cross the river. Everyone said their prayers and gave a group shout of hosanna and watched for the carriers with the Ark of the Covenant. Joshua told the Ark bearers to go first. God would lead the way. Eight Levite priests, four on each side, had the carrying poles on their shoulders and on the poles was the sacred Ark of the Covenant, where God lives. They were facing certain death in the dangerous waters before them. They were responsible for the most precious cargo in all of Israel. Even with God on their shoulders, they were still scared. That was a big river out there and it smelled of danger.

This was a major test of faith. The pole bearers carefully stepped up to the river's edge. The two men in front hesitated, but the two in back pushed on the poles and the front men stepped into the river's edge. The cold water rushed into their sandals. The chill ran up their legs and their bodies gave a shiver. The water was as cold as the snow on Mt. Herman. Even on the edge of the river, the water was gritty from the sand particles it carried. They could feel it rushing over their toes and on the bottoms of their feet. They were suddenly cold from the water and the fear of the river.

The Levite priests had as much faith as anyone else in the group but they were still ready to break and run when the two men in back pushed on the poles again and the front men were forced to take another step into the river. That is when they saw the miracle beginning.

As they stepped into the water's edge it only covered their sandals up to the top of their feet. Nothing more. They took a third and a fourth step and the water was no deeper. A dozen steps later down into the steep riverbed, and the water was no deeper. They were descending down into the riverbed, but the water did not get deeper. It never covered their ankles. Instead, they could see how the water was becoming less and less. The river was drying up. The water was no longer flowing. Somewhere up stream something had stopped up the mad river! The priests could see the sand bars and the debris on the river bottom. They could see where to step and carefully negotiate a way for the Ark.

With each step, the water to their left was flowing away from them. On the right, an invisible wall was holding the water back somewhere upstream. They could see how God was working to prepare the way for the crossing. The further down into the river they ventured, the more it opened for them, but only as they went down into the raging water. When they paused, the pathway ceased to open. Only as they stepped forward did the river open up for them. Only until they got half way, a point of no return, did the river completely stop flowing and the river bottom began to dry.

Their fear was replaced by confidence. The eight priests were witnesses to God's blessing in their lives and that of the nation. The two front men led the other bearers out into the river, down into the river bed, until they could no longer see across the river because of the depth of the bed. Down into the canyon they took their place. They were more than 100 feet below where the surface of the water had been raging only minutes before. Yet, they stood on dry ground. They stood among the stones, old tree trunks, and debris that had been under water for centuries. Now everything was dry. All that the priests could see was the canyon wall ahead.

Forty thousand Israelite soldiers from the tribes remaining in Moab lined up in single file. They formed a line of attack for more than 50 miles along the banks of the dry Jordan. Carefully, but majestically, they began to come down into the riverbed. Every few feet there was an armed soldier ready for battle. They wore metal helmets with face guards, metal breast pieces with ornate designs on them. The breast pieces covered their pure white tunics with rich colored borders. They carried metal shields to deflect any arrows or spears sent their way. They wore heavy desert leather sandals with high shin guards. This great flank of physical power was overshadowed only by the mighty power of God. The Army of God was ready to flex its muscle. They had come to take the land God had promised them.

The soldiers marched down into the riverbed and up onto the Land of Promise. They secured the perimeter, although there was no one visible and no forces to contend with. As the soldiers moved out taking the land step by step, they were closely followed by the citizens and their flocks. In great waves of people and possessions, they came. Step by step, they witnessed where the great river had been but now was dry ground beneath their feet.

There was no hurry. God was proving their way. The first families to cross worked at clearing some of the boulders out of the way to make room for carts and wagons. The first ones cleared enough for their wagons to cross and those that followed improved the way so that the traffic could move faster. The old women slowly made their way over the rocks. The sick rode through the river on carts. Children danced on top of the dry flat rocks in the riverbed. Old men leaning on walking staffs carefully picked their way across. There were wagons of household goods, of tents, of clothing. There were herds of sheep, and goats, and oxen. There were families rejoicing to be a part of leaving the desert and entering the Land of Promise.

The News Reports

The sun was barely up when a runner came with a desperate cry for Jericho to open its gates. As he ran through the courtyard he was shouting, "They're crossing the river! They're crossing the river!"

No one could believe it. How could they get across such a turbulent river? The runner called out that the river had stopped up. The water was gone! The strangers were crossing over on dry ground! The spotters were guessing that hundreds of thousands of people were at the river's edge. The front line was more than 50 miles long and was as deep as anyone could see.

The runner told the King, "Sir, they are coming across the Jordan right now. They started this morning at daylight. They are carrying a strange box balanced on eight men's shoulders. I saw them this morning just at first light. The carriers came down to the water's edge and when they stepped into that mad water, the river stopped flowing! I'm not lying, sir. The flood water just stopped flowing. The river began draining and in just a very short time, the water was gone. It's an empty river bed." The runner was talking so fast so as to get all the details in before he fainted.

"Your Majesty, when the box carriers took a step forward, the water's edge receded from under their feet. Every step they took meant less water in the river until they got to the middle of the Jordan. Then the water just went away. The box carriers are more than 100-feet down in the river bed. They are still holding that box on their shoulders. On dry ground!

"I swear it. I haven't had a drop to drink. It's all true," he said as he was running out of breath. He was all sweaty from the long run. His bare arms were cut by the bushes he had run through. There was a gash in the calf of his left leg where he stumbled on a rock trying to get to the King as quickly as he could.

The King told the courier to sit down and rest and instantly called for his senior council to meet in his chambers.

Soon another courier approached the big gate on a sweaty horse. In his stirrup was the banner of Adam, a town about 30 miles north of Gilgal. He begged that the gate be opened because he had a desperate message for the King. Guards were sent to the front gate and as the gate was opened Jericho's guards held the courier on his steed until they had examined his horse and saddle. Then they let him get down and they searched him again and removed his dagger and banner. Once he was disarmed they tied a strong cord to his right wrist and left ankle so he could hardly move. The guards led him through the courtyard to the back wall and up to the second level. There they called for the King's permission for an audience with the man from the city of Adam.

The courier had ridden so hard and so fast that he, too, was out of breath. As best as he could, between gasps for air, he made his report to the King. "The Jordan River is stopped up. The flood waters are being heaped up near Adam; close to where the Jobbok River flows into the Jordan. The waters are somehow being kept in the basin, so its dry ground all the way to the south. Sir, they told me to report that there has been no earthquake, no landslide, no storm, no way is visible to stop the flow of the river. Something invisible has stopped up the river. It's not flooding the town nor is it even getting out of its banks. It has just stopped flowing. It is some kind of a sign. Our city fathers believe that it is a message from a god, but they can't interpret it. Is there anyone in Jericho who can tell the meaning of this sudden change?"

The king ordered that the man be released from the restraint and be given some water to drink. "Even in a crisis, we must show hospitality," the King said.

How could this be? Nothing like this is possible. The messages were so hard to believe that the King immediately dispatched four guards experienced in information gathering to verify the story. They were to go to different sections, the upper and the lower points of the crossing place, and tell from those vantage points what was happening. Each guard took two runners with him. Each had orders to dispatch a runner back as soon as they verified the account of the incident. Then the guards were to remain there gathering as much information as they could about what was happening and then dispatch their second runner. Later the guards would return to make suggestions on how to prepare for a defense. They would stay no more than two hours and then hurry back.

All that day at the river, the people, family by family, experienced God's miracle. They all understood, again, that God could solve any problem when He was ready.

Every hour the Levites holding the Ark were replaced with a rested crew. They each demonstrated his faith by standing in the center of the river with half a mile of dangerous riverbed in front and another half mile in back of them and a hundred feet below the flood line of the river. The water was being held back somewhere, but they knew not where. Water could come crashing on them without warning.

The families kept demonstrating their own faith by coming to the edge of the riverbed and moving all they had down into the river. Entire families and all of their possessions were at risk in the dry river. They experienced how deep it was and recognized how broad it was. They were amazed that once down in the river they could only see across the river bed. They could not see the land beyond. It was a world all of its own. It was a point of separation from the old life to the promised life. They had to climb up out of the bed to see the Land of Promise. It was like being born again.

The children would run and play as the wagons crossed so slowly over the rough makeshift trails. Two little boys and a little girl climbed up on a flat boulder and began singing for everyone to hear. They were waving their hands trying to encourage the adults to join them. But the adults were busy getting the carts, wagons and animals over the rocks and fallen tree trunks. As the last of their parent's possessions passed them by, the children would jump down to catch up with their family. Then some more children would take the stage and watch their family's possessions pass them by.

In the crossing, one old woman became confused in the crowds and started going back to where she had entered the river bed. But before she got very far, a friend turned her around. One baby was born in the river — they named him Jordan —and several others were born just as their mothers completed the rough journey across the rocks. At least five old men lost their lives. Death most likely was caused by stress, and exertions on the heart. The sheep and goats that broke their legs or other wise didn't make it across became food for dinner that night.

Council for the Defense

Meanwhile, the Jericho King called a conference with his experts on Israel to determine what might be happening. One historian suggested, "This is an interesting situation. The parting of the Jordan is similar in a way to the tale of the parting of the Red Sea some 40 years ago. You may recall, your Majesty, that this parting of the waters permitted the Egyptian slaves to escape Pharaoh's army. How the sea was parted has never been explained. Except, of course, to attribute it to the power of their invisible God. I would say, that if this is another act of that God, then Israel will be difficult to defeat."

Another historian spoke up. "As for the strange box, it probably contains no secret weapon. It is most likely the Ark of the Covenant - where their invisible God is said to live. Only certain people are qualified to touch the carrying poles. All others will die instantly."

"You mean that where we have several gods who stand on the ground or on our buildings, the Israelites hide their God in this box?"

"It's not an ordinary box. I've heard that it's made of pure gold and is considered so holy, that it is constantly kept covered. Not even the people carrying it can see the box or what is in it," the first historian explained. "The Israelites have carried their boxed-up God through the desert all these years. Some say that is where the Israelites power lies."

"Do I hear you men saying that if we were able to capture the box, then we could control their entire nation?" The King was summarizing.

"Correct, sir. But this will not be easy, because first, they guard the box very carefully and some say that anyone touching the box will die instantly. So to capture Israel by first capturing the box, you must have a plan to capture it without touching it. But if you can do that, we would have instant victory." So the King's men set out to determine how to do it.

Shortly before noon, a third runner had more news. "I don't know how much you have heard, Your Majesty, but here is what I have to report," said the runner. "While the Israelites started early this morning, the crossing is likely to take an entire day or even more. Your Majesty, there must be a thousand times more people crossing over than live in Jericho. The first ones to cross through the Jordan seem to be gathering near Gilgal. If they do settle in Gilgal vicinity, their camp will be only a mile from Jericho."

"What are they doing with the box in the river?" A man asked.

"They rotate out with fresh men about every hour so they keep the box steady. They wear brown tunics and stay near the box," the runner said.

"How many people are there?" The King was asking.

"Thousands upon thousands. These people are streaming through the mountains up to the edge of the river bed and breaking into nine or ten groups. We guess that each group has about 175,000 people or more. They far outnumber the ability of the usual fords to handle their traffic. They're using every possible inch of the river bed they can to make the crossing."

Throughout the day, more runners reported how the column of people in the river bed had widened. Each group moved to a pre-assigned place and began setting up camp with its own banner.

Well after dark, another runner reported, "Your Majesty, the strangers have crossed the river. After everyone had cleared the river and was on this side, 12 men with torches went back into the riverbed and each carried out a stone from the center of the river."

"Why would they collect stones from the riverbed? There are plenty of stones all over the ground," the King asked.

"I don't know, sir, but when they came out, the men in the brown robes carried the blue box out of the river. Then the waters blasted back into the canyons. The Jordan is now as it was early this morning before daylight. It is flowing at normal spring flood stage."

The people of Jericho had heard the sound of thunder but it was the river recharging. A wall of water 100 feet high, came roaring through the canyons devouring everything left in its way. It covered the wagon tracks. It swept away any trace of a crossing. The rushing sound of the mighty river passed as a rolling storm. The mighty Jordan was as it was the previous dawn. The force of God that held it back, had now filled it as though nothing had ever happened.

Jericho's first line of defense was down. The enemy had crossed the mighty Jordan. It was a massive enemy, much larger than anyone could imagine. The invasion had begun. Rahab went upstairs to check her scarlet cord.

The next day, several runners were reporting back to Jericho with word about the Israelites. They had camped near Gilgal. Their huge encampment had overtaken the small open town. One of the runners described it as a whale snuggling up to a shrimp. The number of visitors was so massive in size that the group's camp started near the edge of the Jordan and went past Gigal to within almost a mile of the walls of Jericho. The runners guessed that the encampment was about 20 to 30 miles long.

The Hebrews had set up camp quickly after the crossing, working through the night. Apparently, this was a skill they had acquired through their long journeys in the desert. They were well practiced in the art of nomadic life. The tents were in long, neat rows. They were big tents with six foot walls and pitched roofs; all of leather. The sides could be rolled up or closed completely, depending on the weather and the needs of the families living in them.

The First Memorial

When the Israelites came out of the bowels of the Jordan it was the tenth day of the first month. And Joshua called a meeting on their first morning in the new land. The elders and other leaders came to build and dedicate a memorial. After the group had sung a song of praise to Jehovah; the priest, Eleazar, lead them in prayer. He prayed, "Oh great Father of Abraham, you have brought us to the Promised Land. This time you permitted your people to step inside the boundaries you promised Abraham so long ago. This time you have shown your strength and your glory by opening up the river for us to cross over. For which we are eternally grateful.

"Lord, we now dedicate these stones in memory of your great miracle. We dedicate this site in appreciation for your love and concern for us."

Then each of the twelve elders picked up his river stone and brought it to Joshua. He gave each man instructions on how to place the stones. They were carefully stacked with a broad secure base and rose in the air to a single stone at its peak. The top stone was from Judah. As it was placed, everyone in the area applauded the work.

Then old Joshua told the Israelites who were present, "In the future when your children ask their fathers, 'What do these stones mean?' Tell them how Israel crossed the Jordan on dry ground. Tell them for the Lord your God dried up the Jordan before you until you had crossed over."

News of the memorial spread quickly from the Jordan basin to the coast of the Great Sea. It spread as quickly as news of the Jordan being stopped up.

While the Hebrews did not act like an enemy, the King knew better. So there were conferences all day, everyday, in the King's chambers about how to capture the Ark. But there was no news of how they were to do it, or even if they could do it. The strange box had disappeared inside the camp.

During the day, especially in early morning, the strangers took their animals out to pasture. Shepherds stayed with the sheep and goats, overlooking their safety and searching out good grass for them to eat. At night the Hebrews retired to their own tents and the camp was quiet.

As far as anyone knew, there were no Israeli spies. The King's thick network of spotters and runners reported that no one left their camp at night. None of them ever came close to the walls of Jericho, nor did they go to any other city. They didn't seek out information from anyone. There were no envoys from their leader to establish contact or relations with anyone in any of the other towns around. They seemed to be very private people. They bothered no one.

The King of Jericho periodically sent out couriers to the other towns around, especially to Ai. It was a town not far away, high up on the ridge with a very long view. They could see the Hebrew encampment better than the guards in the turrets of Jericho. But they reported no contact with the strangers. No one came from there to inquire of them.

The weeks turned into months and Israel remained calm and peaceful. Perhaps they were just here to become new neighbors. They were not aggressive at all. Perhaps Rahab had been worrying for nothing. She wouldn't need that silly red cord after all.

6

Call of the Rams' Horns

Life eventually returned to near normal in Jericho. Over the weeks the runners and spotters brought back less and less interesting news. The spotters worked during the day and returned home in the evening. A few lookouts from the turrets remained on duty through the night.

Jericho guarded the entrance into the fruitful Jordan Plains, so the King did maintain a defense force of soldiers that kept the peace within the walls and with the farmers and fruit growers surrounding the city. They served as lookouts and were trained to defend the city from the top of the great wall. No one in Jericho could remember the last time that the strong walls were attacked.

Before daylight one morning, Jericho citizens were jolted from their sleep by an ear-splitting, paralyzing sound. Rahab shot straight up in bed like a wild woman. Her hair felt like a bird's nest and her night clothes were twisted around her. She must be having a nightmare.

There in the darkness of the room came the piercing sound again. Like a dagger of sound stabbing the air. It was off in the distance. The sound was somewhat muffled by the walls around the city and the thickness of her own apartment walls, but it was a strong sound. She had never heard it before. The brassy, eerie, haunting, frightening call of death in the darkness penetrated her brain and body as easily as it penetrated the walls around her. It left tracks of terror through her arms and legs. Her heart was racing. Her breath was shallow and rapid. She was so nervous, so frightened, she was shaking.

As she sat frozen in bed, she could pick up a cadence of trumpets, much like rumbling, distant, musical thunder. Could it be a call for soldiers to assemble? She couldn't make it out in her dull head; her hands against her face. She still wasn't sure if it was real or a nightmare, until she clearly heard another single blast followed by a rhythmic calling signal. It *was* the call for soldiers to assemble!

Rahab swung her feet to the floor and ran fingers through her hair one more time. This was no dream. It was real! Was that a drum cadence in the distance? *O, God, no!* She reached for her robe and ran barefoot out the front door. She ran right into a throng of frightened people. Others had heard the sounds too. People were coming into the courtyard in their night clothes, some pulling robes around them. More guards ran to their turrets on top of the walls, strengthening the night crew, and called back down that the enemy was leaving camp. They were marching to Jericho!

"Oh, Lord can this be your time?" Rahab cried into the hands covering her face. God heard her call, but Rahab wasn't ready for his answer.

The Captain of the Guards sounded the general alarm. A series of beats on big gongs that hung around the turrets signaled the harvesters to come inside the safety of the wall. More of the guards came running out of their homes to claim their defense battle positions.

Volunteers followed their practiced drills and began filling big cauldrons with water and the fires were started to heat them to boiling. They could be used later to pour on any soldiers who tried to scale the walls.

Others ran to the storage closets on the top rim of the great wall, making ready the spears to be hurled down on the attackers, They brought from storage the hurling knives and daggers to be thrown into the attackers below. Makeshift catapults were assembled to hurl big buckets of boiling water, or oil, — even large rocks, and other things at the enemy.

Within minutes the peaceful, sleepy town was in a strong defense mode. Jericho was ready. The day of battle had arrived.

The first reports came in the gray of the early morning. The invaders were carrying torches to light their way. There were thousands of torches in long rows. The men in the turrets said there must be more than 100 torches across the front and they went for miles back into the Hebrew camp. The torch light was reflecting off shiny armor.

It was a nerve chilling scene. Out front, at the head of a very wide column, were hundreds, maybe thousands, of armed men with shiny spears, shields and swords. Even at that distance and in the early light, the lookouts could tell they were strong, fierce and determined. This was a massive army. There were many more soldiers than there were people who lived in Jericho.

"They're coming this way! They are coming to Jericho!" one of the guards shouted down to the courtyard. But that wasn't all. As the huge army pulled out of camp, there came a separation, a distance in which marched only seven men with rams' horns. They were blowing those trumpets in a heralding fashion; announcing some news that came in a foreign tongue. What did it mean?

The people of Jericho could only understand the feeling, not the message. They had never seen an army that sent trumpeters into battle. What were they for? Rahab ran back into her apartment to quickly get dressed.

When she returned, the dust of the land was billowing up from the column of marchers. The lookout called down from his post, "They must be marching at least 500 men across. People are still coming out of the camp. There are thousands of fighters coming. I've never seen so many people."

Everyone inside the walls fell silent. People would rush out of their homes into the courtyard with the same question on their faces, but said nothing. When the courtyard filled, citizens hung from their windows and rooftops, searching for answers to silent questions. Everyone rushed into a time warp that froze them instantly. They were all motionless: Petrified in fear, with silent, pounding hearts. Jericho heard only the rams' horns. They came closer and closer.

The people listened intently to the running commentary of the breaking news from the different lookouts on the turrets. Different messages came from different advantage points.

After the trumpeters had cleared the front of the camp there was a long wait. (Perhaps this was the size of the army they were to face.) But, then, eight men appeared carrying a strange box on their shoulders. Perhaps the one that Jericho had heard so much about. The lookout above Rahab's apartment kept calling down information. "The box is covered in blue cloth. It's draped and tied so that the wind won't blow it off. It's not as large as I had imagined. It's not very heavy, because the carriers march easily with it on their shoulders.

"Now, here comes a big empty space all around the box. There must be at least 1,000 feet of empty space all around the box.

It's hard to judge, but I would say that the space is larger than the grand courtyard here. It's completely surrounded by armed soldiers. They're marching almost shoulder to shoulder. I have never seen so many soldiers."

Rahab broke from her trance and ran back into the house, up the steps to her bedroom window to check the scarlet cord. It was still in the window. She held it in her hand and prayed. "Oh, God of Israel, I pray you remember the oath your men made with me for my family. Have mercy on us, Lord. Have mercy on my family this day."

She ran back downstairs and nearby to her mother and father's place. "Mother! Dad! Get your servants and come over to my place. Now! Come before the battle starts. I'll get the others."

She didn't wait for answers. She ran down several more apartments, elbowing her way through the people. Her brothers and sisters were already outside their apartments, trying to figure out what was going on. "Everybody! Come to my place before the battle begins. Mother and Dad are coming down. We can all be together when the battle begins."

As they made their way to her apartment another lookout was calling, "That blue box is now followed by even more soldiers. The rear guard is as big as the front guard. They're in no hurry. I tell you folks, this is an eerie feeling. I wonder what they will do first."

The rams' trumpets got louder and louder. The fighting men marched with confidence, but their swords were not drawn. As they got closer to the walls, they began to circle around the city, out of range of Jericho's archers and spear men. It was a show of strength. Mighty strength. The closer they came, the faster the reports.

"That front group of soldiers must be 500 men wide and 30 rows deep. Maybe more."

"Yes, and every one of them is carrying a spear or sword. They have breastplates and shields."

"The early estimates were right. Their front guard is much larger than the entire population of Jericho."

"They're marching in a huge square around that little blue box. There are soldiers all around it Some of the soldiers have bows and arrows. There must be 10,000 men guarding that little blue box."

One of the counselors cautioned the King, "Your Majesty, I believe we can say that Jericho is being surrounded by more than 40,000 soldiers. That is four times the size of Jericho itself."

"Son, I know the size of Jericho. I just don't know what to do about the size of the enemy," said the King.

An historian joined in, "I can tell now that the box is the Ark of the Covenant. They are carrying it with them into battle just as they carried it throughout the Sinai Desert. They have brought their God into the battle. In fact, their God is leading them into battle. They mean serious business."

Rahab's family made their way to her place and they went up to her sleeping room and shared time looking out the window at the throng marching by. From the high window, they could see the soldiers below. There were so many of them! Rahab offered to make tea for everyone, but everyone was focused on the invading army. The attack was only moments away.

The men in the front guard were divided into two groups. The ones in the first few rows all wore metal breast plates and carried a spear in one hand and a shield in the other. They had matching shiny, metal helmets with low hanging face pieces that guarded the brow, eyes, and nose; like a mask would. They were scary looking with the dark metal strip down the center of their noses. Frequently, as if on some silent command, in unison they would lift their shields up to their faces and they would be completely protected from their heads to their knees. Then, they relaxed their arms to carry their shields by their sides.

They wore brown sandals of highly polished leather with shin guards that came up to their knees. From the front they were a marching wall of metal and leather that no sword, arrow or spear could penetrate. From the sides they could see their pure white tunics with short sleeves and the color borders at the bottom that came to just above the knees. This was the same blue color border Rahab had secretly seen months before. They wore heavy armor in front but their backs were not protected. The family guessed the Hebrews never needed to protect their backsides.

The second group of fighters wore much less armor and got their protection from thick leather breast pieces and a wide leather belt that divided into long leather strips extending down to mid-thigh and swung as they walked. Under this leather vest and skirt were their white tunics with different colored borders. They carried taut bows and big quivers of arrows across their backs. At their sides were holsters with short swords. They, too, wore the leather sandals with the high shin protectors.

The attackers were all business. They did not look right or left.

They were not scouting out the place. They seem to already know what they were going to do. No one spoke a word. No command was given. They just marched; out of range, but not out of sight.

As the front guard passed Rahab's window, Jericho was more than half way surrounded by thousands of soldiers, hundreds of rows deep. At any moment they could turn and attack.

They kept marching.

Stories had been told of attackers in small bands that would come and try to beat down the front gate and that is why Jericho had built the gate towers and focused most of the defenses at that point. But this was no ordinary army. They were surrounding the entire city and the front gate was of little interest to them.

They kept coming.

After the front guard passed, Rahab's family could see a break in the pattern. The front wall of soldiers broke into two long narrow columns, each about 20 or 30 soldiers wide. There was a long column on each side of the marching wall up front, forming a square in the parade. Within the safety of the guarded square came the trumpeters in tan tunics blowing their ram's horns. They formed a single file and marched about 20 yards from the big group of front soldiers. They had no armor and carried no swords. Their protection was the thousands around them.

Behind the trumpeters, at a respectful distance, walked three men. The one in front was tall and slender with long flowing white hair. He must have been 80 years old, but he was strong. He had marched all the way from Gilgal and around the city. And he was still going. He carried no weapons, wore no insignias, and carried nothing in his hands except a staff to help in his walking. He looked straight ahead as though he had little interest at the size of the great wall. Closely behind him were two other, younger men. Mother thought they might be advisors, or perhaps priests because these people were so religious.

Then there was a lot of open space. In the very center of the square surrounded by the soldiers, came the blue box. It was smaller than most had imagined but still impressive. It looked like it was about two feet by two feet by four feet long. Eight men carried the box with poles on their shoulders. They wore only a tan shawl over their heads and their tan tunics girded with simple leather belts and leather sandals. They looked like typical desert people, except they had neatly trimmed beards and hair, and wore fresh clothes. They carried no weapons. Their defense was the thousands of soldiers 1,000 feet around them.

Quietly they marched.

Rahab's family took turns looking out the little window. Olmad held up his two little boys so they could see what was coming to take the city. Although no one ever mentioned a word in front of the children, they were beginning to question the strength of Jericho's walls against so many soldiers. No one had never seen, nor even heard, of such a massive army.

Silently they marched.

Then came the rear guard. Much like the front guard another entire army that, itself, was twice the population of Jericho. Olmad said he believed the whole army must be four times the size of the city. Like those in the front and side guards, these men were young, strong, and determined fighters. They, too, wore the leather vests, and wide leather belts with the swinging leather straps and the leather sandals with high shin guards. They carried short swords that remained in their holsters. On every eighth or twelfth step they would clap their hands to keep the cadence. It was an eerie sound of so many hands coming together in a single stroke. The clap was not loud or pretentious. It was just strong. It was a solemn, scary feeling; a sound of death.

All those sandals stirred up a lot of dust in the air. It came settling through the open window. The family noticed something else, too. There was a new odor. It was the smell of leather polish

The front guard had marched out of view. The trumpeters had passed by and only heard their sounds from the rear, — muffled by distance. The three men and blue box and most of the soldiers had gone by and still the army was marching past the little window. With most of them out of view, the family members could not figure out what was going on, or where they were going. This was not an attack formation — even Rahab knew that. So she went downstairs to get a report from the turrets.

The courtyard was filled with people and animals. They were quiet, only occasionally whispering among themselves and listening to the information being relayed by the men in the turrets. The defense of the city was ready.

"Jabu. Jabu. Can you hear me?" Rahab was calling to the turrets.

"Hello, Rahab. I'm here."

"Jabu, tell me what's going on. What's happening now?"

"The Israelites seem to be returning to their tents. The front guard and the blue box have already passed around the city and they seem to be headed back to Gilgal."

"Thank you, Jabu."

She went back into her apartment. The children met her at the front door with the scarlet cord from the window. They said their daddy had taken it down. Rahab hurriedly thanked the two boys for it and raced back up stairs where she immediately re-tied it to the window frame and let it flow out the opening. Her brother teased her about it and she only told him it was her good luck charm. This was her house and if she wanted a good luck charm, she could hang one from the window if she wanted. He only held up both hands in mock defense and then smiled. It was the only levity all morning.

Rahab reported what her friend had said about the army passing around the city and appeared to be heading back to Gilgal. They were expecting some kind of surprise move, some strange attack pattern, but so far it had not happened. The storm seems to be passing without any damage, but Jericho's soldiers kept their positions on the mighty wall.

It took them more than an hour to reach the city, and more than two hours for the group to march around the city. However, just as they had come, the Hebrews marched back to their camp in Gilgal. Not one word was spoken. No threatening signals. Not one sword was drawn. There were no battering rams. There were no ladders to scale the walls. It made everyone feel so strange. The family had been at Rahab's most of the morning witnessing this unusual event. It was all they could talk about.

The people of Jericho did not understand the Hebrew parade but they were all glad that it was over. Rahab's family went back to their own apartments to eat a late breakfast.

Defense Strategies

The King's Counsel stayed in chambers all day and was up much of the night trying to figure strategies for an enemy that did not fight. What would they do next? How could they defend against such a huge army? There was no telling what kind of reserves, if any, were still back in the enemy encampment. Should they post some surprise fighters in the palm trees? Should they make small rushing attacks at various points in the Hebrew encampment to cause distractions while they started fires in other portions of the camp? As close as the Hebrews were camped, a good wind and a small fire could solve the King's problem.

Another possibility was that Ark. If everything they did came from their God in the blue box, then whoever had the blue box would be in charge. So they again spent hours on how to steal the blue box without touching it. If they could get a few good men inside the camp and pretend to be Hebrew, perhaps they could find and steal the box. Maybe, they could even kidnap some of the priests in the tan robes and force them to carry out the blue box.

Then, maybe they were getting over excited over nothing. Perhaps this march around the city with such a show of strength was a scare tactic. Perhaps just flexing their muscle kept people in line around them. They discussed it, but no one believed it.

Through the day the King's Counsel made no announcements of defense strategies except to rely on the great wall as the city always had. The King waited for someone from the enemy camp to come make an offer of surrender or cooperation, but none came. The Hebrews just went back to their homes and did their chores as though nothing had happened.

All of Jericho was frightened. They kept listening for the return of the enemy. None of the spotters were outside the walls. The harvesters stayed in. Everyone was locked in the safety of the great walls. People often talked in whispers as though they expected to hear the invaders again. But nothing came by afternoon. And even in the darkness of the night, there were no attacks from the strangers. The Hebrews had come, marched around the city and then went back home. Nothing else happened.

Before bedtime, Rahab went back to her little window, took the red cord in her hand and said, "Thank you Lord for sparing our lives today. Thank you for sparing Jericho. Thank you for being my God." She let the cord slide through her fingers and watched it dance in the wind outside the window. There was freedom and hope in the way the ribbon danced.

Second Day

The next morning at daylight, Jericho heard the rams' horns again. This must be the day. The defense team sprang to their positions on the turrets. The fires were started to boil the water. The catapults swung into positions. Within minutes, Jericho was ready.

Rahab ran to get her family as she did the day before. The wind was sharp against her cheeks. She unconsciously pulled the shawl over her lower face. Still sleepy-eyed the family and their servants gathered again in her sleeping room to look out the window. Yesterday must have been a practice run. Today would be the battle. This would be the bloody battle she had seen in her nightmares; where the mean soldiers would reach inside her chest and pull out her heart and squeeze her blood from it. This must be the day.

Again, the long columns of soldiers marched around the city, followed by the little band carrying the Ark of the Covenant and then the rear guard of more soldiers. This time they were more efficient. Wider flanks meant shorter columns; more men were in position faster.

Everyone in the massive army was quiet. Not a word spoken. No directions. No orders. No drawn swords. No battering rams. No long ladders. Nothing threatening. Just like the day before, the soldiers lead the group around the city. The men with the shields and spears were out front, followed by the men in leather armor. Then came the big open square surrounded by thousands of soldiers protecting the trumpeters, the three men in white and the Ark on the shoulders of eight carriers. Then thousands of more soldiers in broad flanks like the front guard. They marched around the city and back to Gilgal. Jericho was left with settling dust and the smell of leather polish. Fortunately, a gusty wind pushed the odor away before noon.

Once the group got to Jericho, it was all over fairly quickly. The whole episode was eerie, almost amusing. Were they going to take the city with the sound of rams' horns?

During the day a few men stopped by the idols in the courtyard to say prayers and make offerings. That was unusual because generally the idols were ignored, but the people were truly worried about these unusual happenings. The big moon god got the most attention. The enemy was so massive, so strong, how could there be any defense except these walls?

The King cautiously sent out three spotters. Perhaps the Israelites were leaving a few people behind, perhaps hiding in the brush or up in the Palm trees or something, ready for a surprise attack. But the spotters confirmed all of the Israelites went back to camp. The Israelite soldiers changed out of their uniforms, and put away their swords and spears. The people cooked meals, did laundry, fed their animals and tended to housekeeping chores. They gathered corn and flax and more fruit. They didn't act like fighters. No one could figure out what was going on.

Third Day

Jericho slept easier that night. But all were awakened at daybreak with more rams' horns. It was a repeat of the day before. This time the guards did little preparation for battle. They even let some women and children up on the great wall to see the strangers who had come to entertain with their ability to march and play trumpets at the same time.

Rahab's family did not come over. Again, the event started at about daylight and lasted until mid-morning. There was no sun and the gusty wind was blowing up sand. Little whirlwinds of desert sand made columns of dust and sand in the air. It was hard to breathe, but the soldiers came anyway. They came in their same formations. Their armor looked dull without the sun.

The principle conversation in the courtyard that day was about the standards that marked different groups. One of the off-duty lookouts said he had counted twelve banners around the army. Perhaps there are twelve groups within the Hebrew encampment. Beyond that the parade remained a mystery.

About noon, there was a soft shower that cleaned the air of dust and the smell of leather polish. When the sun did peek out, the wet fronds of the palm trees were glistening. Rahab thought that maybe it was a sign from God that there was hope in this mysterious world. Again, she caught herself saying out loud, "I wished I knew more about this new God."

Fourth Day

On the fourth day it was an automatic repeat of the same show and the people began to make jokes about it. The tension relaxed. Few people paid much attention to the daily event. The preparations for defense remained ready around the wall but no one seemed to care. If the big army began to attack then the cauldrons could be heated fairly quickly and the spears and hurling knives remained ready. But no extra soldiers were called to the walls. It was just routine observation.

"I wish they would learn to play another song."

"Can't they march easier and not stir up so much dust?"

"Where are they keeping all their pretty girls?"

"They don't have any back bone. They don't fight like men."
"They think their bad music will make us surrender."
The trumpet players sounded off and everyone took the tour around the walls and went back to Gilgal. And Jericho went about their usual tasks inside the safety of the walls.

Fifth Day

Again, the next morning, Jericho was awakened with the approach of the heralding rams' trumpets. This was the fifth day in a row. Again, they came, circled the city and left without speaking a word. They made no sound other than the rams' horns. Most of Jericho didn't even bother to take notice of the mighty power the invaders represented but did not use. All the tension of a possible attack had vanished. The invaders just seemed to be out for their morning exercise. Rahab's folks didn't come over. No one could understand what the army was doing. They certainly were not a warring party. They didn't fight. They didn't attack. They didn't carry ladders or catapults or battering rams. They had nothing to attack the walls and gates. Despite their mighty strength, they were not serious contenders. There were no envoys sent to talk with the King. There were no attacks on the farmers and fruit growers outside the walls. The Hebrews were only men who liked to parade. It seemed to be some sort of religious practice.

Sixth Day

On the sixth day, it was the same thing. Just after dawn, thousands of soldiers armed with spears, swords and arrows were sounding off and leading the three men and then that box draped in blue cloth, then even more armed soldiers. There were so many soldiers, yet they drew no weapons, made no advances on the walls of Jericho. No one had ever seen such a massive army that did not fight. All they did was repeat their previous performance of marching around Jericho and going back home to do their chores. No one in Jericho could figure out why they would go to so much trouble of getting dressed for battle, go out and march around the city and then go home. Were they afraid? Were they shy? What is going on here? No one had answers to their questions.

The Hebrew soldiers didn't even much look in Jericho's direction. The men carried the blue box just behind the trumpets, but the men on the walls said they could not see any God behind the wrappings. The soldiers were much more efficient now. They used wider lines and compacted more people into the march so that the parade was shorter from front to rear. Before breakfast was ready, they had come and gone. Rahab didn't bother her folks about coming over. Everyone slept in — as best as they could — and then Rahab went upstairs and took down the scarlet cord from the window. This whole thing must be a joke. So she spent the day with a friend weaving flax into linen.

7

The Seventh Day

Again, on the seventh day, Jericho was awakened early. The noisy neighbors were out for their morning exercise. The trumpets sounded in the distance, playing the same chant as they marched before their God's box. The soldiers wore their armor and carried their spears and swords. The people of Jericho were wishing they would learn to sleep later. Only the regular night guard was on duty in the turrets. All the guards had seen the parades and this was just a repeat, boring performance. No one bothered to call out the emergency group.

It takes a while for the front contingency to get from Gilgal to Jericho, so most of Jericho slept as best they could through the noisy approach. Then it takes almost the same amount of time for the first group to march around the city. This is always the loudest part, however, when the people in the square with the rams' horns and blue box get past the city on their return, the world becomes a quieter place.

The front bunch with the trumpeters marched around the city and then everything fell silent. Usually, the trumpets faded away as they marched back to camp, but not this time. After six days, all of Jericho knew their routine, but today, they were doing something different. Rahab grabbed for her robe and ran barefoot outside to see what was going on.

"Jabez. Jabez. What are they doing?" Rahab called to her friend.

"They just stopped. They seem to be resting. The front people made the circle around the city and then stopped. Oh, and there are some other people coming in from Gilgal. They're sitting down in a large ring on the far side of their soldiers. They're just watching. They must be the late sleepers, Rahab."

Second Circle

After a short break, there was a surprise move. The rams' horns took up the chanting tune and the soldiers paraded around the city a second time. By the time they finished their second round, the sun was up and spotters could see that they had brought in a few more of their own people to watch the parade around Jericho. Again, they stopped at their beginning point and took a little break. More people were pouring out of the encampment and forming a wide circle outside the soldiers' circle. The Hebrews were quiet. Softly, they talked among themselves. They must have been whispering. They were by the palm trees and at the edge of the fields and near the roads that lead to the front gate. They were forming a complete circle around Jericho.

Third Circle

When the soldiers started their third parade, Rahab became worried. This day was different. She went back to her upstairs window and replaced the scarlet cord. Then she got dressed and went to her parent's place to try to convince them to come spend the day with her. They said they had things to do and would visit later. Neither her brother nor sisters showed any interest.

Olmad told her, "Rahab, you are just getting nervous by all the weird sounds from the horns. Jericho had never been beaten, even by people who used heavy weapons. These people have only come to play awful music and parade. You have seen them. They carry nothing with them to get through the front gate. And no one can get inside Jericho except through that big, heavy gate. Just relax a little. Everything will be all right."

Fourth Circle

Rahab's friends in the turrets called down answers to her questions as the strangers started their fourth parade of the day. The guards said that a ring of the people was forming around the city just beyond the parade route of the soldiers. These were the ordinary people, not the soldiers. The army was parading closer than usual to the walls, yet still out of spear range. The citizens were probably 200 yards away from the wall, out among the palms and acacia trees. They were bringing bags and baskets of food. It looked as though they might be camping out. They talked very quietly among themselves. Some of them seemed to be praying.

Some of the soldiers rested as others marched. Less than half of the fighters were now marching while the remainder rested. The Ark carriers and the trumpeters changed off when the fourth parade concluded. While some rested, others marched, and then they changed places. For some reason the soldiers seemed to be conserving their strength.

Fifth Circle

Some of the Jericho guards became suspicious of how the soldiers were conducting themselves. They agreed to talk with the Captain about it. They all agreed that this was an unusual day and that it would not hurt anything to call the rest of the guards to duty and prepare for battle. So the guards in the turrets sounded the gong and called for the full contingency to join them. The King was alerted of the extra step of alertness. The fires were started to boil the water for the catapults. Men claimed their supply of hurling knives. The towers at the gate were fully staffed. But the Israelites still had no battering rams for the big gate. There was no way to get into Jericho.

It was already noon. The people ran shifts of parading and resting. More and more of their people came from their Gilgal camp and joined the great outside circle. It was now almost completely around the city. But there was nothing threatening about them, only a strange feeling. They made a fifth parade. As the bulk of the army marched around the city, more and more civilians joined the big circle around Jericho.

Sixth Circle

During the sixth parade of the day, jeers were beginning to come up out of Jericho's grand courtyard.

"Those guys have too much sand in their sandals."

"You mean, sand on the brain."

Everyone was laughing and jeering the strangers for having nothing else to do but run around the city all day. They were a bunch of sissies.

The strange, haunting, and overpowering feeling was coming over Rahab again. The same spirit that guided her when the spies came to her apartment was now coursing through every inch of her body. Something was about to happen. These people were not here for a camp out, they were preparing for battle!

Rahab went back to her mother and father and desperately

insisted they come over and stay with her. She became frantic to get the family to come to her apartment. "Rahab, if you are worried, you can stay with us. Here, make yourself comfortable," her father insisted.

"No, you don't understand. You must come to my place. Something bad is going to happen. You must come now!" Rahab was in tears trying to persuade her parents to bring their servants to her apartment. They didn't understand, but they reluctantly agreed. Anything was better than for Rahab to have another one of her spells in front of the family.

"Perhaps it would be quieter in her apartment," they said.

Her desperation finally moved her brother and his family and her sisters to come, bringing their servants. "Hurry," Rahab pleaded. "Everyone *must* come. You *must!*"

They kept asking why, but all she could say was, "*Because you must!*" At last, they all went to Rahab's apartment — family and servants.

Dust sifted down on the courtyard. The odor of pungent leather polish stifled the air. People were milling about, some worried, some sarcastic, some mystified. A few were praying to the moon god. Probably, they were praying for the removal of those awful trumpets. Rahab's group elbowed their way through the crowd and went inside her place.

Seventh Circle

The soldiers' break was over and for the seventh time — now late afternoon — the rams' horns sounded their call and the full contingent of soldiers began their circle. When all 40,000 of them marched, they formed columns about five hundred men wide and the length was enough to entirely encircle the outside walls of Jericho. They marched around with the soldiers in front, then the trumpeters, the three men, then the Ark of the Covenant and finally the rear guard. The front circle of soldiers was only a few feet from the back of the columns of the rear guard — that's how big the army was.

This time, as they went around the city, a flood of citizens from the Israelite encampment came to the larger outside circle, multiplying the ranks of those that had camped out during the day and provided support for the army. Now they all stood up and shoulder to shoulder took small steps toward the walls of Jericho.

The lookouts were relaxed and were even getting bored by

the whole exercise. There was just no meaning to all this. However, they kept their posts under the King's orders and kept reporting the running commentary. The catapults were ready to be loaded with the boiling water. Every guard had swords and knives at his station. The reserve guards filled in the defense gaps between the turrets. Jericho was ready if the enemy should decide to attack.

From Rahab's front window, she could see most of the people in the courtyard were in conversation with friends. The worried looks had just about disappeared. A few people were standing in front of the idols in view of her window. The great fear of the first visit of these noisy neighbors had completely evaporated. A little goat had broken away from its owner and was romping through the crowd — a delight for all the children.

Except for the trumpets, all was quiet outside. The men in the turrets said there were more than 500,000 people gathered around the walls of Jericho. There were 50 times as many people outside the walls as there were inside Jericho, but not a sound. Only the crunching footsteps in the sand, and the occasional ping of sword sheath against shield.

The soldiers stopped marching. They were changing their formation. They had been in big blocks of soldiers on parade. Now, the Ark of the Covenant was moved away from the soldiers, and out beyond the circle of civilians. The front guard with their metal armor and spears formed the thick front circle all around Jericho. They were backed up by a second thick circle of men in leather and swords. Behind them were several more rows of armed soldiers. There were so many of them! Quietly, they moved closer to the wall. Still out of range, but closer and orderly, they stepped forward. They were preparing to strike. They were not concentrating on the front gate as enemies always did. There were as many people concentrated on the sides and on the back of Jericho as there were in front by the gate. They still carried no ladders. They had no battering rams, yet, somehow they were preparing to strike.

Silence shrouded Jericho. The silence of the outside penetrated the walls to the courtyard inside. The jeering stopped. Not one word was uttered inside the walls. All hearts froze in their chests with paralyzing fear

Rahab's family moved away from the window and they sat close together on the bed pallet. Olmad and his wife were holding their little boys as close as they could. The storm was coming and they could do nothing about it. God Almighty was ready to release His wrath and *nothing* could stop God's fury.

There was a long pause. Everyone held his breath.

Finally, a single piercing tone from the trumpets filled the air. Then a soul wrenching cry erupted from half a million throats. The mighty shout was a roar of thunder which seized control of every heart in Jericho. It was the sound of volcanoes erupting, lightening stabbing the earth; mighty winds tearing at everything in their way. It was a pounding heart trying to express extreme fear. It was an execution.

People inside the walls responded with their own screams of fear. Rahab ran to her front window to look into the courtyard. People were running here and there like crazy goats. They were yelling, "The walls are breaking! The walls are breaking!"

A section of the wall across from her, between rows of apartments, began cracking. Two gashes began at the top of the 30-foot wall, maybe 40 feet apart. The magnified snaps and pops sounded like giants stomping in the forest. The thunderous gashes ripped and tore their way to meet at the bottom — like a slice of pie. A giant invisible hand was pulling at the wall and tearing it from its history.

"The walls are breaking!" Cracks became gashes and with slow, explosive cries of their own, zigzagged their way around the huge building stones — the very stones that gave the ancient wall its mighty strength. The biting cracks chewed at the foundation of the entire wall.

With each lightening snap of the cracks, the people in the courtyard screamed. Their gasping breaths could not fend off the fear. Their hands were over their ears, but it was no defense from the gouging sounds of the crumbling wall. Their hearts poured out their fright.

Rahab cried, "O Lord, have mercy!" And God heard her cry. Rahab's heart was ready for God's answers to her prayers.

The chunk of wall between the gaping cracks gave a mighty sigh, hesitantly quivered, and then crashed to the ground, exploding into a cloud of dust and debris. Big chunks of rocks slammed into apartments injuring the people huddled nearby. Human bodies spewed fountains of blood. The boiling water meant to keep the enemy off the walls was now spilling down inside and burning Jericho's own citizens. Knives and spears came spraying off the top of the wall, like a rain storm, striking people and animals in the grand courtyard. Rahab watched a guard lose his balance on the swaying wall and fall to the courtyard – onto his own sword. Then a large stone from the wall fell and crushed him.

The people of Jericho were being killed by their own fighting materials. They were captured within their crumbling defense. The wall wailed again of its own misery, nervously wobbling in the air. More cracks were forming and a turret with the lookouts on top began to sway and fall into the people's living quarters -- crushing everyone in the way. Another cloud of dust rose taking up the cry of its people.

The invader's army instantly filled the hole in the wall and poured into the city by the thousands. It was a rushing river of glistening swords and shields. The invaders flooded into the city. Shoulder to shoulder they wedged through the opening with swords swinging.

The first men were stabbing Jericho's guards. Anyone with a weapon of any kind was an instant target. They were running across the courtyard and taking the ladders two rungs at a time to the second and third levels.

The next wave of the surging army started pulling down the idols. They were crushing them as best they could. Six men attacked the moon god on her pedestal and pulled it down breaking it in two. Within a minute or two not one idol was standing.

The next wave of soldiers came stabbing all the men, women and children stifling their screams and cries for mercy. Everyone within reach was killed. First, the people in the courtyard were stabbed with bloody swords. Then a search was started house to house with doors being knocked in and strong men marching in and stabbing everyone without saying a word. Another wave started killing the cows, sheep and donkeys. The waves of terror were not distinctive. They were all happening at once; much like the waves on the Great Sea.

New cracks were forming in the giant wall around the city. Each crack had its own wailing, crunching, piercing, awful, alarming, crying sound.

In a matter of minutes the Israelites were on top of the wall going through the remaining turrets stabbing any lookouts and guards remaining there. The soldiers used pieces of support beams as small battering rams to knock open the locked doors. They knew exactly where to go. They were in the royal chambers of the King and his counselors. They were in the granaries, the treasury, the stores, and every house in the city. Three soldiers brushed against the adobe exterior of Rahab's apartment. She held her breath, but they didn't come in. Perhaps, her place had been overlooked. There was such confusion out there. Jericho was like a bunch of ants when their hill is disturbed.

In half an hour it was over.

Ten thousand people lay dead in their homes and in the courtyard, face down in their own blood. Ten thousand lives had been taken in just minutes. The friends were gone. The government was gone. The herds were gone. The food was gone. Everything. Gone.

The city was filled with dead bodies in pools of dirty blood. The stench of death began to fill the stale, dusty air. More sections of the great wall were crumbling and falling down with clouds of dust and ear-piercing thunder. The walls that were meant to provide safety had actually imprisoned the citizens and prevented their escape. Although it would have been to no use. The enemy was stationed all around the city to kill anyone who might try to escape.

All were quiet in Rahab's apartment. The siege had passed over them. They had been overlooked. They turned to hug each other for strength and encouragement just as God was about to answer the rest of Rahab's plea. Something suddenly rammed her front door and crashed it in! Two soldiers burst into Rahab's apartment like a blast of desert wind. They were standing tall. Feet apart. Their bloody swords drawn. Somebody's blood was dripping on her floor. Everyone gasped. Their turn had come.

One soldier shouted, "Rahab! Come quickly. We must leave now. This part of the wall is about to fall!" They were the two spies who had come to make good on their promise. The family was stunned. The soldiers insisted, "Come! Come! All of you. We must leave!. Hurry! Not much time!"

Dazed by the shock of the intrusion of the enemy, Rahab's family began to move in obedience without knowing what was going on. Rahab and the other women in the group automatically grabbed their shawls while the men were pushing them towards the door.

Gently, the two Hebrews escorted the amazed family out of Rahab's apartment and into the courtyard where other soldiers took them through the maze of bodies to the section of the wall that had just fallen.

The sky was all red from the dust of the disintegrated walls. The dust was so thick it was making everyone cough. No one could breathe. Rahab saw one of her neighbors lying in a pool of blood, holding her bleeding child. There was a runaway sheep struggling from its wounds. Rahab's family was in the middle of a great storm of destruction. The crumbling wall wailed of its thunderous pain. Thunder you cannot touch. Thunder you cannot forget.

As they trudged toward a gaping hole in the wall, climbing over large pieces of furniture, bedding and clothing, another section of the wall made a gasping sound. It quivered in the late afternoon air. Then it collapsed to the ground like a cookie in a one-year-old's hand. Cautiously, the soldiers lead the family from the city. They were climbing over fallen stones, wall sections, broken furniture, and bodies.

Rahab saw a neighbor crushed by a big boulder. He had run outside when the storm came. Rahab's gate keeper friends had glazed eyes and gaping wounds in their chests. Unconsciously, she stooped to pick up a baby's rattler, but had second thoughts and threw it back to the ground. It had blood on it. Death was everywhere.

Rahab looked back to see a giant crack coming in the wall over her house. She screamed and then held a hand over her mouth. Her family turned to see the wall split. The late afternoon sun stabbed through the cracks with long dagger-rays of sunset. Then the wall weaved slowly back and forth before it slammed down on her house; crushing everything she owned. A giant door had been shut in her life. Her mother cried and her father held her close. The Israelites grabbed up her two sisters to hurry them along.

After what seemed an eternity, they were outside the rubble. A man and his family waved to them. The woman called out, "Woman with Scarlet Cord, over here." Rahab and the entire family walked with shaken steps to a wagon drawn by a donkey. The man held back but the woman came forward and gave them all hugs. "May God bless you all for He has chosen you above everyone else in Jericho. Please, come with us." The stranger held the reins of the donkey and motioned for everyone to climb into his wagon.

Rahab's parents looked at Rahab with questions marks on their faces but said nothing. Her father helped her mother into the wagon and then the younger sisters. Olmad helped his family and then took Rahab's hand and guided her to the steps up into the wagon. The servants managed for themselves. The Hebrew's wife handed out blankets as each sat down.

"Scarlet Cord Woman, you are blessed," said the woman sitting by her husband. "Blessed, indeed."

None of them knew where they were going. They only knew that they were going away from the disaster scene with its danger and terrible smell. As they pulled away they heard the screeching sounds of another portion of the wall caving in. They did not look back.

They began a slow journey to Gilgal. The family rode in silence, too shaken to speak. The children clung to Olmad, with frightened eyes. His wife hugged the two sisters. The parents and Rahab sat in one big hug. Another section of the wall made its last roar and crashed into the city rubble.

The outer circle of civilian Hebrews began slowly to make their may back to camp. They spread out in a long horizontal line reaching from north to south of Gilgal. There were clusters of neighbors traveling together. Some of the Hebrews began clapping their hands and singing praises to God for His mercy, His love and His victory over idols. They were singing, "Holy God of All Creation, maker of people and nations, we praise you as you reign over everyone and everything. Praise you for victory over idols. Praise you for loving and caring, Praise you for protection from the evil one. To God be the Glory. Blessed be God for His mercy, love and glory. Blessed be God for His Glory."

The Hebrews had prepared tents and bedding for Rahab's family. They explained that because of their religion, non-Jewish people could not live inside their camp. However, they were welcome to stay next door in Friends Camp; which they did, with about one hundred other families.

A stranger appeared at their campsite about the time the family arrived. He brought some big mats which he dropped to the ground covering the sparse grass. Onto them he dropped blankets and a few cushions to sit on. There was no real order to the things he dropped in front of the tents. He just dropped them and figured the servants could arrange them to suit everyone. "You have been chosen, my friends," said the man who provided the items.

"What do you mean? Rahab's father asked.

The stranger's voice was low and gravel-like. "You are chosen by God to be survivors of Jericho. God chooses everyone who wants to be chosen. Your daughter pleaded before the Almighty and He has answered her. Shalom."

The family began to cry. Each took a cushion from the pile and sat down. There was no order, no formality. They were sharing their loss with each other. Mother said, "I have nothing to cook with. We have no clothes. We have nothing."

"What am I going to wear tomorrow?" One of the young sisters was worried.

"Dear," said her husband, "Its all right not to have anything to cook with, because we have nothing to cook." And then he smiled a little, but there were tears in his eyes. "But we have each other."

"Yes, Dad, we have each other," said Olmad. "We will work something out when the sun shines tomorrow." Then he stretched his long arms out to each side and embraced the next two people and they each did the same thing. Quickly, the entire family, including their servants, were one big hug.

Rahab's Confession

"I have something to tell you. All of you," Rahab began hesitantly. She was brushing the tears from her face. "I have a confession to make."

"You have what, dear?" Her mother was asking.

"I have a confession." Rahab paused, gathering up her courage and her strength. "Several months ago — when I was so sick and a mystery to everyone, and a horrible family member — I was carrying a secret; a horrible secret. Now, I can tell you. I knew that this day was coming. I knew that Jericho would be attacked. I've known for several months. I didn't know when or how it would happen or whether or not we would survive the attack on Jericho. But I knew that the Hebrews were coming to destroy Jericho."

"You knew what, dear?" Mother asked.

"Remember when the spies came in and then disappeared?" Everyone was quiet and all eyes were on Rahab. "Well, the spies came to see me. They had already been in Jericho for some time and they broke into my apartment and held me captive for a little while until I promised to give them information. All I really did was confirm their suspicions. But while they were in my apartment, the city guards came and ask me to turn in the spies. But something, — some strange feeling — came over me and because of this strange feeling, I protected the spies and told the guards that they had already left. The guards went out of the city to search for them. When the guards left, I went upstairs and talked to the spies on my roof. We swore an oath. Because I had protected them from being arrested in Jericho, they in turn wouldn't kill my family. There was one catch. I had to swear that I would tell no one about them being there or what they were doing, or anything else."

"Oh dear, you should have told me," her mother said.

"I couldn't tell you, Mother, because it would cancel the oath. And we would be killed along with everyone else. The hardest part was that I never knew if the spies made it back across the river. Or if their commander would accept the agreement they made with me. All I could do was trust that their God would take care of it. That's why I was driven to break up the fertility god in front of my place. I had to get the idols out of my life if I was going to follow their God. I never knew whether I was doing right or wrong. I knew that everyone was in danger — everyone was about to be murdered — and I couldn't breathe a word about it."

Rahab paused to wipe her eyes and face, then she continued. "Anyway, that's why I was so insistent about getting everyone into my apartment when they did come to destroy the city. The agreement was that only the people in my apartment would be saved. There were times when I doubted that, especially when the walls began crumbling. I've never been so frightened in my life."

"We were all frightened, Rahab. We were all frightened very much," Olmad said as he reached over to hug her. "So, that is why the scarlet cord was in your window. It was a signal to the Hebrews."

"That's why the Hebrews have been calling you Woman with the Scarlet Cord," someone else reasoned.

"Yes, but I couldn't explain why the cord had to be there. And you don't know how many times I became discouraged and took it down, or became frightened and put it back. Because I never knew if there would only be a handful of spies who would sneak into the city and destroy it or an army with battering rams come marching up to the front gate. It's been a long, a very long, nightmare, but now it's over. Thank God."

Her dad reached over and lovingly, patted her cheek and then placed his hand on her shoulder. "You did just fine, darling. You did just fine. I'm sorry for the misery you had to go through. I wish I could have helped. but I'm glad you stuck with it and kept your word. Because of that, we're all alive and sitting here tonight. While we look around to see what we don't have, we should be grateful for what we do have. We still have each other."

Her mother had listened with her hand over her mouth. Her father had this amazed look on his face. Olmad, his wife and sisters just couldn't believe it. Rahab felt relief, a new air of confession sweeping through her insides. Every sentence was a lift of the weighted burden she had carried for months. Each word was a chip off the jagged rock that had taken over her insides. Rahab took a deep breath and slowly let out the giant sigh. A refreshing sigh that cleared her body of the dark secret.

Then looking away towards their crumbling homestead, Rahab so very slowly said something. It sounded, so hesitantly, like it came from an old woman. The words were hardly joined at all. Her voice was sad, heavy and dark.

"What did you say, dear?" Her mother asked.

"I said that the Almighty God has answered my prayers. He has kept His promise. We live to see a new beginning. A life without walls."

A Hebrew couple brought them a pot of vegetable porridge and fresh baked bread. "Careful," the man said. "The bowls are hot."

"Thank you so very much," Rahab's father said, as he stood to receive the gift. "I'm not sure what we would do without the gracious help everyone has been offering. How can I repay you?"

"Not us. You owe us nothing. It is our gift in God's service. This gift comes from God. We only provide the hands and feet to offer it to you. You will have many opportunities to offer God's gifts to other people. When you do, remember this night of salvation. Remember the day God saved you."

"Thank you, my friend. Thank you again," Father said.

The family and servants scooped up the porridge with chunks of the bread and realized how hungry they were. They sat there on the blankets looking at the cloud of dust in the air and the broken wall around what had been a beautiful city. They heard the last section of the wall split, crumble and crash into a new pillar of dust and smoke. Two thousand years of history came to an end in a single afternoon.

Darkness was falling over the land, yet there were still soldiers at the battle site making sure that everything that had been alive was now dead. They gathered all the gold, silver, bronze and brass articles out of the treasury and sent them to their God's treasury somewhere inside the big camp. Everything else was destroyed and then Jericho was set on fire. The family gasped when they saw the first flames reach for the sky and encircle their homes. They soon smelled the smoke as it was lifted up towards heaven and then spread across the sky. It was an awfully sad sight. Their hearts were burning with each body in the flames. The city had been sacrificed. It was a burnt offering.

Another Hebrew and his two sons came up to the family with arm loads of firewood. "Here's some wood to make a fire for tonight. It will make a little light for you. We'll try to do better tomorrow," offered the new neighbor.

Rahab's father was on his feet again to receive the offering. But the boys placed the sticks of wood on the ground near the center of the circle where the family was sitting. One boy expertly arranged some of the short logs, placed some twigs and then some leaves underneath the top log. Only then did the older man stoop over and light the leaves from his torch. Soon the fire was giving off some light. When the new neighbor was satisfied with the progress of the fire, he turned to the family and said, "May you give as much love as this fire gives you warmth and light. May you find peace with God." He and his boys walked from the circle of light. No one said anything. They just watched the new fire.

Out of the gray dusk of evening a gruff and angry voice shouted, "The prostitute! Where's the prostitute?" The calm of the sad evening was broken by this angry man.

Olmad stood up and went to meet the shadowy man outside the circle of light. "What do you want, my friend?"

"I'm not your friend. I want the prostitute. They tell me that a prostitute has come into our midst and she can't live here. She must go away. We can't have evil people living in our midst. No prostitutes allowed. Where is she?"

"My friend, your God has just saved this family from the destruction of Jericho. We're the only survivors of that great city over there. Can't you leave us alone in our grief? We have lost all of our friends. We have lost all of our belongings. All we have here is each other right now."

"I'm not your friend. I only want to chase the prostitute out of this camp. We can't have unclean, defiling, detestable women in this place, or God, himself, will come down on all of us. Now, where is she?"

Just at that moment someone else came up behind the shadowy stranger and whirled him around. The shadow man grabbed the intruder's arm and with a single motion pinned it behind his back and the other hand went for his face, clinching his jaw so he could not speak.

"That is enough, my brother! Leave these people alone. They're new to Friends Camp and they're here by God's will. You have nothing to say about it. Whom God saves and whom God destroys is His business, not yours. Don't hinder the will of God. Now, go your way." And as easily as the stranger was caught, so he was released. His shadow against the darkening sky faded away.

"Sorry for that intrusion," said the tall stranger. "My name is Salmon. I was one of the people who were blessed by God to assist you out of the danger up there." And he pointed back to the burning city.

They all stood up to greet him. "I don't mean to disturb your peace, but I just happened to hear that fellow talking loudly and you don't need any of that — especially this evening." He paused for a moment and then continued. "Let me assure you that you're living in the will and the grace of an Almighty God. He has saved you from the idols of Jericho by the might of His army. He did that so that you can learn to love Him as He provides for you. He is here to love you, protect you, and care for you. I trust you will learn more as the days go by."

Olmad was closest and extended his hand to Salmon's shoulder to greet him. "Thank you for coming."

"Where is Rahab?" Salmon asked.

"Over here," she said as she stepped toward the front of the group.

"How are you doing?"

"I guess all right. Shaken. But all right."

"Rahab, you are a very brave, young woman. I suppose you have carried a tremendous burden over these months. I want you to know that you've played an important part in a mission of God. You probably have very little knowledge of what we are doing here — I'm not sure we even understand it all — but we are here by God's will. I just wanted to wish you well. Perhaps I can come back by in a few days, after you get settled, and we can talk some."

"That would be nice." Rahab's voice was squeaking.

"Oh, one other thing. If you don't mind..." Salmon was asking permission to speak again.

"Of course."

"I recall that once you were seeking a better understanding of the God of Israel. I remember that you wanted to know more about the Almighty and renounce your idols in Jericho."

"Yes, that's true and I still do, but look where it's got us. Our homes are destroyed. We have no place to go. No jobs. No furnishings.

No clothes. Tonight we have nothing. Not even food for breakfast." Rahab had her arms extended in the survey of nothings.

"But that is the best beginning," said Salmon. "The very best beginning. Now you are dependent entirely on God. Now you can recognize His help and see His wonderful assistance in your lives. You'll learn so much faster that it is not by your own will that you live, but it is by the glory of the Almighty that you even breathe, much less accomplish anything. Just as He has provided for you this evening with these gifts, so God will bring you blessings you never dreamed possible, when you ask of him.

"To answer your prayers, God has already sent you an army of 40,000 men to take the idols out of your life and He has sent two million new friends to help you adjust to God's way of service." Salmon turned to the circle of people. To them he said, "Do me a favor and concentrate on what you have and not on what you believe you have lost. God will do amazing things in your life.

"Rahab, you've had an encounter with God. You have seen His grace. It was by the grace of God that we crossed the Jordan on dry ground. And today you've seen God's strength and might by taking down the walls of Jericho. You've seen His wrath in eliminating the idol worshipers. I know that this is sad for you now and you see it as a terrible loss. But I pray, in time, that you and your family will have a different view of this act. While you have loss, you also have great gain. You have gained much more than you will ever lose. Never underestimate the will or the love of the only true God."

"That's kind of difficult to see right now," Olmad spoke up. "Why would your God want to work in our lives? How do we rate His interest?"

"Of course, it's difficult for you. Very difficult indeed. Let me come back sometime when you are not in shock from this encounter and we can talk at length. But let me give you one example."

"Fair enough," Olmad agreed.

"You and your family are destined to be great — in Godly terms. Your greatness may not mature for many years but it will come.

"Take our father, Abraham, for instance. Four hundred years ago he was promised children like the stars of the heavens. The problem was that he was 99 years old and he had no children. At that advanced age, God gave him two sons. God also promised him that someday his offspring would live in and occupy Canaan. And here we are. We are His seed, two million strong. That may be less than the number of stars in the sky, but I believe you will agree it's a pretty good start. We don't control Canaan yet, but God has given us our first major city. We now have the gateway into the land. He has given us the whole land of Canaan in our Father Abraham's name. We only need to claim it. That is greatness on the grand scale.

"But God's holy blessing, comes on much smaller everyday scales, too. Today, you've received substance from strangers you've never met, and you may never see them again. You have a need and God is filling that need by sending His servants to you. It's the servants' holy love to be able to fill your need; the need God has chosen to supply you."

Salmon made a sweeping gesture with a long arm and continued, "What has God planned for you? Each of you? Your greatness may be in starting a little ripple on the Great Sea. A ripple that God will grow into a major wave to lift a boat off a sand bar somewhere. Your little ripple may save the lives of all on that boat. And you may never know it. Perhaps you will give food to a child who will live to be a king one day. Or maybe you give a cup of cold water to a stranger who will bring peace to a troubled land. Perhaps you will speak an encouraging word to some person and God will love you for it. You may never know the results. But great results will come because God has ordained it. Your love of God will be reflected in the way you love the people around you — and extend for untold generations yet to be born.

"Well, you see how I like to talk. I'm intruding on your peace. God loves you and is with you. May you walk with God for the rest of your days." Salmon was ready to leave.

"Thank you for coming tonight. I'm sure we all have a lot to think about." Rahab reached for his hands but the man in the shadows had already turned and was absorbed into the darkness of the night.

Silence fell on the campsite. Every one resumed their places before the visitors came. While it was encouraging to hear about the new God and how blessings were suppose to be flowing to them, there was still an empty place in each heart. The blessings had not solved their loneliness. No blessing covered the emptiness of being uprooted from their homes. No blessing covered the sadness of losing their friends. Perhaps they will understand tomorrow, but tonight they were mourning.

Gradually, the soldiers returned home. It had been a long day for them too. Some came with the treasury spoils of Jericho. Nothing else was taken from the city. So most of the soldiers returned empty handed, tired from a long day of work. Many of them were carrying their small children and had their wives along side. There was no bragging. No down playing their enemy. They seemed to have had a job to do and they did it and now they, too, were coming home. Some soldiers, however, remained around Jericho to keep watch over the total destruction of the city. They were there all night.

Rahab and her family huddled together and watched as their city burned. They watched how the smoke rose in tall columns and ate at the dust in the air. The whole sky was red. Dark palm trees were silhouetted against the red-orange horizon. Now and then there was a burst as pots of oil or something else would get too hot and explode. It would send sparks hundreds of feet into the night sky.

The family stayed huddled together all that night watching their city and their homes burn until there was nothing else to watch. There was not much talking. Mostly just watching. It was their history, their heritage, their home and their friends that were going up in smoke and flame. Sadness filled their bones.

It was a long night. A very long night.

8

A New Beginning

As the night grew quieter and darker, the frightened family became calmer. They were totally out of tears, but they still cried in their hearts. Gradually, they became accustomed to the smell of the smoke. The children went to sleep and gradually others of the family would lie down on the pallets that the new neighbors had provided. The Hebrews had prepared tents, but no one went into them. They all stayed together, touching and holding each other. Holding hands was a way of holding hearts, staying connected. It helped to calm their fears.

Rahab was thinking. *Our lives have been ripped apart. Our friends and homes are gone. Everything we owned is gone. All we have is us.*

They were desperate for each other's comfort throughout that very long night. Dad was holding both of his younger girls with his wife leaning against him as she had often done through all their years of marriage. Nearby, Olmad and his wife clung to their little boys as if they had to breathe for them. Rahab was next to Olmad, but not far from her father. As the flames of their homes stopped their popping and crackling sounds and ever so slowly faded into the silent night, they began to relax and with the ease of tension, came a little rest and some sleep.

"I was just thinking," Olmad said, "that if the Hebrew God had made the great wall crumble, then isn't it possible that He rescued us from the disaster? And if He did that He will provide for us."

He gave Rahab's shoulders a gentle squeeze then he went to sleep wondering how things were going to be from here on.

Rahab was thinking: *What a nice thought. Could it be the work of the Hebrew God that saved our lives instead of the two spies? Perhaps the two spies were acting in behalf of God — like angels. Lots of strange things have happened today. God saved the family through the spies and all of these charitable people we met tonight. I'm doubting my own faith again. Thank you, Lord, for answering my prayers.* With a small smile on her face she closed her eyes and slept with her brother's head on her shoulder.

Dawn stole in silently, sweeping away the stars and fears of the night before. When Rahab's eyes opened, the sun was shining. She jerked awake, alarmed by being in a strange place. Then she remembered yesterday's nightmare and the salvation at the end of the day. She looked around. Her father had already received breakfast from one of the Hebrew women and had placed it on a table someone else brought over. The family was sleeping wherever they wished. Her mother was sitting up and looking around. Her brother was back with his family and sleeping with his two boys under his big, long arm, with his wife on the other side. The air still smelled of smoke.

Her father had been up for a while and was walking around surveying the area. To the north were tents as far as he could see. To the south were even more tents, he guessed all the way to the Dead Sea. He couldn't tell how far back the tents went, but he guessed all the way to the Jordan. They were on the front row of Friends Camp facing the ruins of Jericho. He had met a couple of the neighbors. They seemed friendly. He turned to Rahab and said, "Good morning, sleepy head. Ready for some breakfast?"

"Good morning, Dad ...Are you serving?" He smiled as though nothing had happened. But his eyes were strained and his shoulders were drooping from the weight of yesterday's devastation and a long night with little sleep. He doesn't hide sadness very well, as hard as he tries. He handed his daughter a new kind of bread still warm from a stranger's oven. Then he shared his pot of honey.

Rahab's father said that the woman who brought breakfast was a very kind person. She chatted with him for a short time. What he remembered most from their conversation was that she was telling him how they too were beginning a new kind of life. God had brought them to the land. God had blessed them by being able to harvest crops they didn't plant, and drink from wells they didn't dig.

"She said that it seems that God has blessed us that way too. We could all start over together. Frankly, dear, I don't understand it. Last night we had nothing. We lost everything we owned. And this morning we awake in a place that is not our own and we eat food we didn't cook. Can you image that?"

In one afternoon, the family had gone from one of comfortable living, with their own places, work and friends to a family destitute, homeless, and completely dependent upon others. All they had were the clothes on their backs. They had no food, no place to live, no belongings, no toys for the children, no future — except what might be provided by the strangers who came from across the river to destroy their city, kill their neighbors and burn their homes. They were totally dependent on the enemy. They were living with the enemy. They had no possessions, yet they were the lucky ones. With nothing to touch, they were the blessed residents from Jericho.

As father and daughter were trying to size up the day and the events, her mother joined them and soon the rest of the family.

Then Olmad summed up their situation. "We may have lost our homes and businesses, but I believe we can earn them back, because we still have our lives. And all because of the faith of the Scarlet Cord Woman, here." Olmad gave his sister a hug and one of his little boys came to sit in her lap as he continued, "Because of Rahab's faith and trust, we live today. I suggest that we all learn more about the Hebrew God and we, too, place our trust in Him."

"I think we should see what they gave us in our tents and then plan our day," Rahab's father said. "We have new lives to begin." And so they all went to inspect the tents and walk around a little.

More of the people from Friends Camp came up to speak and wish them well. A few invited them back to their tents to get better acquainted. All offered their services to make them comfortable.

From a distance came a greeting and laugh all rolled into one. No one understood the "Welcome, welcome, welcome – anyone here?" But everyone turned to see who was calling.

The Long Legged Priest

"Hello, my name is Jonathan. I'm one of the priests that work in this end of the encampment. And I'll bet you are the new folks: The ones chosen by God Himself to escape the wrath on Jericho. Am I right?"

Olmad was closest to the new person, so he turned and introduced himself. "Yes. We are the new folks. How may we help you?"

"I just came by to offer God's blessings on you and to wish you well. I know that all this is different than where you lived yesterday. And it's sure different than your old comfortable home is today," and he turned to see the smoldering ruins of Jericho. "But this is a beginning: A new beginning that can bring you many blessings. Blessings not are only for you, but for your children and their children's children." Jonathan insisted on hearing something about everyone, including the servants.

The group wandered back to their camping area and each took a cushion. Then Jonathan went into great detail to reassure everyone in the circle that this was the perfect time for a new beginning. Every one in the giant encampment was at the same starting point.

"But we have nothing," Mother said. "How can we start?"

"I'm glad you asked that. Your family here is at the exact right spot and the exact right time for a new beginning: a time chosen by the Almighty, himself. Your biggest blessing right now is that you have God Almighty on your side. He has saved you from those idols of Jericho. All you have now is the grace and blessing of the Almighty Creator. Everything that comes to you now, you can recognize as coming from Him. Your dinner last night came from God. Your breakfast this morning came from God. The sleep last night restored you to face this new day came from the Almighty One. I am sure this is strange talk to you now, and you don't understand everything, but that will come in time. I promise to share the story of Almighty God and His ways with you any time you are ready to learn more. Neither God nor I expect you to suddenly be great believers. But you have such an excellent position to start learning. You are close to His people. You are on a new adventure as God's people possess the new land. You have talents and skills that I'll bet, outshine most of the people camped along this river. You have no idea of how God can bless you, when you let him. I pray you to open your hearts, look for His ways, and receive His blessings.

"Now, there I go sounding like a priest...next you will expect me to want to take up a collection." Jonathan was laughing to relieve any tension he may have imposed by coming over.

"If you expect to take up a collection here, I'm not sure you will get very much," said Olmad, meeting the preacher's jest. "Tell us how we can best go from here."

Jonathan took his time studying each person's face. He was a tall man, athletic built, broad shoulders with a nothing waist line and small hips. He could have been a swimmer or a discus thrower. Probably 24 or 25 years old. Trimmed short beard, stylish of the young Hebrews. A wide, brown robe covered his legs when he spread out over the cushion with his knees wide apart and long legs extended. His hooded robe and handsome thick rope sash were the only things that identified him as a priest. There was nothing stuffy or pious about the young man. He enjoyed his work and his life and thought everyone else should too. The Almighty God was his friend, not his chastiser.

Finally, he said, "First, tell me how you were working – how were you making a living and contributing to your neighbors until yesterday?" He looked at Olmad for the first answer.

"I am a trader," said Olmad. "I negotiate with the caravans and others who have things to offer and I try to provide them with things they value and can use. I have several years experience as a trader. We have lived here on the Jericho Plains all my life and I know the territory like the back of my hand."

"And you, sir," Jonathan pointed to the father.

"I have years of experience in growing crops, raising sheep, and trading. I taught my son, here, how to trade," said the father.

"And Mother, what kind of skills do you offer a new beginning."

"Oh, I don't know. I'm just a mother. I keep house, keep children out of trouble, cook, wash, and mend their scratches and bumps. I don't know that I have anything worth while to offer," she said with hesitancy.

Without saying a word, Jonathan turned and looked to Rahab.

"Well, for a few years I managed an inn. I received guests, treated them well, and saw to it that they were up and on their way each day. With mother's help I often fed them and saw to it that their needs were attended to," Rahab said. She had her mother's hesitancy.

Olmad broke in. "The women here are modest. Mother makes great date cakes and other party items. She's an excellent cook. She weaves great linen from flax. Rahab is also a great weaver. The gown she has on is an example of her weaving ... turning flax into gowns fit for a queen. In fact she did do two gowns that the king accepted for his wives. It may not be very ladylike but Rahab also has talent for making strong ropes from the fronds of palm trees. But, sir, why do you ask these questions?"

Jonathan leaned back on his cushion and scooted down into the folds around his body making his legs thrust dangerously out into the circle. He believed in being comfortable.

"This is forward of me to even suggest, but I sense we have

an excellent opportunity of becoming friends, I am going to be as bold, as if we were already friends. God has saved you from Jericho to the Hebrews for a reason. I am just guessing, but I suspect that one of those many reasons is for the talents and skills you have to offer to His work in possessing the land. You see we are the new comers here, and you know the land around here. We have a million head of cattle, sheep, oxen and horses, perhaps more, that must be fed from the land. We are going to run out of pastures before we can be ready to move from here. I'll bet that if you go visit the trader tents just down the way from here, you can pick up some work as a guide to the chief shepherd. If you talk to the same people about the items you can make and offer, I'll bet they will take everything you can make. I mean everything from 50-foot ropes to a platter of date cakes.

"I can't give you advice, but if I were in your position, I'd head out to the trader tents and make friends with everyone of those fellows." He thought for a moment and then concluded. "If I were in your position I wouldn't be sitting here listening to a long legged priest when you could be working on your new beginnings."

"Just a moment, please." The voice came from the back. One of the servants had his hand raised.

"Yes, sir, what is it?" The priest was looking at the servant.

"Perhaps I shouldn't be speaking, but I have a question."

"Then ask it, my friend."

"When the Hebrews came across the river, you moved in and around Gilgal, but I heard nothing of your destroying the city. Yet, when you were ready, you conquered Jericho in one afternoon. Why did you destroy Jericho, but not Gilgal?" The servant was timid, but asked the question, anyway.

"Here is why, my new friend. We are the people of God. We are the ones He has chosen at this time to represent His causes on earth. As a result, we do what He tells us to do. I can give you a full blown sermon on how God led us through the desert, how He has disciplined us many times and how He has blessed us many more times. But the short of it is God has directed us to come possess the land He had promised to our forefathers. When we crossed the river with His miracle blessing, we saw that Gilgal had no idols standing in its square. It was an open town and we could see that Gilgal had no other gods before our God. Now, if there had been idols, then God's Army would have taken them down and the idol worshipers would have been destroyed. That is the difference between Gilgal and Jericho. Because you had idols all around the center of your city, God gave us directions to destroy and burn the city and the idol worshipers."

"But you destroyed only the city is that right?" The servant was on to something.

"Yes, that's right. We did not touch anything outside your great walls. God said to only destroy the city, its contents, and idol worshipers."

"Thank you for being so kind to answer a servant's question," the humble man in the back said.

Then Jonathan smiled and offered his hand to one of Olmad's little boys to help him stand up. The second little boy rushed in to take the other hand of the priest. There was a lot of grunting, groaning, starts and restarts, but the little boys were excited about helping Jonathan stand up. As a result, they were already fast friends with their guest.

"I must leave you to your day. And I must get to mine. I am usually out for my morning walk at this time each day. And I will be happy to help you any way I can. Just ask anyone around for Jonathan ... and don't believe everything they say about me. OK?"

With those words, he placed his hand on Olmad's shoulder and said, "May the Lord be with all of you this day and all the days for the rest of your life. Amen." He lifted the big hand from Olmad's shoulder and waved it across the group to extend his blessing to everyone there. He smiled and turned to walk on down the row of tents, waving back to the children.

The Discovery

When Jonathan was out of hearing range, the servant began jumping up and down, calling, "Master, did you hear what the priest said?"

"What did you hear, Joseph?"

"If the Hebrews only destroyed the city, then your flocks and herds are still alive and awaiting your kind attention. You're not without means, as you thought you were at dawn this morning. Their God has left you with wealth in the fields!"

"Good work, Joseph. I am proud of you and your discovery. Thank you for asking that important question that we all overlooked. That means we should be on our way out there to check on things. Go through Friends Camp and see if any of our new neighbors has a cart and animal to help us reach the fields. We will bring it back before dark and bring them a lamb in payment."

"Yes, Master. I'll be back as soon as I can." And the servant hurried back among the tents.

Olmad rose before the group and said, "I think we should plan our day. I would like to go visit those traders up front and see what they know and what they have and what they need. Maybe they have spotted some advance people for caravans that I missed because of the city being shut down. Maybe I can do something about getting some pots and pans, and food stuffs.

Rahab stood up for her turn, "Dad, let me ride out to the orchards with you and I'll see what I can gather while you are looking after the sheep and goats. Perhaps your other servant will stay and help me."

Mother and Olmad's wife and the two little sisters agreed to meet some of the women in Friends Camp.

"Then it's agreed," said Rahab. "Let me say one more thing before we take off on our first day without walls. She bowed her head and said, "Lord God of Israel, You have shown us your mighty power. You have sent your servants to provide for us. Now we pray for strength to accomplish the tasks that lie before us. Please bless us as we learn to love you in our new beginning. Thank you, Lord, for saving our lives from your wrath on Jericho. Bless us, Lord, and please continue to show us your mercy."

A sound of clumping hooves and the squeak of wheels were heard coming up the pathway. Joseph was leading a horse and wagon. He was smiling. "Look, Master, what Rahab's God has provided."

"I can see. Where did you find such a fine steed and wagon?"

"Almost next door. They were very kind. They said we could borrow it for the rest of the day. They even loaned us a big sack and a basket to put things in."

"Then it looks like we should be on our way. It will take us some time to get to the herds from here. Are you ready, Rahab?"

"Yes, Dad, I suppose you are going to take Joseph with you since he found the horse and wagon. Is it all right if Ari El goes with me, to help in gathering the fruits and dates?"

"Of course," her father replied. "Ari El, go with Miss Rahab. You keep her safe today."

"Yes, Master," the young man replied and climbed into the wagon.

"You people be careful today and have a good harvest. I'm going to need lots of stuff to trade tomorrow. I'm on my way to the trader tents." Olmad was waving good-bye, anxious to begin a new experience.

The remaining women and girls stood waving to the departing family members and then began to wander back into the long row of tents.

Joseph took the reins and headed towards the ruins of Jericho. It was a sad sight:There were big chunks of wall, left over building stones, smoldering oil lamps, and the lingering smell of death. There was nothing recognizable. It had been reduced to a pile of rock and ashes. Little whirlwinds dipped down and tossed bits of ashes from place to place. Rahab began to cry and everyone else turned their faces. No one could look at the devastation of their home place.Joseph cracked the whip and sped the horse on past the scene.

The palm trees had been untouched by the fires and soldiers. They stood as sentinels to remember the past.The nearby orchard was empty of people. Everyone had run away when the walls began to crumble. The orchards, the fields and the trees were available to anyone who wanted to harvest. God had provided it all for them.

"This will be a good spot," said Rahab.And Joseph pulled back on the reins and the wagon stopped. Rahab climbed down and Ari El handed her the big sack and basket.They brought nothing for lunch, but they could eat off the land. God would provide everything they needed.

"Are you sure you will be all right? We probably won't be back until late afternoon." Dad was asking like a dad asks.

"Of course. Be on your way and see how many sheep and goats you still have up there.We will be fine."

And with that Joseph snapped the reins and the two men were off to the hills and the animals.

Olmad's Discovery

Meanwhile, Olmad was going from tent to tent talking with as many head traders as he could find.Almost all of them recognized him as one saved from Jericho. He guessed it was his robe. Maybe it was the news that a family was saved from the attack.They all had respect for him because God had saved him from the idols.

Olmad offered his services as scout. He and his dad could show them where the better pastures were for their animals.They could show them how to rotate the grazing places so the grass would last longer. He offered to show them some linen tunics and gowns better than anything from Egypt. He also offered to show them premium woven robes suited just for this climate. Of course, he said it would take a few days to get production started.

Olmad was having a field day. Yes, the traders would take strong rope. They could use cooking lessons and recipes for the local foods, because no one in the group had ever cooked. Before they crossed the Jordan, God had provided everything. This generation of Hebrews had never prepared fruits and vegetables. They could use a roughed-out map of the area — locating the major towns both north and south, especially the fortified ones. Olmad thought that Rahab might be able to do that since she had dealt with many travelers.

He learned a good deal about the Hebrews including the fact that they didn't know how to weave or make garments. They wore the same garments their grandparents left Egypt with. While they were in the desert, God did not permit their clothes to wear out. But now that they were in the Promised Land, their clothes were beginning to become thread bear and even have holes in them. Olmad promised that he and his family would show them how to remedy that.

On his way back to the family tenting area, Olmad was thinking that the greatest need for the Hebrews was instruction. They were willing to learn how to cook, how to make clothes, how to make soap, how to make tents, banners, and even how to grind wheat and barley into flour. Of course, they would be willing to pay for their services.

The Women's Discoveries

While the men and Rahab were away, the women were visiting with the new neighbors. In the course of the conversation, Mother mentioned that she surely missed her big black pot for cooking. And a neighbor simply reached behind a little screen and brought one out to her and said, "Here, this is for you."

"Oh, I couldn't take your pot," Mother was defending her action. "You will need it when all your family comes over."

"We don't have a big family. The pot just came with some other things my husband traded for and I don't know how to use it," said the wife. "Please, take it and please your man."

"Very well, if you are sure your husband won't mind."

"My husband has no idea what I have to cook with. He just wants food on the table when he gets hungry. Take the pot and please your man."

"Then, thank you very much." Mother said. And the girls were off to see another family's tent.

By mid-afternoon, Mother and the girls had gathered several pots and other items to cook with. They were all gifts – "in the service of God."

When they got back to the camp they found several other gifts. There were extra blankets, more firewood, flour and yeast to make bread, a lamb hind quarter for roasting, and a homemade broom for sweeping the area. Mother was overjoyed. God was providing for them. And this was only the first day.

"I've got to get busy," said Mother. "These blessings are covering me up. How will I ever catch up?"

Father and Servant Discovery

When the father and his servant rolled into the high country, they began looking for the herds. They soon spotted them at the foot of one of the mountains with a large cave in its side. This was just where the master had left them three days before. He was not able to get back to his herds on the Hebrews' seventh day of circling Jericho because he did not know what to expect in the sudden turn of events. But the herds knew how to fend for themselves in this location. The cave provided shelter in bad weather and there was plenty of grass and water to keep the sheep and goats happy. Dad had marked the area with his banner pole and everyone in the area respected his property. He and Joseph took turns counting the animals. There were 306 sheep, and 347 goats. Some were very small because it was still late spring and the new arrivals had not had much time to grow.

Rahab's father was amazed that the herds were still there. He had only lost his house and belongings in the wrath of God. He still had his family and his fortune. "God is good." He said it again, "God is good." Tears were filling his eyes. Joseph looked away out of respect.

They found some peaches on the short trees in the area and pulled two each and ate them quickly, with juice dripping from their chins. Then, they picked some more and put them in the back of the wagon. They wedged the fruit with rocks, so they would not roll around and get bruised on the way home.

Joseph picked out a young lamb and a young goat and tied their feet with the rope he had around his waist. He was only wearing a servant's tunic and now it flowed loosely around him.

The goat was tied with one end of the rope and the lamb with the other end.

"This has indeed, been a good day. Let's head back to the family, Joseph," said the man with the big smile and a thankful heart.

The servant climbed back into the driver's seat and cracked the reins one more time. Gently, he turned the horse and wagon around and they headed back toward the encampment. On the way, they would stop and pickup Rahab and Ari El.

But Rahab and Ari El had to face danger while in the orchard.

9

Up from the Ashes

The orchards, were familiar grounds to Rahab. She and her family went there often for their fruit and vegetables. When the Hebrews began circling Jericho, the residents of the area ran away for their own safety. Now the entire area was unattended and unsupervised. Anyone could harvest as he wished.

Rahab and Ari El took the basket and large bag with them and began to scout out the area. They found some small spades and went to work digging up some root crops. They dug several nice size potatoes, carrots, onions, and scallops which they placed in the bottom of the bag. On top of that went some squash, and green beans. They gathered some soft fruit and vegetables like tomatoes and ripe peaches and placed them in the basket. Although the better grapes were grown south in the Mamre, the Plains also had some grapes with a tangy taste and they took a few bunches of them. The olives were past season, but there were a few still clinging to the branches. They collected some of them for their oil as well as their meat.

Digging and pulling in the giant garden was tiring work and Rahab's back was beginning to hurt her so she suggested that the two of them take a break and rest a while. They each chose a piece of fruit and headed for a tall, straight date palm tree to lean against. Ari El decided to demonstrate the endurance of youth by climbing the 20-foot tree and resting in its branches.

They had been alone all morning, but as Rahab settled against the tree, she could hear the squeaking wheels of a distant wagon. Could it be Dad returning so soon? Not likely. Rahab called to Ari El to stay still in the tree and not reveal himself for safety. She would handle the visitor.

When the wagon left the main trail and pulled into the orchards,

Rahab could see that there was a lone man in the front seat of the wagon. She stood up to greet him as he came near. He called to her and pulled up nearby and jumped down from the wagon. He was in his late 20's, maybe 30 years old. He wore a dirty robe he must have lived in for weeks, judging from the way he smelled. He had big hands and hairy legs from the end of his old, soiled tunic to his battered sandals.

"You're a mighty pretty sight for these tired eyes," he began the conversation. "What are you doing out here?"

"I'm just gathering some food for dinner tonight. My people will be here almost anytime now. I don't really have time to visit. Can I give you some directions?" Rahab was anxious to get him on his way.

"Oh, I have all the time in the world to visit. I don't have to be no where at anytime. My time is my own. We do a little trading, my horse and me. But I'm not tradin' today." He was avoiding her put off. "You're sure pretty."

"Maybe you would like to give your horse a drink from the pool over there and then be on your way."

"That's mighty nice of you, but the horse is all right." He stepped closer and held Rahab's chin in his grimy hand. "You're right pretty. You're just what I've been looking for. You're just right."

Rahab stepped back while grabbing his wrist and removing his dirty hand from her chin. "I'm not available to you. And you don't want to do this. You had better be on your way."

"Oh, I'll be on my way, all right. As soon as I get some of what I found here. Just as soon as I get what I want." And he stepped closer and reached for her chin again, but this time he found a surprise. With one strong wallop, she drove her right fist into his mid-section at the same time her knee came up straight for his groin. The man bent over from pain to his sensitive spot.

"You don't want to mess with me, dirty face. Now, get out of here while you still can." Rahab was no longer the quiet, little, defensive girl. "Hear me now! Get out of here, before you get hurt." She was shouting in a strong, determined voice; much like a mother to a two-year old.

"Oh, a fighter! I love a good fight. Especially, when it's with a pretty girl. And you sure are pretty. I can fight with you all night. Heck, I can fight with you until this time tomorrow." He was grinning and intended to claim his prize. He was coming towards her again.

Rahab doubled up her fist to wham him again and stepped forward. The man stopped advancing and his eyes opened wider, but, then, he stepped backward out of her reach. She stepped forward again and held up both hands with her long finger nails open to look like eagle claws. While he was distracted by her hands, she let go of a powerful kick to his groin again. This time her pointed sandal was on target. He fell back, bumping the back of his head on the tree trunk. His slid down the trunk, grimacing in pain.

"You had better be moving on, mister. For you are in trouble."

The dirty man sat for a few seconds, trying to endure his pain and gather strength to mount his attack. Then he leaned forward to lift himself up by his hands. "Man, you are some prize. I can't wait to get hold of you. And I'm going to have you right now."

With both hands he reached behind his head to the back collar of his tunic and started pulling it up to take it off over his head. Just as his tunic covered his face and arms Ari El leaped from the high branches and fell directly on the attacker, smashing a 40-pound cluster of dates over his head. The man fell to the ground under the pressure of Ari El's fall. He was helpless inside his tunic. With the tunic over his arms and head, he couldn't see. His arms were caught in the double strength of the folds of his tunic over his face. Like a straight jacket.

Ari El struck the attacker again and again across his face with the cluster of dates. The over ripe dates broke open and the sticky juice ran onto the man's covered face. The wet cloth cut off the air to the attacker's face.

The stranger struggled in his efforts to get free. He gasped for breath, making strange, desperate sounds. He managed to turn over, and to throw the boy to the ground. He was crawling blindly on his elbows and naked knees. He couldn't see where he was going. His clothes were stuck to his sweaty arms and face. He was panicking, gasping for air.

Rahab and Ari El were in shock as the imprisoned attacker tried to get a toe hold in the soft earth and push himself upright, but he couldn't do it. He didn't have the strength. He collapsed back to the ground and fell into the pool. It was the deep end of the natural springs. He fought the cold water but he could not free himself from his tunic. The saturated cloth cut off the air to his face. He could no longer scream or cry. He couldn't get his balance. His hairy legs and belly beat the water. He was suffocating. He became limp. The struggling stopped. He was dead.

Rahab and Ari El watched the dirty man float face down. They were frozen in fear. After two deep sighs, Ari El got to his feet and tried to pull the man from the pool. He got him to the edge, but the dead man was more than the boy could lift. So, an exhausted Rahab crawled to the site and helped the boy pull the attacker from the water and then drag him over to some bushes.

"We'll let Dad and Joseph take care of him," breathed Rahab. She was exhausted. But modest Ari El tugged at the man's dirty tunic until he had it down from his face, and then worked it back down over his naked body.

"There, I think that's better." He spoke quietly, reasoning that even the dead should be properly covered. Then they both went back to the palm tree and sat down to recover from the fight.

Rahab and Ari El said nothing for a while. They just concentrated on relaxing and releasing the tensions their bodies collected while watching the man drown. But finally, Ari El whispered, "You are *some* fighter."

Rahab chuckled under her breath and whispered back, "And you sure know how to end a fight, jumping down from the tree like you did. You are a brave man, Ari El."

"I've never killed a person before. I am sad."

"Neither have I. And I am sad with you. Perhaps this was God's will. Maybe we will learn more about him later." Rahab was still exhausted from the use of so much adrenaline. All was quiet for a minute.

"Let's go see what's in the wagon," said the curious boy. He reached for Rahab's hand and pulled her up.

The horse snorted as the strangers approached him. Ari El petted the horse's face and neck and lovingly pulled on his mane. They looked into the old wagon. Although it had been in service for many years, the wagon was in good shape. The metal bands around the wheels had recently been repaired. There were sides on the flat wooden bed that stood up about a foot all around. Half of the wagon bed was covered by a dirty brown blanket. Probably where the owner had often slept. The other half of the bed was full of mostly junk: odds and ends that he had collected and never threw away. Behind the driver's seat were a couple of baskets for food and two bags. Ari El opened one of the bags and said, "Look, a statue."

"Ari El, put that down. It's an idol! Put it down now! That's Baal. You don't want that. What's in the other bag?" Rahab was suddenly frightened at seeing the god of the Canaanites. Her faith had brought her so far, so quickly. She was scared at the site of idols.

The boy picked up the other bag and looked inside. It was another statue. He began to pull it out of the bag and Rahab stopped him. "No. No! That is the moon god. Put it back in the bag. We must destroy them."

The servant boy did as instructed and threw the bags of idols from the wagon. They both found big stones and threw them at the bags until they crushed the idols.

"Ari El, will you take that old, dirty blanket out of the wagon and cover the dead man with it? And then pour these rocks on top of him." Rahab was trying to figure out what was happening. Why would God send her an experience like this?

Before the boy could move, she started thinking out loud. *He was driven by lust. When he began to undress, his arms were caught in his clothes because he was so excited about raping me. But his haste tangled his tunic and when he fell into the pool, he drowned.* She was reasoning, looking for a solution. Then she had it. "Ari El, you have just witnessed another case of the wrath of the Almighty. The man drowned because he worshiped idols. He's a part of the wrath that destroyed Jericho. Remember this line: You shall have no other gods before me, the Almighty God."

"After today, I will remember it for the rest of my life." The young man covered the dead man with the dirty blanket. Then, poured the crumbled idols over the body, as though he were pouring poison on a monster. This was a new experience for him and he didn't want to do it, but he did it. Sadness weighed on him as a load of adobe bricks.

The two of them then leaned against the wagon and talked of what they needed to do before her father and Joseph came to get them. They reasoned since the owner was dead that they could keep the horse and wagon. They guided the horse to the pool and let him have a drink from the upper, clean part of the springs. As the horse drank, they began to load their produce onto the wagon. Then they decided that they still needed some more dates and fronds from the palm trees.

Ari El climbed the trees and tossed the dates and fronds to Rahab who placed them into the wagon. As they finished their loading, they heard the squeaking wheels of Dad and Joseph's wagon.

"Where did you find the wagon and horse?" Dad asked.

"It's a sad story, Daddy, but a man came here and started to attack me when Ari El jumped out of the tree and knocked him down. The man fell into the pool and drowned. His body is over there in the bushes. When we looked in his wagon, we found idols of Baal and Moon. So we broke them up and poured the stones on his body."

"Are you all right? Did he hurt you?"

"Oh, no, I'm fine and so is your servant."

"Master, Miss Rahab is a good fighter. You should be proud."

"I am proud of all my children and my servants too. Thanks for helping out, Ari El. You, two, did a good job. I'll get the details on the way home. Joseph, help Ari El tidy up their wagon and then let's head home."

Rahab joined her father in the borrowed wagon and Joseph jumped into the driver's seat and snapped the reins. Joseph guided his horse to the worn pathway. They could hear Ari El talking to the new horse and clicking his tongue in encouragement for the new horse to follow the lead.

Father and daughter caught up on the day's events along the way. As they pulled up in front of Friends Camp and their campsite, they could smell the stew that Mother had bubbling in her new big pot. It smelled good and everyone was super hungry.

The Family Circle

When the family gathered for dinner, they were excited to share what had happened that day.

"Before anyone speaks, I've got to tell you what happened here in the camp today." Mother said. "Is this good stew or what?"

Everyone was nodding their heads while stuffing their mouths and asking a general question, "Where did all this come from?"

Mother surprised everyone by saying, "From Rahab's new God." The clicking of spoons against bowls stopped. "The bunch of us went visiting, you know, to say hello, and almost every time we met someone they had a gift for us. I tried to turn some of them down, but they insisted that we take the items. They said they were from God Almighty, that He is the great provider. I should accept the gifts because they are given in God's name. So here we are...dinner from God. Today, I received the pot, the rack to hold it, wood for the fire, and the vegetables to go in the stew. We even got a hind quarter of lamb. Now, what do you think about that?"

"I think it is great, Mother," said Rahab. "We are all learning that the earth is the Lord's and everything in it. For all these things we are grateful. Amen. Ari El and I found some good things to eat as well. We got fruits, vegetables, olives for oil and grapes for juice to drink. And Mother, we just happen to have a few dates that we found ripe.

You might like them when you're ready to celebrate something."

"You just want to see me work, that's what you want me to do," Mother enjoyed teasing her daughter.

Then Dad took his turn. "This morning before daylight, I was sitting over there looking at the ruins of Jericho in the moonlight, feeling sorry for myself. I was sad to have to start over at my age. I was wondering at how we could start from nothing and keep together. I was asking myself, "Are we going to be prisoners of these new people who destroyed our home? How are we going to find food? How would we find or uncover things we could trade to get the necessary things to live with? I was feeling very sad about the future of our family. I was sad about losing all our friends, our contacts, our businesses. What would we do?

"Then a nice lady from the Hebrews came up with the honey and warm bread from her own oven and gave it to us. A person right behind her had a table that he gave us to put breakfast on. Someone else had a big bag of tea leaves and the little pot to brew tea. So, before you all were awake, our problems were being solved.

"I had a feeling that this would be an unusual day. There was a new Force that was in charge of our lives. This was the beginning of something different. I still can't explain it. I certainly don't understand it, but it's different. And we are being taken care of by a generosity that is much greater than human kind. I have never seen people be so generous in their gifts and interest. We called these people our enemy, but now they are our friends."

All eyes were on Dad as he looked up into a sky filled with brilliant colors that only the Jericho Plains can generate. He swallowed hard, a little hesitant, and a tear ran down his strong face. "Then ... then, came that long legged priest. I don't think I have ever seen a man with such long legs."

Everyone chuckled and nodded in agreement.

"From his good nature and willing spirit, we learned to take hold of this new way of living. Concentrate on what we have: our skills and talents, and what we can do for others. His suggestion was to become as generous to others as they have been to us. Then Joseph asked him that big question about what was destroyed. The priest said only Jericho was burned. Everything else was left. So Joseph and I went out to check on our herds and we found them all still there. We have things we can begin trading with. We are not devastated. We have most of what we did have, except for clothes and household furnishings. But we have the means to regain them. Our lives continue, but now with much greater opportunity. I would say we have been blessed many times over."

The family circle applauded the patriarch. And Olmad stood up to speak. He was always one to walk while he spoke. He headed to the back of the circle addressing himself to the family across from him as he touched the back of each person he walked behind. "Well, I have a little something to say. Saving the best for last."

The family began booing him. He loved the attention and it was a good release of tension from what his father had to say. "Now, now, now. Just listen to what I have to say. I found more work for us than we can ever do. I am going to suggest that we organize ourselves to incorporate others in Friends Camp here to help us. Just listen to this. The Hebrews have been traveling in the desert for two generations. With very few exceptions, all of these people have been born in the desert, just as most of their parents. The only life they know is life in the desert. Today, they are struggling with how to cook foods that they have not seen before. They don't know a salt sea cabbage from a peach. They don't know the difference between boiling and baking.

"This does not mean they are dumb. Far from it. They are very smart people. But this is an entirely new life for them. They have never had to make clothes before. They tell me that their sandals are the ones worn by their grandparents. Their robes are the ones that came from Egypt 40 years ago. While they were on their journey their God provided for them in such a way that their clothes never wore out. They did not have to cook because manna and quail were provided for them. Now things are different. Perhaps we were saved from Jericho to help teach them how to live in their Promised Land.

"I talked with their traders most of the day today. They will take everything we can provide them. Yes, Rahab, they need your ropes. Many more ropes than you can make yourself. Dad, they need someone to show them how to harvest the grain out there. They are dependent now mostly to trading for flour, because they don't know how to grind wheat. They have been wanderers, so they must learn about crop rotation and pasture rotation.

"Mom, they need to learn how to cook. These women can't read, so they are ready for classes on what foods go together and how to prepare them. They are experimenting now and eventually they will learn. But their men are hungry for good dishes now.

"Because they have never had to sew garments, they must learn to sew and weave. I tell you, family, that opportunity is everywhere. We have so many blessings that we can't count them."

The servant, Joseph, surprised everyone by saying, "And this is just the first day."

A Cry in the Darkness

Everyone seemed to be reflecting on what had been said that night, when a booming voice shouted out of the darkness. "The prostitute. Where is the prostitute? We can't have prostitutes living amongst us. They are evil. God will punish us. She must leave or die."

Two men emerged out of the darkness. "Where's the prostitute?"

Olmad, who was already standing, immediately reached the men before they got to the family circle. "What are you saying, my friend?"

"The prostitute. We've come to get the prostitute and throw her out into the desert. She can't stay here." Their steps were uncertain. Their speech slurred.

"Where do you think such a person would be?" Olmad asked them while he wormed his way between them and had his arms on their outside shoulders.

"She's here in Friends Camp. Somewhere in Friends Camp. We've got to find her."

Olmad guessed that they were not sure where they were going. So he gently turned them around and walked back out into the darkness. "Tell me where have you looked?" He kept them talking while leading them away.

"Everywhere. We've looked everywhere. But we've got find her. She must leave the camp."

"Then maybe you should look some more — closer to home."

"Yeah, closer to home."

Olmad was gone for several minutes, but he soon returned and told everyone that he lost the two intruders back in the tents of Judah. "I spoke to the guard at the entrance and he said he would have someone care for them."

Rahab mumbled that she was afraid she might get everyone into trouble by staying with the family. Perhaps she should move away from the group; perhaps sleep outside the encampment. But everyone in the family rejected her idea. She had been saved by the new God and she should remain with the family. Regardless of what might happen, the family would be together. They had been saved together, therefore they would stay together.

They stoked the fire for the night, and headed for a tent.

Tonight, they would sleep inside.

The Big Decision

Only Dad was up in time to see the sunrise. He had been an early riser all his life and now was no time to change. He had recharged the fire and had the flames ready for flat bread cooked in olive oil and topped with left over honey. While his wife cooked the bread, he made the tea and the two were sitting around munching and sipping as the others began to awaken.

Rahab was next in line. She came out of her tent, holding her head. She had a worried look on her face.

"What's wrong, dear?" Her dad asked in greeting.

"Good morning, you two." Rahab was still searching for daylight. "I just had an awful time last night. I was still remembering that man who came to the orchard while we were there. I must have had a dozen nightmares about him. And I bet Ari El did, too. He was concerned about the man's death. Dad, you might want to talk to him about it today. He thought he had killed the man, but Ari El had nothing to do with that."

"Sure, I'll speak to him as soon as he comes in for breakfast," her father said. "Hey, look who is out walking around this morning."

"Good morning everyone," Jonathan, said. "How did you make it through your first day in Friends Camp?"

"Very well. In fact, extremely well," Father said. "We got quite a bit accomplished and will set some directions this morning. We believe we have found a lot of opportunities that we can be of service here. Getting out of Jericho could be the best thing that ever happened to us."

"I'm glad to hear that. May God continue to bless you."

"You know, I am amazed at the generosity of your people. We were all around the campfire last night and each one of us expressed amazement at how generous everyone is; not only in information and kindness, but in goods and services, too. We saw it at the traders' tents and here in Friends Camp. It amazes us."

"I am happy that you noticed. It's one of God's cardinal rules. He says that we are to love one another as we love ourselves. We are created by God, and when we express our love for his creations, we love God. The things you have been given, the services that have been extended to you are gifts of love in the name of the Father in Heaven. You will do well to imitate the gestures."

"Oh, we plan too," said Dad. "We talked about it last night and we have a meeting planned this morning with that very principle in mind.

"Rahab, are you doing all right? The priest asked.

"Oh, yes. I went to the orchards yesterday and was able to harvest several days' worth of food stuffs for the family. We even obtained a horse and wagon to assist our work here. It was a good day."

"Hey, I must be going and get my hellos said up and down the row. You folks walk with God, today." The priest turned to leave and waved.

As Jonathan stepped out of the tenting area to the walkway in front of the family's tents, another man came up to him, patted him on the back and the two walked off together. The second man seemed familiar to Rahab, and then when he turned and smiled at her, she recognized him as Salmon who had visited them on the first night. He just smiled, turned back to Jonathan to say something and then turned back to see Rahab and smiled again.

One by one the family awakened and came to the fire for their flat bread and honey. When breakfast was over, Olmad wanted to talk.

"It seems everyone is here. If you don't mind, I'd like to make a couple of suggestions," Olmad had the family's attention. "Dad and I were talking some last night after most of you were asleep. We were having a time of grasping this new beginning. Rahab paid a very big price to save our lives. Living with that terrible secret for months on end and then to see the walls of Jericho come down without knowing whether the oath was good or not, required a tremendous amount of faith. So, first, I wanted to acknowledge Rahab's faith, the salvation of our lives and this turning point.

"We now acknowledge that something we were all innocently taught all of our lives was not true. Despite our heritage, with no fault to our parents, idols are not worthy gods. There is one God, the Almighty God, the God of creation. We have seen Him work in our lives the last two days and I suspect we will see Him work in our lives today. So I am suggesting that we all dedicate ourselves and our work to the service of the Almighty God of the Universe." Olmad looked down to the ground and kicked at a tuff of grass as he gathered his thoughts.

"Last night, we all talked about the many opportunities before us. We could gain a lot of wealth from marketing our services and goods to these people around us. We find ourselves in a very distinctive advantage, but I have a strange suggestion. That instead of performing our work for gain, I am suggesting that we try giving it away. Let's work for other people without price or negotiation.

Let's extend love to these people around us. Much as they have shown their generosities to us, let us now return it. Let's work for God Almighty to benefit His children and receive any blessings that He may send us.

"Day before yesterday was the funeral day for everyone in Jericho. If it had not been for the faith of Rahab, all of us would be in the ashes out there. So with this new life, this new beginning, let's not only dedicate ourselves to God, but also dedicate our work to His glory. We will need to learn a lot over time but these are bonus days. We should have been in the ashes day before yesterday, so let's rise up from the ashes and begin this new life and see where God takes us." Olmad brought his hands quietly together in front of him. His long fingers extending toward the center of the circle of family.

"Olmad, are you saying that when I make a rope, that I give it away? And not trade it for something of greater value to us?" Rahab was first to get clarification.

"That is exactly what I am suggesting. When we first talked, we saw ourselves with nothing. What can I do because I have no more clothes. I have no food. I have nowhere to sleep. And almost immediately, our needs were met. We jumped overnight from a place of helplessness to one of being helpful." Olmad was sounding like a school teacher.

"Give us some more examples," his mother inquired.

"Very well. Yesterday, we identified a great need here for people to learn how to cook. There is a whole generation of women in this camp, hundreds of thousands of women who don't know how to cook. They have never had to cook. Their grandmothers probably did the cooking, but their grandchildren didn't need to cook. God provided their food and they lived on manna they gathered each day. So, one of the opportunities here is to teach half a million women to cook the food grown in Canaan. The first thought is to set up classes and charge some sort of fee and teach those who can afford it. But I'm suggesting that we announce your services, Mother, to the leaders of the different tribes and let them invite you to meet with their women. You teach them for free, not expecting a reward. The first reward is that you have done a good service and many more people will understand the differences between peppers and olives and grapes. Then they will be blessed by knowing how to prepare the food that God has blessed the land with."

"And how are we going to support this gift? How can we afford to be the free teacher of Israel?" Dad was not objecting. He was seeking clarification.

"Dad, I'm not sure. But I feel that if we approach these people's needs and provide them with the best services we know how, that their God will continue to bless us. For instance, there are hundreds of heads of cattle and sheep and goats out there in the pastures whose owners died in Jericho. They need owners to feed them and take care of them. We know better where they are than anyone in Israel. But is it better to gather them and divide them among the families here or shall we keep them all to ourselves in some secret range somewhere? We have enough to get by on. We don't know what blessings God has for our future. But I feel the right thing to do is to gather the wealth of the animals out there and give them to the families of Israel who want them. And the same thing with the grain. The harvest is in midstream. Do we go hire thousands of men to harvest the fields the way we show them and then hoard the grain until they can afford to pay for it? Or do we teach Hebrews to harvest grain and keep it in their own storage?

"Let us teach them to harvest, son," said the father. "Whatever comes our way will be a blessing from Rahab's God."

"God gave us life from Jericho. Now what we do with that new life will be our gift to Him," Olmad said and the family all nodded in agreement.

The patriarch stood to conclude the family meeting. He never liked long meetings. "I think of most importance is the remaining grain left in the fields and the harvest of food stuffs that can be saved for winter time. Olmad, why don't you take this idea to the leaders here and Joseph and I will take a tour of the fields and see what kind of equipment is available and how some storage might be found. Momma, look at your food stock with the rest of the girls here and see how you might go about teaching these people how to cook Canaan style. But don't give away all your secrets. Rahab, think about how you would teach people weaving and how to make strong ropes."

"But what about me? What am I going to teach?" Ari El. called out.

"Hummm. Let's see," the master said. "You can teach them how to fall out of palm trees." And the master hugged him. "You be Rahab's first student and learn how to teach rope making."

"All right!" The boy with the big shinny eyes and even larger grin on his face, said. He jumped down from his perch to sit by Rahab.

So the family concentrated on their individual tasks that day. Toward evening, Rahab and Ari El were busy at work in front of their camp site working the palm leaves into ropes when a shadow crossed over their work space. Rahab looked up to see a tall man standing.

"Hello. Remember me?"

The voice was very familiar but the sun cast a shadow over the face. "Let me see," she said. And she stood up to shade her eyes and get a better look. "Oh, Salmon! How nice of you to come by."

"I was just in the area running some errands and was wondering how everyone is adapting to the new life," he said.

"Pretty well, actually," Rahab was smiling. Her voice tightened and she began to sound like a little girl.

"I'm glad to hear that. Someone at the council said your brother came by this morning and offered the services of your family. I believe they said that your family could teach cooking, food storage, harvesting, rotation of pasture lands and a lot of other services. That's very nice of your brother."

"He got the idea from the visits of those offering us their services and bringing us gifts. Olmad thought it was in order for us to give back what little we know. And father agreed. In fact father and one of his servants are out today surveying the nearby lands for what is left in the grain harvests. I think they were going to try to round up some of the animals and divide them out to those people who want them. It's important now to take care of the animals and to get the harvest in before the summer sun burns it."

"And you are making ropes," he said.

"Yes, I'm teaching Ari El here how to make a rope and then we both can teach others. I understand that soon the ropes on your tents will be getting weak and you'll need to replace them."

"And you are not charging for your services?"

"No, we are relying on God to take care of us. We had some of our own goods and materials that were outside the walls of Jericho and with what has been given to us we can get by. We believe that God will bless us for helping others."

"Excellent. I am so glad to hear that. I would love to talk some more, but I must be on my way. Perhaps, I can stop by again. If you are not too busy," Salmon was grinning.

"Please, come any time. It is always good to see you." And she looked down to her sandals with her hands behind her. How else can you say good bye to a good looking man?

When she looked up, Salmon was sauntering down the trail. He was whistling.

10

The Price of Stealing

The die had been cast for their new lives. The family was busy organizing a hundred thousand volunteers to harvest the grain from the vacant Jericho Plains to the Salt Sea. Rahab's father taught the men and women to use all of the Canaanite equipment to continue the harvest. As the caravans came by they ordered more equipment. As the new equipment arrived, more workers went to the fields. As the fields were harvested nearby, they crossed the first mountain ridge and entered the central fields of Canaan. They would need a lot of food to feed the large group through the winter.

Olmad took on the task of storage. He chose the caves of the nearby mountains where his father tended his livestock. He recruited volunteers to help clean out the caves and in many cases strengthened the interiors with support beams, ceilings and massive doors of Acacia wood. The caves were unassigned. They belonged to the people in need. All were unassigned except one. The workers decided among themselves that the contents of that cave would be for Rahab's family. They marked it with a scarlet cord near the top of the heavy front door. The harvesters only took home the grain they needed. The remainder was placed in storage to be used later. As a field was cleared, it was plowed and replanted for the next harvest. This would be a fruitful summer and autumn.

While the harvesters were working in the fields, Rahab's father organized additional men to care for the stray animals. God was generous; so generous, that there was a problem feeding them all. In addition to the animals already on the pasture land, the Hebrews had brought a million head with them when they crossed the Jordan. The solution was to organize a rotation plan in which the animals were moved continuously from one pasture to another so the grass could recover.

The animals were divided into manageable herds with a shepherd or two to watch over each herd and to keep thieves and desert wolves away. The shepherds worked 24 hours on duty and 24 off. As the relief shepherds reported they would move their herds to a nearby place for better grass. The grazing area now was bounded on the north by the mountain ridges near Ai down to the greener fields around the Salt Sea.

These were busy days inside the large campsite, too. Rahab taught the Hebrews spinning and weaving. Some of the Israeli tents had spinning wheels and a few small looms saved from previous generations. Almost all of them were old and needed repair. But Olmad came to the rescue and started ordering the items through the caravans that frequented the trader tents. In fact, three caravans did nothing but search for the items that the Israelites' needed.

Rahab taught the women how to spin yarn from flax, goat hair, camel hair and horse hair. Soon, she and her mother had classes going daily. Although they concentrated on teaching others to teach the new skills, many women wanted to come to Rahab personally for instruction. Gradually, new clothes in new colors began appearing. Then everyone wanted new clothes.

Surprise Announcement

Late one afternoon, when the sky was beginning to turn violet and crimson, Salmon pretended to be on errands that led him in front of Friend's Camp and just happened to see Rahab in front of her tent. "Oh, hello, Rahab," Salmon called in mock surprise. "How are you?"

"I'm doing very well. Thank you for asking and how are you?"

With that question, he felt he had her permission to enter the campsite and talk with her. After all, if a pretty woman should ask a man a question, he must be obliged to answer, right?

"I understand you have been teaching a lot of our people here," he said.

"Yes, they come everyday to improve their skills. We are sending farther and farther away for supplies. I try to teach the women how to teach others, but many of them want to come here and so they come."

"And you are still giving away your services?"

"Oh, yes. There has never been a need to mention pay. When classes are over for the day, they bring us gifts of many different things. We have never needed a thing. It's amazing how we are being supported."

"I have some news," the tall man said and he smiled a little, but he had a serious look on his face. "God has called us to enlarge our territories and we are preparing to take a few soldiers up to Ai and capture that area. Joshua has been in prayer for several days about it. That is, he and his team have been praying and we are moving out tomorrow morning.

"Did you say we? You are going with them?" Rahab was concerned.

"Yes. It's my honor to go. This is how I serve God. The people of Ai worship idols and the idols must be removed along with the idol worshipers."

"There will be more bloodshed." Her hands were against her checks.

"Our spotters tell us it's a small place, a little larger than Jericho, so we are only going to take a few soldiers. The city will be captured and taken care of in one day. We should all be back day after tomorrow."

Salmon reached for her hand and held it against her cheek ever so gently. Her hand was warm and her face was flushed with the sudden news. His strong hand completely covered hers. His gentleness flowed from his fingertips comforting her cheek bone. "We must possess the land," he said quietly. "God has given us a mission and we are His army. I wanted you to know about it and I wanted you to know that I will miss walking by here and seeing you. When I get back, perhaps, we can spend an afternoon together."

"That would be nice," she whispered. Her other hand reached for his hand against her check and tried to hold him even more against her face, but he politely removed his big hand in case someone might be watching.

"Then I trust you will have a good evening with your family. I plan to see you in a couple of days, if that is all right." Salmon was polite again as though her father was watching him touching her hand and face. A young man and a young woman must leave a proper impression.

However, proper or not, Salmon was moved to stay one extra moment and look deeply into her brown eyes. And with three fingertips he reached once again to touch her warm cheek. Gently, he drew his fingers down her cheek to her neck. There was electricity in the air, as he slowly turned and walked toward the Judah camp. The sky was now filled with pink and gold rays hugging little puffy clouds together.

Attack on Ai

God brought the Hebrews into Canaan near the center of the land. By capturing Jericho they had split the land into north and south portions. By occupying the Jericho Plains, the northern people couldn't come down and assist the southern armies if a war should break out. It was good military strategy. Now they needed to complete a line across the county's mid-section in order to exert more control and safety.

Ai was about 15 miles west of Gilgal, up a steep ridge and just to the east of Bethel. Occupying this point on the ridge would bring them into the interior of Canaan. Ai was a little larger than Jericho (about 12,000 people) and Joshua sent a few spies up to check out the area. The spies reported back that there were not many men there to fight, so Joshua only needed to send two or three thousand soldiers to take the city. Rahab couldn't help but wonder if the spies had stopped by an innkeeper in Ai to get their information.

Early the next morning, without fanfare, several wagons pulled by strong mules, left the encampment and headed northeast towards the high mountain ridge. There was no attempt to hide their journey. They were on a mission for God. The wagons creaked and groaned under their load of soldiers and supplies. The mules strained at pulling the load up the steep inclines. They had to travel in a zigzag fashion to mount the ridge. It was midday when they finally reached the top of the ridge.

The soldiers and their officers dismounted from the wagons, lined up with their leather vests, high shin guards, spears, swords, and shields. They were ready for battle in only a few minutes. However, as they marched out of the few bushes and trees that surrounded the city, they were surprised.

Ai's army was waiting for them in front of their city walls. The king of nearby Bethel had also sent his army. Although both armies were small, they bravely engaged the larger Israelite army. In the fierce hand to hand battle, the Hebrews were driven back. They killed some of the local soldiers, but their own army suffered 36 casualties, Ai and Bethel's armies continued to route the superior Hebrews. God's Army was chased from Ai's city gate as far as the stone quarries. Then they were forced back down the side of the mountain ridge. The strong men of God's Army became afraid. Their hearts melted like butter, and that evening they hurried home in shame. The Hebrews were beaten by the little local army!

Joshua was surprised and angry with the report his captain gave him. Joshua wanted to know why his army was defeated. He tore his clothes and fell face down on the ground before the Tent of Meeting.

He lay there in torn clothes until evening time. He continuously prayed to God. He tried to seek the answer. His question was, if God had given them the land, why was His army defeated?

The elders of Israel joined Joshua. All were prostrate with their faces in the dust. All were asking the same question. Joshua was crying out to the Lord, "Oh, Sovereign Lord, why did you ever bring this people across the Jordan? Was it to deliver us into the hands of the Amorites? Was it to destroy us? If only we had been content to stay on the other side of the Jordan!

"Lord, what can I say, now that Israel has been routed by the enemies? Lord, you know how fast news travels in this land. The Canaanites will hear about this and they will surround us and wipe out our name from the earth. What then will you do for your own great name?"

Joshua felt the word of the Lord deep within his body, *"Stand up! What are you doing down on your face?"*

Joshua and the elders with him stood up. They were the men of God and they should look like it. "Oh Lord, what have we done?"

And God answered him. "Israel has sinned. They have violated my covenant I commanded them to keep. They have taken some of the devoted things from Jericho. They have lied. They have stolen. They have put them with their own possessions. That is why the Israelites cannot stand against their enemies. They turn their back and run because they have been made liable to destruction. I will not be with you any more, unless you destroy whatever among you is devoted to destruction."

Joshua was surprised that the people had stolen something from God. They had been in the land such a short time. The battle for Jericho had gone so smoothly. Now God was pulling away His support until the matter was dealt with. The old man would get to the bottom of this quickly.

Joshua turned from facing the colorful Tent of Meeting and faced his elders. They saw his strained face. They saw his nervous hands. They saw his torn clothes. They felt the fright that was coursing through his veins. At the same time he was both angry at the people and fearful of the Almighty God. Joshua had seen how Moses dealt with the misbehaving people and had saved them from God's wrath many times, but this was the first time that Joshua had to do it himself.

Call to Judgment

Joshua raised his right arm until his bony fingers were reaching towards the clear sky. "Signal for all the elders, judges, and leaders. I want them here now!" He was as stern as a father to little children. The ram's horns sounded the special signal that was repeated by other horn blowers up and down the elongated encampment. Everyone could hear them. Everyone was worried by the alarm. Generally, this meant danger. Even Rahab and her family became concerned at the desperate sound of the alarm. They feared that some army was coming out of the mountains to attack them. Everyone became afraid.

The elders, judges, and other leaders in any kind of governing capacity rapidly began showing up at the Circle of Government in front of the Tent of Meeting. Some came with their assistants. The captains of the army were arriving. The priests were there in their brown robes. One governor came in a cart because he was sick. Within an hour, the big circle of space in front of the Tent of Meeting was filling with the leaders of Jericho.

As they arrived they met Joshua's fierce eyes staring at them. They knew instantly that something was very, very wrong. Out in front of him came that long arm with the ancient fingers. "Go. Consecrate the people," he called to the gathering. "Tell them: Consecrate yourselves in preparation for tomorrow. For this is what the Lord, the God of Israel, says: 'That which is devoted is among you, O Israel. You cannot stand against your enemies until you remove it.' In the morning, you are to present yourselves tribe by tribe. The tribe that the Lord takes shall come forward clan by clan. The clan that the Lord takes shall come forward family by family, and the family that the Lord takes shall come forward man by man. He who is caught with the devoted things, shall be destroyed by fire, along with all that belongs to him. He has violated the covenant of the Lord and has done a disgraceful thing in Israel!" The old man was shouting so loud, his face became red. His eyes were strained. His brow wrinkled. He was hurt that someone would steal from God.

So, that evening by bedtime every man in the large encampment bathed, washed his clothes, and refrained from intercourse. More than 600,000 men were consecrated by such acts that night.

Early the next morning, in front of the Tent of Meeting, Joshua had Israel come forward by tribes until Judah was taken. The clans of Judah came forward and he took the Zerahites. He had the clan of the Zerahites come forward by families, and Zimri was taken. Joshua had that family come forward man by man and Achan, son of Carmi, the son of Zimri, of the tribe of Judah was taken. Achan was very nervous but he stepped forward in front of Joshua.

Then Joshua said to Achan, "My son, give glory to the Lord, the God of Israel and give Him praise. Tell me what you have done. Don't hide it from me."

Achan replied, "It is true. I have sinned against the Lord, the God of Israel." His mouth was dry. His hands nervous. He kept running his fingers through his hair, trying to look calm. Then he straightened up and with a stronger voice he said, "This is what I have done: When I saw in all that plunder, a beautiful robe from Babylonia, two hundred shekels of silver and a wedge of gold weighing 50 shekels, I took them. They are hidden in the ground of my tent with the silver underneath." Then the 30-year old man fell to his knees in front of Joshua. He was holding his face in his hands.

Joshua sent messengers running to Achan's tent and found the items as Achan had described them. They brought them to Joshua and spread them out.

Joshua looked sternly at the young family man and said, "Why have you brought this trouble on us? The Lord will bring trouble on you today." Then they took him and all he had to the Valley of Achor.

Messengers ran through the entire encampment, including Friends Camp, for everyone, who could, to hurry to the Valley of Achor to fear the God Almighty. Soon the rim around the narrow depression began filling with the thousands of people. Rahab thought how similar this gathering was on the seventh circle on the seventh day at Jericho. Everyone was quiet. Many of the women were softly crying into their scarves. Everyone was sad. Rahab and her family were not sure what was going to happen. All they knew was they were suppose to be there.

Execution

Because Achan did not destroy the things he was told to destroy, all he owned would be destroyed before the eyes of the people. So the people gathered all of Achan's household goods, his animals, all his possessions, even his wife and children and took them into the narrow valley.

Armed men went out to the general grazing pastures and took his cattle, his donkeys and his sheep and brought them to the valley. Even the children's pets were brought down. The men tied the animals' feet so they could not get away. Achan's relatives carried his tent, furniture, grocery items, clothing, and all they had - even the children's toys - down into the valley. Everyone was crying.

Then the soldiers came for the family. They led Achan, his wife, his little girls and his young son to a place near their belongings and tied their hands behind them. The children and his wife were crying so hard, they fell down. The wife fell on top of her children to protect them and a soldier came back into the valley and pulled her away from her children, totally exposing her offspring to the storm that was about to begin. Achan turned to kiss his wife, whispered something to her, and embraced her as well as he could. It was good-bye.

Quiet fell across the valley. It was the same quiet that shrouded Jericho before the attack. Even the family's screams stopped. The sun went behind a cloud and a great shadow covered the land.

The people began hurling stones at the poor family and listening to them cry and scream. It was awful. The animals were trying to break away and escape the massive rain of stones from every direction. The wife and children fell quickly. Achan was knocked down, but he got up, and while bleeding, he stood until he was knocked down again by the storm of rocks.

Rahab remembers being handed a stone as it came her turn to be in the front row. She stepped up then closed her eyes and threw it out into the air. She didn't know where it went, and she didn't want to know.

More than a million stones were thrown into the valley killing the family, the animals and destroying the household. After everyone had thrown their stones, some men went into the valley and set fire to everything. Later they went back and covered the bodies with the stones, marking their graves.

Thus, it came true what Joshua had said the day before: "He who is caught with the devoted things, shall be destroyed by fire, along with all that belongs to him. He has violated the covenant of the Lord and has done a disgraceful thing in Israel." Everyone was crying. Every fellow soldier had tears in his eyes. Every face was pale with sadness. The people had carried out judgment on their relative and friend. It was a sobering experience.

The wind blew the smoke from the funeral fires over the

camp and throughout Gilgal. Rahab was sick from that awful stench of the burning bodies. Her head was filled with the cries of the family. She couldn't erase the screams and the stomping and snorting and the hurt of the animals. She couldn't breathe, and she was afraid she would lose everything in her stomach. It was such a hurtful experience. It was reliving Jericho all over again. How awful it was to see the punishment of sin. Because one man out of 40,000 soldiers disobeyed his God, the entire nation of Israel was punished by having to take the life of their relative and friend. They would remember this for the rest of their lives.

The smell of death lingered for hours in the calm day. Most of the women held scarves over their faces to try to filter out the smoke and stench. Rahab had pulled her pale blue shawl over her nose and mouth. Still she could hardly breathe the fowl air. All hearts were very heavy. Everyone was silent. Hardly a word was spoken. All the people were reminded of the great Law given to them by God through Moses: "Thou shalt not steal." They were reminded again all sin is punishable by death. These are everlasting laws.

Rahab was awake all that night. This was a troubling experience. Her father came and sat with her until very late into the night. They didn't talk much. They just sat there with his arm around her. But in sentences separated by very long pauses, they reasoned how important God was to these people, how He had guided them, took care of them and purified them by such strict laws. Jericho gods were nothing like that. They were just wooden statues that stood there and didn't do anything. And now they didn't even exist because the Israelites had destroyed them. This invisible God was very different than any god they had ever heard about. He was all powerful. He was in control of everything, including their lives.

While they couldn't see the Hebrew God, they could see how He worked in His people. They saw how He worked miracles through them, such as the crossing of the Jordan and the crumbling of Jericho's walls. They understood how important it was to do as God said to do, and now they understood the consequences of ignoring His directives.

Rahab was starving to know more about this God, but she was afraid to ask. She sat there in front of her tent watching the sky. She saw the gathering of the clouds and they covered the stars and she felt the cooler breeze sweep in. The day ended with a somber gray sky as if it, too, was in mourning. Were the clouds, the stars and the cool breeze a message from God, too?

The next day there was a soft, gentle rain. It was so gentle it caressed the land with new hope and new beginnings. It cleared the air and it cleared their minds. However, everyone was still very quiet. Sadness remained everywhere. The people in the Israeli camp hardly moved. They were very reflective on the price of sin. Everyone was in mourning. The place where the Achan family tent stood was swept clean and remained vacant for a long time in memory of the young family.

On the evening after the soft rain, a good looking man passed by Friends Camp on his way to the Israeli camp. Rahab was outside, as she usually was. She was sweeping the pathway to the front of her tent. As she looked up, their eyes met. Salmon politely asked, "How are you doing? How is your health?"

"Very well, thank you," she answered. "But I am terribly sad about the stoning. That was an awful experience. How are you doing?"

"My health is fine, but my heart is sad. Like yours. Would you like some good news?"

"Yes. Anything," Rahab looked up with expectations.

Salmon took her left hand and held it as he said, "Last night in Judah, three new babies were born. Two boys and a girl. The Lord has replaced the children destroyed because of their father's sin. I wanted you to know that. I wanted you to understand that God is merciful." Then, he politely turned to leave. As he walked away, he looked over his shoulder at Rahab and smiled.

The New Attack

After three days of mourning, everyone went back to work. The Lord spoke to Joshua again and told him to not be afraid; he had delivered Ai into his hands. The Lord told him to take the whole army and go attack Ai. "For I have delivered into your hands the King of Ai, his people, his city and his land. You shall do to Ai and its king as you did to Jericho and its king, except this time you may carry off their plunder and livestock for yourselves."

This time, Joshua, himself, would lead the attack according to the strategy given to him by the Lord. Joshua chose 30,000 of his best fighting men and gave them instructions to leave that night and set an ambush between Bethel and Ai, but behind Ai.

Quickly, several advance spotters struck out for the high ridge to secretly mark the trail. They were dressed as nomads riding donkeys. They scuffed up their beard and hair, smeared ashes on their faces, and pulled on old tattered robes. They set off with distances between them so if they were spotted, no one would associate them with the mighty Israeli army. Along the way they marked the trail with stakes and ribbons that could be spotted that night by the army. Before sundown they were in place, hiding on top of the ridge safely behind Ai.

The captains and other leaders gathered their things and with sadness still in their hearts, kissed their families good bye and loaded the war wagons. Well after dark, the wagons began to roll out of camp. Each wagon traveled alone with several feet distance between the other wagons. If they should be spotted, they would not easily be thought of as an army. With only the moon light and the small stakes in the ground to guide them they slowly and quietly began to climb the mountain. There was little conversation. They arrived at the campsite and they all hunkered down until daylight.

Early the next morning Joshua and the remainder of the army of about 10,000, rode out of camp with their shiny sandals, white tunics, shields, swords and spears reflecting the sunlight. They could be easily seen and that is what Joshua wanted. They headed for the worn pathway to the mountains, up the ridge, past the crevices and to the trees and bushes that lined the narrow flatland on top of the mountain. They could see Ai beyond the bushes.

Just as God had said it would happen, the armies of Ai and Bethel were waiting at the front gate of the city. The two little armies came out to fight the Hebrews as they had a few days earlier. When they came out to fight, the soldiers of Israel fell back as though in fear, and the armies defending Ai charged even harder. Israel retreated even more, farther and farther from the city. Both Bethel and Ai were open and unguarded.

When they were far enough away, so that every man in both Bethel and Ai were chasing the Israelites, Joshua stepped out of his hiding place on top of a high point overlooking Ai. God told him to raise up his javelin toward Ai and the men in ambush rushed the city and set it on fire. When the men in retreat saw the smoke rising from Ai, they charged the armies of Bethel and Ai. Joshua's remaining men lying in the ambush charged from the rear. The city's defense system was crushed by the Israelites. They cut down every fighting man, leaving neither survivors nor fugitives.

The Israelites captured the King of Ai alive and brought him to Joshua. Joshua had him hung on a tree and left him there until evening so all could see the price of idolatry. The Israelite army went back into Ai and tore down all the idols. The soldiers killed all the women and children. In all, twelve thousand people died that day.

This time God gave Israel the spoils of the city, so Joshua told the men to gather up all the cattle, donkeys, and sheep, all the household goods and all other valuables to take them back to Gilgal. The soldiers gathered the wagons and horses and mules of Ai and loaded them with plunder. Israel's war wagons were brought out of hiding and filled with the remaining plunder. At sunset, Joshua ordered them to take the king's body down from the tree and throw it at the entrance of the city gate. They raised a large pile of rocks over it. Then they burned everything that remained of Ai. The plume of smoke was dark and tall in the calm evening. The plume was so tall everyone in Gilgal could see it. They knew that God had given them the victory.

The men of God's Army rested that night, but as the sun was rising over the distant horizon, old Joshua was ready for his breakfast and the journey home. His dagger like finger was pointing the way. This time the procession was victorious. Slowly the animals were driven down the mountain side. The advance men rode swiftly ahead and spread the good news to the waiting families. God's Army was victorious and there were no casualties.

As the plunder wagons and the herds of animals arrived in the Israelite encampment, the spoils of Ai were divided between everyone in the camp who wanted or needed something. Rahab's family got some basic household items to furnish their tents better.

The army's return was followed by three days of celebrating. They had received God's favor again. God had given them the victory over the idol worshipers. Everyone expressed their happiness with a lot of singing and dancing until the sun rose over the eastern mountain ridge and gave its light to a new day in Gilgal. In all the merriment in front of the trader tents, someone touched Rahab's shoulder and said, "Hi." Then, as Rahab reached to hug Salmon, he quickly kissed her for the first time. He said that he missed her.

The First Date

Several days went by before Salmon came back to the front of Friends Camp. When Rahab saw him, she went out to meet him and to speak. "How are you doing?"

"Just fine, Rahab How are you doing?" He asked.

"Just fine. It's good to see you, Salmon."

"I want to ask you something. Some friends and I are going out to the Palms this afternoon. I was wondering if you would like to go along? It could be fun," he added.

"Sounds like fun. Yes, I'll go with you. It will be a good break from this routine around here." This was Rahab's first invitation to join with others.

Salmon came by later that afternoon with four friends carrying a big basket. One of the friends was Daniel. They got into a cart pulled by two donkeys and rode off to the Palm trees.

The group asked Rahab about her life in Jericho. "Losing my friends and home and everything was a terrible loss, but I'm grateful that my family was saved and we have enjoyed the company of being close to the camp at Gilgal."

Daniel asked Rahab how it was that God had chosen her to be saved from Jericho. "You must have been a very special person to avoid His wrath."

"I don't know how I would be special," said Rahab. "I am just an ordinary person who worked for a living. I had a small inn just inside the gates of the city and I provided travelers a place to stay overnight. My family lived several apartments down from me, but I was on my own for three years and was beginning to do pretty good managing my affairs."

"What do you suppose made you stand out in God's favor?" Daniel was trying to bring her back on the subject.

"I don't know. I had heard about your God through the caravans. They brought us a lot of news. I learned that He was much more powerful than our statues. So, often, late in the day I would look into that great open sky I couldn't understand, and I would wish to know more about how it came to be and what I was suppose to be about. — I have never told this to anyone — but I have always been full of questions about what I would become. What is it that holds the day together and prepares us for a new one? What is it that guides us throughout our entire lives? But, do you know what concerns me most? It is the little two word question, 'Why me?' How could I be worth the attention of your God? I don't qualify on any grounds. No training. Born to the wrong people. Surrounded by idols. Brought up in the wrong business. Everything about me is wrong. I keep wondering, did Joshua send two spies to Jericho to discover information or were they sent by God to prepare a way for saving my family and me?"

"I'll answer your question," said one of the young women. "God saved you in answer to your prayers. And as for your question did Joshua or God send the spies to Jericho, possibly both. Joshua commissioned the men to seek information, but God uses people to do His work. So while the men sought out information from you; the events that lead to the oath of salvation, most likely was the work of God."

"That's right," Daniel said. "When you were wishing into the sunsets, you were actually praying. Think about it. If the Lord took the time to see that you were born and looked after you while you were growing up, and cared for you to this day, and heard your prayers and answered them, then you are worth it. You are worth more than you can imagine because you have God's love in you and all around you. God makes you worthy of his calling."

Then it was Salmon's turn to speak. Very slowly he looked deeply into her eyes and with a stern, sober look, he wrinkled his forehead and spoke very softly, "Rahab, you have invited a tremendous Force into your life. The power that raised up the mountains, the Force that caused these beautiful palm trees to grow so straight and tall, the Force that feeds the Jordan River, — that is the very Force that is filling your life. All the tenderness of a newborn lamb, the gentleness of a mother's touch, the soft colors in the flowers, the comfort of a friend's arm around you when you are sad, — all of it — is filling your soul with His love. God is not just our God. God is God of everyone and everything. The earth is the Lord's and everything in it. Including you and me and all of us. He is the Creator of all things large and small. You called out to God and He is answering you. Listen with your soul and hear His love." Then he reached for her hand and held it for a long time. A gentle breeze wafted through the group and everyone smiled.

Daniel broke the silence by getting up and saying "I've got to get some more tea, who wants some?" He walked around the circle and put his hands on Rahab's shoulders and then went to the cart and picked up a big jar of berry tea. He went around the circle filling everyone's cup, and wisecracking something about each person. Daniel did a little jig, balancing the clay jar of tea on his forehead, but still holding it with one hand and making waving motions with his other arm. The friends began to laugh.

Daniel came to his place in the circle and sat down. "As I was saying so long ago: The mighty power of the Lord is available to everyone who obeys God's will. It is available to everyone who asks."

One of the young ladies sitting next to Daniel, turned to Rahab and said, "This is probably the first time in my life that I have ever agreed with Daniel," she said, punching him in the ribs with her elbow. Everyone laughed. "We are happy you do have an interest in God. And that you are here today with us. I want you to know we love you as God loves you." Then she got up and walked across the circle and gave Rahab a hug. Everyone else applauded.

"Just so Daniel won't tell another one of his jokes, I want to say something," and the second young woman jabbed Daniel in his other side with her elbow. While everyone was laughing again, he fell back into the sparse grass and lay there listening. "A priest told me that in Moses' Book of Law, God gives several illustrations of things He does so that the people will know who God is. The enslavement in Egypt, the deliverance from slavery, the parting of the Red Sea, and the provisions of food during the travels in the wilderness are examples of signs of who God is. I would suggest that most recently, the stopping of the Jordan River, the crumbling walls of Jericho, the defeat at Ai, and even the stoning of Achon, were all signs to remind us of who God is. We need to keep watch for other signs, not just the miracles, but watch for the people who come into our lives in everyday life. Things happen in our lives so that we may know who God is."

The circle of friends was quiet. Everyone was thinking. The young woman reached back to help pull Daniel upright. He reached over and hugged her and then asked, "Now can I say something?"

But everyone in the circle shouted "No!"

And the friend placed her hand over Daniel's mouth to keep him quiet. "No more jokes."

Daniel mockingly hung his head and pretended to cry. This caused the friends to jointly say, "Ohhhhhhhhhh." And everyone laughed yet another time. It was a good day for all. A little whirl wind caught up some dust and leaves and danced them in the air and then moved on. The sun was beginning to set and they needed to get back home. The men loaded the cart and the people got in and rode back, but Salmon asked Rahab if she would like to walk. She said yes, of course. He took her hand and they walked a little distance behind the cart.

Along the trail they chatted, but they said nothing of substance. Rahab sensed that Salmon wanted to say something more than small talk. She wasn't sure how to encourage him. Then she asked about what he really wanted to do with his life. A bright beam came into his eyes and he said, "Oh, get married and have lots of kids." And he squeezed her hand and looked into her face. She looked back and smiled.

"Sounds nice," she said.

"But, first," Salmon began hesitantly, "I must help with the settling of this land. You need to know that I have some duties and pledges — some vows — to complete before I have much of a life other than the army. It's only fair to say I would like to get to know you better and spend everyday with you, but it's unfair to seek your favor when I may be away so much and one never knows what will happen as we take over the land."

She felt he was making more excuses than saying what was on his heart. From her years as innkeeper she could still read a man's face. And this time she saw a face that was in love. So she took charge: "Well, Mr. Salmon, perhaps I should be a help to you. You just keep calling on me and I'll tell you when everyday is too much. Is that a deal?"

"A deal," he said. He hugged her up close and kissed her quickly behind the ear. He smiled and kissed her again on her cheek; just as cheers and applause came from the wagon in front of them.

11

Deception

The hot days of summer swept the land as if someone had opened a giant oven. The grass turned as yellow as straw. The trees stopped bearing. All the farm work was laid aside until the fall showers and a chance for rebirth in autumn. The animals lay in whatever shade they could find. At midday there were few people out.

To see travelers at that time of day was odd, but here they came. A half-dozen beleaguered men with tattered clothing and dirty faces, walked beside their tired donkeys burdened by worn out baggage. Almost all travelers came from the north, but these came from the south and made their way slowly in front of Friends Camp. Rahab and her family offered them a drink of water. The tired and dirty men drank hurriedly, gulping down the water as if they had none for days. The water ran from their lips and dripped onto their bare chests. Dust flew from the hood of one man's robe when he touched it in appreciation of the water. The men were invited to sit down and rest a while, but they declined. "Thank you for your hospitality, but we have come a long way to see the king. Where will we find the king?"

"Israel has no king, but the leaders are inside the encampment behind the traders' tents. Just inquire at the trader's tents, and they will help you."

Olmad and his father got water for their donkeys and helped the men refresh a little. Olmad could see how worn the sacks and wineskins were on the beasts. The wine skins had been mended many times. They were dry and cracked. It was doubtful they could hold any water at all. One man opened a food basket and they could see that the bread was dry and moldy.

Rahab collected her mugs from the six travelers and felt sorry for them. They must have come such a long ways. Their sandals were patched and worn. Their travel robes were shabby and dirty and torn. They had no sashes to hold them closed, so she could see their tunics were in no better shape. They were soiled so badly from things spilling on them, one could hardly tell their color. They were so ripped and shredded. One man's tunic was torn at the collar and laid bare his chest with matted hair. Another man had a split down the side of his tunic exposing his upper leg. His body was crusted with sweaty dirt. They smelled awful. Their hair and beards were filled with sand and brush. They had been in the desert a long time.

Olmad agreed to show them to the traders' tents and let one of the Hebrews seek council with Joshua. The chief trader sent a messenger to Joshua, who was in a council meeting at the time. The chief trader's message said that six members of a delegation from a foreign country had arrived and wished a few moments of his time to make a treaty. Joshua granted the time and the messenger escorted the six men and their donkeys back into the maze of tents to the Tent of Counseling in the Circle of Government. Joshua brushed back his hair and rose to greet them just outside the tent.

"May God be with you," the visitors called to the thin man.

"And also with you," said Joshua. "How may I help you?"

"We have come a long ways. From a distant country. Will you please make a treaty with us?"

When the councilmen heard the word treaty, they, too, came out of the tent and examined the visitors. They agreed among themselves that the men had come a long ways. This treaty must be very important to them.

One of the councilmen asked, "I see you are a Hivite. Perhaps you live nearby. How can we make a treaty with you?"

"We will be your servants. We will live a life in submission to your rule, if you will let us live." The travelers were looking at Joshua.

"Tell me first, who are you and where do you come from?" Joshua was showing some doubt as did the councilman.

The traveler doing most of the talking, smoothed his matted beard. Then he wiped his hands on his dirty tunic and then said, "Your servants have come from a distant country because of the fame of your God."

A second traveler broke in, "We have heard reports of your God and all that He did in Egypt, and all that He did to the two kings of the Amorites east of the Jordan."

The second traveler was interrupted by an excited third man,

"Yes, yes, yes, we have heard all about Sihon, King of Heshbon, and Og, King of Bashan. We know how he reigned in Ashtaroth. We keep up with the news. We follow your travels, and we know how you destroy everything in your pathway."

The appeal swung back to the first man. "Our elders said to us, 'Go, take provisions for your journey. Go and meet with the Israelites and say to them, we are your servants, make a treaty with us to let us live.'"

"Just look at this. Our bread was warm when we packed it at home on the day we left to come to you. But now see how dry and moldy it is." The dirty man reached into the food sack and broke off some of the dry bread. "See how dry and moldy it is."

A second traveler picked up an empty wineskin, "And these wineskins. We filled them when they were new. But see how cracked they are."

The third man pulled at his robe and tunic, looking down his body to his feet and quietly said, "And our clothes. Our sandals. They are worn out by the very long journey we made to come appeal to you for this treaty."

The council members sampled their provisions but they did not inquire of the Lord. "Very well, then," said Joshua. "We will make the treaty and you shall live in the land and we will protect your city." All present ratified the treaty by oath. But, still, no one took the matter before God.

The messenger escorted the travelers outside to the traders' tents and told them good-bye. The men continued northerly from Gilgal.

The councilmen retired to their meeting and Joshua took up other matters, dismissing the alliance for the moment. However, that evening, the chief trader sought Joshua and told him he was worried about something.

"What's that," asked the old man.

"I'm concerned about an odd thing. Those travelers we had earlier today? They came from the south and wanted to make a treaty. Is that right?"

Joshua answered, "Yes, that's right. We made a treaty with them. Why are you asking?"

"Well, those travelers came from the south. Said they had traveled a long distance, but they left going north. I was wondering why would somebody so destitute for food and rest would take off in the direction that would lead them farther from their destination?"

Joshua raised his eyebrows and gripped his friend on the

shoulder. "That's a very good question."

"I just can't figure out why they would make such a long journey in this heat? Why wouldn't they go back the way they came?"

"You're saying that they came from the south to make us think they came a long way. Are you saying, my man, that their visit was a deception?" Joshua was thinking more than talking.

"I am reporting that the travelers came from the south and left going north in the heat of summer. You would expect that after they had done their business, in this heat, they would head back home. But they did not go back in the direction they arrived. Perhaps a couple of men should see where they go."

"Good idea," said Joshua. "It's the end of the day now. Would you say that the travelers are most likely to stop soon and rest for the night and then begin again in the morning?"

"Probably so, Joshua."

"Then we would be able to catch up with them in the morning if we needed to. I think we should see what they do tonight and then check them out tomorrow morning. Let's pray for guidance tonight on what to do."

"Of course, Joshua. As you say." And the big man returned to his own place, and Joshua headed for his home tent.

Before the sun had peeked over the distant mountain on the other side of the Jordan, Joshua was already at work. One of the tribal representatives, who had attended the midday council session, approached the leader. "Joshua, I have a concern about those men who came to see us yesterday."

"You, too? That makes two of us," said Joshua.

"We were so busy listening to all their hard luck that we didn't really get a look at the men, themselves. We saw what they wanted us to see. They said they came a long ways. They showed us their dry bread and empty wine sacks. They showed us their worn out clothes. But did you listen to their voices?"

"What are you saying, my friend?" Joshua was asking.

"Their voices were strong. People living in the desert, out in the open, weary from travel, dirty and sunburn, are going to have weary voices. Their whole body will be weakened. These men appeared to come a long ways, yet, they had a strong stride and strong voices. This is mysterious. I sense that we may be part of a ruse."

"You may be right. Will you check with the people who have been scouting out the land and see if they have any kind of a map that shows the towns around here? It might be very interesting to see just where these fellows did come from. When you get one, bring it over to my tent." Joshua patted the council leader on the back and pointed him to the scouting office.

Next to Joshua's meeting tent was a cadre of soldiers and messengers. Joshua simply called out, "Messenger," and two soldiers and two messengers stepped into his tent within seconds.

"Yes sir," they all said.

"Remember those travelers who came here at noon yesterday? The ones that were all covered in dust and had tattered clothing?"

"The ones that smelled so bad," said a soldier. "Yes, sir."

"Go up the road north of here and see if you can catch up with them and tell me where they are going. See what you can find out."

"Yes, sir," they all said respectfully and turned to their fast steeds that were always saddled and ready to ride. They raced off in the early morning sun.

Joshua had organized a circle of tents that served as the government facility for the combined 12 tribes. Representatives from various services were almost always present so that quick action could be taken if needed. This was true of emergencies, such as fire, plague, storms or whatever might harm the people. The army had its standby team on site. Joshua walked casually over to the army tent. He was mumbling to himself as old men often do.

"What are you boys doing over here?" The Israeli leader asked.

"We are protecting the encampment and possessing the Promised Land, sir," someone from the back of the room said.

"And you can do that laying on pallets and telling stories?" The leader asked with a glint in his eye.

"Yes, sir. Want to join us?"

"I think I will. I sense that I am about to learn something. I may have spent 40 years doing my job the hard way." So the old man pulled up a cushion and a young soldier took his arm and helped him lower himself. "Now, the next thing is to figure out how I am going to get up."

There was a soft chuckle in the room. Joshua had a sense of humor, but he seldom showed it while he was conducting business.

"What's going on, sir?" A young soldier asked.

"A mystery, son. A real, honest to goodness, mystery." Joshua's voice fell silent, but his brain was still whirling. "Yesterday, we were visited by six men all covered in dust and weary from travel in the sun. They were thirsty and hungry. They said they represented people far away and wanted a treaty. We gave them the treaty and now I and some others are having second thoughts. Something unusual is going on. I'm afraid that we may be set up for a surprise attack of some kind."

"Joshua, at the snap of your fingers, I can get you 5,000 men in a half circle guarding all the entrances into this encampment. From the high points we can watch by daylight great distances to see if anyone is approaching and signal here for more protection if we need it. At night we can have the men standing guard every few feet to detect any one moving out there. Just like a seine catches fish in the water, so we can catch anyone moving out there heading towards Israel." The suggestion came from the captain on duty.

"Let's do that for a few days, until we learn what is going on. Put out your sentries this morning. And, tonight let us use two rows of men out there. Place one about a mile away from the camp, and the other one two miles from the camp. Make sure there are several messengers and signalers in the group who can run back with reports if they should need to," the commander in chief said. Then he looked up to the captain on duty and tried to snap his old fingers. It took three times but the popping sound came from the fingers. And everyone grinned as they jumped into action. Then he reached up for any hand that could help him stand up. "You boys, need thicker cushions, if I have to come over here and help you do your work anymore." And from out of the sea of movement, came a stranger's strong hand and helped the leader to stand.

Before Joshua was standing straight and gaining his balance, the ram's horns were sounding three short blasts and one long one. It was the emergency signal for a cadre to form outside the Circle of Government. The men in the tent were drawing up plans for the circles of protection. The casual room had sprung into action. As Joshua was making his way across the circle, soldiers from the Transjordan group were reporting in with swords and shields, ready for work.

As Joshua left the army tent, the councilman handed him a rough map of the general area. It was the earlier work of different spies who had mapped the area and developed strategies. The leader returned to his tent to study it. "Thank you, my friend. I appreciate your getting this for me."

On the Trail

Meanwhile the two soldiers and their messengers made up lost time quickly. They were on fast steeds and the travelers were on donkeys. They were only a few miles out when the lead soldier signaled to halt. He had spotted a campsite. They stopped to examine it and found the coals still warm. They found an old worn out robe thrown down, yet there was a wineskin, practically new, laying on the old robe. The six travelers only had stale food and battered wineskins. Where would they get a new wineskin?

"Boys, let's get on down the road and see what these mysterious men are doing now?" The leader of the group got back on his horse and off they raced in a cloud of dust. When they topped a little rise in the ground, they spotted the six men on donkeys still a good distance away. They seem to be talking and waving their hands at each other. They were not as weary as they seemed to be the day before. Even at that distance, the soldiers could tell that the travelers were happy about something. They decided to approach carefully and see what the men did.

The more the soldiers watched, the less weary the travelers seemed. In a few minutes they turned off the trail and headed for a large sand dune and a couple of dilapidated buildings. The old buildings appeared to be abandoned and wrecked by storms.

"Why are they heading for those old buildings?" One soldier asked.

"This is beginning to get interesting," said another.

They were in a low ravine area in the roadway, but on their horses they could watch the travelers, even though they were more than a half-mile away. "Let's stay right here for a few minutes and then let's move over to that scrub brush and watch from there."

The six travelers rode up to the abandoned building and dismounted. They pulled off their old robes and threw down the burden they had packed on their donkeys. One of the travelers went into the falling down building and took out a new skin filled with water and began pouring it on himself. Then he hung it up on a swaying board and re-tied the bottom so that the water came out slowly. He turned it into a makeshift shower. Another man hung three other water bags up and soon all six of them had pulled off their clothes and were taking showers outside, in the middle of the desert.

"Now, it is getting interesting," said the first soldier.

After their showers, they dried off with new towels and pulled from their hiding places the fresh tunics and robes of wealthy people. As soon as they were dressed, they pulled out some fresh food and wine and began to devour it in the shade of the fallen building. They were satisfied they had pulled off their ruse. They seem to be celebrating.

"One of you messengers, make a big circle and come up behind our friends down there and see what they have to say. Tell them you're lost or something. Ask them where they're going. You know, the usual stuff."

One of the messengers nodded his head and turned his horse around to go galloping off to the side, crisscrossing as he went. Finally, he headed towards the old building and came up to the travelers. From the back of his sweaty horse, he called out, "Oh, my friends, can you help me?"

"Why would we want to help you?"

"Because I'm lost. Which way is it to the nearest town that has an army? I want to help them beat off the Israelites," the messenger raised his hand like he was stabbing something with his invisible sword.

"But you dress like an Israelite. Why do you want to attack them?"

"I've been with them learning their methods and their plans. I have important information. Where are you people from?"

The travelers looked at each other and shrugged their shoulders. "We come from all over. We are with an alliance of several small towns near here. We might have a market for your information. Come join us. Have some food."

"I don't have much time. I should be talking with a king as soon as I can, but I thank you for something to drink." And the messenger sat with them and sipped their wine and ate some of their bread with a tangy sauce on it. Where is the nearest king?"

"Probably, Gibeon. That's where we're headed. You can ride along."

"I thank you for the invitation, but I have important news and must ride quickly. Which way is Gibeon?

"Continue with the roadway over there and down the ridge a little ways you will see it. It is not far. You can be there by sundown."

"Gentlemen, I thank you. I must be on my way. Thank you for the directions. I must go see the king." And with that he jumped back on his horse and headed for the worn roadway. The travelers watched him ride as a fierce wind until he disappeared over the next little rise in the road to Gibeon.

"Where's he going now?" Ask one of the soldiers.

"He's covering his story, I guess."

"I hope he remembers where we are."

Soon they could see the dust of a whirlwind with a horse and rider inside it. The messenger was making it back to them as part of a large circle to protect their hiding place. Out of breath, the messenger reported to the rest of them, "These are the same men who were at Gilgal at noon yesterday; the ones pretending to be travelers from far off. They are diplomats from several towns but they are headed for Gibeon to report on the treaty they got from Joshua."

The soldier in command looked at his fellow riders and then decided, "My friend with the news, why don't you hurry back to Joshua and tell him what you discovered. The rest of us will follow these interesting people some more and see what else we can learn from them."

So the messenger snapped the reins of his steed and headed back to Gilgal and an audience with Joshua. All the while the travelers sat in their new clothes munching tangy sauce on warm bread and drinking a skin of new wine.

An Interruption

But back at Gilgal, the afternoon sun was beaming down so intensely the messenger could feel it stinging his face. The encampment was lifeless. Few people had the energy to move around. Rahab had opened both ends of her tent in an effort to catch any breeze that might come around. Nothing was stirring. She had changed into her lightest weight linen gown. The soft peach color was a beautiful contrast to her darker skin. It was sleeveless, low cut and cut high enough so her ankles would show. She would never consider wearing it outside, but in the tent she felt it was all right. She kept a robe handy in case someone should call to her. But who was there to call? No one was moving.

No one, except two men with ugly black beards, bushy eyebrows and matted hair. A slim man and a man with broad shoulders had been secretly watching Rahab's tent. The slim, little man came to the front of the tent as the bigger man went to the back. As if on cue, they both entered her tent and grabbed for her. They both snarled, "Prostitute! God will get you."

The startled woman reacted instantly. Without thought, Rahab reached for the closest hand, grabbed it and swung with all her might to bring the smaller man around her and into the heavier one. The collision threw both intruders off balance, falling to the ground just outside the back of her tent. Rahab screamed as loudly as she could. "Get out of here! Get out of here!"

The two men did not expect such a challenge. They had talked of just coming in and getting the prostitute for themselves and taking her away, but instead they found a hornet's nest. Her adrenaline rushed at top speed, her defense system was on automatic. Blindly, she reached behind her for something to throw. Her fingers found a pot of hot peppers she had brewing in the heat of the sun. Her fingers grabbed it and flung it toward the intruders. The pot itself was heavy with hot water which burned their skin. Then the pepper juice got on their eyes and hands and burned them even more. The men were scrambling around trying to get back on their feet. When they did, they ran as best as they could. "And stay out!" She screamed.

Her father, brother, and the two man-servants were at her tent in seconds, but the two intruders were running into the desert.

"Rahab, are you all right?" Her father asked.

"Rahab, what happened here?" Her brother asked.

"Just a little surprise visit from a couple of outcasts with no manners. Yes, I'm all right, Daddy. Just mad," said Rahab. "Why can't people learn to do their fighting when it's cooler? I just wasted my best peppers."

"I told you she was *some* fighter," said Ari El. He sounded as though he was an expert on classifying fighters. Rahab was one of his favorites.

"I'll go after them, Miss Rahab. I'll get them for you," said Joseph, looking out of the tent towards the desert.

"Joseph, don't waste your energy. Maybe they've learned their lesson." Rahab was reasoning without sentences.

"Thank you, Joseph," said his master. "Rahab's right. There's no need to go chasing them. God will provide the time of judgment."

Ari El brought back the pot where the peppers had been simmering. "I'll clean up the mess, Miss Rahab, but here is your pot. There is a crack in it."

"Thank you, Ari El. You are very kind," said Rahab.

The Messenger Reports

A whirlwind of dust chased after the messenger's speeding horse. He was spotted by the sentries and a ram's horn signaled his arrival. Joshua was waiting when the messenger rode up to the Circle of Government. "Joshua, you were right to suspect the travelers. We spotted them just north of here a little ways where they had hidden clothes, water and food. All that dust and dirt they had on them and the donkeys was something they had put on themselves to make you and the others think they had come a long ways. In fact, we believe that they're from Gibeon. They may represent other towns, as well. The rest of our team is following them to see if they can learn more. I talked with the travelers briefly and they offered me food and wine from their hideout just a few miles up the road. All that stuff they had packed on their donkeys and their old dirty clothes, were things to miss-direct you and get your sympathy."

Some of the councilmen were eavesdropping. "Just as I thought," said one councilman.

"I told everyone to be careful. To go slow," said another.

"Thank you, my friend. Now, come into the tent and tell us what you do know, what you think is happening, and the difference between the two." Joshua brushed his silver hair back behind his ears and walked into the council tent. "Now start at the beginning and tell us everything that happened."

The messenger began recounting the experience. He told of finding the campsite with the new wineskin and discarded old robe. He told of watching the men shower in the open at an abandoned house and then dress in rich robes.

"They shared a meal with me and I learned that they were diplomats from several towns but they reported first to the King of Gibeon. They never did say directly, but, from what they did say, I'm guessing that they rode from Gibeon to the hideout, stowed their things, rubbed dirt on their faces, wet them down and rubbed some more on. They changed their clothes and baggage to the worn out stuff and then rode in a big circle for a day or two to come up from the south, say Jerusalem or somewhere. By then they smelled of the outdoors and were ready to play their part."

"Well done. You have solved one mystery and started another one," said Joshua. "And the rest of your group is still out there?"

"Yes, sir. They're following the men slowly to see what else they are up to," the messenger said. "It'll probably take them a couple of days to get to Gibeon at their pace."

"Thank you again, son. Now, go get you some rest. We'll try to decide what to do next." Joshua stood up to dismiss him by placing his hand on the young man's shoulder. When the messenger left through the open entrance to the big tent, Joshua turned to the others and said, "Men, it's at the end of the day. Let's explore this matter more tomorrow. Be sure to pray for guidance tomorrow." And the day was finished.

New Sleeping Arrangements

Over in Friends Camp, Rahab's family was finishing up their evening meal together. They were laughing, joking, and fielding a few serious questions and answers. They talked of possibly teaching the children of the camp to read and write. Rahab liked the idea. They could hold classes in the mornings before it got so hot. Finally, the talk turned to what to do for the evening to provide safety for Rahab through the night. While several suggestions came up, her father decided that the thing to do was simply for Rahab and Joseph to exchange tents for the night. Joseph was a strong man and could alert the rest of them if someone came back into the tent.

After some objections from Rahab, her father overruled everything and the two prepared to exchange tents. Joseph took Rahab to his tent back a ways into Friends Camp. He picked up a dagger and put it into his belt. Then he went to the long narrow pallet and pulled back the top cover exposing the pillow. "Have a good night, Miss Rahab," he said and turned to leave.

Rahab pulled off her robe and stood in her gown for a moment surveying the tent. *It smells like a man*, she thought. Then she lay down on the pallet and buried her face in the servant's pillow. *Like a man.*

Joseph went up front to Rahab's tent and walked into it. How different hers was from his. She had so much more color in her tent than his. She had the little projects that she had started from flax and palm fronds and other things. Most of them were in soft pastels. Her linen things she had woven from flax and had them dyed in pinks and yellow, and light green and blue. There was the smell of perfume. Where would she get perfume? Then he smelled her. He smelled Jasmine. He undressed from his robe and tunic and left only his basic loincloth. He placed his dagger under the soft pillow. Then he stretched out, his feet going beyond the end of her pallet. He smelled of the pillow, relaxed his body, closed his eyes and thought, *Ah, Jasmine.*

Daylight was just creeping into the day when Joseph was awakened by his master calling. "Joseph, are you awake?"

"Yes, sir. I'll be right out," called Joseph. He quickly pulled on his tunic and stepped out of Rahab's tent. The night had gone without incident. All was safe.

"Did you sleep well?" His master was asking.

"Like a rock. And you, sir?"

"Like a rock. I just wanted to mention something," Rahab's father was almost whispering.

"What's that, sir,"

"I don't want you to make this a habit of coming over here and sleeping in my daughter's tent," said the father.

"Not to worry, sir. Too much perfume."

And Rahab's father took the servant by the shoulder and grinned.

Time for Action

All of Israel became angry within two days of the treaty with the Gibeonites. Out of two million people, there seemed to be three million ideas and solutions. The anger turned into protests and threats of violence. The treaty was in contradiction of Holy direction to possess the land and rid it of idols and idol worshipers. Many feared the consequences of not following through as directed by the Holy One. The common theme through the day's debates became: *Why wait for the facts? Let's jump in and go take care of the Gibeonites now! Why risk God's wrath?*

The men of Israel began protesting to the councils. They pointed out over and over again how bad the treaty was and everyone needed to rise up and go take the towns as God had ordered. Joshua feared that he might lose control over his people and prayed for God's direction.

The army was assembled and they rode out that very day to the mountain ridges and paths that led past the ruins of Jericho and the ruins of Ai and then down the ridges to Gibeon, another oasis in the desert. Soon they were near the city gates of Gibeon, Kephirah, Beeroth, and Kiriath Jearim.

It was a very strong show of force. The frightened citizens of the little towns could feel the power and the anger of the Hebrews. It was a mighty show of force. So many soldiers. So many swords. So many daggers. There was no escape from the 40,000 soldiers at their front gates. Fear was in the eyes of every Gibeonite. Was it better to die now or to be the slaves of such strong masters?

However, the Hebrews did not attack. The captains of the army reminded their soldiers of the oath. The leaders of the assembly had sworn an oath to the Gibeonites by the Lord. Joshua called out to them, "We have given them our oath by the Lord, the God of Israel, and we cannot touch them now. Listen to me. This is what we will do to them. We will let them live, so that the wrath will not fall on us for breaking the oath we swore to them. Let them live, but let them be woodcutters and water carriers, for the entire community."

The angry fighters understood that this meant that the Gibeonites would live by becoming common slaves to everyone in the Israelite encampment. They would also be slaves for the tabernacle because the sacrifices required much wood and water.

Joshua summoned the Gibeonite leaders and asked them, "Why did you deceive us by saying, 'We live a long way from you while actually you lived near to us?" He did not wait for an answer. "You are now under a curse. You will never cease to serve as woodcutters and water carriers; you shall be slaves for the house of my God."

The Gibeonite council answered Joshua, "Your servants were clearly told how your God, had commanded his servant Moses to give you the whole land. We know that your God has commanded to wipe out all its inhabitants. So, we feared for our lives, and that is why we did this. We are now in your hands. Do to us what ever seems good and right to you."

So Joshua accepted their surrender, and they did not kill them. "Captains, go now into Gibeon and take the first 100 young men, men of fighting age, and bring them with us to serve as slaves to the Tabernacle. They shall provide the wood and water needed for our sacrifices and feasts."

The captains and their helpers went into the city and took on sight the young men who were strong and healthy. They bound their hands behind them and placed them in Gibeonite wagons, drawn by Gibeonite horses and took them back to Gilgal as slaves to the Tabernacle. At Gilgal an iron band was welded to the right upper arm, marking them as slaves.

Taking this small amount of slaves was only a token gesture, but it made the point that Israel was in charge. But not much. The deception was not over for the Gibeonites. The ruse had only begun. This time Israel had turned its back on what was to come. Everyone in Canaan was fearful of the huge army. Everyone had heard of the mad destruction of Jericho and Ai. So, recruiting massive numbers of resistance was easy. All the peoples of the hill country, in the western foothills and along the entire coast of the Great Sea as far as Lebanon, came together and laid plans to make war against Joshua and Israel. "If they have 40,000 soldiers, we shall have 100,000," became the secret cry in the midnight meetings across the land.

12

The Proposal

Rahab and her family developed an interest in teaching the girls and women of the camp how to read. This was a bold movement because women had never been taught before. As a custom of the times boys and young men were taught reading, scriptures and other subjects, but girls were never invited to public classes. After all, why would they need to read?

Rahab answered, "Why not?" She could read, why others shouldn't be allowed to read as well. She reasoned that if she taught the classes then whoever came could learn but there was no direct support from the Hebrew government. Rahab started with a few little children and the classes often included mothers who brought their children and stayed.

At the end of one of the classes, Salmon came by and asked Rahab to take a walk with him. She agreed and told one of the servants that she should be back shortly. Salmon took her hand and they walked past the front of Friends Camp without looking either way.

"I hear you are still having trouble with intruders in your campsite," Salmon began, with a worried look on his face.

"A little. I try to brush it off, but it's hard to do. I guess, regardless of what God does, your past still stays with you. As they say, 'God forgives easily, but neighbors are reluctant.' There is an element here that is determined to get rid of me. Maybe I should put up a sign that says, "Leave me alone!" But I'm not sure these men know how to read.

"You're probably right," Salmon said. "How are you coping?"

"My father is now insisting that I sleep in different tents and one of our servants usually sleeps in mine. But weeks have gone by since the last experience. Maybe they have grown bored and found something else to do."

"I'm thankful that you have not been hurt," said Salmon. "There has been no report of anyone breaking our defense perimeter. It must be someone inside the camp here. Someone who just doesn't accept God's will."

"Probably so. I have faith that God will take care of me."

"Me, too," he said. "But I can talk to Joshua about a guard along the front of Friends Camp. Just let me know if you want one."

They came to a couple of trees and a few little bushes that offered some shade and privacy from the public trail. Salmon turned Rahab out to the trees and they found a flat rock that made a perfect seat.

"I've been concerned about you," he said. "You are in my thoughts all of the time. Every time I smell Jasmine, I think of you. I have associated that scent with you ever since we were in your Jericho apartment. You have become so very important to me."

"You are just saying that because I had a strong rope that night when you and your friend came tearing into my apartment; a rope for your escape." She was teasing him while he was trying to be serious.

"Well, I am thankful for the escape. But to tell the truth, when I first smelled Jasmine in your apartment and saw your directness in dealing with the surprise visit, I knew I needed to get to know you better. When we finally got my friend squeezed through that window in the wall and it was my turn to leave through it, I came so very close to taking you with me."

"Really! You were ready to kidnap me?" Rahab was surprised.

"I certainly had those feelings. You were pretty. You were confident. You showed you could take care of yourself. You were kind. You had a temper." Salmon grinned and reached to touch her necklace at its lowest point.

"You like your women to have a temper?" Rahab quizzed him while taking his hand from her necklace.

"I'm not sure. I never had someone that attracted me so much."

"You are serious."

In a soft sincere voice, he pleaded, "I'm very serious. I wanted so much to kiss you through the window in your apartment, but our rules would not permit it. I just had to come back and get you when the time was right. I prayed every day for you. I prayed that it be God's will to bring us together And now that you are here, I still want to spend more and more time with you. I still pray everyday for you." He turned his head to kiss her cheek.

And she turned her face to his and kissed him back. "I am growing fond of you, too," Rahab said quietly. She looked down to smooth out a wrinkle in her robe. "You don't know how often I think of you, but I also remember that you need someone else. Someone of your own tribe. Someone who has not had the background that I have. You should not be harnessed to a woman like me"

"Oh, I know about your past, but your past is not as important as your present and your future. God knows about your past and He has forgiven you. So why not me and everybody else? You are living a beautiful, giving life. You are a very loving person. I can't wait for an opportunity to speak with your dad about giving me his blessing to sweep you away into life in the Judah Camp."

"What is it like inside?" Rahab asked.

"That's right, you haven't been inside. Tomorrow, I'll come and get you and give you a tour. Meet my folks. Everything. Do you have time tomorrow morning?"

"I'll make the time. I would love to see inside."

"Very well, it's set. Tomorrow is tour day of Judah." Salmon stood up and picked her up in his arms and twirled around as if the world were standing still, and it was all his. Then he kissed her softly and very carefully he let her down on her feet — as if she were a fragile beam of sunlight.

Announcement of a Journey

That afternoon a messenger came through Friends Camp announcing that everyone was invited to make a trip with Israel to Mt. Ebal for the renewing of the covenant given by the Lord. Not many seemed to understand what the young man was talking about, so he explained it. "Moses said when we were in the Promised Land that all of Israel should go to Mt. Ebal to renew the covenant. Joshua and his team believe that it is safe enough for the entire nation to make the journey. Especially, since the Gibeonites had been enslaved.

"Joshua and some of his staff are inscribing all ten commandments on large stones to be carried and mounted on top of the mountain. After Joshua reads the commands from the mountain, then some of the tribes will shout blessings from one side of Mt. Ebal to the other tribes that are on the side of nearby Mt. Gerizim. Then the people on Mt. Gerizim will recall curses and call them out to the tribes on the side of Mt. Ebal. It will help us all to remember the purposes for which we are in the Promised Land. It will renew our relationship with the Almighty." The young messenger was excited about the proposed journey. "We will be leaving in a few days."

"Hey, what's going on over here?" The strong voice came from the pathway in front of Friends Camp. Everyone in Rahab's family looked up and saw that it was the long legged priest.

"Jonathan! Come in. You are just the person we want to see."

"I bet you say that to all the good looking priests who come by here." Jonathan was smiling and reached down to pick up one of Olmad's little boys and then swooped up the other one. "Boy, you guys are getting heavy. Have you been eating rocks?"

The little boys giggled and hugged Jonathan's neck and then he let them slide down his lanky frame. By that time everyone in the family had gathered in the family circle and Olmad asked the big question. "What is this all about: a renewal of the covenant?"

Everyone took a cushion for a long explanation. Jonathan took a guest cushion and promptly spread out those long legs into the middle of the circle. The little boys were back to sit on each side of him. "So you have heard about the trip to Mount Ebal?"

"Yes, but we don't understand it," Rahab's father said.

"So, you are going?" He looked up from tickling both boys.

"We're thinking on it. We'll leave one servant to look after things."

"That's a good idea. Joshua will also leave a cadre of soldiers here to protect the camp. We will be having many of the members of the tribes from across the Jordan join us and some of their people are likely to stay and protect things, too. So your belongings should be safe."

"So what is this about?" Rahab wanted answers.

"It's a big deal. It is a very important mission for all of us. And it would be very meaningful to all of you as well. But I think you should experience everything first hand. You will be better off to learn these things as they happen. Let me to just urge you to come with open hearts and expect to feel the glory of God. You'll be amazed." He paused and then roughed up the hair of the two boys and said, "And stop feeding rocks to these old boys. They're getting too heavy." And with that the boys started pulling on Jonathan's arms trying to get him to stand up. It was a mock struggle for everyone's entertainment, but finally the little ones were able to get the big one to his feet.

Jonathan flashed a loving smile to everyone in the circle, put his hand on Rahab's father's shoulder and said to all, "Walk with God."

Touring Judah

About mid-morning the next day, Salmon stopped by Friends Camp and was greeted by Rahab's mother. "And what are you doing here, young man?"

"I have come to ask a girl to accompany me," Salmon flashed his big bright smile to the grandmother.

"Well, how about me? I'm a girl."

"Indeed you are. I have one major test for all the many women I date," he was wondering what kind of answer he would get.

"And what kind of a test is that?" The older lady shot back. She was still drying her hands on her apron.

"Come here and I'll show you," Salmon walked towards the woman with the big smile and sparkling eyes. "It's my super hugging test. Let's see how you do." And he reached out and politely hugged Rahab's mother around her shoulders and waist, almost tipping her off her feet. And she hugged him back like a mother would a new son-in-law. And they both chuckled. "Hey, you're pretty good. I'm going to have to add you to my list of world's best huggers."

"And how long is your list?" The breathless woman asked.

"Well, to be honest, you are the first one. You are actually on top of my list." Salmon was enjoying the banter.

"Well, I guess I should call Rahab, while I am still on top," her mother said. Then she called for Rahab to come to the front.

Rahab quickly changed sandals, brushed her hair and was ready to take Salmon's arm, and head towards Judah. The mother watched her daughter and the good looking young man walk off to see the massive Hebrew settlement. Then she went back to her chores, mumbling to herself, "On top, he said. Can you believe that? On top of the list."

The camp was actually a very large city. It just had tents instead of buildings. In contrast to Jericho there were no walls, gates or fences. The camp surrounded Gilgal's stucco buildings.

The place was huge. Almost all of the inhabitants had spent their entire lives living in these big tents with six foot sides and pitched top. Across the front of the camp were the leather tents for the general public, where the vendors traded items to people passing by. Behind this row were the warehouse tents that contained the backup supplies and the shops for the little stores out front. They also served as storage.

Salmon and Rahab turned into one of the roadways that led behind the public stores and warehouses and she saw that across from the stores was a group of tents where people lived.

Salmon explained, "The whole camp is divided into twelve communities that house each of the decedents of the twelve sons of Jacob. The arrangement of the groups was organized by Moses. When we were traveling through the desert the nation moved with the Levities carrying the Ark of the Covenant, and in the front row were the tribes of Judah, Issachar, and Zebulon. They were followed by the Tabernacle, and the tribes of Reuben, Simeon and Gad. After them was the Tabernacle furnishings carried also by the Levities, and followed by the tribes of Ephraim, Manasseh, Benjamin, Dan, Asher and Naphtali." Salmon sounded like he was teaching class.

"Whenever the journey came to a rest for weeks or months, the encampment also had specific order as directed by Moses," Salmon continued his lecture. "Each tribe had its own place in a basic square around a major Central Courtyard in which is located the Tabernacle containing the Ark. This placed God within the center of our homes."

"So that is how your people were able to set up camp so quickly when you crossed the river! We were amazed at how fast so many people could establish order," Rahab said.

"When you have two million people in the family then you had better have a plan or there will be no order. Nothing would ever get done," Salmon was talking with his hands. "And remember we have been doing this since before I was born. It has always been Judah, next to Issachar next to Zebulon, all my life. But I am prayerful of seeing that change when God gives us the land and we receive our inheritance."

Salmon was trying to give Rahab the scope of the nation and break it down into some order. "I'll show you the Central Court so you can see how everything is managed. It is the main lifeline of the nation. On each side of the Central Court are three tribes that average about 50,000 families each. Some a little more, some a little less, but you get the picture."

"I am amazed at how it's organized. I had no idea," said Rahab.

"It all came from Moses and his direct relationship with God. After we crossed the Jordan each tribe took up its normal position here at Gilgal"

Salmon was taking Rahab down a road between Judah and Issachar. Everything was so orderly. The tents, some well worn by the desert winds, were all in straight lines with little places for the children to play and for the parents to sit in the evenings and visit with their neighbors. Children were running and playing everywhere. It seemed to be a happy place.

After a long walk, they suddenly came to a big open area. It was about 1,000 feet across and 1,000 feet long, at the far end was a giant tent of goat hair with support poles of gold. Salmon explained that this was the Circle of Government and that the big colorful tent was the Tent of Meeting or Tabernacle that housed the sacred Ark of the Covenant."

"So that is where they keep the blue box?" Rahab asked.

"That is where God lives," he said in a rather strong voice, correcting her attitude toward the Ark of the Covenant. "That is where Moses received his commands from the Holy One. It is where the sacrifices are presented by the High Priest. It is where Joshua prays. It is where many of us go to pray when we have something very important to take before God." And in a softer tone, he said, "And it where many come to rededicate their lives to the Almighty."

There were soldiers standing at the four corners of the tent, guarding it. Two Levities guarded the entrance. No one went in. The ground was too holy. People came to an area in front of the tent and quietly prayed to God. There were about a dozen people quietly praying as Rahab and Salmon stood at the edge of the courtyard.

Rahab could see the tents that lined the central court were specially made tents with little signs on them. "Joshua calls it his Circle of Government. This is where he meets with his various counsels and his High Priest. This area contains the nations' treasury, its archives of history, even the bones of Joseph, who had asked to be buried in the Promised Land.

"With this arrangement, decisions can be made quickly and actions taken quickly. Here is the central command of the army, its intelligence, quarters, supply, logistics, and other services that a well equipped army needs on the move. Even though the soldiers live with their families scattered throughout the maze of tents, we have signals from the rams' horns so Joshua can gather as many people as needed for a particular objective. There are always some soldiers on duty and an army of almost any size up to half a million fighting men can be assembled in minutes. You know what's funny about living here?"

Rahab caught his arm and looked up to his face, "What's that?"

"In this mass of people everyone is in some way related to everyone else," Salmon observed. "We all share common forefathers, all the way back to Jacob and his father Isaac, and his father Abraham. We are at least some distant cousin or distant something." And then he flashed that big smile.

"Where do you live? Which is your community?" She asked.

"I'm a descendent of Judah," he said and pointed to a large area across the square, towards the front of the city. "Want to see it?"

"Sure," she said, with great anticipation.

So they turned to walk back towards the front of the encampment. Each of the twelve communities had representation on the square. This is where each community's governor lived — usually the oldest direct descendent of their son of Jacob. Roadways ran off the Central Court like spokes of a wheel to connect each community to the others and to the Circle of Government. As they walked down one of the roads next to the Judah community, Salmon again pointed out that on the other side was the community of Issachar. "Always has been."

They came to a cross street that ran the entire circle of the encampment. Salmon said that they always have a midway access path in case of emergencies. "In case of a fire, or a storm, or a need to get the army out quickly, then this midway cross street helps expedite traffic. When you have as many people as are living here, you are going to have a lot of traffic."

At the cross road they turned into Judah. There were children playing everywhere. Some of the tents were open with people coming and going, others were closed for privacy. In the open tents she could see the heavy rugs on the ground and a few pieces of furniture. They were still living in the style learned over the years from the desert.

"And where do you live?" Rahab asked her tour guide.

"Right over there," he pointed about six tents away. They walked over and a woman and her husband were sitting on individual benches at the entrance to their area. Salmon said, "Rahab, I would like you to meet my parents, Nahshon and Bethel." His father stood up.

"I am Nahshon, Salmon's father," the man said. He was a thin, wiry, little man with gray hair and shoulders that stooped under a life of hard work. There was a mysterious sparkle in his eyes. He was a happy man. "And who are you?"

"I am Rahab." She started to say, when Salmon broke in.

"This is the Woman with the Scarlet Cord that God saved from the fall of Jericho," Salmon said. "She has been living in Friends Camp. I'm showing her around."

"You do that. You do that," the old man said and sat down. Salmon's mother smiled, but said nothing, according to their custom.

"It's good to meet you," Rahab said.

"Shalom," the father said, as if excusing them.

Salmon touched Rahab's elbow and pointed her on down the broad way, then said, "Excuse, me" and ran into his parents tent, picked up a basket and quickly joined her, saying nothing else.

"They don't talk much with new people," he said, and they walked on, taking some little paths built for donkey carts. Soon they came to another clearing. There were a lot of children playing in the area. Adults were sitting on the grass, visiting. It was like a park in the middle of the community. "How nice," she exclaimed.

Then Salmon told her that each community had at least one such gathering area. This is where they come together as a community to play, worship, and hold their community meetings. Sometimes they had fairs or exchanges: where a family could offer things to trade or give away to other families of the group. Children's clothes were especially popular. Almost all the way around the gathering area were vendor tents where merchants of the group sold their wares for a living. There were tents for leather, vegetables, meat, clothing and other items. People usually traded what they had for what they wanted. There was a Defense Tent where the soldiers gathered to get information quickly if an alarm sounded. There were other tents for similar purposes but Salmon rush her by them.

They sat down on a grassy knoll, away from the other people, and he opened the basket, serving lunch. "Well, what do you think? Think you could find happiness in such surroundings?"

"It's very nice. The people all seem happy and are making do with what they have and the conditions as they are. I have liked all of your people I have met," she answered.

"You didn't answer my question. Could *you* find happiness here?"

"You mean here in Judah?"

"Yes, here in Judah."

There was a long pause, to make sure she understood his question. "Yes, I could find happiness here in Judah. I already have happiness and I have many of the blessings of your God in my life. I still miss my walls, my windows, draperies, and flat roof, but I'm adjusting. What are you asking?"

He looked straight at her and his eyes grew big and for an instant Rahab thought she saw him hesitate. He was searching for a way to say something important and he wanted to say it correctly. Salmon had always been so positive, so determined, so assured of himself, it seemed odd for him to hesitate. It was only for an instant: a blink of an eye, a twitch in his jaw. Then he immediately had composure and the decision was made. He just said it straight out.

"I'm thinking of asking your father for permission to marry you and bring you here to live with me. Would you marry a soldier?" There, he said it. But he rushed on with a long explanation. "We still have the southern campaigns and the northern campaigns which may be tough and may take several years, I understand. But I won't be gone all the time and you'll still be close to my family and your family when I'm gone."

He had done a lot of thinking about his question and had worked out all the answers. Salmon was such a methodical person. He was spilling out reasons and excuses like stars falling from the sky. Rahab placed her hand over his mouth and said, "I would be honored."

He didn't have to ask her. He only had to ask her father. "But there is something you need to know about me. I may not be the kind of person you expect me to be."

"You mean about your life in Jericho? We have already been over that," Salmon was second guessing her and doing a good job of it. "The past is behind us. How you made your living before is not important any more. We only have the present. We have only the future that God will provide us. All of the tomorrows are in God's hands."

"You mean you would accept me even knowing that I had lived for years earning my living as a prostitute?"

"I know that you had to earn a living. Keeping an inn and serving men is one way of doing it," Salmon answered her directly. "I also know that your faith saved you from those crumbling walls. Your faith in God saved you from the spears of our army. That little red cord in the window didn't save you, Rahab. God saved you. God saved you because you had been asking about Him. You wanted to know more about Him, so God provided the way, as he always does. He knows the quality of person you are."

Rahab started to say something, but Salmon raised his hand.

"Out of 10,000 people, God saved you and your family because of your faith. And He brought you to me. Those are the two most important things about your life you must remember. God loves you and I love you." With that the conversation fell silent. Salmon had made his case. He leaned over and kissed her and they got up to leave.

A mysterious ball rolled into their area and Salmon automatically picked it up and threw it high in the air in the general direction from wince it came. Two little boys ran in an effort to catch the ball as it fell back to earth. They were excited about the ball being thrown so high. "Mister, you really can throw a ball. Wow! Look at it!" Salmon just smiled his big grin and said nothing. They stood there watching the boys run and play.

After a long pause, he said, "Someday, God will clear the land of idol worshipers, and we will all build real cities of brick and stone. Real houses where children can run and play. Where neighbors can talk and visit. Real houses with walls, windows, drapes..."

"Draperies," she corrected him.

And he went back to counting off the items on his fingers. "... Draperies and flat roofs." Then Salmon looked across the play area and pulled Rahab up close to him. "Someday soon, we will be able to plant gardens, grow big trees, dig ponds to catch the rainfall. Someday soon, I just know that we will be able to claim all this land in the name of God Almighty and live in peace. The times could be so happy with you by my side."

He paused and then said, "And a household full of babies." His strong arm pulled her up close again and they made a turn in the road.

Exiting Judah

A tall, lanky fellow darted out of a side trail and almost ran into Salmon. "Oh, no. Not you two," he said as a greeting.

"Hey, watch where you are going, Daniel," Salmon was grinning again. "Rahab, do you remember Daniel, from the time we all spent the afternoon under the palm trees? This is the guy with the one line jokes."

"Of course, I remember. How are you, Daniel?"

"Don't tell me you are still hanging out with this guy?"

"Well, for today anyway," she shot back. "He served me lunch"

"Good for you. I just pray that he didn't cook it." He placed his hands on their shoulders and quietly said, "Walk with God," and disappeared across the roadway.

A few tents down the road there was a vacant spot where a tent had stood. Now it was empty, swept clean. Rahab asked, "What's that?"

Salmon squeezed her hand and then quietly uttered "That is where Achan and his family lived. He was my cousin."

Rahab was thinking hard as if she should know about Achan. Then she remembered and let out a gasp. "You mean the family that was killed? The one we threw rocks at in the valley over there?"

"Yes. This is where they lived. My cousin had a good life and loved God very much."

"I felt so sorry for him and his family. Those precious little girls."

"Unfortunately, Achan let greed and temptations cloud his eyes. He sinned and God called him into account. When Joshua called him to the Central Court, he admitted his sin, and he was stoned by his relatives and friends."

"How awful," Rahab muttered. She had both hands over her cheeks, holding her head in grief. The whole scene swept back into her mind as a great storm would sweep up the sand and rearrange everything. They kept on walking slowly. "How terrible you must have felt. Having to stone you own cousin. You poor man." She hung to his shoulders like a sad thought clings to the mind.

"It was a tough time for all of us, I agree. There is no doubt about doing God's will. If God punished Achan by having us destroy his family, then that is what must be done without hesitation or question. But when the punishment is taken against someone you know and love, when you have enjoyed their little children and knew his talents and how he loved his family ... that is the tough part. It wasn't just Achan who was punished. We were all punished. The entire community of Judah was punished. We all were reminded of how important obedience is to God."

"It just doesn't seem fair," Rahab gasped again. "His wife and children suffered for his sin, not theirs."

"We are all one in God's eyes. There is no such thing as fairness. If God has the power to raise the sun in the morning, then he has the power to determine how we shall live and for how long," Salmon stopped walking and pulled Rahab close to his side. He was almost whispering. "God is good and provides for us. God brings us the fruit on the trees, and the grain of the harvest. It was no accident, you know, that we should arrive just as the fields were ripe for harvest. And there is grass for our livestock. And fresh fish from the river. And those round fuzzy things, what do you call them?"

"Peaches," she said.

"And peaches," Salmon squeezed her again. "We are His creation — everybody is His creation, including you, — and just as God said that the creation of the earth was good, that the Heavens were good, and the animals were good, so He said His creation of mankind was good.

"God loves each of us and knows what is best for us. His taking Achan and his family reminded us how powerful God is, and that He disciplines us for our good.

"We keep the empty spot in our community to remind us that God is steadfast. He never falters. He keeps his promises. The wages of sin is death and that is why Achan and his family died. That is why 36 of our soldiers died in the campaign against Ai. But since the sinner was removed, God has shown us His mercy. God is the supreme ruler and justifier. We obey His will, without hesitation," he said.

"But I still don't understand why his family had to be killed, too," Rahab said as they picked their way over some small stones.

"That was God's decision. I don't have an answer for you," then he looked up and saw a man in his twenties coming towards them. "Here comes someone who can answer your question. Hello, my friend," Salmon called to the man approaching them.

"Hello, Salmon. Who do you have here?" The tall man asked.

"Jonathan, please meet Rahab, the Woman with the Scarlet Cord. This is one of my best friends, Jonathan, a Levite, and priest."

"I know Jonathan. He stops by Friends Camp often and has been very helpful to our family. Hello Jonathan."

"My dear, it is a pleasure to see you again, and right off I want to extend my condolences." Jonathan reached for her hand with both of his.

"Why thank you," she said, thinking he meant sympathy for the loss of her friends in Jericho.

"I am sorry you have had to spend time with this fellow here. I'm sure he has been heavy on your ears, wasting your time, and telling you how strong he is," Jonathan said with a big smile and winked at Salmon. "Please understand that you must reconsider everything carefully that Salmon says. Especially about being the fastest runner in the camp." And with that he comfortably burrowed his way between Salmon and Rahab and with his arms over each of their shoulders they continued their walk along the path. Jonathan was right at home walking between them holding them close just as though that was his spot.

"Jonathan is gloating over the fact that he beat me slightly, ever so slightly, in our race last evening," Salmon explained.

"He hasn't told you about our race?" Jonathan sounded as if Salmon had been deliberately keeping this earth shattering news from Rahab. "I am shocked at Salmon! There you go, you see my dear, already Salmon is keeping important information from you. Salmon never likes to admit defeat, especially when it is little old me that grinds him to pulp on the races."

"Jonathan has a slight problem with exaggeration, but he is rather harmless. He won by less than an inch. And it was his first time in two forevers."

The two men laughed at having a good time at the other's expense. "Rahab has a question just for you, Jonathan. Rahab this is your authority, ask any hard question you wish," Salmon had to lean forward to look around Jonathan to see her.

"I was just asking Salmon why Achan's family was killed when we all stood up there on the rim of the valley and threw our stones. The family didn't do anything."

"I am tempted to make a sarcastic remark in jest to belittle my friend here. Rather, let me say, my best friend here, but you ask a serious question." He paused and they stopped walking, but he held on to both of them with his strong arms. "You deserve a serious answer."

The priest paused a moment and then said, "God does mighty things. And He does many small things. He does them so that we may understand who He is. God is here not to punish us but to love us. But punishment is often an act of love. It teaches us authority. It teaches us presence. It teaches us that God is still with us; among us.

"To answer your question, I think there are at least two or three reasons. Only God really knows, of course. But first, I believe that God was showing all of Israel who He is. He was showing us, even in the midst of His powerful miracle, that He is in charge. God is the maker and keeper of all things. Including Achan. It seems that as people, we have very short memories. It is not enough that God sends us sunrises to demonstrate His power. Or that He sends us great love with spouses and children. Or that He can part the waters at will. We are so frail and God is so patient, that He sends us special lessons, trying over and over, so that we may each know who God is.

"Second, God was showing us the importance of the individual in His great love. God doesn't just love Israel as a nation. He loves individual people. Further, He loves all individuals, not just Israel. He loved the people of Jericho, but they were idolaters. They were putting other gods before him and God doesn't like that. It is forbidden. Therefore, the idolaters were eliminated. Many more idolaters are likely to be eliminated as God gives us more and more of Canaan. From out of Jericho, God chose you and He loves you, Rahab," Jonathan paused. There were tears in his young eyes.

"Third, God took Achan's family so that they will all be together. What we see as harsh judgment, God sees as great love. The Achan family spirit is still together. They are one family in the bosom of God Almighty and only He understands how great, how tall and how deep is that love." Jonathan's voice was very quiet and slow. "But God tries everyday to teach us that love. It is our most important lesson to learn."

There was silence and Jonathan squeezed on their shoulders and then stepped out from between the two of them and turned to face them. His eyes were glistening from tears. He touched Rahab's face with a single finger, and lovingly drew some pathway across her forehead down between her brown eyes to the bridge of her nose. He turned to his friend and tugged at his hair as a gesture of departing. Then, he took a step backward and said, "But watch out for this guy. Regardless of what he says, there really is someone who can run faster than ol' Turtleman here. Otherwise, he is occasionally a fairly good guy."

The mischievous grin appeared and disappeared and seriously he whispered, "Walk with God."

Then he smiled at both of them and abruptly sprinted past his two friends, down the trail into the maze of tents. Salmon pulled Rahab close to him one more time and they quietly walked toward the front of the encampment.

13

The Renewal

Excitement for the journey to Mount Ebal was building everyday. So when the people heard the rams' horns signaling the early morning call to assemble, they were ready. They were ready to head for the mountains.

Israel formed their standard order of march used throughout their journeys in the desert. First was the advance guard of about 10,000 soldiers armed for battle. They were grouped by the wagonfull. Then the marching soldiers guarding the open square which protected the Ark of the Covenant. The Ark with its familiar blue drape was surrounded by 1,000 feet of respectful space. Soldiers rode on each side of the long train with another 10,000 troops in the rear guard. The soldiers were constantly rotating in and out. They would march for an hour and then be relieved by members of the front and back guards. The soldiers took turns guarding and traveling with their families.

Israel marched three tribes wide with Judah, Issachar and Zebulun tribes along the front. The people of Friends Camp were at the very back. It was a festive occasion. Each family decorated their wagons with streamers and flowers. Some had little bells on their horses and donkeys.

Rahab's family could not tell from their rear position, but Joshua had sent spotters to search the land in front of the train. They were moving just a few hours ahead of the mass to check for safety, good trails and land and other matters that would keep the group of more than one million people moving to Mount Ebal.

The journey was slow and tortuous because of the steep mountains. The wagon train only stopped briefly at noon to give the animals rest and to feed the people and animals. Then it was moving on again to a mid-afternoon break. About an hour before sundown the wagon train stopped for the night.

The wagons groaned under the strain as they climbed the steep ridges to the ruins of Ai and Bethel and followed the trade route along the broad ridge to Shiloh and Shechen where they would sleep in the presence of the towering peaks of Mount Ebal and Mount Gerizim. Up high like this, the air was thinner and cooler.

The first day out Salmon had to work the front guard and did not get back to see Rahab. But that evening he made his way back to the group from Friends Camp and went searching for Rahab and her family. Guided only by the light of the camp fires, he searched from one fire to another until he saw a familiar shape. It was the plump shadow of Rahab's mother. He was so glad to see her that he raced over and grabbed her up with a hug.

"Oh my, you caused me to lose my breath," said the grandmother.

"Hello, I am out of breath too!" Said Salmon. "Can you tell me where my girlfriend is?"

"I thought I was your girlfriend."

"Oh ... oh, you are. Definitely. My – girl friend. Yes, ma'am'. You ... certainly are." Salmon was trying desperately to get his bearings. Mother was sharper than he supposed. "Well, you see, honestly, well, what I am trying to say..."

"Y-e-s..."The female voice came from in front of him.

"Well, to be honest, I have two girlfriends. I have you and one other...you know the rope maker."

"Oh, you need a rope? What do you need a rope for young man?" Mother was blocking the way into their campsite.

"Well," he was trying to think fast. "Well, I may need one to hang myself with if I don't get to see Rahab soon."

"Then, I've got one question for you. Am I still on top of your list as best hugger."

"Yes, ma'am', you will always be on top."

"Then I'll call her. Rahab. Rahab, come here. There's some scary fellow out here mumbling your name." And Mother reached over and squeezed the boy with her top of the list hug and swatted him on the back side. Then she whispered, "Now, have a good time."

The young couple strolled to the edge of the campsite, just out of the flickering campfire and behind one of the wagons. Rahab's parents could hear them talking softly but couldn't understand their words. Now and then they recognized giggles that reminded them of their courting days.

"He's a good boy," said Mother.

"I think he is, too," said her father. "I wonder what is taking him so long to ask for our blessing?"

"It will come soon enough. Never you mind. Here, hold my hand like you use to 30 years ago."

"What will the children say?" he whispered back.

"Maybe they will think that we are still in love," she said. And the two held hands and snuggled up close to each other. The flames of the campfire cast moving shadows on the wagons, the bushes, and the people. The moon came out. Salmon had to leave for his shift of guard duty. He told Rahab that tomorrow would be different because he got to guard the rear section of the movement.

Second Day Out

Little wisps of clouds passed in front of the moon and over the stars until it was time for the sun to make its announcement of a new day. From the high ridge of the mountains, the sun seemed earlier and shown clearer than when they were down on the Jericho plains.

The call to rise and eat breakfast came quickly. They must all move out soon in order to be to Mount Ebal by sundown.

The massive caravan of people, wagons, and animals moved off the high ridge and followed the trade route slowly descending to the valley floor by noon and then to the little nondescript town of Shiloh. It presented no danger because it was part of the surrender pack with the Gibeonites. However, the Hebrews did not stop there but moved on past it as the local Hitites watched.

The people of Israel saw that the mountains were getting taller and rougher. They were happy to be on the valley floor. They were happy to be so close to the farm land and see the good grass for their herds and flocks. For the first time they were experiencing something of the promise God had made to the people. What a contrast this was to the desert where they had all grown up.

Throughout the day, Salmon would listen for the wagon with the clicking wheel and stop in to say hello. Sometimes that was about all he could do while he was on duty, guarding the rear of the caravan. Then when he was off duty he spent as much time as he could with Rahab and her family.

The broad vistas of the grassland gave way to the entrance of a beautiful valley between two large mountains. At the gateway to the valley was Shechem, a small fortified town of Hitites, who were also included in the surrender treaty with the Gibeonites. The citizens had been notified by the advance spotters of the coming mass of people. The spotters steered the mass around the little town and directed the wagons to form a giant half circle around the bases of the two mountains. Israel had reached its destination point. They would rest here for the night and tomorrow morning they would renew their covenant with the Holy One as directed by Moses.

As the wagons took their places, the soldiers guarding the Ark of the Covenant, escorted the Ark through the valley between the mountains to the far end of the valley, opposite of where the Israelites would be sleeping. The guard remained there protecting the Ark throughout the night.

Day of Renewal

At sunrise the rams' horns signaled the call to awaken and eat breakfast; the big day had begun. It was a bright and beautiful morning. From their spot in the encampment, Rahab and her family could see about a dozen men climbing to the top of Mount Ebal and looking for natural stones. As they found a certain kind of stone, they stacked them on top of each other to make an altar to the Lord God. No iron tool was used on them.

When they had finished, Eleazar climbed the mountain in his special colorful robes decorated in precious stones, designating him as High Priest. With him were two other priests. One of whom was carrying a lamb without defect. The other carried wood for a fire. A man already nar the top had a lighted torch.

Eleazar was a man about Joshua's age. He, too, had long, flowing, white hair. He was the son of Aaron, who was Israel's first High Priest and a brother of Moses. Eleazar was comfortable with performing the offering and sacrifices in front of the Tent of Meeting as commanded by the Lord, but this was a special occasion. He had trouble steadying himself with the incline of the rugged mountain path. From the top of the high mountain, he could see all the people gathering on the two facing hillsides. He turned and faced the crowds, and held his hands together in front of him.

The crowd began singing, "Holy, Holy, Holy is our Lord, the God Almighty. Holy, Holy, Holy is the one true God. Holy, Holy, Holy is the Maker of the World, Our God, our one and only true God. Holy, Holy, Holy is He."

The valley was filled with the richness of echoes resonating from the million voices singing praises. Even the Gibonite servants in Shechem were standing in awe of the sacred moment of worship.

Then in the quietness, the old man in the beautiful robes, raised his hands above his head and cried, "Blessed be the Lord Almighty. Blessed be the Lord God of Israel. Bless us, O Lord, as we bring this gift to you."

Quickly and efficiently a priest placed the wood on the altar and started a fire. While the fire was gaining intensity, the priest with the live lamb, placed his hand on the lamb's head and with a sharp knife drew it down the lamb's chest and loins. The lamb tried to resist the grip on him and cried out as he gave his life to God. The priest slaughtered it in full view of the massive audience. No voices were heard. Even the breeze had stopped. Every eye was on the sacrifice. Then the priest reached into the warm cavity of the lamb's body and scooped out a handful of blood. Ever so carefully he sprinkled the blood onto all four sides of the new altar. Then the priest placed his bloody hands back into the lamb's body and tore out all the fat he could find. The fat around the kidneys, the loins, the covering of the liver and even the tail were ripped out. He threw the fat into the roaring fire as an offering to the Lord.

By sacrificing this perfect lamb and burning its fat on the altar, the people present were offering an atonement for unintentional sin in general. It was an expression of devotion, a commitment and a complete surrender to God.

A third priest came up the mountain with a young male goat. This animal also, was without defect. He, too, was sacrificed on the same altar for thanksgiving and as a fellowship offering. Everyone on the two mountain sides could smell the burning fat.

Eleazar came back in front of the altar and prayed again for the God Almighty to bless the people assembled and reminded God and everyone there, that they all rested in the faith that the Lord would protect them and give them victory in possessing the promised land. Then, the lamb and the goat were cooked on the fire and a group of Levite priests came to the top of the mountain and ate the sacrificed animals representing all the people so gathered.

The crowd sang another song in praise of the Almighty One. Several men in Levite robes carried large, heavy stones up to the side of the altar. They had been painted white with plaster and the people could see there was writing on the stones. Eleazar took Joshua's hand and helped him stand straight and safely in the place beside the stones. Joshua held a long thin stick, a pointer, and he pointed to the words as he began to read out loud to everyone.

The thin man did his best to stand straight; the wind caught up his silver hair lifting it from his shoulders and then laid it back down again. His colorless, undecorated robe was a sharp contrast to that of Eleazar, but everyone knew it was Joshua. In the style of Moses, Joshua raised his ancient hand for everyone to be quiet, but all were already quiet.

"Hear the word of the Lord, O Israel." Joshua began his speech. "On these tablets are written the law that God gave to Moses on Mount Sinai." Joshua paused and took a deep breath. "Write them on your hearts. Write them on your children's hearts. Remember them forever more. And when you feel faint, come back to Mount Ebal and read them again out loud for everyone present to hear them; even as I read them to you now."

Joshua looked across the crowd and then to the sky. He could see the clouds circling as they did 43 years ago on Mount Sinai. He remembered climbing part of the way up the mountain with Moses. He remembered how Moses went on up a little ways and met with God.

"These are the words of the Most Holy One:'I am the Lord your God, who brought you out of Egypt, out of the land of slavery."

These were the grandchildren of those slaves. What do they know about the God Almighty, Joshua thought.

"You shall have no other gods before me." His words were deep and penetrating. Of all the Laws given to Moses this must be the most important one. This one Law had given more trouble to Israel than any other. How can he make it live in their souls as it did his?

The sky turned dark with new born clouds. The wind silently puffed in gusts, catching up loose leaves and sandy dirt, whipping it in circles across all the people. There was an invisible force moving among the people. They could not see it, but they could feel it. They knew in their hearts that it was there.

Then a blast of cold air brought chills to the desert people. It was almost bone chilling. The people huddled together. A blinding bolt of lightening stabbed the earth from dark clouds. A roll of sudden thunder shook the mountains. Every single soul could feel the awesome power in the air.

How do you read the words of God so the people will remember them? You read them again. Joshua raised his hand and pointed his finger to the masses as if they were an orchestra and he was conducting. He repeated himself. "The Lord God of Israel said, 'I am the Lord your God, who brought you out of Egypt, out of the land of slavery.'"

And a bolt of lightening cracked open the cloud and shot to the earth. With it came the sharp report of the power of thunder that only God can send. The very power that had raised the mountains they were sitting on was the power that stirred among them. They were totally at its mercy.

"You shall have no other gods before me," Joshua was trying to out shout the thunder. However, he did not need to shout, because the wind carried every word directly into their hearts. "You shall not make for yourself an idol in the form of anything in heaven above or on the earth beneath or in the waters below. You shall not bow down to them or worship them for I, the Lord your God, am a jealous God." Joshua was pointing to each word.

Everyone felt the power of God in the whirling clouds. The wind that was blowing so hard now that Joshua could hardly stand. His robe was being whipped one way and then another. His hair was like a sail above him. Joshua had seen the majestic beauty of God's power before. He was not threatened by it, but he had great respect for it. There was so much energy charging the air between the two mountains and all the people, that it could take Joshua or anyone else, or everyone else, and snatch them up in the next puff of wind.

The people were filled with awe. They were still as if frozen. All the women had their heads covered with their shawls. The men had their hoods pulled up. Most of them were bowing in prayer. They all felt the Presence. They were on holy ground. They took off their shoes and stood in silence.

"You shall not misuse the name of the Lord your God, for the Lord will hold no one guiltless who misuses his name." The lightening raced in a jagged line seeking a place to strike. Its crackling sound was electrifying.

"Remember the Sabbath day by keeping it holy," Joshua was shouting, but the wind was carrying every syllable to the people. "Six days you shall labor and do all your work, but the seventh day is a Sabbath to the Lord your God. On it you shall do no work."

The wind seemed to calm down and a split came in the clouds overhead. The light began to shine through in long streams. "Honor your father and your mother, so that you may live long in the land the Lord your God is giving you."

And the people broke into applause, shouting, "Amen! Amen!" It was the first audible response of the masses. Joshua lifted his old crooked finger and stabbed it towards the millions in front of him. "You shall not murder." Joshua read it as the breeze came to a halt in mid air. "You shall not commit adultery. You shall not steal. You shall not give false testimony against your neighbor." The old man was breathless from shouting. He paused again and took a deep breath and pointed to the line of letters across the bottom of one of the stones. "You shall not covet your neighbor's house. You shall not covet your neighbor's wife, or his manservant or maidservant, his ox or donkey, or anything that belongs to him."

And the people roared with shouts of "Amen! Amen!" And thunderous applause vibrated in the land. As they cheered the reading of the Law, the dark clouds parted and light began to shine through again in the late morning. The light seemed to warm the air. A sudden isolated boom of thunder melted every heart there. God was still very present. The people began to praise God by singing, "We praise you, O Great Jehovah. We know your powers. We know your tests. We know your love. We praise you for the protection you give us. We praise you for saving us from the evil one. We praise you and love you, O Lord, our God."

The mountains grew quiet. The pillars of smoke from the altar were gone. The cold breeze had blown away any of the odor of the burnt offerings. Joshua's old crackled voice was still ringing in their ears. Everyone came down from the top of Mount Ebal except Joshua and Eleazar. They took their place on a bench that had been placed for them near the altar.

The service switched to the other mountain. Slowly, very reverently, thousands of Levite priests climbed up both sides of the crowds seated on Mount Gerizim. There were 22,000 priests, all dressed in their brown robes with ceremonial ropes at the waist. They concentrated on climbing the mountain, row after row of them. Their heads were bowed. They were humming and then softly singing, as if to themselves. "Bless us O Lord, for we are your children. Bless us O Lord, for you know the way we should go. Bless us, O Lord, for we are your children. We are your children, O Lord, God Almighty."

They turned to face the massive crowd and said to all Israel, "Be silent, O Israel, and listen. You have become the people of the Lord your God. Obey the Lord your God and follow his commands and decrees." Then small groups of the priests began to call out curses to the people and the people responded.

"Cursed is the man who carves an image or casts an idol – a thing detestable to the Lord, the work of the craftsman's hands – and sets it up in secret."

"Amen!" shouted the people.

"Cursed is the man who dishonors his father or his mother."

And all the people said "Amen!"

Cursed is the man who moves his neighbor's boundary stone."

"Amen!" The throng called in agreement.

"Cursed is the man who leads the blind astray on the road."

"Amen!"

"Cursed is the man who withholds justice from the alien, the fatherless or the widow."

"Yes! Yes! Amen!"

"Cursed is the man who sleeps with his father's wife, for he dishonors his father's bed."

And all the people said "Amen!"

"Cursed is the man who has sexual relations with any animal."

"Amen!"

"Cursed is the man who sleeps with his sister, the daughter of his father, or the daughter of his mother."

And all the people said "Amen!"

"Cursed is the man who sleeps with his mother-in-law."

And all the people said "Amen!"

"Cursed is the man who kills his neighbor secretly.

The people cried "Amen!"

"Cursed is the man who accepts a bribe to kill an innocent person."

And all the people said "Amen!"

"Cursed is the man who does not obey the words of this law."

"Amen! Amen!" They shouted. Then one million people began applauding and stomping their feet in response to the reading of the curses.

The scene then changed back to the other mountain. Eleazar, the High Priest, rose from his bench on Mt. Ebal. He lifted his deep voice and cried out, "If you fully obey the Lord your God, and carefully follow all His commands I give you today, the Lord your God will set you high above all the nations on earth. All these blessings will come upon you, and accompany you if you obey the Lord your God."

Eleazar paused for a moment to catch his breath. He looked

across the throng and then continued, "You will be blessed in the city and blessed in the country. "The fruit of your womb will be blessed, and the crops of your land and the young of your livestock –the calves of your herds and the lambs of your flocks. Your basket and your kneading trough will be blessed. You'll be blessed when you come in and when you go out. The Lord will grant that the enemies, who rise up against you, will be defeated before you. They will come at you from one direction but flee from you in seven. The Lord will send a blessing on your barns and on everything you put your hand to. The Lord your God will bless you in the land he is giving you."

The throng erupted in joyous applause at this blessing. Eleazar waited for a moment of silence and then continued. "The Lord will establish you as His holy people as He promised you on oath, if you keep the commands of the Lord your God and walk in His ways." Eleazar glanced at the clearing sky, and with a sweeping motion of his long arm said, "Then all the peoples on earth will see that you are called by the name of the Lord and they will respect you. The Lord will grant you great prosperity – in the fruit of your womb, the young of your livestock and the crops of your ground."

Thunderous applause interrupted the gray haired man again. Eleazar quickly put up both hands to quiet them and continued. "The Lord will open the heavens, the storehouse of His bounty, to send rain on your land in season and to bless all the work of your hands. You will lend to many nations, but will borrow from none. The Lord will make you the head, not the tail, if you pay attention to the commands of the Lord your God that I give you this day and carefully follow them, you will always be at the top, never at the bottom. Don't turn aside from any of the commands I give you today, to the right or to the left, following other gods and serving them."

Thunderous applause interrupted Eleazar's blessings. Everyone was happy to hear and to accept the blessings. These were happy days. These were the days where dreams come true. However, the High Priest was not finished. He raised both hands so that the long full sleeves formed a diagonal line from his wrists back to his waist. The sharp sun was shining through them. He began speaking again.

"However, ... however, if you do not obey the Lord your God and do not carefully follow all of His commands and decrees I am giving you today, all these curses will come upon you and overtake you: You will be cursed in the city and cursed in the country. Your basket and your kneading trough will be cursed. The fruit of your womb will be cursed and the crops of your land, and the calves of your herds and the lambs of your flocks. You will be cursed when you come in and cursed when you go out. The Lord will send on you curses, confusion and rebuke in everything you put your hand to, until you are destroyed and come to sudden ruin because of the evil you have done in forsaking him. The Lord will plague you with diseases until He has destroyed you from the land you are entering to possess. The Lord will strike you with disease, fever and inflammation, with scorching heat and drought, with blight and mildew, which will plague you until you perish."

His last sentence was punctuated with forceful jabbing of his long finger. The curse was delivered one emphasized word after another. The throng was quiet for a moment. They were still in the holy moment. Sowly applause began in a far corner of the crowd and quickly spread throughout the mass gathering. They all began chanting, "Our God is Holy. There is but one God. Our God is Holy."

Joshua leaned on his walking staff and pushed on one knee to raise himself up and slowly made his way to the side of his good friend Eleazar. They spread out their arms to say the concluding prayer. One began the prayer and the other would join in. It was difficult to tell who was praying. But the people heard: "Holy Father in Heaven, Creator of everything, Maker of the mountains here, of the seas, of the trees, Maker of sky and water and wind: We feel your presence in our souls. We praise you as the eternal God and we praise you as your children. Today, we renew our vows to you as we hear your sacred word. Weld it to our hearts, Lord, inscribe it on our brains, instill it in our children, so we may never forget, we may never go to the left or to the right. Bless us, O Lord, with your kindness and your mercy. Help us to follow your paths. Help us, O Lord, to always remember that you are the potter and we are the clay. Mold us into your grateful likeness, keep us pure, keep us holy as you are Holy. May we always remember your presence here in the mountains and within our hearts. We love you, O Lord."

And all the people shouted, "Amen! Amen!" The service was over.

The day's sun had dropped behind Mount Gerizim and the people realized that the worship service had taken the day. Everyone was suddenly hungry and ready to break for their individual campsites.

Rahab and her family had been sitting at the base of Mount

Gerizim. They were able to make their way back through the immediate campsites to their own in relatively short time. They had not seen Salmon all day. Rahab was so inspired that she thought that the service had been planned just for her.

"Oh, I know that it wasn't," Rahab told her family. "But this is just what I needed. I felt so close to God. I felt His very Presence."

Olmad said that he felt the presence of God, too. Now he knew he wanted to know all about their Law and how the Hebrews lived by it.

At their own campsite, the women hurried to start supper and feed the family. Dad was wondering how Joseph was doing in guarding their campsite in Gilgal, but the subject was changed to what was happening with them and of the journey back home. They would see Joseph in a couple of days, but where was Salmon?

As the family was rolling out their bedrolls under the stars, Dad asked, "Where was the boyfriend today?"

Rahab blushed a little at her father calling Salmon her boyfriend. It was the first time he had done that. Olmad picked up the pace quickly and murmured, "He was probably working. I noticed that they were changing out the soldiers pretty often around the Ark at the end of the valley. They also had guards posted all around the encampment here. No enemy could surprise this group. I don't guess there was any trouble. I just suspect that they had everyone available to work at least part of the day."

"And in this large group it would be hard to find just one family if you didn't go to that spot with them," Rahab defended Olmad's theory.

Darkness swept into the land, the moon began to glow. Its soft light encouraged everyone to pull up the covers and close their eyes. Tomorrow would be a full day of traveling again. The little boys snuggled between their parents. The sisters fussed about not having enough room. Ari El stoked the fire one more time and then pulled up his cover. Mother's bare foot slipped over and touched her husband's toes and he gave them a secret, little love wiggle and they, too, drifted off to sleep.

The Fourth Day

All too soon the rams' horns sounded the rise and shine call and sleepy faces all around the mountains began to recognize the new day. Breakfast was quick and simple. Packing was hurried; everyone doing his part. Soon Ari El was in the driver's seat, snapping the reins and joined half a million other wagons heading towards home.

The spotters took the wagon train passed Shiloh to the very base of the tall mountain ridge they needed to climb before sundown. It was at the base of the incline that they called for a lunch break. The break was welcomed by everyone, especially the animals. All the harnesses were removed and the horses and mules were well fed by the Shiloh slaves. It was a longer than usual break, but the spotters wanted the animals to be in their best shape for the steep road ahead.

While everyone was resting and recalling their feelings of the day before, who should wander up to Rahab's side, but the tall fellow who had been missing. "Rahab, I just got to see you," said Salmon.

"Oh, hello. We can step over here behind the wagon," she said.

"I've been missing you terribly. I couldn't find you yesterday in all the mass of people."

"I know. We guessed you were working, too," she said.

"There were so many people and there was no real order to anything. I just couldn't find you. And I wanted to be with you so very much," Then Salmon took her in his arms and hugged her up close and then kissed her for a long time. A very long time. "Is your father here? I have something to ask him that is very important."

"Yes, he is here. Let's go find him." Rahab had a misty twinkle in her eye. A twinkle anticipating the question that Salmon was going to ask. "There they are," she said pointing to her father and mother. "Father, Salmon would like to speak with you."

"Hello, Salmon. We missed you yesterday," her father said.

"Thank you. I just couldn't find your family. There were so many people and everyone was out of place. Could we walk a little ways? Would you mind? Just down here a little ways?" Salmon was nervous.

"Sure," the father said. And they started off away from the people, but the father looked back over his shoulder and winked at the family. They had not gone 20 feet, when suddenly Salmon turned to Rahab's father and picked him up in a bear hug and was dancing around and around in joy.

"I guessed he asked the question," Mother said.

"I guessed he got the answer he was seeking," said Olmad, grinning.

Rahab was speechless and had tears of joy in her eyes.

Salmon left the father and ran back to pick up Olmad, who

was much larger than their father, and in a mighty hug danced around in circles. He was shouting, "We are going to get married! We are getting married!"

Salmon picked up little Ari El and tossed him in the air and shouted, "We are going to be married!" He picked up both of Olmad's little boys, one under each arm, and twirled around, almost taking their breath away. "We are going to be married!"

He ran from one girl and woman to the next and kissed them all. When he got to Mother, he kissed her and then said very softly, "But you are still on top of my list." And Mother kissed him back.

Then he went to Rahab, the one with the glowing face, and presented her to her family, and said so loudly that all the people west of the Jordan could hear, "And this is the bride to be. The bride for me." And he held her around the waist, and then the cheeks and then he kissed her for the first time in front of the family. "As soon as we have time to plan a wedding, then we shall be married. And I want everybody to come."

And so all the family was happy. All of the neighbors close to the wagon were happy. The whole day was happy. The news circulated faster than a rumor. *There's going to be a wedding!*

No one remembers the steep climb up the mountain ridges to the travel routes or when supper came or sleeping that night or how they made it through the next day along the ridges and down the other side past Bethel and Ai and on to Gilgal. *There's going to be a wedding!*

14

Someone Is Missing

"Where in the world have you been?" The bridegroom was standing in front of Friend's Camp waiting for the wagon with the clicking wheel.

"Looking for you to help unload this old wagon," Rahab's father called back. "That's the advantage of you Judah folk; you get home first and the rest of us have to wait in line."

"Ah, but you are here now. Just look what Joseph has for you," said Salmon. Joseph was standing beside Salmon waiting to be spoken to, so he could speak.

"And, Joseph, how did things go for you?" His owner asked.

"Just fine, Master. Everything is just fine. I have some peasant stew for you after your long journey."

"It smells delicious. Help us down, will you?"

Joseph extended his hand and reached for his master and helped him down from the wagon. And then Joseph helped the rest of the family. Afterwards he and Ari El began unloading the luggage, bedrolls, and other items.

"What smells so good, Joseph?" Rahab was asking.

"Its peasant stew. I hope you like it."

"I am sure we will and I am starving. Did you make enough for Olmad's boys and me too?" The little boys were each leaning against Rahab, hiding behind the folds in her robe as they hugged her legs.

"I think we have enough for the boys, too," Joseph was pointing his finger at the closest boy, aiming it at his tummy. The boy giggled like a little girl and then squealed. They were all happy to be home.

So the servants unloaded the wagon and un-harnessed the horse and stowed away the wagon. While they were doing this, the family was rearranging their things in their tents. Then they all came back to the family circle to savor Joseph's dinner.

For the first time Salmon was invited to eat with them. He was smiling. Everyone could tell he still had marriage on his mind. The sun had not yet set and they could all see the love-sick expressions on his face. He was beaming almost as much as Rahab was.

Her father then said, "Mother, I think you had better get your tonic out for both of these kids. They look love sick to me." He had that mischievous glint in his eyes.

"Now, Dad, you stay out of that. Wedding planning is women's work. We don't want no man stepping in where he don't belong. Isn't that right, Rahab?"

"Mother, you said it. Now let's see if you can enforce it."

"I think I am getting into a tough family," Salmon was sitting there looking from face to face, not sure how to react.

Then Ari El said, "And I bet you haven't seen her fight either. She is some fighter."

"Thanks for the warning, Ari El. I'll be sure to keep that in mind."

A gentle chuckle rippled through the family circle as everyone was getting to know Salmon better. But a sudden blast of the ram's horns broke the fun. It was an emergency call that the family had not heard before.

Salmon looked up when the signal was repeated. "Sorry folks, I must go. That's the emergency call for the entire army. Something very important is happening." He automatically reached over and hugged Rahab and kissed her again in front of the family and said, "I'm going to miss you. I'll see you later." And he started running back into the Judah camp before Rahab had an opportunity to reply.

The family in the circle had never heard the signal before. They could not imagine what kind of an emergency it could be since they had just arrived from Mt. Ebal. They sat there guessing. Olmad went to check with the neighbors to see if they had an idea of what was going on. No one knew.

Just as the sun was about to disappear behind the western mountain range, Jonathan came walking up with a serious look on his face. Olmad ran out to the pathway to greet him and invited him to the circle. "What's going on, Jonathan?"

"I don't have very much information, but messengers have arrived from Gibeon and they're saying that some armies are coming up to fight them. They reminded Joshua of the treaty that we are to protect them. So Joshua is making his plans now and will likely send some soldiers there to protect the city. I'll have some more information in the morning and I'll come tell you. In the meantime how are you doing?"

"Will Salmon have to go?" Rahab was asking; her hands shaking.

"I'm not sure who will have to go. The signal was for everyone to report, but that doesn't necessarily mean that Joshua will use everyone. I hope not," said Jonathan. "I just dropped by to see how you made it through the Renewal of the Covenant?"

"It was an awesome experience," said Rahab. "It was so good to see the High Priest and witness the sacrifices and offerings. We had never seen anything like that before. It's different than the sacrifices in Jericho."

Olmad was standing next to Jonathan and said, "I appreciated seeing the sacrifices and to hear the High Priest. Those were beautiful robes."

"Yes, those were fashioned by God. God gave the instructions to Moses. He had the people do the embroidery and jewel smiths to fashion the precious stones. Only the High Priest can wear the garments. They were made for Aaron, Eleazar's father. Then when Aaron passed from this life, Eleazar inherited the position and has served as High Priest ever since."

"The storm that came up while Joshua was reading the Laws was frightening," said Mother. "There was so much power in it."

"You're right. The words of God are powerful words. They carry the strength of the Almighty. To disobey any one of the laws is a cause for death. If you accidentally break one of the laws then you are able to have an animal sacrificed in your stead. Always remember, this is serious business.

"Let me mention one thing. As you saw the power of God at work when His Law was being read, you also saw God's strength, and in it His great love for people. The same strength that God used to raise those tall mountains is also the strength God uses to bring about His will in people's lives. When you ask for a blessing of the Almighty, you now know that He has the power and strength to provide it in His time, if it's right for you. God loves every one of you. He can save you from the evil one and He can raise you up from all your troubles. Whenever problems befall you, you can call on God and you can feel His power and His strength at work in your behalf. God is stronger than any other force on earth. No man can break God's Law and win. God is the Creator. He is always stronger than anyone He has created ... and He has created us all." Jonathan's words beamed into their hearts. They were words that would take on new meaning; words that were prophecy.

"God is love," he continued gently. "When you express your love to another person you are performing a godly act. Always remember that. Loving people, forgiving them, helping them, understanding them, — all are godly acts. They are Holy acts. You love God by loving people."

Jonathan reached out his arms toward the little boys and they ran over and grabbed his long legs and giggled. Jonathan ruffed up their hair and in great compassion for them, mumbled something about them having grown over the last week. Then the tall man placed his big hand on Rahab's shoulder and looked into her eyes. "Whenever you feel weak, remember there is strength in prayer."

The world was quiet as Jonathan turned to leave. He was adjusting the priestly rope than bound his hooded, brown robe. The moon was rising to give its first glow of the evening. Friends Camp was silent in thought.

Messengers of War

Meanwhile at the Circle of Government, Joshua had received the messengers from Gibeon. They had come directly over the mountain on their fastest steeds and were escorted directly to the commander in chief. They explained that armies from Jerusalem, Hebron, Jarmuth, Lachis, Debir, and Eglon had joined forces and were marching on Gibeon. They needed immediate help from the Hebrews. That is when Joshua stepped to the entrance of his command tent and called to the army tent just a few feet away.

"Yes sir," was the reply.

"Step over here a moment, will you?" Joshua was starting to give orders. Then he turned back to the Gibonites. "How do I know you are telling the truth? Your people are not known around here for truth."

"We're your people. We're your servants. We are not your enemy. If our people are killed and the city is overrun, then it is your loss. You will know by this time tomorrow, whether we lie or tell the truth. But by then it will be too late. You will have lost 15,000 slaves or more. Will you come and honor your treaty?" The messenger asked.

A group of soldiers were at the doorway to Joshua's tent. The commander turned to them and said. "It seems that Gibeon will be under attack soon. We've got to go stop it. Sound the general alarm to gather all the army in their local tribal areas. Get their representatives over here for some instructions. Get me a dozen spotters out here now to leave immediately. I want some captains and commanders in here to start planning the campaign. We'll finish it in the wagon on the way. I want to see some people standing here when I get back from asking the Almighty to bless our efforts. Is that understood?" With each order, Joshua was pointing to a different soldier.

That is when the general alarm was spread throughout the big encampment by the rams horns signal. Men were beginning to come to the command center as Joshua walked over to the front of the Tent of Meeting and fell to his knees and then with his forehead on the ground he prayed: "Almighty Creator of the earth and all that is in it. You have been so good to Israel. You have blessed us when we did not deserve it. And, thankfully, you have blessed us when we were trying to do all your will. I ask you now for your guidance. Are these men from Gibeon telling the truth or not? Will Gibeon be under attack by the multi-city force or is this another deception? Lord, I need to know whether to go to Gibeon with your army or shall we sit it out? I pray for your guidance at this time. I am thankful for all your blessings. Please bless me now with this measure of wisdom. Please bless me, your servant."

The wispy, old man pushed himself up by the hands until he could sit up on his knees and then pushed on his walking staff until he was able to stand up and look around. There at his side were the leaders of the 12 tribes of Israel, the 12 commanders of the individual armies ready to call their men into action. And there were 12 spotters, armed and ready to go. As he looked around in the gathering lamp light of the evening, he felt the Lord say to him, "Don't be afraid of the attackers; I have given them into your hand. Not one of them will be able to withstand you."

That was all Joshua needed. He sounded like a young man again. He stood straight and started pointing and barking orders. "All right men, here is what we're going to do. The Lord is with us. I want these messengers from Gibeon arrested and held in camp."

Instantly, some soldiers from the army tent stepped forward and took the Gibeonites by the arms, then disappeared in the group of tents.

"I want you spotters to go make a safe path for the whole army to cross directly over the mountains to Gibeon. You are to leave now. Mark your trail well. Some of the army will be following closely behind you. We will be marching within the hour. The army is to be followed by the mess wagons and the supply wagons. So the armies don't need to wait to pack their things or make arrangements for food. They will be following you. The same thing for the spotters. Leave now and take turns waiting for us to catch up with you with supplies and something to eat. I want a safe path, as straight as you can make it. Time's important. I want to attack before sunrise. Is that clear?"

The spotters nodded and ran for their horses. They left with only the clothes on their back and bundles of cloth strips to mark the way.

Then Joshua turned to the tribal commanders. He wrinkled his forehead. "Men, this is sad to say, but I don't know when we will be back. I don't know how long this is going to take. It is the greatest battle we have faced but the Lord has given us His blessing and the enemy has been turned over to us. All we must do is obey the Lord and go get the enemy. There are at least five kings and their armies on the way to Gibeon and I want to be there before they are and have a little surprise party waiting for them. So, go get your men organized and ready to move out within the hour. As soon as you are ready meet in front of the trading tents. The first ones there will be the leaders. As the others arrive they will take their turn in the order of march. Speed is of the essence."

So the lieutenants hurried back to gather their men.

"Now the rest of you get some wagons for those soldiers. Get some more wagons for the mess tents. Get me some more wagons for tents, clothing, and other supplies. Each tribe should have three or four wagon loads of Gibeonites to help in the make-ready. Any questions?"

There were no questions. The remainder of the command channel vanished into the maze of tents using the emergency middle pathway to get back to their people on horseback.

The bony man in the colorless robe reached for a towel to wipe his face. And his young aide offered him a mug of water. "Thanks," he said. "I needed that." And he drank it in one big gulp.

Joshua looked up from his place in front of the command tent and saw Eleazar standing near the front of the Tent of Meeting. The two friends started walking towards each other. They reached out their tired arms and hugged each other. "Eleazar, this is a sad time. We are off to war, before we get to rest from the long trip from Mount Ebal. I expect to go up there and get things started and then be back in a few days. I'll let the youngsters clean things up." Joshua was looking tired. His eyebrows were drooping and the flesh on his cheeks was sunken in. He was stooped over with a tired back.

"The Lord will protect you, Joshua. May He give you strength to fight His battles and bring you safely back here. The Lord is with you. Just follow the way He leads you." And Eleazar placed his hand on Joshua's shoulder and blessed him. He was so gentle, so kind, that the glory of God shown through him and comforted the tired commander-in-chief. The little command wagon pulled up beside them and the two friends climbed in and the driver took them to the front of the trading tents. Some men were already gathering there.

When Olmad noticed a lot of activity in front of the trading tents he called back to his family, "Look, there are some soldiers in front of the tents up there. Let's go see if it is Salmon's group? Maybe we can learn something."

The family dropped what they were doing and each one joined Olmad in the short walk up to the trading tents. The guards standing there held them back and would not let them get very close. They kept looking for Salmon to see if he was going to leave them, but they could not find him in the torch lights. There were too many shadow faces in the Judah group.

Within the hour after the first signal, Judah was assembled in the war wagons and pulled out for Gibeon. Other groups were following, taking their places where Judah had assembled and heading out behind them. The good-byes had been said. The hugs and kisses were over. Wives clinging to their husbands' tunics trying to keep them from having to go — it was all over.

Except for Rahab. She did not get to say good-bye. Only, Salmon's voice was ringing in her soul, "I'll see you later." He didn't know then why the horns were signaling. Rahab was crying softly. To her, the rams' horns were signaling that their wedding was off. No getting married now. How can you love a vision? Just when they were getting to really know each other someone calls a war, and Salmon must go. He must leave her — without getting married. It was a sad moment. Very sad.

The moon rose full and beautiful. The soft glow lighted the way for 40,000 soldiers in a long line, 50 wagons wide and miles in length. As they were leaving, their support wagons with clothing, shelter and food were being prepared. Soon they joined the long lines of the march. As the main army was leaving, a second army was called on alert. If they needed them, there were more than half a million men of fighting age ready to take their places. Creaking wheels and snorts of sleepy horses could be heard all night long.

A Night for Shadows

Before the first watch started, all was quiet around the encampment. Rahab, Olmad and his wife, their parents, children, siblings, and servants were back at the camp. It was time to turn loose of the day and let God be in charge of the army's safety.

It had been a long day. They were ready for some rest. Everyone headed for their tent to sleep from the long, tiring journey. There was almost a collective sigh as the family gave up the day and slipped into the night's sleep. But not everyone was sleeping.

Into the still of the night, two shadows stole into Friends Camp and tip toed to Rahab's tent. They were carrying a small cloth that was dripping with a strange smelling fluid. They eased open the back end of her tent to match the opening in the front. It let in more moonlight. They stood perfectly still watching her breathe. She was lying on top of the cover. Her right hand was up under her head. Her thin gown was kicked up above her knees. They could watch the muscles in her legs twitch with tiredness from the day's journey. Slowly, ever so quietly, they lay a strong strip of cloth on her sleeping mat so that when she straightened her legs, they would go over the binding strap. Two other matching straps were placed above her waist, as one would place a fishing line, to catch her hands. One lay on each side, so regardless of which way she turned, her arms would likely be on top of a binding strap. Quietly, they patiently waited, watching her sleep. They admired how pretty she was. They stared at strong cheek bones. They saw the little mole on her neck. They watched as sometimes she wrinkled her nose as she took a deep breath. They watched the muscles of her diaphragm and chest moving in and out, up and down with the very breath of life. No one knows how long the shadows watched her sleep. One was squatted down near her feet, the other near her head and arms.

At long last, one foot and then the other kicked over the lower binding strap as she turned to her side. Her arms went to the front of her with her hands above the upper binding strap. The shadows' patience had paid off. Very gently, so as not to awaken her, they carefully tied knots over her feet and hands. Then she jerked and tested the bindings on her hands. She tried to move again, without awakening.

Rahab sensed something was wrong: Perhaps a bad dream or

something. That is when the man close to her head, reached for the dripping cloth. He softly squeezed her nose, causing her to open her mouth to breathe. He rammed the saturated cloth into her mouth and covered her nose. Her eyes stormed wide open with fear. Her cries were muffled with the wet, smelly cloth. Her fear caused her to breathe deeply of the fumes that blocked her nose and mouth. In three or four breaths, Rahab lay motionless. She was completely in their control.

The two men closed the ends to her tent and then very gently picked her up. The stronger man placed her over his shoulder and they stole her out of the camp. They left as quietly as they had arrived. The moon hid behind a cloud and the night was dark. The three went out of the camp, down a ways to a waiting cart and very slowly, quietly, they stole out of the campsite.

When the sun was about to appear, Dad was up ready to make tea. Joseph put wood on the overnight fire. He greeted his master. They didn't say much as was their early morning custom. Everyone needs a few minutes to grasp the day and make the transformation from sleep to alertness. The master took a cushion and faced the western sky towards the mountains and watched the sky grow light. Joseph just squatted down, his bare feet in the sand and his elbows on his knees, his hands supporting his face. He was watching the same sky. A new day was beginning.

Joshua's Surprise Attack

Across the mountain ridge Joshua's army was gathering forces for a surprise attack on five armies. The soldiers took turns sleeping in the bouncing wagons. The spotters laid out a gathering place for each of the 12 tribes. They ordered the slaves in Gibeon to prepare tea and biscuits for the men and bring them to the gates at the back of the city. The opposing armies were hunkered down in the woods in front of Gibeon, waiting for the last of the armies to arrive. The battle would begin at sunrise, as was customary.

Breakfast was brought out to the soldiers in carts and wagons and fed to the massive army scattered through the woods opposite their opponents. So far, they had not been spotted. The slaves had been warned that if they made any noise in feeding the soldiers, they would die instantly. Everyone was careful. There was little if any whispering.

As the fighting men were preparing for the new day, spotters were out checking the woods across from them. They were noting every camp they could find of the enemy. When Joshua was ready, he could literally pounce on the enemy in total surprise; which is what he did.

Gibeon was an important city, like one of the royal cities. It was larger than Ai. The five Amorite kings were angry at Gibeon because they had made the life saving treaty with the Hebrews. Now, they planned to take it down to spite the Hebrews. however, Joshua had a surprise for them.

At first light Joshua's cavalry burst from the darkness and onto the enemy. Soldiers of the opposing armies were awakened with screaming shouts as stomping horses trampled on top of them. They ran off the enemy horses as best they could in the opening blow, land eft many of the enemy dead. As the foot soldiers came in with their daggers and spears drawn, the hand to hand battle began. The Amorite soldiers were confused by the surprise attack. They didn't know who was attacking them, how many they were, or even where they were located. The Amorites were frightened and many started running away from the battle. As best they could, they headed toward Greater Sidon down to Misrephoth Maim and to the Valley of Mizpaah on the east. The Hebrews were in hot pursuit.

Surprise Breakfast in Gilgal

Back at Gilgal, the family began coming to the fire for their early morning tea. Mother was ready to toast flat bread on the griddle over Joseph's fire. She already had the dough ready to pour on the griddle when Olmad and his family came to the circle. The sisters came in. Ari El was last, still wiping the sleepy from his eyes. They started talking about how long the journey was the previous two days. They all agreed on how nice it was to sleep on their own mats again.

"I wonder what is keeping Rahab?" Olmad ask the question everyone wanted to ask. "She is probably just sleeping in, but it's not like her."

"I'll bet she is dreaming about her wedding," said Ari El. "I'll go check on her." He was closest to her tent. He simply took the three or four steps and called to her. There was no answer. So he opened the tent flap for a little peek inside. There was no Rahab.

"She's gone!" Ari El screamed.

Everyone was shocked! Mother put down her bowl of dough and subconsciously placed her two hands on her cheeks, in total disbelief. "What do you mean, she's gone?"

"She is not in her tent, come see," and Ari El threw back the front entrance flap as the entire family gathered around.

"Perhaps, she has wondered off to see some friends down in the camp. Maybe she is just out for a walk." Olmad was trying to rationalize the situation, but he didn't believe his own words. Instead, he ran to the tent and ducked his tall head to go inside.

"Dad, I'm afraid, someone has taken her. See, here is her shawl. She would never go anywhere without her shawl." Olmad was trying to figure things out. "Her nightgown is not here. Wherever she is, she is still in her nightgown."

"This is so strange. Poor dear. I heard nothing during the night," her father was trying to be logical.

Everyone was trying to contribute. "I heard nothing."

"No strange sounds, and I sleep right next to her tent."

"Who could have come in here without waking us up?"

"Yeah, because she is sure some fighter. I'm going to go look around and see what I can find." Ari El was the first to take action. He raced off down between the tents of Friends Camp. People were still waking up. Some were still asleep. But it didn't stop Ari El from calling out as loudly as he could, "Rahab. Miss Rahab. Where are you?"

Joseph was quickly behind him taking the other side of Friends Camp. He was going slower, checking between tents and calling out, "Miss Rahab! Miss Rahab, where are you?"

The people coming out of their tents were all asking the same question, "What is going on here? Is someone missing?"

Olmad and his father were walking more carefully checking for her between the tents and telling all who asked that Rahab was missing. No one reported hearing strangers in the area.

After a search of Friends Camp, Olmad decided to call in the troops. He headed off to the armed soldier tent that acted as a communications post for aliens. "My sister is missing from Friends Camp. We just went through there and we can't find her. Can you alert the soldiers to help us?"

"Of course, my friend," the guard was calmer than Olmad, and asked him, "Who is this person that may be missing?"

"My sister, Rahab, the Scarlet Cord Woman."

"Oh, yes, I remember. Just a moment." The guard turned to his messenger sitting in the tent. "Quickly, go get me a dozen men from the ready tent and tell the captain on duty that there has been a kidnapping from Friends Camp. The Scarlet Cord Woman is missing."

The young man said not a word but instantly ran as fast as he could to the Circle of Government and made his report. In a very few minutes several soldiers were at the front and told Olmad they would do all they could. "First, we will search the encampment here and see if someone brought her into their tents. That is the most likely thing to happen. Now tell me how we can spot her."

"Rahab has long coal black hair. We believe she was kidnapped in her night gown. She has no shawl with her. Probably barefooted. She is the woman that taught so many children and their mothers to read. She is the one who taught many of your men to make ropes. She and her mother taught many of your women how to cook. Many will recognize her."

"We will send a messenger to each of the 12 community tents and each tribe will be searched this morning for her. We will see if any of our people are holding her. When that is done then the captain will make more extensive plans, probably going to the mountains over there and search the caves. We will find her. We will find her as quickly as we can. Go tell your folks that." The soldier was confident. He nodded to the messenger with him, who nodded, turned on his heels and ran back to the command tent. Even though the command was now staffed by alternate soldiers, they had good training and this was a big deal to them. "If anyone can find her, we can," the first soldier told Olmad and then suggested that he get back to his family. "Just tell them we are on it."

When Mother is worried, she begins cooking, regardless of the time of day. So she picked up her vat of flatbread dough and began pouring it onto the griddle. When her vat was empty, she made another and without counting what she had cooked, she grilled another stack of flatbread. She was worried about her daughter who had done so much during her short life. She was worried because of all the good things that were about to come true for Rahab. Where could she be?

Dad was so worried that he walked quietly out in front of Friends Camp and was staring into the western plain that lay in front of them. Could they have taken her to the mountains? Could she be in one of the caves where his flocks and herds often stayed? Who could take his baby away?

Dad was standing there with his hands on his hips, staring at the mountains, when someone placed a big hand on his tired shoulder. "What is wrong, my friend?" It was the deep voice of Jonathan.

"Rahab is missing. We all went to bed at the same time last

night. This morning when she didn't come to breakfast, Ari El went to her tent and she was gone. That is all we know."

"You have told the soldiers, I guess," Jonathan said.

"Yes, Olmad has just returned from there and they have started a search of all the tribal tents and we have gone through Friends Camp, here. I am very worried about this."

"Of course, you are." Jonathan stood directly in front of the worried man and placed both hands on Dad's shoulders. He bowed his head and privately, but reassuringly said, "Lord, we don't know what is going on here, but you do. We ask you take care of Rahab and cause her to be safe, until she comes back to us. We know, Lord, that you have the power and the will to save her. You have already demonstrated that in Jericho. Remember her faith, Lord. Remember how she has helped so many people. Remember what she still has to contribute to your people here. Watch over Rahab and keep her safe, Lord."

Then Jonathan brought his hands together behind the father's back and hugged him close. There were tears in both of their eyes. They held each other with compassion for a long time.

"Come get you some breakfast, Dad. You can't solve anything on an empty stomach. And bring Jonathan with you," Mother was calling. "Come, let's talk about this while we get some food in our bodies." Her voice was nervous. Her hands were shaking. She didn't hide her feelings or her fright very well. None of them did.

Rahab opened her eyes. She could see nothing. It was as dark with her eyes opened as they were closed. "Have I gone blind?" She was asking herself. Then she tried to rub her eyes but her hands were bound together. Fear stabbed at her heart. Terror zapped her body. She couldn't move her feet. She couldn't sit up. She couldn't see. "Help!" She yelled.

Rahab knew nothing of the two shadows from the night before. She cried out, "Daddy! Daddy! Come here, I need your help!" But there was no answer. So she cried out even louder, "Olmad! Olmad! Come here, now. Help me, Olmad!" But there was no response in the inky blackness.

Rahab had gone to bed like she had for 23 years, but now she can't see and her hands and feet were tied. *What's going on? Where am I? Why can't I see? Where is my family? Has somebody stolen my family?* "Daddy!" *Why is there an awful taste in my mouth? Why is my throat so sore?* "Olmad! Come here. Help!" *Why can't*

I see? There were no responses. There was no one to help her. As frightened as she was, she began to slowly reason things out. She must not be in her tent at Gilgal. She must be somewhere else. "O Lord, let it be that I am in a dark room. Lord, please let me still have my sight, Lord, I'm scared. I don't understand this. Help me, Lord, to find out what is going on here. Lord, have they buried me alive? Has someone taken away from my family? Help me, Lord to calm this wild, beating heart. Lord, I'm so terrified. Help me! HELP ME, LORD!"

She turned over a little and felt dirt on her face. She was laying in dirt. "Help! H-e-l-p! Someone. Anyone H–E–L–P!" She was on the ground, in the dirt and it was dark. That was about all the reasoning she could muster for the moment. She pulled her knees up to her chest and tried to turn over to sit up. She almost made it, but bumped her head on the ceiling of the place where it was so dark. She fell back on her side. Her heart was racing. Her breath was shallow. Could this be a grave? Had she died and they buried her? She was so frightened! Every one of her nerve endings was burning in terror.

Before she could try to escape, she had to get her hands free. So she pulled at the wrist straps. No luck at all. She couldn't see the knots but she could feel them with her tongue. She took the knot in her teeth to untie it. The knot was so tight, the work would be very slow, but what else was there to do? Gradually, the panic subsided. She began to work for her freedom.

Miracle from the Sky

Across the mountains, past Gibeon, the Hebrews attacked the Amorites fiercely in their surprise early morning blows. The Amorites were confused and began deserting. They were fighting haphazardly. Some tried to escape the battle they did not understand. By the thousands, they headed for the trade route of Gibeon towards Azekah and then on to Beth Horon.

The bright morning sun was giving way to a dark cloudy sky. As some of Joshua's army remained in place to battle the five armies at Gibeon, Joshua ordered a large group of his men to chase after the Amorites and kill them where ever they found them. The Amorites were running on foot to escape. The Hebrews were still on horseback, but were having a hard time maneuvering around the trees and rocks. It was faster to run on foot.

The clouds got darker and then opened up over the Amorite

runaways. The gray-green clouds pounded the Amorites with balls of ice from the sky. No one had ever seen anything like this before. The hail stones fell on the enemy but not the Hebrews. They watched with wide open eyes stepping back from the isolated storm in full wonder of the miracle. They knew then that God was on their side. They would later report this event to the people back home as a miracle where God rained hail on the enemy but not on them. The hail stones killed more of the enemy than did the Hebrews.

However, some of the enemy escaped the hail and made their way to Beth Horon where they were able to work their way down a steep and dangerous mountain side to Lower Beth Horon which introduced the beautiful Aijalon Valley. There was a steep declining path about two miles long that connected Upper Beth Horon with the lower part of the city. It was too rugged for ordinary pathways. The little crooked trails were dangerous with thorny bushes, jagged rocks, and sudden cliffs. Joshua was going to need more of God's help to get his army down such a steep slope.

The Search

Back in Gilgal, the soldiers alerted each home team in the tribes to search for Rahab. Before the noon watch, every tent in the encampment of 2,000,000 people had been searched. Rahab was neither in the encampment of the Israelites nor in Friends Camp. One of the captains came to Friends Camp and inquired for Rahab's family. They offered him tea and a cushion in the family circle. Jonathan came with him.

"We have completed a cursive search of the encampment and we are reasonably sure that Rahab is not there," said the captain. "Will you tell me again what happened and how you are sure that she was kidnapped?"

Her father answered the soldier's question: "We had just returned from the journey to Mount Ebal. We were tired like everyone else, and we ate supper and went to bed soon after sundown. We all fell asleep and this morning when we began breakfast, we noticed that Rahab was gone. That's about it. We heard no noise. There was nothing to awaken us. And that in itself is strange because we have had a little trouble before about people coming into our camp wanting to run Rahab off; calling her a prostitute. But they were always noisy. They seldom put up a fight. One time they did get to Rahab, but she was able to defend herself and ran them off before any of us could get to her."

"Would you guess then that her kidnapping would be related to those calling her a prostitute?" The soldier was trying to get additional information.

Olmad answered this time. "No one knows, but my guess would be that it is. That is the only trouble we have ever had. The people around here have all been so generous to us. So many people have accepted us and welcomed us.

"On the night that Jericho burned, two men came up in the darkness and wanted to see the prostitute and run her off, because the Law prohibited a prostitute to live among you. But they never saw Rahab. Salmon was here and he showed them the way back into the encampment. He told them that God can save anyone He wishes and that no one has the right to question what God does."

"There have been other threats?"

Olmad continued, "A few more times. The men would show up in pairs, always after dark, so we couldn't get a good look at them. One time, they were drunk on wine and I escorted them back into Judah. Now, I don't know if that is where they live or somewhere else, but since that is the tribe that is closest to us, it was my guess that is where they lived. Anyway, that is where I left them. The last time they came here it was daylight, but only Rahab was up front here. She was in her tent and two men came in, one at each end of the tent. They called her a prostitute and grabbed for her. But Rahab is well trained in self defense and she threw them into each other and then hurled hot pepper sauce at them and they fled into the desert. We never saw them again."

"And last night?" The soldier wanted to hear the story again.

"Last night, we heard nothing." Olmad was trying to think of any clues. "I could hear the wagons leaving the camp up there by the trading tents, but I heard nothing here in Friends Camp. Like everyone else in the family, I fell asleep and heard nothing during the night. She just disappeared."

"May I see her tent, then?" The soldier asked.

"Of course, over here." Olmad stood up with the soldier and Jonathan, and they walked over to Rahab's tent. "My guess is that she must have been caught in her sleep. Otherwise she would have cried out and someone would have heard her. Her shawl is still here and she wouldn't go anywhere without her shawl. Her good sandals are here, all her dress robes and gowns are here."

"What is that smell in here?" The soldier asked.

"Rahab likes perfumes. They all pretty much smell alike to me."

"I can smell something a little like sleeping salts. Most of the odor is gone now, but it's possible that someone crept in here and smothered her with a cloth dipped in a strong sleeping salts solution. That could knock her out before she awakened and then there would be no fight. Probably little, if any noise. I think some sleeping salts came in on a caravan a few weeks ago. I'm sure that a strong enough solution could drug someone"

The soldier was thinking with his hand cupping his chin. "It seems like the people after Rahab are getting smarter in their attacks on her." The soldier paused and looked back over the tent. Then he saw a long strap across the corner of her bed. "Is this strap hers or someone else's?"

"I hadn't seen that before. No, Rahab has no straps like that. That must have come from the kidnappers." Some pieces were beginning to come together.

"I would like to take this with me. With this strap and the smell of something like strong smelling salts, I am going to pursue this as a kidnapping rather than as a missing person. And for now, I am going to concentrate on the Judah tribe ... my tribe, where I live." The soldier was still examining the contents of Rahab's tent. "Let me go do my work and I will get back to you. I'll probably have a team go out to the mountains and begin to search the caves. If any of you are out there, you might keep an eye out too. There are a lot of places to hide there. In the meantime, I'll be back in touch with you soon. We will find her, believe me." The soldier raised his right hand with open fingers and faced the family. "We will find her," he said as he left.

It was still dark where Rahab was. The drugs still made her sleepy. She would be awake for a little while and then doze. As she could, she would get the knot binding her hands in her teeth and pull at it and try to bite it in two. For most of the day, she worked at chewing the knot in two. Once when she was awake there was a little beam of light coming into the area where she was. She could see! She was not blind. She could see that the light was restricted by something. The light flooded in through a few jagged cracks in something. The floor was dirt and the walls were dirt. She must be in a cave. A very small cave. Once she thought she heard bells outside. Gentle, tinkling bells. The next time she awakened it was dark again.

The captain of the guard reported back to the command tent in the Circle of Government. He told the officers that they had a kidnapping on their hands. The Woman with the Scarlet Cord was missing. And he said the first place to look for the kidnappers was in the tribe of Judah. Two important clues to search for were for any additional straps like the one he brought back to show them; and containers of something that smelled like hypnotic smelling salts. He said he was afraid that they had sin in the camp, again.

"We had better notify Joshua. If we do have sin in the camp, it could certainly affect the way the battle goes for Gibeon. We don't want another Ai on our hands." The officer was thinking as he was talking. "Better get a messenger out to Joshua right away. And ask them to search all of the provisional wagons. They may have slipped her body in as part of the baggage. I'm going to go talk with the High Priest."

Several men answered "Yes, sir," and a messenger left immediately on one of the standby horses. He was headed for Joshua 20 miles over the ridges.

Finally, the drugs seem to be gone from Rahab's system. She could concentrate on undoing the knot. The light came back through the crevice of the rocks. She kept calling out but there was never an answer. She was totally alone. At last the knot binding her hands came lose and she was able to free her hands. Once her hands were free, she worked on getting her bare feet loose. It took a little time, but what else did she have to do? "Thank you, Lord, for giving me the sense to get untied. Now, please, help me get out of here."

The light went out again for a moment and then came back. It was a mystery to her. How could such a thing happen? While she had light she looked around the room where she was. It was dirt on the floor and walls, probably a cave. There were some sticks on the floor and a bag of some sort. In the bag was some food: several pieces of fruit, raw vegetables and several pieces of bread. She didn't know how long it had been there or who it belonged to, but she wasn't asking questions. She tried a piece of bread. It was dry, but a lot better than nothing. There was also a clay jar with something in it. She lifted it to her lips and discovered that it was water. So at least she could last for a few days until she could find a way out. But before she could get to the front of the place, the light went out again.

Battlefront Receives Word

The messenger raced to get to Joshua at the battle scene. Salmon was working in the command center helping to set up an administrative and logistical center for the attacks on various cities. He was the first man that the messenger saw. "Quickly, I must see Joshua."

The old man turned to face the young man dismounting his sweaty horse. Joshua pushed his hair away from his face, "What can I do for you?"

"Joshua, there's been a kidnapping in Gilgal. We are afraid there is sin in the camp and it may affect your battle here. They sent me to tell you this. The captain back in Gilgal is seeking advice from the High Priest, but he wanted you to know it as quickly as I could get here."

"He was right. And you are winded. Sit down here and get you a mug of water. Salmon, get one of the servants to bring in some cool water for this young man and to take care of his horse. Now start all over again, and give me the details."

One of the slaves appeared at the entrance to the tent with the water and the messenger drank it thankfully. Then he began to tell his account.

"Slowly, now," said Joshua. "I don't listen very fast any more."

The messenger began, "Remember the Woman with the Scarlet Cord? The one that was saved in the fall of Jericho? The one in Friends Camp?"

"You mean Rahab," jumped in Salmon. "What about Rahab?"

"She turned up missing this morning and we suspect that she was kidnapped during the night from her tent. There are few clues. The kidnappers made no noise and awakened no one. But she is gone and we have searched Friends Camp and the entire nation, except for the freight wagons that came out here during the night. The men back in Gilgal are searching Judah even now for two men who have visited her family campsite before."

"Joshua, please let me go back and help hunt for her," Salmon was pleading. "Rahab is my betrothed. I got her father's blessings on the way back from Mount Ebal. I was one of the two spies who she protected when we went to Jericho. I helped her and her family get out of the falling walls of the city. I've got to help her somehow." Salmon was holding his cupped hands at arm's length.

"We all need to help her, son. Call me a Captain of the Guard and I want a council of the commanders right away."

"Yes, sir," said Salmon. He stepped to the front of the tent where the messengers were waiting. He dispatched one to summon the captain of the guard and three others to round up the commanders of the different army groups. "Quickly," Salmon admonished.

The Captain of the Guard was the first one to appear. "Yes, sir," he said as he stepped into the command tent.

"Josh, get you some men and go over all the freight wagons we have here. Look among the clothes, food, supplies — everything— and see if there is a bag big enough to hide someone in. Especially the body of a young woman. Some thoughtless and ruthless men may have tried to sneak a woman out of the Gilgal camp by sending her here as freight. I'm preparing to go back to Gilgal and I want to hear your results before I leave."

"Yes, sir," he said and called some men to help him make the search.

"So you kinda like this girl, do you?" Joshua was talking more as a father than a commander.

"More than that. I love every hair on her head, every bone in her body, every ounce of her heart." How could Salmon be any clearer?

"You sound like a biologist. No, you sound like a love sick biologist." Joshua was grinning and reached for Salmon's shoulders with both of his old hands and gave them a pat. "And I wouldn't have it any other way, son. We'll see what we can do to find her."

The battle commanders signaled to enter the command tent. Joshua had them come in to lay out strategies for the next few days. "I need to go back to Gilgal for a couple of days. Let's try to keep these five little armies corralled so they can be eliminated. Get out a big bunch of spotters all around the back side of their locations so you can watch for any deserters. We have already seen some heading for Beth Horon over there. My guess is that most of the boys out there don't really want to fight and they are going to leave any way they can and head back to their homes and we are going to need to call on them there. You know there are suppose to be five kings out there somewhere. Find them and keep tabs on them.

"Your first duty is to protect Gibeon. Second, stop the fighting here. And third, keep up with the boys that escape from here. They may lead us to other places we need to take care of while we are out this far. This may be God's way of giving us more of the Promised Land.

"Remember to rotate your men so they can get some rest. They are all tired from the journey from Mount Ebal and the travel last night."

Joshua paused. Perhaps, he was thinking of his own tiredness.

No one else spoke, so Joshua continued. "Get some men to work on how we can move this army down the ridge to Lower Beth Horon and find us another place to set up a temporary command center. I'll be back in a couple of days. I've got to go with Salmon here and find his girl friend. Josh will fill you in on everything."

The old man slowly stood up and as they walked outside to get the driver for the little command wagon, the Captain of the Guard reported that there was no unusual freight in the supply wagons. No women anywhere. No bodies.

The driver and Salmon helped Joshua into the little horse drawn cart and then he and Salmon jumped in. Six armed guards surrounded the cart and they headed for Gilgal. The messenger from Gilgal quickly overtook the cart and rode ahead of them several paces as their spotter.

The light came back on in the place where Rahab was. She moved to the opening and could see that the light was shining through cracks between three or four big heavy rocks that blocked the entrance. There was a big goat sitting on the ledge and as he moved away, then the light beamed through the tiny crevices. That was one mystery solved.

She started working at pushing the stones away. They were heavy and she tried to move them with her hands and then turned around and tried with her feet. She did move one rock a little and improved the opening. Her efforts were hampered because she couldn't stand up or sit up and exert any real force. She still didn't know where the cave was or how she got there, but she now had the use of her eyes, hands, and feet.

Fresh air streamed through the improved opening and she stuck her face up close to breathe it. All she could see through the tiny opening was the sky and the few limbs of bushes that were close. She must be on the side of a mountain. Probably up high, but she still didn't know where. Rahab called for help again. There was no response so she turned to prayer. "Lord, they tell me that you can make a way where there is no way. This sure would be a good time to demonstrate that. Have mercy on me, Lord."

Back in Gilgal, Rahab's dad was walking in circles with his hands behind his back. It was his worry walk. "I can't just sit here and wait for the soldiers to do what I should be doing," he said with tears in his eyes. "I want my girl back. I'm going to the caves out there."

"I'm going with you," said Olmad.

"I'll get the horse and wagon," said Joseph. And he disappeared behind the tents to where the horse and wagon were kept.

"I want to go too. The more eyes, the more you see," said Ari El. Everyone was waiting for direction from the head of the household.

"Mother, you had better stay here, in case there is good news from the soldiers. We still have half a day of sunlight. We can do some good searching in that time." Rahab's father had a new determination in his voice.

"Then you should take some clothes for her and some food for her and some other things.

Olmad's wife volunteered, "I'll get some water and a wet cloth and some towels. She may need washing."

"I'll get some fresh clothes. She won't want to be seen in her night gown," her mother was talking as she was racing to Rahab's tent.

Joseph had harnessed the horse and was bringing the wagon with the clicking wheel up front in record time. Everyone was putting the things they had gathered into the wagon. The four men jumped in and took off facing the strong afternoon sun.

"We should be back by sundown," her father called back as they drove toward the mountains.

Joshua Returns

Jonathan saw the clicking wagon heading for the caves and he stopped in to comfort those who remained behind. He hugged everyone and told them that the army was going through Judah camp, one tent at a time looking for anything suspicious. He told them that Joshua had been summoned and would likely be here before sundown. But it was not long before the messenger who went after Joshua can racing back into camp calling out "Joshua is coming. Joshua is coming."

Later, Joshua's cart rolled into the camp and headed straight for the Circle of Government. The command center was already assembled and ready to report to the commander in chief.

"So, what is going on," said the old man as he took his place.

"Joshua, we have done a cursive search of the entire camp and of Friends Camp but have not found the girl. We suspect that she was captured by two men who have sought after her before, in fact, even had a fight with her. We believe they may be in the Judah camp."

"I remember those men," said Salmon. "I turned them away the first night of Jericho. It was dark and the family was grieving over losing everything and two rough looking men came up wanting the prostitute — to use their words. I think they are the same ones that have come after Rahab several times later."

"Can you recognize them?" A commander was asking.

"I doubt it. Possibly their voices. I never got a good look at their faces. I remember they had a strong odor about them. Didn't bathe very often. Alcohol. They drank a lot. The family told me that on most of the occasions, they had been drinking when they came to the campsite."

"I see two major problems," Joshua was quickly drawing conclusions. "If the girl is not in the camp, then she is likely to be in or near the Jordan or out in the caves. The Jordan is pretty crowded. Not many hiding places there. I'd bet on the caves."

"Me too," almost everyone present said.

Joshua raised his almost closed hand. His thumb was shaking. "The other problem is that there seems to be sin in the camp. We must find the person or persons who have committed this sin and deal with it. How are we progressing on that front?"

A soldier raised his hand with his elbow still on the table. "We have consulted with Eleazar and are now doing a tent by tent search of Judah for anyone suspicious. We are talking with everyone in the tribe and asking questions. Nothing so far. But we are working on it. We have a ways to go."

"And you are focusing on Judah because they are next door to Friends Camp? Any other reason?" Joshua was asking.

"We have nothing else to go on. It seemed the most logical place. The men were seen coming out of Judah and they were returned to the tribe at least twice. It's possible they were passing through Judah to somewhere else. It just seems to be a good place to begin."

"I agree. Keep up the good work and let me know when something happens. I'm going to go see Eleazar. Get Salmon a couple hundred men and let him take them to the mountains. If we can find the girl alive, she may help us with getting to the sinners. We must deal with the sinners before they hamper the battle. Salmon, go look for your friend and find her as fast as you can." Joshua got up and turned to leave. Then he turned back to Salmon and whispered, "And give her a hug from an old man." He winked with love in his eyes.

One of the captains crossed over to the army tent and ordered a ram's horn signal for 200 volunteers. Within a few minutes, 300 showed up. They were young inexperienced soldiers, but they had strong legs, good vision and could search caves. They headed at top speed to the mountains.

Rahab pushed and shoved against the heavy rocks blocking her escape. She exhausted herself but with little success. There was nothing in the cave to use for leverage. No poles or tools of any kind. It was just up to her and her faith. "Almighty God, you have given me a big task. I don't know why, but if you gave me the task, then you also have a way for me to meet it. If I could only see where I am then perhaps I could figure out what to do about it. Lord, will you bless me with your mercy and your patience. You know I don't have very much patience, but if it is your will, I had rather learn about patience later, and get this problem solved now. Lord, will you please give me strength to move those rocks up there. Please, O Lord."

Rahab lay on her back in the dirt, placed her bare feet against the top rock and focused all her energy in a mighty strong shove. It didn't move. So she placed her heels against the rock next to it and shoved. Nothing happened. On to the next one she went. *There must be a loose stone up there somewhere. There must be.* Then on the center stone, she placed her scraped and bleeding feet against its rough surface and said, "Lord, this one must be it." She pushed and it moved. She pushed again and the little rock fell out of the cave and down the mountain side.

The light of joy and victory streamed into the cave. It lit up Rahab's dirty face. *"Thank you Lord!"* Rahab turned her tired body around and looked at the five by six inch opening in the rock wall that guarded her escape. To celebrate, she cried out, "Help me!" But there was no response. Instead the big goat came back, lay down on his ledge, and the light went out.

Joshua met Eleazar at the Tent of Meeting and soon they were joined by the leaders of each of the 12 tribes of Israel. "My friend, you didn't stay gone very long," said Eleazar.

"And I'll guess that you didn't get any more rest than I did," said Joshua. "What do you know about our situation here?"

"Probably less than you do by now." Eleazar placed his hand on Joshua's tired shoulder to welcome him. "Our guess is that two men kidnapped the woman from Friends Camp by using something like hypnotic smelling salts to suffocate her before she could awaken. And they then carried her out of the camp without making a sound. No sounds going in or coming out of the camp. Of course, everyone was tired last night because of the trip. Even the young sleep soundly, when they have just come off a trip like we did."

"Then perhaps the kidnappers didn't make the trip? I wonder how many people were left behind?" Joshua was asking.

"Quite a few, I suppose. There was the regular guard detail and their seconds. And the sick. And the crippled, and the very old. And I would suppose some people who just chose not to go. What do you have in mind?"

"Just a thought. Where is my aide?" Joshua called out quietly.

"Over here, sir. I was trying to give you some privacy."

Joshua took hold of his aide as though he might escape. But in reality, he was only using him for support. "Go back to the army tent and tell the man in charge to search first for people who did not make the trip to Mount Ebal. It may save us some time. They would be the fresh guys who could stay up all night and be carrying loads without making a sound."

"Great idea. I'll tell him right now." And the young man ran off towards the army tent across the circle from the Tent of Meeting.

Joshua and Eleazar stood in front of the tent where the Ark of the Covenant was kept — where God lived — and leaned heavily on their staffs as they lowered tired old knees to the ground. Almost in unison they leaned on them again as their upper torso's slowly bent to place their hands and foreheads on the ground in front of them. The leaders of Israel joined them, prostrate before God. They all took turns in approaching God. There were pauses and sometimes two or more men wanted to pray at the same time. They all felt that the nation of Israel needed a blessing. "Almighty God of Israel: We praise you as the highest name in the entire world. We praise you as the Creator of the entire world. We recognize you as our Father, and we are your children. Bless us, O Lord, as we seek your mercy and guidance in determining if there is sin in our camp.

"Lord, if our truth is what we suspect it will be, help us find the evil men in our camp and to rescue the young woman who has disappeared. Lord, we pray that she will be found alive. Lord, we pray that not only we find the sinful men, but that they will help us find the woman. Remember, Lord, that this is the Woman with the Scarlet Cord that you saved from Jericho. This is the woman who has been such a help to us in getting adjusted to this new land. The woman and her family have contributed so much to our well being in this land.

"Lord, we mercifully ask that you not allow this sin to affect the battle at Gibeon. Bless our men at the battle site. Continue to bless our efforts in clearing your land of idol worshipers so that this land may be the land of your peoples in accordance with your oath. We are your people, Lord. Bless us and help us solve this problem."

Finally, the prostrate men began to say "Amen." One after another were almost singing the word. All of them in front of the Tent of Meeting said it all together in full voice. "Amen!" It rang through the tents and into the free air that covered the Jericho Plains. And God heard their prayers and He blessed them.

15

The Rescue

Olmad, his father, and the two servants rolled up to the mountains where there were hundreds of caves. Ari El was the first to volunteer, "I'll start here." He jumped from the moving wagon and ran from big cave to big cave calling out, "Rahab. Miss Rahab. Where are you?" But there was no response.

The others went down a short ways and stopped near the caves that often protected their own flocks and herds. It was familiar territory. They, too, started working the caves near the ground. They called Rahab's name.

Joseph and Ari El began climbing the mountain looking into the smaller caves. There were sheep and goats all over the mountain. The animals enjoyed the higher elevation and the thorny bushes that dominated the mountain side, but the boys found nothing.

After a while, in the distance, they heard the running hooves of three hundred horses. They could see the big cloud of dust they whipped up. "Dad, I think we have some help coming."

"I believe you're right. What do you want to bet that the young fellow in front is Salmon?" Olmad's dad had that glint in his eye again.

"I think I am on your side on this one. He rides straight and tall. A man on a mission!" Olmad, too, liked what he saw.

The leader of the pack raised his hand and all the horsemen came to a stop. Salmon called out instructions. "You men take that mountain. You men take this mountain over here. And the rest of you follow me. Look carefully. Call out 'Rahab' and listen carefully. She could be tied up in an open cave. And she may be in one that has been closed. Look for any ground or bushes that have been disturbed. Listen for any muffled sound." The group began to disburse. Some were on foot and others remained mounted. They were all searching to cover the widest area possible in the time they had left before sunset.

Salmon rode up to Olmad and his father and greeted them. "How is the search going? I heard you were out here."

"We haven't been here very long. No clues yet." Olmad reported. "There are a lot of places to hide a person. If God is on our side we may find her soon."

"My friend, let me assure you that God is on our side. Joshua has returned from the battle to oversee the search and to find the people who took her. He and all the leaders of Israel are praying for her recovery and to find the men who did this to her. Those are heavy weight prayers. God is listening."

"For which we are all grateful," said Dad. "How did you get back here? Aren't you supposed to be at the battle site?"

"The soldiers here sent a messenger to Gibeon to alert Joshua that there may be sin in the camp, because of the kidnapping. When I heard that it was Rahab who was missing, wild horses couldn't hold me there. So here I am. Now, where have you searched? I've got 100 men here who need some direction."

"We have searched the lower and bigger caves around here. Joseph and Ari El are working on the upper levels. So come join us."

"Men, over here. Watch for disturbed rocks, bushes or torn clothing. Anything like that. The culprits most likely have moved some rocks to block an entrance. They may have even moved some bushes. Well, you know what to do. Keep calling out her name, Rahab. When you find her, call me so we may come help you rescue her." The searchers then joined the other two hundred and began combing the mountain.

Rahab had dozed off and was awakened hearing her name called in the distance. It was a fuzzy dream, she thought. Who would be calling her name? Perhaps her father, maybe Olmad had come to the caves to check on the animals. Rahab was not sure whether she was awake or asleep, but the sounds went away. The goat moved from his ledge and the light came back into her cave. She reached for the sack to see if there was anything edible inside. Her head was hurting. Her feet were swollen and bleeding where the rocks had scraped them.

In Gilgal, the search continued for any suspicious men. This was the third time they had searched Judah. The first time it was just a cursive search to quickly determine if Rahab was in the camp. The second time they were interviewing people quickly to see if they could identify any suspicious people. This time they were carefully going through every tent, locating the families living there and asking if they went to Mount Ebal or not. If they said no, then they were interviewed in detail about what they did, what they saw, and what happened during the week that the majority of the people were away. This time the search was slower. Although several hundred soldiers were searching and interviewing, there were more than 50,000 people in the Judah camp. This search would take a great deal of time.

The soldiers were looking for containers of a fowl smelling fluid, red straps, signs of heavy drinkers, unkept hair and beards, loud and boisterous men. The searchers were divided into small groups of 10 and 12 with a team leader who collected the information. As each unit gathered any information or saw any signs or trends, then the team leaders reported that to group leaders who then merged everything together and reported it to the master search leader.

Little by little clues began to come in. There were not many people who had stayed behind. Of that group, most were ruled out as too old, too sick, too crippled and other reasons to not be suspect. There were only a few mentions of some drunkards who drank more than they worked and seem to enjoy living by themselves and make up their own rules, but no one seemed to know where they lived. They were just spotted occasionally. The sun was getting low and a few people were already building fires for the night. Something should break soon.

In the mountains, the searchers were scaling the cliffs, examining rocks against the inclines that could possibly hide cave openings. The calls for Rahab echoed off the mountains as three hundred men desperately searched for the kidnapped woman.

The clouds in the sky began to turn dark and then crimson. The white bright sky itself had tinges of light blue but quickly faded to yellow; almost canary yellow. It was time to call it quits and head for Gilgal. Very reluctantly, Rahab's dad called for Olmad, Joseph, and Ari El to go to the wagon. "We will come back at daylight tomorrow morning," he promised.

Salmon stuck his index finger and little finger into the edges of his mouth and gave a sharp long whistle. When the searchers turned to look at him, he waved them down to the ground. Common sense called for them to saddle up and go home. All 300 of the soldiers volunteered to come back with him the next morning. All the men must leave the caves for the night without finding a trace of Rahab. Perhaps the others in Gilgal would have had better luck.

Rahab looked out her little hole between the rocks and with her hands, she pushed another little rock out. It was small, but it broke off easily and skidded off the larger ledge and she could hear it bounce down the mountain side into the valley below. She watched the crimson clouds and the yellow sky, until darkness closed in. She was alone. Even the old goat was gone. The whole day had passed. She was still alone. "O Lord, will I ever get out of here? Will I ever be with my family again? Will I ever see Salmon again?"

Joshua ordered all the search team leaders to assemble at his command tent. It took a while to get them all there because no one wanted to give up the search. The Woman with the Scarlet Cord had touched many of their lives and the lives of their children. They had to solve the mystery somehow. Even as the leaders were assembling with Joshua, the citizens were taking up their own search. They were comparing ideas of who might have done such a horrible thing.

Joshua began by asking, "What do you men have to report?"

The leaders began sharing notes and ideas. At this point they had not found the kidnappers. All the leads pointed to two grubby men who were drunkards and generally stayed by themselves. But so far there were no clues. The men had been seen in Judah camp and sometimes walked in front of Friends Camp. They had access to Rahab, but the men themselves had not turned up.

"Men, you have had a long day. I thank you for your work. Let us begin at daylight tomorrow. And set me six or eight men inside Friends Camp tonight. Get back out of sight. Leave off your sword belts and anything else that make you look like a soldier. Mix in with the aliens over there and watch who walks by tonight. Sometimes people get curious. Then at the last watch, slowly change out to a new group for the rest of the night so you won't attract attention. You never know who is watching. Let Rahab's family know that some of you are there. It may give them some comfort, but they don't have to know that all of you are there. See my point?"

The leaders agreed. And all were dismissed for the night. Joshua, himself, headed to his tent. An aide brought him dinner and as soon as he ate it, he spread out on his sleeping pallet. Instantly, the tired old man fell asleep.

Olmad, his father, and their servants rode in with Salmon and the 300 searchers. Salmon took everyone by Friends Camp and called out so all could hear. "See, this is where Rahab lives. Pray tonight that by this time tomorrow she will be back with her family." And the soldiers went on to their own families, grateful that they had families who were safe.

Olmad and his father were greeted by their wives and children. They were anxious to hear what had happened, but there was little to report. Salmon had come back and brought a large group of searchers out to the caves and they made a tremendous difference in searching so much territory.

Salmon let the men greet their families and then he stepped out of the shadows and hugged Mother. "I am sorry we did not find her today, but we will be on the job at daybreak tomorrow. I pray to God that we find her tomorrow and that we find her alive." He was speaking softly into Mother's ear as they hugged each other. They both had tears in their eyes. Mother reached up with her dish towel and blotted Salmon's eyes, as she would any of her children.

"Come have supper with us," she said.

"I really need to get to my parents. They don't even know that I am here. I came in with Joshua about noon and went straight out to the search site. I thought you would like to know that when we asked for 200 volunteers to help us search, 300 showed up. They all remembered how much Rahab had meant to everyone. Everybody loves her."

"Thank you for telling me that," Mother said. Then she reached for a chunk of yeast bread and dipped it into her special sauce and handed it to Salmon. "Here, this will hold you until you can get home."

Salmon smiled and said, "Thanks. I feel at home already." He leaned over and kissed Mother. He grabbed Dad's and Olmad's shoulders as he parted.

Then the family came to their circle for supper. As everyone filled their plate and gathered around the campfire, Dad stood up and said in a shaky, uncertain voice, "I pray to Rahab's God.; the God that saved us from Jericho; the God that has provided us these generous friends all around us; and the God that has blessed us so very much. Now I pray that Rahab's God watch over her tonight and keep her safe. I pray that Rahab's God look after us and help us find her tomorrow morning. We miss her very much. We all love her very much. Amen" And he sat down.

There was little talk that evening. It was a sad time. Tomorrow would be better. Tomorrow they would find her. Tomorrow they would find the people who stole her away. They promised themselves that tomorrow would be better.

A stranger stepped out of the night and came to the fire. He was rather short and skinny. He was dressed in a very common tunic and wore no head covering. "Hello," he said. "May I come in?"

"How may we help you, my friend?" Olmad was on his feet in front of the stranger. Olmad was several inches taller than the stranger.

The stranger stepped around Olmad and went to the circle and squatted down, much as a servant would do. He spoke softly. "I apologize for the intrusion, but I wanted you to know that both God and Israel are watching after you tonight. There are some soldiers who are visiting with families around you and we are watching for any strangers who might pass this way. I come not to frighten you, but to reassure you that even though it is dark, we are still on the job. We are searching for Rahab's kidnappers through the night, as best we can. The Army of God wanted you to know that."

"Thank you. We appreciate your coming to tell us," said Olmad who was still standing. "Are you one of the soldiers?"

"No. Not me. I'm not tall enough. But I work with them and they sent me. They said that if anyone was watching they wouldn't suspect me as being a messenger. Please be assured that the power of Israel surrounds you tonight." And with that he stood up. "Understand more than anything else, the power of God is with you. Please, ... rest well." The skinny man went to the campsite next over and greeted that family, stayed a few minutes and then left.

There was a little small talk around the family circle, but it soon stalled to nothing and there was talk about going to bed. Then one by one, the members retired to their tents.

Dad was the last one at the fire. Joseph came over and stoked it for the night, but Dad just sat there and stared into the flames. The servant's worried look penetrated his touch as he placed his hand on his Master's shoulder. "Tomorrow will be better. You'll see."

And Dad reached up and touched his loyal servant's hand and said "I know. I know. Thanks for your help today."

The silent servant walked towards his tent. And Mother came up and called her husband to come to bed. "Tomorrow will be better," she said as if confirming prophesies. He took her hand and they went in to lie down. Both were very tired; worry tired. This was the first time they had ever gone to bed not knowing where all their children were. Still her bare foot found his bare toes and they touched each other. She reached around his tense shoulders and kissed him near his ear. No words were spoken. They had been in love so long that words were not needed. She reached for the light weight blanket and pulled it up over both of them. When Dad stuck one foot out from under the cover, Mother knew that he was feeling better.

No one had noticed but six men had come into Friends Camp and were visiting as if they belonged there. They looked like everybody else in the camp. As the light disappeared and the night reigned, the men were sitting in the shadows as still as tent poles. A trap had been set.

The moon rose high and wispy clouds played tag in the sky. The stars flashed messages to each other. A little breeze flirted with the bushes out front, but nothing else moved. Across the camp, the snores of old men began to sound like a symphony out of tune. The honks and snorts each added their own part. Some were loud, others soft. Some were high and others low. Each snorer had his tune. It was a strange symphony without a leader, but it announced that Friends Camp was asleep.

At last the silhouettes of two men with scruffy beards came stumbling down the trail. Their walk was weaving in and out. They were talking and laughing softly to themselves so as not to disturb anyone. They kept calling to the other one, "Shhhhhh. You got to be quiet. You don't want to awaken anyone." And then they would softly laugh as the other one said the same thing. There seemed to be no hurry. No time line. They were just two guys out for a walk. Apparently, they had been drinking and now they were out for a little night air. Their coy laughs and the tenor of their hushed voices indicated they were probably talking about women.

Finally, they stopped in front of Friends Camp. They looked at each other and then one said loud enough to be clearly heard, "Well, you can see there ain't no prostitutes here tonight."

Just then four men reached out of the darkness and grabbed the two drunks. Strong hands reached for the men's jaws crushing their back teeth so they couldn't make another sound. Hands reached around them and pushed the strangers' arms up their back bones. One of them cracked, breaking his arm but it stayed behind his back. Two other soldiers jumped out of the bushes and reinforced the hold on the two strollers. The trap was sprung.

"What are you doing out here?" The soldiers asked.

"Just, just out for a little walk. Can't a man go for a walk?"

"Not tonight. Not here anyway. Where do you live?

"Back over there. Just outside of Judah. We ain't done nothin'. What do you want with us? We ain't nobody."

"You're coming with us." The soldier ordered. And the soldiers took the two men back to the army ready tent in the Circle of Government. There, the soldiers on duty questioned the two men until almost daylight but they admitted nothing. They were just men out for a little night air. That's all. They wanted help with the broken arm, but were only promised help when they told what they had done with Rahab. They confessed nothing. At last, the man's arm had a splint placed on it and bandaged. They were placed in detention until morning.

But at first light, two soldiers were sent to find their tent and to search it. They found two tents. One was used mostly for storage and contained some ceramic jars that smelled of sleeping salts. They found three more red straps like the ones in Rahab's tent. They found several items of women's clothing. The searchers guessed they must have been trophies from their escapades.

At daybreak, the Israelite encampment smelled of camp fires, smoke, and baking bread. Friends Camp has its own flavor of baking bread and campfire smoke. Joseph came out of his tent rubbing the sleepy from his eyes as usual and headed for the fire to add some more wood to it. And sure enough, his master was there with the pot of water to start the morning tea. The master took his place on the cushion facing west; facing the mountains where the caves were. He wasn't watching the sky so much today. Joseph perfected the wood placement on the fire and squatted down on his heels, placed his arms on his knees and rubbed his hands in front of him. He watched his hands and didn't look at the skyline very much. Slowly and quietly he mumbled. "This is the day that is going to be better."

"Joseph, if there is any power in the spoken word. This day is going to be a whopper of a better day!"

Out in the mountains across the Jericho Plains, Rahab opened her eyes but she didn't smell breakfast. She turned to the opening she had punched out of the rocks that imprisoned her and said, "Good morning, Lord. This is the day you have made and I will be glad in it. I look forward to see what you have planned for me. Bless me with your mercy. Bless me with patience. And, is it selfish to ask, bring me Salmon. Lord, you know my needs and you know my future. Give me the strength to be what you would have me to be, Lord." Then she turned to the bag to see if there was anything left to eat.

At Gilgal, the soldiers were beginning to report in to volunteer for the search party. Salmon was among the first. He went to the army tent to see if there was anything new from overnight. When he learned that two men had been arrested, he couldn't wait for them to be brought in. When the men arrived for him to identify, he jumped from his bench, shouting, "Yes. YES! Those are the two who came to Rahab's family the first night of Jericho. I remember their smell. I don't think they have had a bath since that time. Look at their clothes; they haven't been washed since then either. All of these months and they are rotting in their own filth."

Salmon was in rage. He was screaming at them. "Where is she? Where is Rahab? What have you done with her?" He lunged for one of the men's throat. "In the name of God, you will tell me where she is!"

Two of the other soldiers jumped on Salmon and pulled his hands from the grubby man's throat. "WHERE IS SHE?" He was screaming loud enough for all of Canaan to hear. The two soldiers could hardly contain him. "WHERE IS SHE?"

Joshua stepped into the tent and placed his cold, wet hand on the back of Salmon's neck. "Save your voice, son. Let me ask the question, Salmon," Joshua said quietly, and authoritatively. Then he walked up to the one with the broken arm standing almost nose to nose with him. And then he yelled, 'WHERE IS SHE?"

The two prisoners said nothing. They knew the tension of the room, but they didn't have to answer. Joshua turned to the team of soldiers. "What do we know about these two?"

"We had a secret team posted after dark near the front of Friends Camp as you ordered. And late in the night these two showed up. Our men were trying to arrest these two when one of their arms got broken. They have admitted nothing. They were very drunk last night and we are praying for something better this morning. We have found their tents. One is a junk heap and we found these things," the soldier was holding up a jar where sleeping salts has been stored, two red straps like the one found in Rahab's tent, and some women's underwear.

"It seems like the better day everyone was talking about, began about midnight," Joshua said calmly. He took a big sigh. He looked the two grubby men over. Then he pulled Salmon over to the entrance of the tent. First, for some fresh air after being close to the dirty men, and then to say to Salmon, "Son, I think your best efforts would be to take your men out to the mountains and begin searching. As soon as we get something of value out of these two, I'll get it rushed right out to you. Why don't you go by and pick up her folks and let them ride out there with you. I'm sure they will need some comforting too."

Second Day of Searching

"Thank you, Joshua. If I stay here much longer these suspects will either be dead or deaf from my screaming."

"Exactly. I'm glad you see it my way." And Joshua squeezed Salmon's upper arm. "Now go out there and find that girl. Do you hear?"

"Yes, sir," said Salmon and he left the tent. A soldier was waiting for Salmon to report that the search party had assembled by the trader's tents. They rode out front and Salmon saw the group of volunteers was larger than yesterday. "How many men do we have here?"

"When I assembled the men an hour ago, there were a little over 400, but it looks like some more have arrived. They all want to help find the Scarlet Cord Woman."

Salmon led all the search party to the front of Friends Camp just as Joseph was bringing out the wagon and horse. Mother was checking to see if the clothes, food, and wash cloths were still in the wagon. Olmad, Dad, and Ari El joined Joseph in the wagon and they rode off with the entire search party. It was now almost 500 strong.

The wagon was slowing them up, so Salmon started riding to the different leaders and gave them permission to go on and begin the search. Soon there were men and horses climbing over the mountains and peering into open caves.

Rahab sucked in the fresh air like it was life itself. The sky was clear. It would be a hot day in the sunshine. Her cave was cool though. She began to look around one more time to see if there was anything she could use to attract attention in case someone came looking for her. She reasoned that anything left in the cave was God-given and she could use it to aid in her escape. All she saw were the two red straps that had bound her, the bag that held the stale food, a few little rocks and some clumps of dirt. Not much to go on. She would have to rely on her faith that God would send someone to get her. She did take one of the red straps and pushed it outside her cave opening onto the ledge. However, when the old goat came, he picked it up in his mouth and carried it off.

Back at Gilgal, the questioning of the two dirty men drew little response. They simply said that they did not remember anything about an alien helping anybody. They knew nothing about a kidnapping. They knew nothing about any storage tent, evidence, women's panties or anything else they were being accused of. The two men only claimed one tent that they lived in; they had no storage tent. Different men tried different approaches, but they got nowhere.

Eleazar, the High Priest, came to the door of the army tent but did not come in. He asked how the interviews were going. He was told they weren't going anywhere. He asked if he might try and would they bring them out into the sunshine. The two were brought out.

"Good morning. I am Eleazar, the High Priest. I am the one who conducts the sacrifices and makes the offerings in behalf of people who have sinned. Should I prepare for a sacrifice in your behalf?"

There was no response.

"You understand that it is not up to me to determine who sins and who doesn't sin. Only God knows, but that is enough. If you have sinned, then God already knows it. He knew it the minute you sinned and you already know that there is only one punishment for sin. Its death. You break any of the rules and God takes your life. Unless...unless you make an offering and have an animal killed in your behalf. Someone is going to die for a sin. It is either the one who commits the sin or an animal offered in his behalf. Now, which is it with you two: Do you want to make an offering or shall I go call this whole matter to the attention of God Almighty?" The old man raised his shaking hand to his chin and looked at the two men. He seemed to be looking directly into their souls, but they said nothing.

"I have scheduled a prayer time shortly, what would you have me say?"

The two scruffy men looked at each other and back to the

High Priest. They were hesitant. They were trying to arrive at a decision. Finally, one said, "Sir, do as you wish. We ain't committed no sin. We ain't done nothin' that would involve you, God, or these soldiers. We ain't got nothin' to say."

"Then, I commend your souls to the Almighty God who created you," and the High Priest looked them over again. The men felt that Eleazar was going to bring judgment upon them directly. Instead he said, "You are at the mercy of God's judgment." As he walked away the men's hearts hung heavy in their chests. Their chance for salvation was walking away from them.

Two soldiers took the dirty men back to the holding area. They had them strip off their clothes and then threw buckets of river water on them in an effort to clean them up a bit. While they threw water on them, other soldiers brought them two dry tunics.

Back at the mountains, more than 500 men were combing from top to bottom looking for Rahab. Each was frequently calling out the name of Rahab. The name Rahab was bouncing from mountain side to mountain side in a continuous echo and Rahab heard it. The sunshine moved from the sky to her face. There were people out searching for her! *"God, how can I help them find me?"*

"If I can only get that old Billy goat away maybe someone can find me," she was talking to herself. She reached through the hole and pushed at the goat, but he didn't move. She shoved at him again, but he only became irritated. The ledge belonged to him and nobody was going to take it away from him. He turned to look at her hand trying to push him away. He stood and stared. In disgust, Rahab reached out and grabbed his leg and pulled it into the hole. The goat began to squirm trying to get out of her trap, but she held on. Then he started bleating, crying out for someone to help him. The longer Rahab held on to the goat, the louder he cried. The harder she held on, the harder the goat pulled at her grasp. The old goat was crying as loud as he could, straining against Rahab's hold. Slowly the goat was winning and was pulling his leg out of the hole along with Rahab's hand. She was about to lose him.

Ari El was only a short distance away from the troubled goat. He raced over to see what the matter was. How could a goat be caught in something this high up on the mountain? Rahab yanked on the goat's leg again, harder and harder, and the goat yelped louder and louder.

Ari El was on top side of the goat and then saw a woman's hand holding onto the goat's leg. He yelled, "Miss Rahab is that you?"

"Yes, Ari El. Can you help me?"

Ari El stuck two fingers into the corners of his mouth like Salmon did and tried to whistle, but only air came out. So he did what he knew to do best. He yelled. "Hey! Everybody! OVER HERE! I've found her! I have found Miss Rahab! Come here. Help me!" Six big, strong soldiers came running over and moved the stones from the mouth of the cave. By the time they were ready to reach in and extract her from the prison, Olmad, Dad, and Salmon were at the opening.

"Oh, baby, I'm so glad to see you," her father said. With gentle and trembling hands he reached for his daughter's hands and began to gently pull her from the narrow cave.

"Oh, Daddy, I'm so glad to see you," Rahab was crying. "I was afraid I would never get out of here. Thank God for this chance to be with you."

Olmad reached in to get her under her arms and to support her. "Just take it easy. We will have you out in a minute. Are you hurt anywhere?

"Olmad, you look so good. It is so good to be coming out of that hole. My feet hurt. I hurt my feet."

When Salmon saw that she could not stand because of her sore feet, he reached under her and picked her up and carried her out to the ledge. "Come here, darling, let me carry you to somewhere safe. Here, sit on this ledge and let me get a look at you." He carefully placed her down on the ledge so she could sit up and then he reached around her and hugged her and kissed her. "I thank God you are back with us," he said as he wiped his tears on her shoulder.

Olmad and Dad were right there to hug her and kiss her and look her over. Everyone was crying.

Rahab was crying. Salmon was crying for joy. "Praise the Lord, He has answered my prayers," said Salmon. 500 soldiers began to applaud and cheer across the mountains. The sounds bounced from one mountain side to another. It was an echo of happiness and victory. Victory was in the air. However, the soldiers maintained their distance so the family could share some element of privacy in the saving of Rahab.

Olmad stood tall in the sunlight with tears of joy coming down his face. He reached over and hugged his father with his father's head on his shoulder hiding the older man's tears.

When Ari El made the big announcement, Joseph had the sense to run for the wagon and bring it closer. He brought her food, and clean, wet towels. Rahab began to wash her face, arms, and hands. Through her tears, she kept repeating herself. "Oh, this feels so good. Oh, this feels so good. This water feels so good."

Five hundred soldiers began climbing down the mountains, clapping their hands in unison and singing, "Blessed be God from whom all blessings flow. Bless this creature here below. For she is found and is alive. Blessed be the Almighty." And the world was filled with music. The lost had been found.

After everyone had caught their breath, they looked for a way to get her down the mountain side. She was almost 100 feet above the wagon trail. She could not walk, so first Salmon picked her up and carried her part way and then Olmad carried her further. Then Salmon again, until they were at the wagon. They sat her up in the rear of the wagon.

As the family moved away, five soldiers, trained in spotting, came to the cave site and began examining it. At first there was not much to see. But closer examination revealed a set of two-wheel tracks not far apart. Probably from a little two-wheel cart used to pull her up the incline. They collected the two red straps that had bound her, noting the teeth marks on one where she had chewed herself loose. They found the bare spots from the ground around the cave opening where the rocks had been moved. The soldiers followed the wheel tracks and discovered a dirty old blanket with blood stains on it and they included it in the evidence.

At the wagon, Joseph gave Rahab some water to drink. Her mouth was dry and her throat was sore, so the water felt doubly good. Salmon was beside himself. How could he help her? Between his own tears of happiness and joy, he reached for a piece of bread, dipped it into some sauce and offered it to her mouth. He sat beside her and fed her several bites.

He was so concerned over getting Rahab back, that he had forgotten his duty. As he remembered, he called one of the soldiers over and told him to ride like the wind back to camp. "First, go to Rahab's family in Friends Camp and tell her Mother that we have found Rahab and she is all right. Then go to Joshua and tell him the good news, too. Like the wind. Race like the wind. This is great news!" And the messenger sped away with the good news.

The lieutenants began gathering their men back to their horses and they rode by slowly, shouting "Hosanna! Hosanna! God is great!"

Soon the area was quiet and only the family and Salmon were at the wagon with Rahab. Olmad examined her feet and saw how bruised and cut they were. He got a cloth that Mother had included and began binding her feet.

Ari El reached for the robe and brought it to Rahab. "Miss Rahab, your mother sent you a clean robe. She said that you would not want to be seen in camp in your nightgown. I have a shawl here for you, too."

Then Rahab looked down and for the first time realized that she was there in full view of everyone in her night gown. It was all dirty and muddy. Olmad and her father stood there not sure what to do, but Salmon took charge. "Let me help you. Just take the straps off your shoulders and I'll slide your robe over your head, then run your hands up the sleeves one by one. After that, I'll let it down over your chest and you can slip off your gown. Take your time. I know that you are sore. Just take it easy."

Rahab hesitated a little, but then obeyed the man who can now be her husband. Slowly she slipped the right strap down and then the left strap, holding the gown in place with her left arm. Salmon ran his hands up the loose robe until he found the neck and sleeve openings and gently placed it over her head. Rahab felt his gentleness until both of her hands were in the sleeves and the robe fell down over her gown. The men slowly lifted her to her bound feet and the gown fell to the ground. Then they sat her back down and helped her to lie down.

Olmad picked up the gown and began loosely folding it until he noticed something. There was a blood stain in the center. A dirty, blood stain. His first thoughts were that his sister had been raped. He wasn't sure what to do. Then he decided that the others should know it also. So when Rahab was comfortable in the wagon, he told his father and Salmon within hearing distance of the two servants that he thought Rahab had been raped by the kidnappers. Salmon's face turned beet red and fury rose from the collar of his tunic up his throat, face and hairline. He punched the side of the wagon to release his anger. Her father's reaction was almost the same, but more controlled.

"We should be getting Rahab back to the camp so her mother can attend to her," said her father.

Joseph took the driver's seat and the other men took turns

ministering to Rahab on the way back.

The Good News

A cloud of dust marked the trail of the messenger of good news. His horse was at top speed as he leaned on the neck of the stallion to encourage even more speed. Some people in front of Friends Camp were the first to see the approaching cloud. They had gathered near Rahab's family site. The rider came to the front and pulled the horse to a stop, leaping down before the dust could reach him. He ran to the waiting arms of Mother and hugged her so tightly, as if to snap her in two. "I have great news! Rahab has been found and she is all right! She is safe and sound!"

Every one present gave a mighty shout of happiness. Mother wouldn't let the young messenger go. She held on to him with her top of the list hug so he could hardly breathe. She started kissing him and saying over and over again, "Praise the Lord, thank you my boy. Praise the Lord, thank you my boy. My baby has been found!"

When the messenger finally got loose from Mother, he excused himself and told everyone he had to get to Joshua and tell him. So he rode straight for the Circle of Government shouting from his entrance. "Rahab has been found! She is alive and well!"

The shouts of joy brought everyone out of the tents in the big circle and they all began applauding the good news. Joshua and his attendants came out of their meeting and the young messenger ran to him to repeat the good news. Instead, Joshua reached out and hugged the boy. "You did a fine job, young man. Take a seat here and catch your breath." Then he turned to his aide and said, "Take care of his horse. This boy needs some rest."

The messenger began giving details. "She was in a very small cave high up the side of one of the mountains. It had been closed off with stones. It was hard to find. We probably would not have found it but for a Billy goat. Rahab had been able to push out a few small stones and a goat was lying nearby. She just grabbed one of the goat's legs and pulled it so hard that the goat began crying and that attracted one of their servants and he found her. Then they pulled her from the cave. She has some scrapes and gashes on her, especially her feet, but nothing appeared life threatening. She is alive and well. The family is returning together in their wagon. Salmon is with them. There was a team of spotters searching the site for evidence. I expect that they will be in shortly."

"You have done a good job, young man. Thank for you being

able to bring us such good news," said Joshua.

The council waited until the family had brought Rahab into camp and they were able to determine her injuries and condition before they met to consider judgment. They also wanted to see the report from the men collecting evidence and to hear Salmon's report.

Rahab was received at home with open arms from all the family. Her mother examined her carefully and rebound her sore feet. She determined that Rahab had been raped.

Meanwhile, Salmon reported into army headquarters and helped the others bring focus to the evidence and prepare for judgment. Joshua had to move quickly. He had a battle going on.

So, that evening after dinner, Joshua moved the judgment hearing to the front of the camp behind the trading tents for the convenience of Rahab. The men brought out oil lamps to light the area. Then, Joshua sent a cart down to pick up Rahab and her family. The two suspects were brought out in their clean tunics to hear the evidence against them.

The Charges

One of the soldiers opened the trial. "Your Honor, we are ready to provide evidence that will prove the following facts and charges: Rahab, the Woman with the Scarlet Cord, was asleep when these two men stole into her tent, bound her and took her to the caves in the mountains. In the mountains, they raped her and hid her in a small cave against her will. Fortunately, after a search by a large group of people, she was found and is returned to us. These men have violated the Laws of God to wit:

"Law number five: Honor your father and your mother. They have brought dishonor to their parent's name by doing such dreadful deeds. We will present witnesses to testify they have been drunk in public. They have brought false accusation against the neighbors. They have conducted detestable acts in public. And they have disturbed the peacefulness of the camp. They have shamed their parents. Breaking this law is a cause for death.

"Law number six: You shall not commit murder. While these men did not actually take this young woman's life, they intended to by leaving her unattended in a place with very little food and water. They sealed the small grave-like cave so she could not escape by herself. They have committed murder in their hearts. Breaking this law is a cause for death.

"Law number seven: You shall not commit adultery. These two men have violated this woman and her mother will testify that rape was committed against this woman while she was in the possession and confinement of these two men. Breaking this law is a cause for death.

"Law number eight: You shall not steal. We have evidence, including the binding straps, containers of a knockout substance that these two men used to steal this woman from her bed and hide her in the caves of the mountains. Breaking this law is a cause for death.

"Law number nine: You shall not give false testimony against your neighbor. These two men have repeatedly denied ever seeing Rahab or her family. Yet, we have witnesses to declare that not only did they visit their campsite last night, but several times before. They have been bringing accusations against these people while in a drunken stupor. Breaking this law is a cause for death.

"Law number ten: You shall not covet your neighbor's wife or anything he owns. We propose that a daughter belongs to the family and the accused have coveted the daughter so much that they humiliated her, kidnapped her and raped her and left her to die in the mountains. Breaking this law is a cause for death.

"But most importantly, sir, they have broken Law number one: You shall have no other gods before me. We are prepared to demonstrate that these men have let greed, selfishness, covetousness, and evil to become their gods in place of the Lord God Almighty. Breaking this law is a cause for death." The presenter of the charges then sat down.

"And what do you men have to say for yourselves?" Joshua was giving the accused a chance to respond.

"This is all a surprise to us. We don't know nothin'. We ain't done nothin'. We was just out walkin' for some fresh air last night when some soldiers come up and grabbed us and started yelling at us. They broke this man's good arm. Besides, this woman here is just a whore. She's the one that needs to be questioned. How can you let a harlot live in the camp? God will strike us all down by letting her stay here. She's just covering us. We ain't done nothin', because, anyways, she don't count. She's just a whore. And whores are things, not people." The accused man sat down, holding his bound hands in front. A booing and hissing noise rose from the crowd.

Rahab's Response

Then Joshua turned to Rahab and asked if she had anything to say to these men. She was sitting in the back of the wagon because of her sore feet. The men pushed the wagon into the light, up close for her to speak. "I am sorry to see you two men here. I am sorry that all these charges have been brought against you. I was hoping you would learn your lessons every time you were escorted away from our camp. But I guess you didn't learn much and today you are accused of crimes that will take your life away.

"I am just now learning how you were in my tent and that you drugged me and carried me away from my family. I know nothing about the trip to the mountains. If I had been awake when you raped me, you are not likely to have any eyes, hair or other parts to your body left. I don't know how you got me into that little cave or how much time you spent sealing over the entrance. But I do know how frightened I was when I woke up in total darkness. I was blind.

"I was terrified when there was no answer to my screams and calls for help. O, how I cried out to your God, the God you have abandoned. I cried for His help and He supplied it. It was His strength that brought me through this awful time. It was His strength that kept me alive. It was His strength and power that brought all those people out to search for me, when you could have admitted it and saved so many people so much effort. I thank each and every one of them. I thank God for each and every one of them." Rahab looked around the crowd that had gathered for the Judgment hearing. She saw soldiers who had been up on the mountains searching for her. She had her family, including Salmon and the servants beside her.

"I'm not sure why God sent you two into my life, except to cause my faith to grow. Well, it has grown by leaps and bounds and I will never again doubt the power and wisdom of God. I can thank you for that.

"I can't imagine why you would want to throw away such a blessing: To go about trying to live your life without God. Don't you remember that it was God who prepared things so your mother would conceive you? Isn't it important to you anymore that it was God who provided the correct environment for that little egg to grow so that one day He could pull out little arms and legs and a head. It was God who decided whether you would have curly hair or straight. It was God who determined the color of your eyes. It was God who determined if you would be a boy or a girl. Yet, you throw all of that away. Isn't it important to you that it was God who gave you your very first breath of air...who gives you the air to breathe even to this day? Isn't God important to you at all? Yet, you live so selfishly that you have deliberately broken 8 of the 10 commandments.

Rahab stopped to wipe the tears from her face and to reach for Salmon's hand. She looked back at the two scruffy men and said, "I feel so sorry for you. You are a very unlovable pair standing there. And I suspect that may be one reason you are in judgment today. You have isolated yourselves from the community and you don't feel their love. And you don't extend any love to them. This is another way you have driven God away, because God is love.

"Let me tell you this. I'm sorry for your decisions, and for your life-style. Someone needs to love you and have mercy on you. So I will. I forgive you for the harm you have done to me and to yourselves. I pray that God will have mercy on you. I forgive you for violating me, for leaving me for dead, for causing my family such a fright, and for causing hundreds of soldiers to come to my aid. I forgive you and I extend mercy to you by making this proclamation to the judge." Then Rahab turned toward Joshua and directed her voice to him. "I know, sir, these two have broken God's law and it requires death as punishment. But can they be taken out of the camp to find God's mercy? And if God wills them to live, then they can live. If God wills them to die then they die by themselves and not by the hands of the community here."

Then Rahab turned back to the men in chains and almost yelled at them. "I say that you two are the prostitutes. You have twisted God's laws to suit your own whims. The very act you sought to save was the act you brought about by your own deceit, your selfishness, and for your own personal satisfaction. You have prostituted the laws of your own Lord. May God have mercy on you." Then Rahab bowed her head and began to cry.

The crowd was stone quiet. Joshua looked at the two men and back to Rahab and her family. He was expected to hear evidence against the two men. Instead, he turned back to the two men with the scruffy beards and hair and said, "So be it. According to the procedures established during the leadership of Moses, you are to be carried out into the wilderness, away from this encampment, with nothing but the tunics you are now wearing. Each of you shall have a travel robe, one skin of water, and one bag of food. You will be at the mercy of God." Joshua paused, then he stood up and said "Men, carry them away."

Four soldiers took the arms of the men and that night carried them deep into the wilderness south of the Jericho Plains, never to be heard from again.

Joshua watched the men lead the accused away. He remained standing and called to the crowd, "Men of Israel, consecrate yourselves this night so that the camp of Israel may be free from sin. The Lord has given us the enemy on the battle field. We must go possess the land, but we must walk the land free of sin. Consecrate yourselves and see the wonders of God tomorrow."

The group was quiet as they began to leave for home. Salmon was standing by the wagon with Rahab and her family. He took Rahab's hand and she turned to look into his face. He smiled and said, "I'm so very proud of you. You are so courageous." Love was radiating from his eyes.

Rahab just smiled at him. Her heart was sad. She didn't know that she was pronouncing judgment on the two men. She only wanted to express her thoughts and tell them that she forgave them for their sins against her. She had never made a speech before. Certainly she had never made one with such results.

Salmon turned to the family and said, "I've got to pack, for we will be leaving for the battle field shortly. Joshua wants to be back by sun up. We have work to do. I am still not sure when I'll be back. But whenever that is, I still want to marry this little girl here and give her all the love in my heart. Can you please begin some plans for the wedding? I'll send my parents over to meet with you. And when I can get free I'll rush back to see you. Jonathan will help too. I would like to see him perform the service, if that is all right with everyone."

Then he turned and hugged Mother and she hugged him back. He whispered, "You are still on the top of my list." And he smiled. Mother was quiet, with tears in her eyes, and she reached up to the tall boy and kissed him. Then Salmon went around the circle and hugged everyone there, including the servants Ari El and Joseph. Then he came to Rahab.

"How do I tell you I love you? How can I express how important you are to me? How can I tell you how proud I am of how you survived this enormous test of faith? I'm sorry that you had to go through all this and for the pain that it has caused you and everyone else, but I am so grateful that God gave you the strength to survive. And that He has blessed you with yet another new beginning: One filled with love all around you. A life filled with respect of all of Israel. A life that has captured my whole heart. I so look forward to spending the rest of my days with you. Living with you will be such a blessing. I love you with all my heart." And Salmon hugged Rahab up close. She whispered something in his ear. He smiled, kissed her again, and slowly walked away into the encampment. At the entrance to Judah, he turned and waved, calling out, "I plan to see you soon."

Rahab and her family went back to their campsite, understanding they were secure and safe for the night. The family was whole again.

16

The Longest Day

A rain storm blew in on the tail of a gusty sharp wind, just before Joshua, Salmon, and the guards left Gilgal for Gibeon. It was coming from the left, bitter cold, and stinging their faces. The early morning hours were dark. The blinding rain soaked into their camel hair robes. The weave of the robes swelled to form waterproof raincoats for the men but they were still damp from the blowing rain.

It was a long, treacherous trip up the ridge of the mountains and then down the other side. The horses kept sliding and faltering on the hard, slippery land. It was slow going. The little group was able to reach Gibeon about an hour before sunrise. Then the rain clouds began to clear away and the dawn came in unusual glory, lighting up a hidden rainbow.

"Ok, men, where do we stand?" Joshua was in command of the battle site again, with no mention made of what happened in Gilgal.

The report from his commanders was brief and to the point. The battle for Gibeon had been contained, there was no more fighting and the city was not damaged. Their spotters had sent back messages last night that most of the few fighters who escaped, were returning to their home towns. The kings had gone to the caves near Makkedah. The spotters were still working on a way to get their army down the steep and dangerous trail to Lower Beth Horon. They had found on alternate way for the wagons farther south of Beth Horon.

This morning they needed to move the army down the slope, verify that there were no enemy in the valley, and regroup near Makkedah in order to take that town. There were seven towns to capture and then the southern portion of the Promised Land would belong to the Israelites.

"Feed your men breakfast and let's get going," said the commander. Breakfast call was sounded and 40,000 men came to breakfast served by the Gibeon slaves. Joshua gathered his leaders around him and began to ask the Lord's blessings on this day. "O Lord of heaven and earth, we glorify your name in all that we say and do. We ask that you accompany us today. Help us to remember that this is your battle and we are clearing your land of idol worshipers. Help us to keep our perspectives straight and our mind on target. Keep the evil one away from us so that we may do your good work. Amen."

Joshua and a few leaders walked over to the ridge and surveyed the scene below. Beth Horon was a town built in two parts on a steep mountain side. The two parts were connected by simple trails that descended 500 feet over two miles. From the top ridge of Upper Beth Horon, you could see across the beautiful Aijalon Valley. The Israelites, who gazed at its beauty, began to understand why this was called the land of milk and honey. Memories of harsh desert fade quickly when men see lush green meadows accented with beautiful trees.

Spotters were posted at the foot of the incline protecting the soldiers from any of the rag-a-tags that might still be hiding in ambush.

As the movement began in earnest, Joshua could see that it would take days to make this one decent. The morning sun was still close to the eastern horizon and the moon was shining low in the western horizon — pale like a ghost. They needed more time, a lot more time. So he gathered a few men around him again and this time prayed very specifically. Looking up into the heavens back toward Gibeon, Joshua lifted up his old arm and pointed his finger to the sky and prayed, "O sun, stand still over Gibeon." Then he turned westward and again lifted his arm to heaven and pointed to the lesser light and prayed, "O moon, over the Valley of Aijalon."

And God heard his short prayer and began answering it immediately. The few leftover clouds from the night's rainstorm simply dissolved in the clear sky. A little encouraging breeze blew in and shoved the loose leaves and dust down the incline to Lower Beth Huron. The leaves danced along, as if saying, "Come follow me."

The men working on the tangled slopes suddenly felt stronger. Three men attempting to move a cart of food to the lower level were straining against the cart to keep it from running away. Their shoulders were pressed against the front of the cart with one man steering the wooden tongue. Then as the sun stood still, their load lightened and their arms and legs were not sore any more from the strain. They began to talk without grunting. Soon they were laughing and telling jokes as they eased the cart on down the long incline. They didn't understand why, but they weren't asking questions either.

Fifty feet to their left, Gibeon slaves were struggling with a cart with a water barrel on it. It was heavy. Some slaves were in the front to guide the wheels down the path and six other men were holding the cart steady with a long rope. Then the magic moment came and the load was light. Something had happened.

Other men got hatchets from a supply wagon and began chopping the prickly vines away from the pathways, making it easier to descend. More and more men began to fill the pathways. But the sun stayed near the horizon. The temperature remained cool. No one was sweating. The men in their fighting gear opened more pathways and soon the hillside was flooded with soldiers and small carts of necessary items. It was a very pleasant day.

In Upper Beth Huron, the war wagons carrying regular supplies moved a few miles down a little road that led to Aijalon. They were able to move several wagons at a time. They, too, noticed a change in the day. Something was happening. Work was easier. There seemed to be no need to hurry. There was no explanation for the changes.

One of the soldiers was heard saying, "I don't know what's happening, but something sure is. Logic tells me we have been working here several hours, yet look at the sun. It's still in the morning sky. This is a different kind of day. I feel God present, just as though He's saying, 'Take your time. It's ok. I'm in control. This is my battle and you're doing fine. You have plenty of time. I'll see to it.' — Does anyone else feel this?"

The soldiers around him agreed, but they couldn't explain it either. The Army of God continued to pour down the mountain side and the war wagons continued to flow down at Aijalon. As the traffic made it onto the valley floor so did the sun progress across the sky. When the army was in place on the meadows, the sun set in the western sky turning the heavens first crimson red and then briefly purple, before white lace appeared around two or three little clouds. Then the full moon cast its reflected light onto the meadow and the army continued to work with the ease and freshness of early morning. It became known as The Longest Day, for there has never been one like it before or since.

Later that evening, Salmon and some of the men recognized that a miracle had taken place. While they were in the midst of the long day they were not aware of it. They kept working without tiring. They were busy encouraging and helping others to make the desperate trip down among the thorny bushes, treating their scrapes and cuts. "Time stood still today," Salmon heard himself saying. "Joshua asked God to extend the day and He did. God listened to a man, and granted his request. Can you believe that?" God was indeed in charge of their mission. "To Him be the glory," Salmon told his group. "We have made up the day that the enemy lost coming down the ridge. Now we can rest."

It took a few more days for the scope of the miracle to sink into the men. God had, again, made a way where there was no way. Just as He opened the river for them to cross, as He had made the walls of Jericho crumble, as He had rained hail on the enemy but not the Israelites, so now God extends the day for His people to make up for lost time. "God is not only the God of earth, but He is also the Lord over the sun and the moon and the heavens," said Salmon.

The miracle of the longest day was peculiar to that one region. The people in Gilgal were not part of it. It was an ordinary day for them. Joseph came and stoked the fire. Then he squatted to his heels with his bare feet in the sand and looked toward the western hills. Dad started water for tea and took his cushion facing west to watch the sky light up. They sat in silence until Mother started breakfast.

Olmad's servant girl tended to Rahab most of the day, keeping her in the tent. She had opened the end flaps to let the breeze blow through and swept the thick rug that covered the ground in the tent. She said it would feel good to Rahab's feet when they healed some. Rahab sat up but did not put pressure on her feet that day. Ari El kept popping in and out wanting to know what he could do to make Rahab feel better. Otherwise, it was a usual day in Gilgal.

God's army marched out into the broad meadows of Aijalon. Forty thousand soldiers saw the trees and flowers everywhere. The reds, purples, yellows, oranges and a beautiful shade of blue caused Salmon to think of Rahab. In the distance were the gently rolling hills. The spotters led the soldiers down the trade route towards Makkedah. The closer they got, the more hills there were. The hills were dotted with caves. The spotters had already reported where the enemy was hiding.

Salmon took his group out to look for the kings in accordance to the instructions of the spotters. The kings were careless in their moving about, so it was not difficult to spot their trail. Salmon and his team crept up to the side of three different caves. At the third one, they could hear the kings and their advisors talking. The kings never heard the Israelites. The men took several big stones, and as quietly as they could, moved them to the entrance and sealed the opening. The kings had a fire going and soon there was a stream of smoke bellowing out the cracks between the stones. The kings were yelling and coughing.

The men posted two guards and left without saying a word. There were many loud threats coming from inside the cave, but the guards only listened in silence. Salmon and his team joined the rest of the army and helped squash some renegades on their may to Makkedah.

Later on orders, Salmon and his team brought Joshua the kings of Jerusalem, Hebron, Jarmuth, Lachish and Eglon. Joshua ordered, "Tie their hands and feet and throw them to the ground in a row."

When the guard detail had done so, Joshua said, "All you commanders come here and put your foot on the neck of one of these kings. Don't be afraid. Don't be discouraged. Be strong and courageous. This is what the Lord will do to all the enemies you are going to fight." Then Joshua, himself, struck and killed the kings and had them hung on five trees. They were left hanging until evening, when he ordered the bodies taken down and returned to the cave where they had been hiding. The cave was then sealed with large stones.

Darkness fell on the land as the crew returned from the caves. Under the night sky, Joshua's army attacked the walls of Makkedah and destroyed the royal city. Not one living thing was left. Everything was reduced to rubble and then set on fire. It burned most of the night. The army took no spoils, because the Lord had not permitted it.

While the fires were burning Makkedah, the Hebrews practiced their custom of spending several hours of quiet solitude, reflecting on the mighty power of God and expressing their thanksgiving for the protection of the Almighty. Joshua had his command post moved from Gibeon to the Makkedah vicinity.

Joshua told his commanders, "Men, I think we can wrap this

up pretty quickly and get back home. These towns are going to be helpless without their kings and armies. I don't think there will be much of a fight in any of the places. Let's divide up the towns and go after them all at one time."

"I'm certainly for it. I'm ready to go home. I hear there may be a little wedding back there soon." And a gruff old man winked at Joshua and Salmon.

"Ok, Ok, you can come to the wedding," Salmon was holding up his hands in surrender. "Just get me home so I can help in the planning. I want to remember who it is I'm marrying."

"Oh, you'll remember that. She's the one with the rolling pin," mocked the gruff man. And the group laughed. Then it was back to serious business.

"Let's divide this up. One group goes after the deep south area, say Hebron, and Debir. A second group takes Lachish and Eglon. And one group stays here for Libnah. Then we all head for Jerusalem, and go home together," suggested Joshua.

"But how are we going to keep up with each other," someone asked from the back of the room.

"Good point. Who has a suggestion?" The commander-in-chief asked.

"We'll have the spotters in front of us laying down the course. How about some additional spotters with messengers in the rear who can be dispatched each evening to bring word back to command here?"

"I had rather see two messages a day. One in the morning and one late afternoon, if all goes as we expect. If something happens then we get additional messengers out, so additional troops can come help. The messengers can make round trips. They'll bring information from the field to command and on the next trip; take command information to the battle front. The troops here in command can act as backups if we run into any surprises. I guess, Joshua, you'll keep your daily messenger service to and from Gilgal?"

Joshua was nodding in agreement. "Yes, of course. I think that will do. Working like this we won't have to move so much material and supplies. You know what our mission is: Search and destroy. Our mission is to wipe out all of the idolaters. So, as you go to your destination cities, cleanse the land as you go. Destroy all idols and idol worshipers. God is with us and has already given us the victory. All we must do is claim it. His mercy is on the land. Is that clear?"

"Very clear," the answer came from every part of the room.

Joshua stood up to make the final announcements. "Team A moves out first in the morning for Hebron and Debir. Team B goes second for Lachish and Eglon. Get your spotters to lay a straight course, forgetting the trade routes, except where it will expedite your journey. Then, when they are on the way, Team C takes on Libnah. When we hear that these cities are destroyed and burned then we'll all head straight for Jerusalem, meeting up along the trail. Get a good night's rest men. Tomorrow is a work day."

"Yes, sir," they all chanted.

The usual ring of guards encircled the Army of God that night, but little protection was needed. All the people nearby where afraid of the power of the Israelite army and they kept their distance.

A Secret Message

The messenger from the battle front rode in fast and furious waving his pouch high in the air. He went right through the entrance guard and straight to the Circle of Government. Two Gibeonite servants were ready to take care of his horse, while the messenger reported to the command tent and brought news of the battle. In the pouch were two scrolls. One was for the people operating the government in Joshua's absence. It told of the battle scenes and asked questions about Gilgal. The lieutenants already had their report ready but read Joshua's and then answered his questions on the end of it and were ready to stuff it back into the pouch for the return journey.

The other scroll was addressed to Rahab. "Who is this Rahab?" One of the young men at the table was asking. "Is this some kind of mail service we started running around here?" His voice had a little sarcasm in it.

"Rahab? Isn't that the same as the Woman with the Scarlet Cord? The one saved from Jericho?" And a conversation was started about how she could rate a personal message in the official command pouch. Then slowly the new men on duty began to put things together. She was the one that had been kidnapped and had spoken at the judgment.

"Her feet were all bandaged up. She had been hurt."

"She's the one who was raped."

"That's right. Poor woman. I'll take it over there," said another man.

"I'll go with you," said another.

"Me, too," said yet another.

And so the scroll was delivered by an official honor guard of Israel. Six men guarded and delivered one scroll to an alien in Friends Camp. Such an event had never happened before. The men marched from the Circle of Government to Friends Camp, asked for directions at Friends Camp and then at the proper place inquired, "Is this the campsite of Miss Rahab? It's official."

The men had all gone to work, but Rahab's mother, met the men and showed them Rahab's tent. She pulled back the tent flap and called to Rahab, "Honey, the army has a message for you."

Rahab looked up to see six men standing there with one little scroll. She accepted it and began to open it. The soldiers just stood there wanting to see what was inside. "It's from Salmon! Salmon has sent me a letter. I guess he still wants to marry me."

The soldiers were leaning forward to hear more of this love letter. But Rahab caught their eyes and mentioned that the letter had nothing to do with the logistics of the battlefront and the men were free to return to their work. "But, thank you so very much for bringing this to me. Mother, can you get them some little cakes, or something?"

On their way back to their post, the soldiers were mumbling something about wishing they could hear more of the love letter. "We don't get love letters through the command post."

Rahab didn't share the contents of the note, except to say that Salmon loved her and was ready to get married as soon as they got back. There was a new glow, a new radiance, about her that lasted all day.

She decided it was important to tell Salmon's parents that she had heard from him. She called for Ari El and asked him to bring the wagon around, she wanted to go into Judah and see Salmon's parents. Mother was shocked that she should try such a journey with her feet still bandaged but agreed that a change of scenery might do her good.

Rahab liked visiting with Salmon's folks. They were older than her parents, and very kind and gentle. She often had long conversations with Nahshon, his father. This time Ari El signaled the horse to pull the wagon up close to the outside bench where Nahshon like to sit. Rahab waved to the old man and called to him, "Good morning. How are you doing?"

"Rahab! The important question is, How are you doing?"

"Just fine. This is Ari El. He's my driver for the day. He's also the guy I choose when I need strong protection." Ari El just smiled as he helped Rahab down from the wagon and to a bench.

"If Ari El is here to protect you, then my dear, I promise not to have a fight with you today." The old man reached for her arm to help her sit on the bench. Then he sat beside her and Ari El went back to the wagon.

"I heard from Salmon today. He sent a letter through Joshua's messenger service. Six soldiers delivered it to me just a little while ago. He is doing fine. Staying busy, but doing fine." Rahab was glowing. Nahshon knew there was more to the letter than what she reported, but he didn't inquire. He was happy to hear the good news.

"That is good news. I'm glad to hear that they made it back and that the battles are going well." Nahshon was looking directly into Rahab's face. He was reading how she was truly feeling. "Tell me again, how you are doing."

"Pretty good. That was a frightening experience of waking up shut up in a dark cave. Not knowing where you are, or how you got there. Or even how you would get out. It was scary. It brought back feelings of Jericho. I guess those are my two most frightening experiences in my life. I remember being in Jericho when all those soldiers came and started killing everyone. I'll never forget all that crying and screaming. I'll never forget that awful smell."

"I know, dear. I know," said the old man. He patted her hand.

Rahab paused to look away, to control her emotions. "And when I woke up in that dark cave and thought I was blind, and I didn't know where I was. I cried when I guessed that someone had buried me alive in that hole. I don't think I have ever been so dependent on God than in those two events in my life." Rahab began to shake in fear as she recalled the episodes.

"Then you have an idea of what purification is like." Nahshon had returned to his favorite subject. "You know something of growing closer to God. You now have an idea of how God can answer your prayers. When you are totally helpless and there is no way out, yet you do get out, then you can give all the credit to God. I have found that so often in my own life and those of others, God often has your solution prepared, all you must do is ask him."

"Like that old goat on the hillside," said Rahab.

"Exactly. You were trying to push away the answer God had sent you. Fortunately, the goat was stubborn and in your frustration set off the alarm that God had sent you days before you needed it."

Nahshon patted his knee, reassuring himself that God has sent the Billy goat to Rahab.

Rahab reached over and hugged him. She held his stooped shoulders that were once so broad. She felt his tough whiskers against her face. She felt his weak arms reach around her in tenderness. But most of all, Rahab felt his wisdom, his tenderness, and the great love he had for God.

"I must get back home, but I hope to see you soon. If I hear anything else from that son of yours, I'll be sure to let you know."

"You do that. You do that," Nahshon repeated himself as he waved.

The First Team

The next morning swept in like a symphonic fanfare. The sky lighted up suddenly and chased away the stars and darkness. A rush of birds flew overhead and a chorus of wolves in the distance seemed to be chanting some mystical song. A gusty breeze darted here and there to see what branches would rattle or whoosh, or sigh. It was work day on the battle front.

Salmon's team had the farthest to go, so they left first. They would take about 10,000 soldiers, some wagons to carry them in and a few more for supplies. They only took about 200 Gibeonite slaves to prepare meals and tend to their day to day needs. A dozen spotters left first, marking the way directly to the southeast toward Hebron and providing guidance for the 12-mile trip.

As they vacated the staging area, Team B came in and took about the same cadre and rations and they too left on a 12-mile trip to the southwest.

Team C decided to wait until the next day to go the short distance down to Libnath. They would be the instant backup team.

Usually when the army got to a city, they went in and looked for idols and made sure they were torn down and broken and then burned with the rest of the city. Sometimes they found idols built beside the roadways and each time they would pull them down and destroy them. They had found some on platforms that were 30 feet in the air. These giant platforms would often support several statues. Typically, there would be a single stairway up to the platform where human sacrifices were made. The soldiers tore down everything, both the platforms and the idols and then burned them. The soldiers did not kill all of the people in their path, however. There were many little villages and clusters of people who were left alone. Those who did not have idols were left unhurt.

The Second Team

The second team moved right past Libnah to Lachish. There was little danger in passing the city because their king was dead and most of their army had been destroyed. Generally, the Israelite army was feared and received little, if any resistance. Lachish was another one of the fortified cities. It was built out on the maritime plain with a breeze coming in from the coast. They could not see the Great Sea from the city but they understood that it was not far away.

The Army of God took their first day to prepare for the attack and then on the second day they took the city. The city and everything in it was put to the sword. As they were charging the city, young King Horam from Gezer, came to rescue the city, but the Israelites turned and captured his entire army in one swoop and put them all to the sword. They watched Lachish burn that night.

Since Gezer was closer to the Makkadeh command center, the commander of the second team sent a message back to command asking for assistance with Gezer. The third team readily accepted the challenge and attacked Gezer the next day and completely destroyed it. Gezer was the most powerful city in southern Canaan, but now it laid a pile of burning rubble.

As the second team was destroying Lachish, Salmon's team rolled into the Valley of Eshcol, where the ancient city of Hebron stood. It was beautiful, a city nestled in a forest of giant oak trees. Father Abraham had lived there with his family. In the nearby Mamre forest Abraham had bought land, lived and later buried his wife, Sarah, there

However, there was no sentimentality on this journey. Salmon directed the army to move in on Hebron and they easily captured the city. Everyone in the city was killed, the city and all of its idols, were destroyed and burned.

As was customary, they took a day's break for reflection. The soldiers enjoyed walking through the oak trees of Mamre. How quiet and peaceful it was. It was only a couple of miles from Hebron itself. No wonder Abraham enjoyed it so much. They did not find the cave where Sarah was buried, but they did find the tall oak where Abraham was said to have pitched his tent and made his home more than 400 years before. At least it was the biggest oak in the forest.

Simultaneous Battles

After a day's break, Salmon's team went out to Debir, only five miles to the southwest. They attacked the city and its villages, killing everyone by the sword and then burning all that remained.

While they were in Debir, the second team moved to Eglon where they took up positions and attacked it. They captured the city the same day they arrived, killed all who were living there and then totally destroyed it.

While Hebron and Lachish were being destroyed, the commander of the third team marched into Libnah only a few miles away and attacked it and completely destroyed it by the sword. They left no survivors there. They attacked, captured and burned the city in the first day they were there.

Great fear of the Israelites rose throughout the land. While they were feared for taking Jericho and Ai, now they were feared for destroying three cities in one day. No one in the southern part of Canaan wanted to challenge them.

The spotters on each team had drawn a line across from Makkadeh to Jerusalem. Each of the three teams would join the others along the line. Then they would move on to Jerusalem. The second team joined the command team in just a couple of days. However, Salmon's group took several days to catch up.

"Where have you guys been? Out sightseeing?"

Salmon replied with a big grin, "If you guys had been where we have been you would do some sightseeing, too. Beautiful land. Gorgeous country. We brought Joshua a surprise. Something he hasn't seen in a long time."

"Did I hear my name being called?" The old man with the flowing white hair was feeling good about the victories without losing a single man.

"Yes, sir," said Salmon. "When we stop for the night, I've got something to show you."

"It's not something for the wedding is it?" The old man teased.

"Oh, no. It's something you haven't seen in 40 years. You'll just have to wait." Salmon was dogmatic.

"Then, I hope it's not an old girl friend."

"No, sir. Nothing like that."

The Army of God came near to Jerusalem and camped for the night. They would attack the city the next day and then go home. Joshua was walking among the wagons and came upon Salmon.

"And what is this big surprise?"

"Just look at this." Salmon pulled back the tarp covering a huge bunch of grapes. He had two of the Gebonite slaves get it out and hold it up for Joshua. The single bunch of grapes measured three feet across and four feet long. Joshua recognized them.

"The grapes of Mamre! How did you get them?" Joshua had to feel of them and picked one grape out of the big bunch and tasted it.

"We were down at Hebron and had to make a run south of there into the Mamre forest after a few Amakites and we saw them there. I remembered the tales of you and Caleb bringing back a bunch of grapes to show Israel how fertile the land was. I thought you and Caleb might like to show this generation what you have just conquered."

"Very nice, my son. Very nice indeed. We sure will. Thank you for being so thoughtful." Joshua took a second grape and put it into his mouth. "Nice," he said.

The day had been a hot and windy one at Gilgal. Almost everyone spent the day inside. Toward evening, the wind calmed down and the family came out to prepare dinner. Joseph and Ari El had the campfire restored to cooking height and Mother soon had her pots smelling good with bubbling stuff. That was about the time when Jonathan came by, apologizing for arriving near meal time."

"No need to apologize," said Mother. "You just pull up a cushion and have dinner with us."

"Thank you very much, but I really came by to check on Rahab. How is she doing?" Jonathan already had a little boy on each leg. They were clinging as fast as they could to hold the tall man in his place. Olmad had to call them off, so Jonathan could get around.

"These boys are all right. God bless them with long lives and good spirits." He said as he looked for Rahab.

"Come with me, I'll take you to Rahab," said Olmad. A priest would never enter a woman's tent alone. Olmad called out to Rahab, "Hey, look who the burning wind blew in."

"Oh, Jonathan, it's so good to see you," called Rahab. "You will have to forgive my rude brother for his remarks."

"No need. Olmad and I have a good relationship and I understand his love for everyone. How are you doing?"

"Better. I can walk a little now. My feet are healing quickly. The scratches are all about gone. It's my heart that is heavy from missing Salmon."

"I understand. I miss Salmon, too. I told you, didn't I that we often run races together. Sometimes with several others. It helps to clear away the frustrations of the day. He's a very good friend. I love him too, but not like you do, I suppose. I expect that we will soon be hearing from them and they will be home in a few days. The last word I had was that they only had to take Jerusalem and then they would be finished with the southern campaign. All has gone well, and there has not been one casualty in the entire campaign."

"God has truly blessed us," said Rahab.

"Yes, He has."

"How are you doing emotionally?" Jonathan straightened the clerical rope around his waist.

"Pretty fair. I still have nightmares but not like the first nights. I've gotten over the feeling of always being dirty. Those first days, I just couldn't scrub myself clean enough."

"I know. That is one reason I came by. You have enough distance from the event now that you may be able to place it in perspective. May I visit with you a moment about it?"

"Oh, I wish you would," said Rahab. She straightened up some on her bench and motioned to Jonathan and Olmad to take two other benches nearby.

"I believe that God sends each of us adventures, maybe experiences is a better word, in order to test us. And to help prepare us for the next level of faith that is available to us." Jonathan began.

"Yes, Mother and I were talking about that a week ago, but continue, please."

"Rahab, sometimes these experiences send us close to our breaking point in order for us to recognize that not only is God great for the world, He is mighty in our individual lives, too. We can see how mighty God is when He stops up the Jordan River, so two million people can cross over. But we don't always recognize that the same God, with the same power, can move our lives individually. God often does this by sending strange people and strange events into our lives to test our reaction." Jonathan was making his point.

"It's tough going sometimes, but I understand what you're saying."

"Our forefathers, Abraham and his grandson, Jacob, both had experiences of strangers appearing in their lives. Sometimes even wrestling with them; only to recognize that they were angels sent by the Almighty. They were there to work in their individual lives. Sometimes these kinds of experiences can be happy ones, sometimes they're sad. Can you see that?"

"Yes, I believe I understand that," said Rahab.

"Your experience was a sad one, but I'm sure that it will have a happy ending. Because of this adventure, you are stronger. You now know how to pray to God for specific things. And, more than ever before, you now know that God hears your prayers and is ready to respond to you. Rahab, you now know that God is listening to your calls. He loves you and will take care of you. Always." Jonathan reached for her hands and held both of them in his big hands.

"Thank you. You are always so kind, Jonathan. I shall remember your words for a very long time. Please stay for dinner. Join our family circle this evening and tell us all about what you have heard from the army."

"Only if you can join the circle, too."

"I can do that. One word though. We both want to get in the serving line ahead of Olmad. Have you seen how much he eats?" And she winked.

"No, but I can see how that would be good advice. Come, let us help you to the circle." And Jonathan and Olmad helped Rahab walk to the family circle and they all enjoyed dinner together.

The next morning, Joshua and his army attacked the walls of Jerusalem and beat them down, destroying the city. There was nothing left of the city on a high plateau between two mountains. All the Jebusites were killed by the sword, their idols destroyed and the entire city and its contents set on fire.

Israel now occupied everything from the hill country, the Negev desert, the western foothills, and the mountain slopes. The land from Kadesh Barnea to Gaza and from the whole region of Goshen (the eastern part of the Negev) to Gibeon was now Israel's. Joshua and his army had totally destroyed all who resisted them in the area, just as the Lord had commanded. All the kings and their lands Joshua conquered in one campaign, because the Lord fought for Israel. Joshua dispatched one final messenger to Gilgal. "Just tell them we are on our way home."

A Little Four Day Party
The messenger ran through the camp with the exciting news. "They're coming home! Joshua and the men are coming home! They'll be here in two days." This called for a party. And the Hebrews

know how to party.

From out of the tents came colored banners. Long cooking pits were dug and the best lambs were prepared for roasting. The best of the vegetables and fruit and sweet breads were started. Someone got long poles and placed banners on top of them and planted them in the ground to form a welcome column along the roadway. The musicians started rehearsing. The welcome home party would be in front of the camp so everyone could attend including the residents of Friends Camp and Gilgal.

The next day Israel sent its own spotters out to watch for their returning men. When Joshua and the army were seen coming up the roadway, the word was quickly passed and everyone ran out to greet them. Rahab and her family went out almost a quarter of a mile and parked their wagon in the shade of one of a giant palm trees until they saw the long column of wagons filled with weary soldiers coming over a little hill. Everyone began cheering.

Many wives and children ran to meet them, but Rahab's group stayed in the shade and waited for their arrival. The soldiers were jumping from the wagons and hugging their families. When they got to the entrance of the camp, already some of the soldiers were carrying babies and small children in addition to their gear and swords. There were so many people out hugging and kissing their men that Rahab did not see Salmon.

Near the rear of the long column of tired men were two men marching with a long pole on their shoulders. Hanging from the pole was the huge cluster of grapes from the Mamre. They were beautiful, large, red grapes. A short portion of the big central vine was still attached and they used that to help tie the bunch to the carrying pole. The giant cluster of delicious grapes was the only spoils they brought in from the campaign.

The Gibeon servants on duty that day gathered the soldiers' armor and brought them basins of fresh water to wash their faces, arms and feet. They had benches and pillows for them to sit on. The priests sounded one long note on the rams' trumpets and the fellow who served as Joshua's assistant, climbed up on one of the wagons in front, extended his hands before the throng and said, "In the name of Jehovah, the Lord Almighty, in thanksgiving for the victories He has given us, we welcome everyone home." There was a roar from the throng.

"There is one short presentation — no speeches — just a VERY short presentation. Will Joshua and Caleb please come forward?"

And the announcer came down from the wagon. From out of a nearby tent the two old friends, Joshua and Caleb came marching out with the huge bunch of grapes. They carried them up a ramp to the wagon bed so everyone could see and presented the grapes to Eleazar, the High Priest, on behalf of the people.

Joshua turned to the crowd and tried to quiet them down some, but everyone already knew what he was going to say and were cheering him on. Finally, he just went on and said it anyway. "Eleazar, 46 years ago Caleb and I brought in a stem of grapes very similar to these from the Mamre in southern Canaan. We brought them to show the people of Israel what lay ahead for them. But the people then chose not to come into the land and we missed the fruit that God had prepared for us. Now, we present the grapes again to Israel but with a different statement. Not as wanderers, but as possessors. See the fruit of the Promised Land that we now possess!" The crowd went wild again. The roar of the cheers could be heard all across the land, reverberating from the mountains all around the Jericho Plains.

"Let the party begin," said Joshua. And it did. For four days the party ran day and night nonstop. God had given the entire southern portion of the Promised Land to Israel in one major campaign. There was a lot to be thankful for and the Hebrews knew how to express it. Long tables were laid out with roast lamb and fatted calves, with all the complements of a wide variety of vegetables prepared by the best cooks in the camp. As soon as one platter was emptied, the Gibeonites brought out another. As soon as one wine skin was emptied, out came two more. Giant bonfires lighted the night and the party continued day and night in front of the camp grounds.

Rahab kept looking for Salmon, but the throng was so thick she didn't find him in the mass of happy faces and cheering arms and hands. People were pushing and shoving in such joy. Once, however, there was a particular bump against her shoulder and she turned to see who it was. There, staring her in the face, just inches away was the very happy face of Salmon. Without saying a word, he reached for her chin and turned her face up to his and kissed her. Then he grabbed her around the waist and pulled her close to him twirling her around in the air. It was the best hug of her life. It was so very good to see him!

They just looked into each others eyes for a long time, with everybody in the world; it seems, pressing by them. Finally, Salmon said, "Let's get something to eat and get out of here. I can't wait a minute longer."

They each got a plate of food and wandered off to a quiet spot away from the people where he told her how much he had missed her. She told him how much she had missed him and how worried something might happen to him.

"Nothing was going to happen to me because the Lord was with us all," he said. "The closest to losing a soldier was when I felt I was almost dying from loneliness for my girl." Then he smiled. Those bright teeth and eyes were glistening. Then he kissed her again. At last they gathered up their empty plates and headed back to the party. The giant bonfires kept the Gibeon wood cutters working all night, again.

17

The Wedding

As the big victory celebration was winding down, Salmon could wait no longer. He was at Friends Camp more than at home. He was ready to get married. "I'll ask Jonathan when he can arrange the ceremony and when we can have the celebration," he volunteered. "Unless you folks have other plans or have any objections, my parents will provide the wedding garments. Friends of the family will provide food and drink."

"Wait just a minute, now, young man," Mother stopped the parade. "We want to be a part, too. This is our wedding, too. We will at least bring some food; just tell us who to coordinate with."

"Sure, that's no problem." Salmon was executing this wedding like he would a military campaign. "We'll just make the announcement in Judah and I'll tell you who to speak with. They are all good folks, and you'll like them."

"I'm sure we will." Mother was a little more relaxed now. This was her first Hebrew wedding and wasn't sure what to expect.

"Of all that will go on, one thing is sure, this little woman here must show up and be as radiant and beautiful as she is right now."

"Salmon, you make me blush, but I love it." Rahab had been silent. She wasn't sure what to expect either. "Look who is coming up the pathway. Hello, Jonathan. We were just talking about you."

"Was it good or bad?" The tall priest had his hands over his face, peeking out between his fingers.

"We'll never tell, my friend. You will have to go through the rest of your life wondering what we said about you." His close friend reached for the tall man's hand and pulled him down to the cushion beside him.

"Oh, the burdens of being a priest!" Jonathan flashed his big smile. "What's going on here?"

"We are detailing the wedding. We want you to perform the ceremony. Can you do that?" Salmon was giving commands.

"Well, that depends," said Jonathan.

"Depends on what?" Salmon asked.

"It depends on whether there will be any date cakes there."

"I think I can arrange that," said Mother. "Any other conditions?" And she was smiling.

"Not at the moment, but I want to keep my options open. That first one went too easy."

"When do you think we can get this arranged?" Salmon asked.

"I'd say in four or five days, if you wish. I don't know of any reason to put it off any longer. You two have had enough trouble and separations. I'd say let's do it."

"Is that all right with everyone over here?" Salmon was asking. "If it is, I'll ask Mom and Dad about it, but I'm sure that one day is as good as another."

"Fine here," said Mother. Rahab didn't have much to say. It wasn't her place to speak up while her wedding was being planned. Brides did not participate much in either Hebrew or Canaanite weddings. They were almost always arranged by the parents. It was unusual for the groom to make many arrangements, but he did so because he was marrying outside the Judah tribe and could not have the formal blessings of his father. However, his father did not object. He just kept a lower profile than usual.

"One more thing, friends: I need to tell you something. That while everyone has been celebrating the victories of the southern campaign there is still more to go. Even while the big parties have been going on, there have been spotters out spying out the northern part of the country. I don't know when, but I expect that I will need to be a part of that movement. I may have to leave in a few weeks or a few months for a while. So I am asking, Rahab, my darling, had you rather marry now and then be separated or wait until the separation is over, whenever that may be?"

"I don't want to wait. We have been separated enough. It has been six years since I first saw you. And that is enough waiting. Whatever separations in the future, at least we will know that we have had some time together."

"Those are exactly my thoughts. The northern campaign will be longer and harder than the southern campaign, but I expect that Joshua will manage it differently and will be rotating people in and out of the battles as God gives them to us. But when we get to receiving the inheritances of the land, we will be ready. Most likely we can have a family ready to place on that precious ground that God has promised us all."

"That sounds fine with me," said Rahab. "Anything else?"

Everyone shook his head, the meeting was finished. Jonathan and Salmon rose to leave, but Rahab followed them out to the pathway. "Salmon, I have something to ask, secretly."

"Sure, what is that, dear?"

"When you pick me up for the wedding, could I ask a favor?"

"Sure." Salmon said. But it was Jonathan who had the inquisitive smile.

"When you come to pick me up for the wedding, can you come on a camel? Mother and I have had a long running joke about my marrying a camel jockey. She will be so surprised if you showed up as a camel jockey!"

"Sounds like fun. Sure, I think I can borrow a camel. The next thing is to see if I can ride one of those things. And you want to ride it up to the wedding site? And let your family follow along behind?" Salmon was trying to figure this out. Jonathan was laughing.

"I've never ridden a camel in all my life," said Salmon.

Rahab just shook her head. "But wouldn't it be fun?"

"What do you think, Jonathan?"

"My friend, don't get me into this. I don't give advice. I just ask the questions at weddings." However, his friend was smiling his biggest smile and reached over and hugged Rahab. "Go get him, Rahab, and then hold on to him."

"I plan to," she whispered back.

And so the men walked away from Friends Camp. Later that evening, Rahab would go to bed, but was still wide awake. After everyone else was asleep, she sat at the back of her tent and looked at the stars. Much as she remembered doing when she was on her rooftop in Jericho. The sky was dark but the stars were bright in contrast. A little breeze was moving about ever so gently. She felt comforted. Words began to spill from her soul.

"God, it's me again. I'm as confused as ever. With all your power and strength, with all your abilities, you must have such a busy schedule of looking after your world, how can you still have time for individuals like me? How do I strengthen my faith to give my whole self to you? How do I go about understanding your laws? At times I feel you in my life and at times I'm confused, as I am now. Help me in my unbelief, Lord. Hold me close so I feel you in my heart. Show me how to live, Lord. Show me how to be worthy. Show me what to do. Lead me in the paths I should go, Lord, to bring glory to your name. Please, Lord. Please."

On the day of the wedding, all the friends in Friends Camp were busy getting chores done so that they could get dressed for the big party at sundown.

Just before sunset, a big camel came ambling up to the entrance to Friends Camp. The camel had bells on over its oriental blankets, headpiece and double saddle. Salmon was in the front saddle, holding the reins and carrying the guide stick. He reached down under the camel's neck and tapped the bell with his guide stick and Mother came out to see what the bell ringing was about. First, she saw the camel and then she recognized Salmon on top of the beast. She placed her hand over her mouth, and then screamed, "O, my Lord!"

Everyone came out of their tents to see what the matter was. Salmon had learned to command the camel to lower himself to his knees and was involved in doing that as Rahab, her dad, Olmad and his family, and their servants lined up in front of the tents.

"Ma'am, sir, I have come to take your daughter away," announced Salmon, just as Rahab came out glowing in her own radiance. She went over to her mother to give her a hug and to kiss her father.

"Mother, can I run away with this camel jockey?"

"Well, let's see. Is he cute?"

"Yes."

"Is he rich?"

"Rich enough."

"Will he take care of you?"

"He already has."

"Will he make a good son-in-law?"

"Yes."

"Then Papa, what do you think?"

"If she doesn't marry him, I might."

Mother brushed her husband's hand away and said, "You're already married. Let the children go."

So Salmon got down from the back of the kneeling camel, took the hand of his bride, and placed her in the back saddle. He took the front saddle and gave the command for the camel to stand up and with a "Hut, hut, hut," they rode off into the camp with the family following behind in their wagon with Joseph holding the reins.

Some of their neighbors followed behind in their own wagons.

The wedding was set in the open area of Judah where the wedding planners had set up two special tents as dressing rooms for the wedding party. There were about a hundred people there, including all of Rahab's family and their friends. While the bride and groom were getting dressed, ushers escorted the bride's family down to the front reserved seats and introduced them to the groom's parents, Nahshon and Bethel. The men said, "Hello" but the women did not speak. They only smiled.

Rahab was surprised when the dressers presented her with a pure white linen gown and a very thin lace head dress. Salmon was dressed in a white robe with a broad, red sash. As they came out of the tents Jonathan met them in his royal purple robe and black turban. Everything was very formal. This was not the feisty, young man everyone was so familiar with. Although he still had that mischievous glint in his eyes, he was a serious priest with an important mission.

As the three entered the approach to the wedding canopy, a group of singers at the front began singing: "O Lord, maker of earth and heaven, maker of man and woman, we beseech your blessings on these two. We ask you to bless these two children of yours. Bless them with fruitful days, with good health, with good fortune, and fine sons and daughters. Lord, bless us all. Let our lives be to your glory. Bless us all, O Lord."

Jonathan led them down the long isle of well wishers and under the canopy. Then he turned to face them and he said:

"Listen to these words from Moses. Moses received them from God. So listen to what God has to say:

"Hear, O Israel: The Lord, our God, the Lord is one. Love the Lord, your God, with all your heart and with all your soul and with all your strength. These commandments that I give you today are to be upon your hearts, impress them on your children. Talk about them when you sit at home and when you walk along the road, when you lie down and when you get up. Tie them as symbols on your heads and bind them on your foreheads. Write them on the door frames of your houses and upon your gates.

"When the Lord, your God, brings you into the land he swore to your fathers, to Abraham, Isaac and Jacob, to give you a land with large, flourishing cities you did not build, houses filled with all kinds of good things you did not provide, wells you did not dig, and vineyards and olive groves you did not plant — then when you eat and are satisfied, be careful that you do not forget the Lord, who brought you out of Egypt, out of the land of slavery. Fear the Lord, your God, serve him only." Then Jonathan paused to look deeply into their eyes. Very quietly, he asked each, "Do you understand this? Serve only God for He is your life stream. He is the fountain from which all blessings flow."

With respect for the solemnity of his question, they each nodded.

"Do you understand that as you begin your life together that there is nothing more important than loving the Lord, your God? Do you understand that to love God is to love each other? For God is love. To express love to another person is a holy act. It is a godly act. Do you understand that this is the greatest commandment for all of your lives? Love God with all your heart, soul, and strength, then you shall live in the favor of the Almighty. Do you each understand?"

And they each nodded their heads.

Then he turned to Salmon and asked, "Do you take Rahab to be your loving wife, to cherish her, to provide for her, to protect her, to love her only for as long as you both shall live?"

Salmon took Rahab's hand, squeezed it, and told his best friend, "Before God, I swear with all my heart I will."

A great shout punctuated his solemn promise. The mighty shout rose from everyone present just as the words came from Salmon's mouth. There were no vows for the bride, because women did not speak during the service. Instead, Salmon, son of Nahshon, reached around Rahab's waist and pulled her close to him and, for the first time, kissed her in public. And a second cheer went up from the party. Someone handed them a cup of wine. They each took a sip from the clay cup and then Salmon threw it onto a special pad and crushed the cup with his heel. They were married.

Another big cheer went up and the musicians played happy songs until almost dawn. However, Salmon and Rahab left around midnight to be alone for the first time in Salmon's tent. There was great joy in their hearts. God had found favor in her by providing such a strong, handsome, kind, generous, loving husband.

Rahab's family stayed for much of the party. Mother received many compliments for her date cakes and several hugs from well wishers. Around midnight, however, the family left to go home. Rahab would spend the night in Salmon's tent in Judah.

The sun was up for some time before there was any stirring in Salmon's tent. All the men were at work and the women had their own chores to do. Only the flaps of the tent for the newly weds remained closed. Finally, there was some movement inside and at last the front flap opened and a sleepy eyed Salmon peered outside. He was squinting in the bright sunshine. Rahab's face was looking over his shoulder. A man walked by, smiled and needed to say something. So he asked, "Did you have a nice night?"

Salmon said nothing. He only grinned.

The Spies' Report

As soon as Joshua had returned from the southern campaign (and while everyone was celebrating their victories), he had secretly sent out 500 spies into the northern territory. The spies were dressed as nomadic travelers and wore nothing that would identify them as Hebrew. They traveled in small bands and split up when they neared a city so only two or three entered each city. They were mapping the way and gaining intelligence for the next major campaign. They would be ready when God gave them the permission to possess the country.

After three months of traveling, the spies began to come back and reported to their chiefs and the summary reports made it to the command tent at the Circle of Government. The spies were telling of tall mountains with snow on top of them. They would have to find a way to get through massive thickets of reeds. There were more signs of human sacrifices. There were tough fortress walls. More cities built on mountain sides so that the lower parts had to be captured before climbing to the upper reaches and then fighting all over again to capture the top city. There were forests, deserts and few roads. It would be difficult to get an army their size through the land with any element of surprise.

"So you are telling me that this one will not be as easy as the southern campaign," said Joshua.

"That's right. And we have a new kind of people to contend with. Some of the people in these cities are of Phoenician stock. They're very intelligent. They have an alphabet that is entirely different from ours. They are very good traders and they love art. They have shared their intelligence and wisdom to nearly all the shores of the Great Sea. But as smart as they are, Joshua, their religion is an abomination. They worship many gods. Their priests conduct orgies to Astarte and Baal. We found many, many followers of Baal." One commander reported.

Another commander summed up the reports of his spies by saying, "Joshua, my men report signs of human sacrifices. They tell of more huge stone platforms, sometimes 30 feet in the air where they sacrifice young virgins and children. This is awful."

After hearing these and other reports it became easier to understand why God wanted the land swept clean of such terrible practices. Joshua felt in his old bones that a horrible war was not far away.

The newlyweds began to adjust to living together and the constant companionship. Although they lived in Judah, they spent almost as much time in Friends Camp. Salmon would have to break away occasionally to tend to his work as a soldier. But there was not much going on, just waiting for orders.

Rahab was having a little trouble adjusting. They had only been married a couple of months when she had trouble with her stomach in the mornings, and she was feeling weak. Her appetite was increasing. It seemed that she was always hungry. Salmon teased her gently about eating because she was nervous, "You always want to do the right thing. Just relax. It's just us. I love you as you are, not for what you want to pretend to be. Just be Rahab."

"You're so nice and I love you too, but I want this marriage to be perfect in every detail. I don't want you to have to be gone for a long time."

"Let's worry about that when it comes; but not before. Just remember, I'm not looking for a perfect wife. I'm just looking for a happy one." Salmon took her in his arms again and kissed her.

"I just don't seem to have the energy to get my chores done."

"Why not talk to your mother about it. I'll get a cart and we will ride over there this morning." Salmon had some concerns about her health.

They rode to Friends Camp and Dad asked Ari El to serve everyone tea. Rahab and her mother took a little walk to talk in private. Her mother listened to all the symptoms and made a fast conclusion. "You've been married how long?"

"About three months, mother, you know that," said Rahab.

"Yes, I do, but do you know it? Time can get away from you when you are in love. If Salmon has to leave you to do his work, I think you should move back over here and stay here until your baby comes."

"Baby?"

"Dear, you're showing classic signs of being in a motherly way. Let's watch it for another few weeks. I think you will be adjusting and hopefully, begin to feel better soon; as soon as your body makes adjustments. You're hungry, because you are eating for two people."

"Mother!" Rahab reach for the woman with the glistening eyes and hugged her. "Oh, I can't wait to tell Salmon." She left her mother standing between the tents and ran to Salmon. She was yelling, "Salmon. Salmon. We're going to have a baby!"

The men having tea were startled at the loud news. This was something shared in intimacy, not broadcast for the whole Jericho Plains! Salmon stood up and caught her in his arms. "A what?" He asked.

"You know, one of those little things that wiggles," she said.

Olmad added to her sentence, "And cries, and keeps you up all night."

And her dad said, "And grows up to make you into a grandparent."

Then mother caught up with the group. "Let's not rush into this, but young man, your wife has all the good symptoms of being in the motherly way. Let's see what happens over the next few weeks."

"Oh, I am so happy. So very happy," said Salmon. He held on to his wife with all his might. "You make me so very happy."

Back at the Circle of Government, another meeting was about to conclude when a breathless spotter came running into the tent. "Joshua, I beg a minute of your time."

"You have it, son. What's going on?"

"My spotters are telling me of a massing of soldiers to the north. It looks like they come from several cities. And they will be headed for Gilgal."

"Where are they now?"

"They are forming up north of a big lake on the Jordan. It's called the Sea of Galilee. There are several armies that are still heading that way. It'll be a very large force. The largest force we have ever encountered."

"So, they are not ready yet?" Joshua was summing up.

"No. It'll take several more days for them to assemble and then march down here, but they're a very large force," said the spotter.

"Thank you, son, for bringing us this news. We'll take care of it from here. Get you some rest now." Then Joshua turned to his commanders. "Get me some information on this Sea of Galilee and how to get there. If everyone else is going, then why can't we? I've going over to see Eleazar."

The commanders went back to the army tent to find out all they could from their men and maps about the Sea of Galilee and the best way to get there.

Joshua went to the tent of many colors and the golden support poles. There he found the High Priest. "My friend, how are you doing today?"

"Kind of slow today. My back probably feels like yours does. What are you so excited about?" Eleazar reached for his friend.

"It looks like trouble is brewing in the north. Looks like some more business for the soldiers. I need to talk with God about it."

Some of the tribal leaders, who were in their tent near the Tent of Meeting, heard the two old men talking and came out and volunteered, "We would like to help." So they all leaned on their walking staffs and kneeled down facing the Tent of Meeting and then leaned forward to touch their heads to the ground.

Eleazar was first to pray: "Lord we call on your name as the Almighty God of all the earth. We recognize you as the creator of all things, master of all things, and the very giver of life. We ask for your attention to a grave matter."

Eleazar paused and Joshua began. "Lord, we hear that a large force is gathering up north and is preparing to come to Gilgal to attack us. I sense that this may be an opening to possess the northern part of your land. Please let us know what to do."

The tribal leaders added their voices saying "Amen, Amen."

Everyone was very still. And from inside Joshua came the voice of the Lord. *"Do not be afraid, Joshua. I have given you the victory."*

Then Joshua said "Amen." He began to get up. Some of the younger men in the group came over and began to help Joshua and Eleazar to their feet again. He turned to his council and said, "The Lord has blessed us with victory. We will leave immediately and give the foe a surprise."

Joshua made his way directly to the army tent and this time found them very busy with maps and logs of great detail of all the northern territory. They were pasting their individual maps together, redrawing some of them for a better fit. Their logs told how the city-states were fortified, where the walls were, where the gates were, where their weak points were. The commanders were able to draw in the deep ravines and hazardous mountains and route their companies of soldiers between them.

Joshua walked into the busy tent and said, "I see you boys are earning your keep for a change."

"Yes sir, how may we help you?" It was a voice a young spotter.

"I want you to concentrate on the Sea of Galilee. I guess you have gotten the same message that I did. A big force of soldiers from different cities is gathering north of there. Will you verify that report and then get me a pathway up there for the full army. Get me a few spotters out there to start flagging the road right away. The army will leave as soon as we know where we're going."

"Yes, sir, we're already working on it, sir." The scrolls were pushed aside except those with the Jordan running through them and a big lake. "It shouldn't take much longer, sir. But I can tell you now that the lake is about 70 miles north of here. Probably the best battle ground is just north of that lake. It's called the Waters of Merom. I'd bet that is where they'll go."

"I hope you're right, son. Get me some directions." And the Commander-In-Chief walked out of the tent and into the sunshine of the day. There under the sun, Joshua heard the call of the rams' horns, signaling for all the commanders to come to the central court and for the soldiers to begin gathering in their own tribal areas. The pace of war was picking up.

Within a few minutes, all twelve of the commanders were present and accounted for in the big command tent. "Men, it's time to saddle up again and this time we are not likely to return for several years. As soon as we get this first battle over with, we will know how to pace ourselves and how many fighting men we will actually need. That is a long way around to say, I think we can furlough a bunch of the boys and rotate people in and out so that no one has to stay on the scene for very long at a time. Any objections, so far?"

"No objections. But for the record, I like the furlough part best." The voice was from the back of the room and was soon covered up with a few chuckles. Then it was back to business.

Joshua still had the floor. "The boys are plotting our trail now. We will be heading to just north of the Sea of Galilee. It's about 70 miles north of here. Several armies are combining forces to come and take us. But they are not quite ready yet. So I think we should throw them a surprise party. Call your men together and we'll leave about midnight. The support wagons will follow so your men can leave that kind of stuff with their families. And it will come up behind us. Be sure to get the cooking wagons in line, or we will be getting hungry up north. Oh, and tell your men to prepare for cold weather. Lay out their heaviest robes and stockings. Any questions?"

The room was quiet. "Then get with your men and tell them the news. They have until midnight to start filling up their wagons. Oh, one other thing. Tell them that the Lord has blessed our efforts and the victories are ours. We just have to show up and fight the battle."

Rahab and Salmon had been married four months when the call to war came. Together they went to tell the news to his parents and then to her parents.

Rahab looked worried. Salmon reminded her, "God will protect everyone in Gilgal just as He protects His army. Darling, you must remember that God chooses lots of people for special purposes. He has chosen us as a nation of people to fulfill His promise to Abraham. Under the protective love of the Lord, no harm will come to us. He has chosen you for another special purpose, just as He has chosen your parents for their special purposes. Therefore, God will protect you. God will provide the circumstances and the teachers to increase your faith, to give you the talents and strengths to honor His glorious name. Love God with all your heart and you will be blessed." Then Salmon touched her hair and reached for the back of her neck to bring her face to his and softly said, "I love you." And he kissed her.

"I'll be right here waiting for you," she whispered. "I mean we will be waiting for you," and she patted her stomach.

The Departure

At the end of the last watch, while it was still dark, 40,000 soldiers got dressed for battle, and headed for the war wagons. Salmon pulled Rahab up close again and kissed her and then held her for a long time. Her heart didn't want to let him go. Her head said she must. She held him as long as she could.

While Salmon had his men loading the wagons for Judah, Rahab collected her family and Salmon's parents and they met at the main entrance to wave good-bye. Thousands of other families had the same idea. They all cheered the men on. The priests for each tribe held a brief prayer ceremony asking God's blessings on the journey and for the men's safe keeping. Many more of the priests formed a line on each side of the entrance leading out of the camp. Family members and people from Friends Camp gathered behind the priests to wave the men on as they rode out of camp.

As the wagons appeared at the entrance, the priests began

singing a portion of the *Song of Moses* that had been remembered throughout all of their travels in the desert. They were singing: "I will sing to the Lord, for He is highly exalted. Who is like you, Lord: majestic in holiness, awesome in glory, working wonders. You stretch out your right hand and the earth swallows the enemy. In your unfailing love you will lead the people you have redeemed. .."And the beautiful singing continued for the entire song.

Joshua had grown up as a military man and had provided the strategy for the encounters of the Israelites during their desert years. So the first people to leave the camp were spotters. They would operate as the advance men, first to gather information and to report any problems that the armies might encounter. They carried no armor, only daggers under their travel robes, very similar to the ones that first came to Jericho. As the spotters left through the ceremonial honor guard, they spurred their steeds into action and raced off into the starlight.

This time Joshua would divide his army into four groups of 10,000 fighters each and they would take similar but separate paths to the battle ground. This helped to maintain some element of surprise on the enemy.

After the spotters, came supply wagons that moved slowly. Each tribe had provided and outfitted long wagons with food, clothing, additional spears and swords, blankets, and tents for about 4,000 men. The wagons carrying primarily food and tents were the first to leave using their own exits from the camp. Each wagon was directed by two drivers. The horses lumbered under the heavy load. The fighters would likely catch up with them and even pass them later, but this got supplies on the road and down a ways before they would be needed. The caravan was escorted by a team of fighters to protect the supplies. This further cleared the way for the army. Spotters rode with the supply wagons that could immediately run back to the column of men and alert them of any danger.

Almost immediately after the first support wagon appeared, came the soldiers. There were so many of them. At a distance they were fierce fighting men with shields, breastplates, spears and swords. Their leather sandals and shin guards were shined as if for inspection. Rahab sensed that familiar smell of leather polish. Up close, she could see the men as husbands, fathers, and sons. So many of them had boyish faces. The armor was dull in the starlight, but when the first rays of the sun streaked across a clear sky, the shields and breastplates would be glistening.

Two wagons filled with soldiers passed by Rahab's group. Each soldier held his sword up high in salute. The third wagon held a thin old man in his colorless tunic. He had two other men with him. This was the chief command wagon. Joshua was standing in the slow moving wagon and the breeze was blowing his tunic back against his body, revealing how thin he was. The long white hair was flowing in the light breeze. His lanky thin arms were bare in the yellow light of a half moon as he slowly waved to the crowds. He held onto the seat to steady himself as the wagon came through the entrance and out to the road that lead to war. One of the men handed him a robe and he pulled it around him and sat down, blending in with the Army of God.

Group after group of the men passed by the columns of well wishers. They went out about a quarter mile from the camp entrance and began splitting into four different pathways. Each group of 10,000 fighters plus support personnel would meet up again near the proposed battle site.

After the columns of men had cleared the camp, then came more wagons of supplies. It was well after sunrise before all the army had cleared the camp. God had sent them back to war.

Early in the afternoon, a cousin of Salmon's came to Rahab and invited her to join some others in the Central Court for a report on the situation. When they arrived, a man was calling names and naming towns Rahab had never heard.

He said the biggest and strongest city up north was Hazor, north of the Sea of Galilee. Its king was a man named Jabin. "We have learned that Jabin started organizing this defense as soon as he heard about our entering the Promised Land. He has formed alliances with the other kings in just about all of the villages and cities to our north. He's going to try to stop us with one big army. Jabin is coming after us with incredible numbers of soldiers.

"Our reports tell us how the fighters are coming out of the valleys, hills, mountain passes, all throughout the northern part of Canaan to form this huge army. They have both horses and chariots. And we know that they are gathering at the Waters of Merom to organize and then they expect to attack Gilgal.

"Where your men are going is a rough place," the speaker told the wives and mothers. "Jabin is no beginner. He has built the largest and most fortified city in Canaan. He's showing his expertise as a commander by having the armies assemble in a particular area that is hard to approach. Our spotters tell us that it is a naturally fortified area near a triangle shaped lake north of the Sea of Galilee. Inside a ridge of jagged mountains lies a level plain. The Jordan River flows through the plain and the Lake of Merom and then falls to the Sea of Galilee. The plain, where the battle will most likely be fought, is about sixteen miles long and about seven to eight miles wide. The spotters expect it to soon be filled with soldiers, horses and chariots.

"To attack this assembly area, Joshua must either lead his men over the very rugged mountains of Naphtali or through a morass of thickly covered canes and papyrus reeds, which are virtually impenetrable. There is one other possibility. It's to use a single gentle slope with irregular hills that will probably be used by Jabin to assemble his men. We don't know how Joshua will attack the position, but we do know that this will be our toughest battle yet."

Eleazar, the High Priest and all the Levites gathered the people of Israel together and for days a constant prayer was sent up to God for the battle. It was a solemn time for Israel.

Weeks went by before there was any real news. Rahab was lonely for her man and was wondering if Salmon's parents had heard anything. So she went back to Judah and to the familiar tent of Nahshon.

"Hello, stranger. Did you get lost? It's been a long time."

"Hello to you, stranger," Rahab returned the greeting. "Why haven't you come to see me?"

"Oh, honey, I don't get out much any more. Besides, my wife would be jealous, if I told her I was going out to visit a pretty girl."

"I would hope you would bring her over, too. My folks would love to visit with you." Rahab was making herself at home on the bench next to him.

"I am sure we would have a delightful time, my dear, but when you get old with gray hair and winkles, you like to stay home." Nahshon was a gentle man with a very big, kind heart.

"I don't guess you have heard anything from your son." The old man just shook his head. "I get to wondering, with him out there on the battle front and all those people getting killed, homes destroyed, and everything. I wonder why is it that God has so many people killed. Isn't there another way?"

The kind man was in no hurry to answer. He looked toward the horizon and grew glassy-eyed. Then he repeated Rahab's question, "Why does God kill so many good people?"

"What we see as good and what God sees as good are two different things. He created people to be His children, to worship Him, to bring Him honor and glory. Some of His children run away and no longer honor Him, or even recognize Him. They no longer appreciate the life He provides them. God gives them an opportunity to return to His love, but when they don't, He removes them.

"God's blessings never flow to anyone until some action is taken. As one example: the Jordan River would have never stopped for us if the Levites had not first had the faith to step into that raging water. This can be a frightening experience. Do you risk your faith in God Almighty or will you be swept away to your death in the raging water? This is the test.

"The closer you are to God, the stronger your tests. Not just in stopping rivers, but in the way you live, the blessings you receive, the strength to overcome sickness, and losses. God blesses your everyday life as you act on its challenges."

Rahab reached for the old man's weary hand. It still had some calluses from days of working. There were rough spots from hard years in the wilderness. While he was talking, she turned his hand over and looked at the big veins running from his wrist to his fingers. There were the aged spots and the big wrinkles left from the days when his hands were big and strong. Now the muscles are replaced with wrinkles. She tried to rub the winkles away, but they remained as sentinels of other times.

"The problem with the people in Jericho," he started again, "and those other cities is that they don't recognize God. They're worshiping man-made gods. They're denying the blessings that God Almighty provides to everyone. He causes the sun to shine on everyone. He causes the rain to fall on everyone. He provides the air to breathe to everyone, whether they are good or bad. Some people begin to think that they don't need God, so He just stops blessing them. And they die. Just as surely as He told Adam and Eve, people who dishonor God die without His blessing. Sometimes it is by the sword, sometimes by famine, sometimes by flood, and, perhaps, sometimes by simply growing weary in old age, or simply lost from His presence. God makes that judgment.

"Oh, I find myself rambling on. My dear, you probably need to talk to someone smarter than me about this big question, but that is how

I see it. Every time you draw a breath, or see a sunrise, or lie down at night and fall asleep to awaken the next day, God is saying He loves you and wants to hear a response from you in appreciation."

"You are such a wise man. I am so very happy that I have this opportunity to receive your wisdom," said Rahab. She stood up to leave.

"You make too much of an old man's thoughts."

"Now that I have checked on you, I've got to get back to Friends Camp and make sure everyone there is behaving."

"I'm glad you come checking on me, but you can't leave."

"Why not?" Rahab was a little confused.

"Because you haven't hugged me. Or don't you hug old men?"

"Well, sometimes. When I'm in a good mood," said Rahab as she reached for his little slumped shoulders.

"Well, I'm glad you're in a good mood," he said as he hugged her.

Battle at Lake Merom

Joshua and the Army of God found the battle site to be as described by the spotters. The high elevation already had cold temperatures in the thinner air. The four groups of soldiers camped in the mountains without being spotted. They could see soldiers still coming into the mass of men on the flat plain. The army was still forming; there were apparently no established lines of command or even a plan of attack. At this time it was hardly more than a group of unorganized renegades. The enemy was not ready.

Joshua was praying to God for direction. This would be the biggest battle so far. How did God want him to handle it? And God spoke inside Joshua and told him, *Do not be afraid. By this time tomorrow, I will hand all of them over to Israel. You are to hamstring their horses and burn their chariots.* So Joshua's army spent the first day at the site resting and observing.

Meanwhile one of the spotters discovered something. "Look, most of the men reporting are all wrapped in blankets. All kinds of blankets. Probably, something they brought from home."

"So, what are you saying?" Ask another.

"I'm saying that after dark, anyone wrapped in a blanket could get into their assembly. No one knows anyone else here. If we went in with a blanket wrapped around us, we could be right there on the plains among them." The word quickly passed to the commanders and then to Joshua.

So, during the night a large group of Israelites were able to slip into the fortified plains as a contingent group of rag-a-tags. The Israelites wrapped in different kinds of blankets over their armor, blended right in with the enemy. Joshua sent another group up into the mountains through narrow crevices to reach a point where they could enter the battleground. Others he massed on the very path that the enemy must use to escape.

As the first rays of the sun reached over the mountain tops, they attacked suddenly. The Israelites stood up from their sleeping positions and threw off the blankets they had wrapped themselves in; thus revealing their armor and swords. Steel swords clanged against steel swords.

Most of the enemy were still asleep, undressed, unarmed and very surprised. As the enemy watched the massive numbers of Israelites sweep down on them from the mountain walls, they discovered that Joshua's men had penetrated their campsite. Everywhere the enemy turned; there was an Israelite ready to stab him with his bloody sword. The men fought most of the morning and the blood ran thick across the triangle shaped plains. Some of the enemy ran away with the little armies separating and heading back to their hometowns. Joshua concentrated on those on the bloody plain and did as God had directed, so God gave them the victory.

Joshua had all the enemy's horses hamstrung, by cutting the tendon above the ankle, crippling the horses so they could not walk. Then he burned everything including all their chariots, corpses, and horses.

Joshua reassembled his men and they gave thanks to God for the victory. They rested, got some food and then prepared to take off for the ones that had escaped through the mountains. Joshua's spotting system was already at work. There was no hurry. He knew where the runaways were.

God's fighting men and their support groups were now about 100 miles from home and communication was slow. It took days for a messenger to make his way through the hills to report the news to Gilgal. Supplies were sent out almost everyday. Reporting stations had been set up to direct the wagons to the ever changing locations. However, there was always more silence than news.

Rahab didn't know where Salmon was or how he was. She learned to pray daily for him and for the safety of Joshua and his army. "Lord, I know that you are in charge of everything. I know that you love everybody, even me. Almighty God, I plead with you to protect your army with your love; that you would clear the land quickly of the evil ones, and that you send your army home soon. Lord, please protect them from the cold winter winds and rain, just as you protect them from the enemies. Have mercy on all of us, O Lord."

The weeks turned into months and the months into years. And the fighting kept on. The harvests came and went. One season melted into another. For seven years the Army of God cleared the land of idols and idol worshipers. In bits and pieces, the people at Gilgal learned that their army pursued the enemy all the way up the coast of the Great Sea to the general area of Sidon, but not Sidon itself. Joshua's army pursued the enemy to the sea coast near Tyre, eliminating them and crushing the idols.

Although many of the armies had been either destroyed or severely damaged, there was still fighting to be done. Joshua's army would attack a city, clear it out and destroy everything that breathed in it except the animals and then the men would rest and meditate. The army was divided so that some of the crew was always ready to fight, but most of them were in periods of resting. Joshua even arranged for furloughs, so some could go home

After the initial battle, Joshua turned the command over to his commanders and let them seek the battle sites in accordance to his instructions. The old man, himself, returned home to Gilgal in one of the furlough wagons.

Thus the commands he had received from Moses to completely destroy the fortified cities were carried out. God permitted the army to gather the spoils of the cities and send them home. All the idol worshipers were killed. Not one person was left alive in any of the cities they attacked. Even the kings of the cities were put to the sword as they had done in the cities to the south. Every city was then burned except the ones built on their own mounds.

Ever more frequently the spotters came back to camp with the wagons of spoils, but there was no word of Salmon. The army sent wagon trains back to Gilgal filled with household items, gold, silver, brass, art, leather, cloth, spices, grain, horses, cattle, donkeys, sheep, and many other things. Almost every week, a wagon train would arrive and as Rahab helped unload the wagons, she would learn the news. Also on the wagons were soldiers on furlough. They would stay for a few weeks and then take one of the wagons back to the area where the next city would be taken. Rahab kept looking for

Salmon but there were always other people to be made happy and grateful. As the wagons returned to the war fronts, they carried back supplies that they were not able to obtain from the ravaged cities and country side. Mother always sent some date cakes.

Not knowing about Salmon and whether he was alive or dead or sick or hurt or well and happy, worried Rahab, as it did many of the family members around the encampment. One day when Rahab was sitting in the sun outside her tent looking towards the old Jericho ruins, a familiar voice called to her. "Hey, you, the woman of the green cord."

She looked up and saw it was Jonathan, "I mean the scarlet cord," he said with his biggest smile.

"Hello, Jonathan. What are you doing on such a pretty afternoon?"

"Just looking for someone to talk to," he said, as he boldly made his way over to her bench in the sun. "May I join you?"

"Of course, have a seat." She moved over a little and straightened her floppy skirt tail so he would have room to sit. "And before you ask, no I haven't heard anything from Salmon. Everyone is always asking."

"I know, I get those same questions everyday, too," Jonathan said.

"I do miss Salmon. In fact, I am depressed not knowing anything about him. Where he is? What in he doing? Is he all right? Is he safe?"

Jonathan turned a little to look into her face. "As a friend of a friend, let me say that God will take care of Salmon and he is always safe as long as he lives for God. Salmon is a strong spirit and I'll bet he is doing better than we are. We are worried but he knows what is going on — so he's not worried."

The visitor paused a little, looking toward the palm trees. "Hey, I've got a problem, maybe you can help me out."

"Sure, what is it?"

"My problem is: I've been put in charge of a little baby and I don't know what to do. I was wondering if you could baby-sit for a while for me. Honestly, I don't know the first things about babies." He had a worried look.

"I guess so. I have baby sat for my brother's two little boys. I guess I could do that. Where is the baby?" She asked.

"Over in my neighbor's tent. Do you mind if I go get the little one and bring her to you for a while? It won't take long."

"Sure, go get the baby and bring her here and I'll watch her."

"Oh, thanks so much," Jonathan said as he was getting up and leaping off in a dead run towards the Judah tents.

In just a few moments Jonathan came back with a blanket in his arms and a big smile on his face. When he was three feet in front of Rahab, he unwrapped the blanket and revealed a baby lamb. Now his smile covered his whole face. "Remember, I didn't say what kind of baby I had."

"No, you didn't," she said, somewhat relieved. "So you need someone to keep her this afternoon?"

"Well, not really," the priest said. "What I really need is for some kind woman to adopt her and raise her and train her as she would a husband. You know, kind of practice until Salmon gets back."

"You are giving me this little lamb?"

"Someone gave me the lamb for some services I performed. It was a gift in love, but I can't keep a lamb, so I am giving her to you in the same loving spirit that I received her." He had those big sheepish eyes that glinted with mischief. "I think this baby will help you pass the time."

"Thank you very much, ... I think," she told him. "I can hardly wait to tell my brother that I'm going to compete with him in sheep ranching. Jonathon, you didn't have to do this."

"I know, but I wanted to cheer up someone, and God provided this opportunity. I must go, but I hope you find contentment and happiness in your new found friend. Now, walk with God."

"Wait a minute. Tell me something. Why do you always say Walk with God? Most other people say, The Lord be with you."

"I know. It's just me, I guess. You see Moses writes that God is always with us. He created us. He loves us. He is with us forever and ever. When he calls us away, as he did Moses, God is still with us. So if we are away from God, it is only because we have strayed. Not because God has. I believe that the proper term is to say something that encourages us to remain close to the Holy Father. We should always be encouraged to walk with God as Abraham walked with God. See what I mean?"

"Yes, that's beautiful. Then my friendly priest, walk with God."

"Thank you, ma'am. I'll be back soon to check on how you are treating my baby." Jonathan smiled and sprinted off down the pathway.

One afternoon several weeks later, Rahab was not feeling well and did not go out to meet the incoming wagons. She was lying on her pallet when she heard a voice at the entrance of her tent calling out, "Is this the place of The Woman with the Scarlet Cord?" It was Salmon!

She rushed to the entrance and into his waiting arms. "Salmon! Oh, thank God you're home!" She never wanted to let him go. He was so strong. He was looking good and had recovered from a few scratches but was well.

"Oh, how I have looked forward to holding you in my arms again!" Happiness ran from the tips of his dark hair to the soles of his feet.

"I never want to let you go. I just want to hold you just like this forever and forever."

"I know. Me too. It's so very good to feel you next to me again. I have missed you so. I thought of you every day. I missed you every night. I would wake up hugging my pillow thinking it was you in my dreams. I love you so very much. You look so very beautiful." Salmon was beaming his biggest smile — the one that starts in his eyes and goes to his cheeks and then to his bright teeth.

"Oh, I must look a mess. I haven't combed my hair. I have no makeup on. Everything around here is a mess. Not much of a home coming for you."

Salmon touched her lips with his finger and said, "You are fine. You are prettier than the oaks of the Negav, and sweeter than the grapes of Mamre. And I've got you, and I never want to let you go."

Rahab broke away from his grip. In a single flowing motion, she puffed up her hair from the back, inserted two ear rings, slipped on a necklace and pulled on a colorful waist band. Her motions were as fluid as the days of Jericho. All while she was asking, "How did you get here? Are you home for a while?" Rahab was full of questions.

"I came in on the supply wagon."

"The very one I missed was the one I should have helped unload."

"You're doing fine. I have a three-month furlough from the war. There are several of us who came in. They are rotating the men on furlough and the married guys got to go first. And I qualified as a married man. I am still married, aren't I?"

"Well, you may have to pass a couple of tests to determine that, but I think you will probably pass. Let's tell mother and daddy you're here."

"And how are you doing down here?" Salmon patted her stomach.

"Just fine. No more morning sickness. Mother says I am doing great!"

"That's wonderful news. We must go tell my parents, too, that I'm back. I came straight here because I guessed that you would want to be close to your folks in my absence." Then Salmon started shouting, "Hey! Is anybody home? Anybody want to hug a poor soldier from the front lines?"

And the family started coming out of their tents. Olmad was first and he said, "Sure," and reached over to give his new brother-in- law a welcome hug.

Mother was next. Her little chubby arms reached around the tall man and gave him a squeeze. "How's that, young man?"

"A top of the list, ma'am," he said and bent over to kiss her.

Dad and Olmad's family and the servants were all in line to welcome Salmon home. "When did you get here?" Dad was asking.

"Just a few minutes ago. I haven't been to see my parents yet. We're going over there and should be back in a little while."

"Be back in time for dinner," Mother had taken charge.

And so Salmon and Rahab went into Judah and made their way to his parents' tent and greeted them. He found them in good health and as eager to see him as his in-laws. Then after they had talked for a little while, Salmon mentioned something about freshening up and they would go to his tent. Which the two newlyweds did, but they didn't come out for a long time. When they did reappear, they were both smiling.

"Welcome home," she whispered.

"Boy, I'll say." And he just grinned.

18

The War Years

As soon as Jonathan heard that Salmon was back in camp, he came looking for his married friends. "Hello, my friend. It's good to see you're back."

"And it's good to be back," said Salmon.

"I suppose your wife told you the news," said Jonathan with a mischievous grin.

"What news is that?"

"That while you were gone, I gave her a baby."

"A what?" Salmon was surprised.

Rahab quickly joined the men's conversation. "A baby lamb."

"And I came over specifically, to see how my lamb is doing," Jonathan was turning to get a better view of Rahab.

"She is not your lamb any more, Jonathan. Remember, you gave her away. Now she is my lamb." Rahab was setting the facts straight.

"Boy, Salmon, you wife is tough."

"It comes with pregnancy, I hear. When a woman becomes pregnant a man must get out of the way until the baby is born. No two ways about it."

"You have to be tough to put up with the likes of you two," Rahab said.

"And how much longer of the tough life do we have to endure?" Jonathan was admiring the glow about Rahab's face.

"Another couple of weeks. The baby should be here before Salmon has to return to battle. He should be here to name the baby and then leave so you can come over and change the diapers."

"See, I told you she was tough." Jonathan reached over and placed his arm around Rahab's shoulders and gave her a love squeeze. "Salmon, are you going to be at the races tonight? I sure would like to leave you in my dust as I take on the championship."

"It sounds like you already have everything arranged but the acceptance speech, but I might come over there and tilt your world a little. Let you know what it's like to have dust in your face, my friend."

"Then I must be going. I just came by to say hello. It's good to see you back."Jonathan reached for Salmon's shoulder in friendship and turned to Rahab. "My dear, you look radiant. I know you're going to be a wonderful mother. God bless you and Salmon and the baby. Walk with God." He touched her check with his finger and walked away.

The days of Salmon's furlough passed faster than any of them wanted to admit.Almost everyday there was a train of wagons from the war front bringing in more spoils from the north. Everyday they were divided among the people who needed or wanted the items. Salmon spent most of his days in the army tent, across from Joshua's command tent, helping the spotters keep up with the places of battle. There were weekly and sometimes daily reports of cities being captured and destroyed.They kept a roster of the kings and the cities overcome.

When Salmon got home one evening, Rahab was in pain and wanted to go to her mother's.The baby was due and she was going into labor. Salmon disagreed about her leaving. The baby must be born in Judah. He could not be born in Friends Camp. He called for one of their servants to rush over to her folks' place and bring Mother back quickly. She could attend to Rahab in Judah.

In a few minutes Mother arrived with her towels and compresses and her gentle baby talk. "Now you just lie still and as comfortable as you can. I'm here to help you. Everyone else get out.You men must wait outside.This is woman's work."

So Salmon and his father went outside and sat on the benches next door.Salmon's mother was in the tent to assist Rahab's mother. The men could hear nothing. People would come by and inquire, but the father-son team could only shrug their shoulders.

"Oh, son, I have always been meaning to tell you how babies are made," his father was talking slowly.

"Thanks, Dad, but I think that we have already figured that out. By the time you get around to telling me this stuff, this baby will be ready for that information."

"You're probably right."The old man smiled a little and then looked down at his hands between his knees.The son hugged his father.

The sun had set and Nahshon brought out oil lamps to light

the tents and the common area between his tent and his son's tent. Olmad and his family and his father made their way to the birthing place and joined the two men. In the flickering glow of the lamps, suddenly there was a cry from Rahab and then in the silence that followed was a wee little cry of the new one. A new life had entered Judah. Salmon took his father's hands and said, "O Lord, let the child be whole. Let the child be fine. Let the child be yours."

And Nahshon said, "Amen."

Salmon's mother stepped to the front of the tent and announced that a new baby boy had been born. He was well and his mother was well. They needed a few minutes to clean things up and then they could see the baby.

It seemed like an eternity, but finally, the women let the new father into the tent to see the mother and baby. Salmon went in and immediately kissed Rahab's damp face. "You're beautiful. You're the most precious person I have ever known. You're the light of my life. You have that new mother look on you. You're just beaming. I am so grateful that God brought us together."

"See what I have for you." Rahab held a little bundle of blanket and pulled a corner back to reveal a tiny, wrinkled face with one eye open, a little nose, and fuzzy hair. "Here is a son for you."

"How beautiful he is! Oh, Rahab, we're so blessed. Look at that hair. Ohhh, he's stretching. Did you see him stretch? Everybody, did you see him?"

"Yes, my son, I think you have a very fine boy. God has answered your prayers," said his mother.

"I've got just one question."

"What's that, Salmon?"

"How do you hold a baby?"

"Very carefully," and Rahab's mother picked up the newborn and handed him to Salmon.

"I've got to show the others," beamed Salmon. "I've got to show the ones outside. I'll be right back." Salmon held the precious bundle cradled in his arms, close to his heart. He stepped to the front of the tent and out into the lamp light and called to the ones waiting. "My friends please come and meet Boaz: Our new son." Then he lifted the baby up towards the sky and prayed: "Father in heaven, you have been creating things for a long time, but you have outdone yourself this time. You have created a son for Rahab and me. Thank you Lord, for this magnificent blessing. Thank you for the care given to Rahab. Thank you for the care given to the baby. Thank you, Lord, for this good company and this good time to bring a son into the world. Lord, we gratefully accept this blessing from you and hereby dedicate our son, Boaz, to your service. We pray that he will grow in the glory of the Lord, and reflect your glory in all that he says and does. Amen"

And all those present said, "Amen."

Nahshon was the first to come see the baby. He gently pulled back the corner of the blanket and looked at his grandson. The baby was wrinkling up his nose and had both eyes open. The grandfather's rough, old hand rested on the soft white blanket that covered the newborn. He only said, "God bless you. You are beautiful."

Then Rahab's family came over to Salmon and touched the baby and made their similar comments. "Uh oh, he's stretching again. Boy, this guy likes to stretch!" Salmon was so excited.

Olmad pulled the corner of the blanket back even further and a little hand and arm were revealed. "Look at this."

"Fingers!" Salmon was in a world of new discovery. "He has fingers! And he stretches!" Salmon was engrossed with this new wonder. He was holding a bundle of love and magic.

Neighbors of Nahshon came over and formed a procession passing by Salmon and seeing the baby. Salmon just beamed in excitement. He was so proud of his gift from God. Every other woman who came by told Salmon to get the baby back inside, out of the night air. So when the last of the line came by, Salmon took the baby into the tent and gave him to Rahab.

"I brought your son back," said Salmon. "I think he is the most popular boy in Judah."

"You had better bring him back," said Rahab's mother. "I was about to come and get you. I was going to get you both back inside." Mother hugged Salmon and kissed him on the cheek. "Now you go outside and be good for a little while."

After the birth of Boaz, time seemed to go by twice as fast. Salmon's furlough whizzed by and he had to report back to the battle front. Boaz was six months old before he saw him again.

The pace of the war was picking up and would soon be coming to a climax at Hazor. This was the most fortified city in the north.

During the course of the war, all of Gilgal depended on the news from the men driving the plunder wagons. The reports told of how the army pursued the enemy, attacking all of the walled cities, tearing down their battlements and defenses, and killing all who lived there. Then they took the animals and the other spoils of each city and sent them to Gilgal, except for what the army could use. Whenever, Gilgal heard of an advance spotter coming in, they knew that a plunder wagon would soon be arriving. Israel was getting richer and richer as the treasure, animals, and other spoils were brought in from each of the cities they destroyed. But more important than the spoils, was the news from the front:

While Salmon was away in the army, Rahab and Boaz lived near her parents in Friends Camp, however, she visited Judah frequently. Once, when Boaz was asleep and under the careful watch of her mother, Rahab went back to Judah to check on her in-laws. When she walked up to Nahshon, she found him working in a flower bed. "Wives! They always have something for men to do," he growled and then that little grin covered his face.

"Somebody has to keep you good looking men in line," Rahab answered. He motioned for her to sit down. "A wagon just came in and the driver said he knew Salmon and he is doing great. He's been promoted to commander."

"That sounds like my boy," the old man leaned on the bench with one arm and then sat down. "Where's the baby?"

"Boaz is asleep now. Mother has him so I could get out for a little."

"Did the man say where they are now?"

"They went into the Misrephoth Maim and are now in the Valley of Mizpah on the east. I have never heard of those places," she told him. "The campaigns are going well. There have been no causalities."

"It's so good to get the news. I'm sure God will take care of all of our boys, but we always appreciate the confirmation, my dear." The old man leaned forward supporting himself with elbows on his knees.

The conversation fell silent.

"I've been concerned about something. I hope you can help me," she pushed forward her quest to the frail, little man.

"What is that, my dear?"

"I sometimes wake up in the middle of the night grateful to be alive and for having found this new life: Meeting these new people: Especially Salmon, and certainly Boaz, and getting better acquainted with you. Especially for all the time you spend with me. But in the darkness of the night I keep asking, Why me? Why would God choose me to be rescued from those falling walls and the slaughter of all those people in Jericho? Why would God have me rescued from the cave? I don't understand it."

"That's a very big question and only the Lord really knows the answer," he said. "But I could make a guess. First, I would guess, because you are special. My second guess is that you had probably been silently crying out to the Lord to know Him better. You've told me that you had been wondering about the power that surrounded the Hebrews as we wandered through the wilderness. I don't know what you heard — stories often get twisted — but if you had been seeking to know about this power, which is God himself, then He simply answered your prayer.

"I suspect that God wanted to show you and others, something of His strength. You had asked to know about God's power, and you saw the waters disappear from the Jordan and then rush back in the next day. You saw and heard, first hand, how God caused the walls of a strong city to crumble. Seems to me, dear, you and your family have been the beneficiary of God's mercy, love and grace. That makes you someone very special."

"I agree," she said with tears in her eyes.

"Now, let an old man get back to his flower bed, so he will be able earn his supper tonight. You know how wives are."

"Well, I wouldn't want you to miss your supper. I'll try to put in a good word for you. That's a pretty good flower bed." Rahab turned to leave.

"Hey, where is my hug? Or don't you hug old men any more?"

"Well, sometimes. When I'm in a good mood," and she reached for his thin, little body.

"I sure am glad you're in a good mood again," he said as he patted her on the back in gratitude for the visit. "And tell Boaz hello from Grandpa."

"I'll be sure to do that."

The Greatest Battle

The war went on. The army's action at Mizpah helped fulfill the promises made to their forefather Jacob about his children's children possessing the land. This was a holy moment. Joshua sent a message back that the army should rest for a few days before they went to Hazor. He was bringing in the rest of the army from furlough. They needed the full army to take the last city.

The army on the front lines rested for several days and then turned south to face the greatest battle of the war. They moved past the smoldering ruins of Kedesh and on to Hazor. This was near the starting point of the northern campaign years before. They had made a great circle and were now within 30 miles of the place where they had started the cleansing north of the Sea of Galilee at Lake Merom. They camped a few miles away from the Hazor fortress and rested in secret for three more days. Meanwhile, Joshua brought in the rest of the troops and they prepared to make their move.

Harzor was a large city with well fortified walls. It was in the midst of rugged mountains. It was so difficult to get an army up close to the city that it became the stronghold of the Canaanites. It was built on two levels. The lower level contained 175 acres within its walls and the upper level was built into the mountains. It was twenty-five times larger and better fortified than Jericho. Here Joshua would virtually complete his victory of possessing the land. This was his last great battle for the glory of God.

On the third day, Joshua and his men rose early and asked God's blessings on their efforts. Then, as the sun pierced the night sky over the high ridge of mountains, they attacked. Because the city was built into the mountain side, it could only be attacked from the well guarded front. Joshua had to capture the lower part of the city before he could capture the upper part where King Jabin lived.

They fought and overcame the embattlements in front of the great wall. They withstood the rain of arrows and knives from the upper city as they mounted the wall. When they got through it, they discovered a second wall, equally strong and defended, but they were eventually able to break through it and sweep into the lower city.

They met stiff resistance from hundreds of soldiers and battle stations. Jabin's army was shooting arrows from many protected places in the upper city. Vats of boiling water poured down on them. Flaming arrows burned everyone they hit and started fires in the lean-to shacks.

After several hours of battle, Joshua's army made its way through the lower level, killing all who lived there. Soldiers would battle for about an hour and then give their places to rested soldiers as they sat out the battle for a while. By rotating troops, the Israelites were able to keep up a strong, barrage.

Then they started their efforts to capture the upper city. It was as difficult as the lower level: More protective walls. More hidden turrets of soldiers hurling more spears and torches. For three days and nights, they waged war non-stop. Eventually, they were able to break through and capture the upper part. Israel had control of Hazor. They put the king to the sword and then totally destroyed everything that breathed in the city. Then the city was burned, reducing to ashes the strongest city in Canaan.

As the flames reached for the sky, Joshua said, "Let's go home." Everyone was ready. Israel had now conquered all of the armies and cleared the land of major resistance. The idols and idol worshipers had been destroyed. They had been at war for seven years. Now there could be peace.

"I said does anyone want to go home?" Joshua repeated.

There was a great shout of "YES!" And a lone voice from near Joshua said, "Just don't get in my way, sir."

The Army of God rested and meditated that night. The next morning at daybreak the spotters rode off plotting the course home. The army, the support groups and the last of the plunder wagons turned south past Lake Merom, the Sea of Galilee and generally followed the River Jordan slowly down the 70 miles to Gilgal where another party was waiting.

Everyone was so glad to see their men returning home. The welcome home party had all the banners on high poles on the roadway to greet the men and there was a general reception party at the entrance to the encampment. It was a massive throng of people. Even before the army was dismissed, families were already infiltrating the ranks and finding their husbands and fathers. It only took five minutes for Rahab to spot Salmon this time and she kept a good hold on him. Salmon held on to Boaz.

Eleazar called all the people together to welcome the men home. From his perch in one of the wagons, he spread his big hands wide and called for all of the people to bow before God. In that great throng of people there was not one little sound. In the deafening silence, the booming voice of the High Priest called out: "Oh Lord, our Lord, King of the heavens, how majestic is your name in all the earth. You have set your glory above the heavens so it fills all the earth. Even from the lips of children and infants you have ordained praise."

His old voice was booming as he called out to his God. A God you realized was his friend. "You have cleared the land of your enemies and silenced the foe. You sent us out to do your work and you brought us back without a single casualty. We glorify your name.

"Now you have cleansed the land you gave to Abraham for us to receive. How majestic is your name in all the earth. It is to your glory that we welcome your army back into our fold and with thanksgiving, we accept your many, many blessings." Then the old man brought those big hands together in a mighty clap that shocked most of those in hearing range. The long ceremonial sleeves were still flowing from the thunder of his clap, when he said, "Let the party begin."

There was a mighty shout from the Hebrew nation. A shout that could have crumbled any nearby wall. The food and wine began to flow intermingled with the welcoming hugs and kisses of relatives and friends. But the real party soon retired to the gathering areas of each community within the massive camp.

Now all of the land that had been promised to Abraham had been returned to his descendants as God had said it would be. Joshua took the entire land just as the Lord had directed Moses and God gave it as an inheritance to Israel according to their tribal divisions. Then the land had rest from war.

Salmon and Rahab found her parents and family and visited with them for a little while and then retired to Judah to see his folks. After they had visited a little, the young family retired to their tent and had their own little party trying to teach 6-year old Boaz his numbers.

The new family slept late that first night together, entwined in each others arms. Well after daylight they made tea together and did everything together that day. They were standing outside the tent while Boaz was playing inside, when Jonathan came up to wish them well. "Greetings," he said as he reached to hug them. "How is married life?"

"After such a long departure and absence from each other, I would say the welcome home night was grrrrrrrrreat," the husband-father said with that smile of mischievousness. To which Rahab doubled up her fist and tapped him on the nearest shoulder. He reacted with mock hurt and leaned forward to cry on Jonathan's shoulder. But the priest stepped back and then beside Rahab.

"Hey, buddy, I'm on her side. I have to be because she has my lamb."

"You don't have a lamb, Jonathan. You gave your lamb away. Now JJ is my lamb."

"JJ?" Both men were asking together.

"She's my lamb and I can call her whatever I want," declared Rahab. I was going to name her after Jonathan. But then we discovered that the lamb was a she, so I just call her JJ for short. Jonathan's initials."

Salmon put his arm around Rahab's shoulders and asked, "JJ. What kind of a name is that?"

"It is one that she has to live with. I fed her with a bottle and when she was old enough I placed her in the herd with daddy and Olmad's sheep. Now when I see or hear JJ, I can remember this tall guy here who rescued me from my sadness and loneliness."

Then Jonathan got to ask his question, "And how is JJ doing?"

"Very well, she already has her first two little lambs."

"Two! Wow, Salmon, this wife is going to make you wealthy."

"I don't care about the wealth," said Salmon. "I just want to know if she can bake biscuits."

"That, old married man, is something you will have to discover for yourself. Now I must go and be about priestly things." He winked as he touched their shoulders and said, "Walk with God."

Jonathan came by often in the next few months as they prepared for new chapters of their lives together.

About three weeks after the return of the armies, and the partying was over and family routine work was the new way of life, Joshua called all the elders of the twelve tribes to the Circle of Government. The time had come for the next phase of life for the Hebrews. The big central government must be dissolved and the people given the land according to the plan of Moses. Two of the items on the agenda were to take the Ark of the Covenant to its final resting place and to bury Joseph's bones at Shechem.

Daniel stopped by Salmon's tent to see how married life was. Salmon reported that all was going fine. And Boaz was growing taller by the day. Daniel said, "I remember our first month together. When Debra came into my tent it was a whole new life. Nice, you understand, but she kept moving everything around and feeding me all that fat stuff. I gained so much weight I had to get a new waistband. Salmon are you still wearing the same waistband?"

"Yes, I think I am. But I haven't got to spend too much time at home. You will have to ask me that question in a couple of months."

"Did you hear the news?" Daniel said seriously.

"What's happening," Salmon asked.

"The council decided today, officially, that there are no plans for replacing Joshua. They think we are close enough to the inheritances that in a few weeks Israel will move to governments among the tribes. Things are going to be different. Did you know that Joshua is over 100 years old?"

"No, I didn't," said Salmon. "I pray I am as strong and healthy when I get to be a hundred. The inheritances are not far away."

"Just think," Rahab joined in. "Soon we will have space. We can have houses with walls and flat roofs. We can have individual yards. We will be out there planting trees and flowers, sowing our own fields and tending to our flocks."

"Sounds a little scary," Daniel looked at the ground and then the sky as he rubbed his hands together. "But lead me on, I'm ready."

"So are we all," Rahab said. "So are we all."

Plans for the settlement were well underway. Israel would develop and grow as twelve nations and cooperate as they needed. If there were a famine in one of the areas then the neighboring tribes would help as they could. If one tribe were attacked then others could help defend and rout the enemy. All of the tribes would remain with God as leader and depend on God's blessings for their daily existence. This fact alone would make them victorious to all their neighboring countries. To insure that the tribes remained close to God and each other, the Levites would be dispersed to 48 cities throughout the Promised Land and live among the other tribes teaching peace and unity in the arms of God. Six cities of refuge were to be established.

The Distribution of the Land from Gilgal

Moses had already given inheritances to the tribes of Reuben and Gad and to half of the large tribe of Manasseh on the east side of the Jordan. Salmon told Rahab, "Today, Joshua had a priest cast lots for land to belong to Judah and for Manassah and Ephraim. The good news is that the land for Judah is just to the south of Gilgal, and we don't have to move very far."

Within the land inherited by Judah was a city to be given to Caleb. The city was Hebron, the area that Abraham had loved so much because of the large oak forests nearby. However, Hebron was once again occupied by idolaters who had moved into the site after Salmon and his army had burned it in the first campaigns. So, being a commander of the Judah army, Salmon chose a few good men and went back to Hebron. They quickly killed off the idolaters but left the city standing for its new residents. Then Salmon came back to escort Caleb and his rich family and servants to their new home.

Everyone gathered to see them off. Caleb climbed up on the front wagon and extended his arms to get everyone's attention. In a very quiet voice he shared with many of his friends how that he was seeing the promise fulfilled that Moses had made him almost 60 years ago. This was the promise made when he and Joshua were two of the spies who got information about Canaan. Only he and Joshua told Moses and the people that with God's help the land could be theirs. But the remainder of the scouting party told of giants in the land and they were afraid to go possess it. Because they disobeyed God (by not entering the land and possessing it) He made them wander in the desert those 40 years until that generation had died off.

Caleb was a very old man when he waved good-bye and headed towards his new home among the giant oaks. His caravan included 45 wagons of silver, gold, fabrics, provisions, relatives, servants, and several large flocks of sheep and goats. He also had his own security force of 75 soldiers.

Preparations for Final Journey

Joshua and his counselors continued to work on the distribution of the land, prepare for the placement of the Ark and deliver Joseph's bones to their final resting place. All the tribes were to receive some land, basically, according to their population, except Levi. The Levites were to maintain their priestly status and their inheritance was God himself.

The land was at peace. The camp was filled with joy. Each day dawned quietly to the sounds of the sheep and goats and other animals ready for breakfast. The Israelites watched their crops grow, the flowers bloom, and listened to the laughter of a happy people. Summer had given away to autumn, and soon the spring floods would be coming and it would be planting time. In order to conclude their tasks before then, the organizational meetings would continue during the trip to secure the Ark and bury Joseph's bones. Everyone in the camp was invited to participate in the long journey to Shiloh and Shechem. A memorial week would proceed the journey.

Six days were set aside to honor the patriarchs, Abraham, Isaac, Jacob, and Joseph. On the night honoring Joseph, his coffin was the center of a processional around the camp's mid-circle. It was at dusk and seven ram's horns were trumpeted, followed by an honor guard of 12 shoulders in full battle gear (one from each tribe) and the coffin was carried by eight Levite priests. Everyone stood on each side of the interior roadway and sang anthems as the honor guard came into view. It was a very touching moment. This was the coffin with the embalmed body of Joseph that the Israelites had carried with them through the wilderness for 40 years. Now was the time to keep their promise of burying him in the Promised Land.

As the memorial was being observed in honor of Joseph, everyone who could was preparing for the journey to resettle the Ark of the Covenant and to bury Joseph's bones. Joshua made an announcement that he had decided to retire to Ephram and claim the town of Tinnath-sera on Mount Ephram for himself, as his own inheritance. He would move there when the final journey was completed.

Rahab had heard that Joshua and his High Priest had spent days in prayer before the Ark so as to know God's will. Joshua sent down a message from the Central Court that all Hebrews were to begin a day of prayer and fasting to purify the camp. This trip would be Joshua's last deed for Israel before he retired. He wanted it to be right. So with military precision he directed that everyone pray for the resettlement of the Ark, that the people would be acceptable for the task, and that all Israel would be blessed. A group of elders had joined Joshua in praying for the location of the new Tabernacle. It would be safe and yet accessible to all Hebrews who wished to come and pray at its site.

The town chosen was a very small place called Shiloh. Rahab remembered going by the little town when they traveled to renew the covenant. Shiloh was about 10 miles from Bethel and not very far from Gilgal. It was near the center of Canaan on the other side of the mountain ridge. Shiloh was a lonely place, on a broad, shapeless plain, absent from any features or landmarks. It was an isolated sanctuary that could easily be forgotten, but it was where a tabernacle was built for the most holy article in the Hebrew camp.

Many of the people from the Transjordan groups began to arrive in Gilgal, staying with friends and relatives until the time to depart on the final journey. The caravan to Shiloh would move at a slow and dignified pace so even the elderly could make the journey. There was plenty of time and plenty of room for wagons. Spotters were sent out to choose the best way to get to Shiloh.

The final journey was about to begin and Rahab would be in it. "Thank you, Lord. I realize now that you have brought me a long ways. I have witnessed your power from the outside when you attacked Jericho. Now, I see it from within the heart of the movement. As your people were wandering in the desert I was wandering in my own kind of desert and did not realize it. How often do your people wander in desert land when your promised land is within reach? Thank you, God, for the rescue. Thank you, Lord, for saving me from idolatry to your grace and love. I love you Lord."

19

Final Journey

The rams' horns sounded a long note and the trip to Shiloh began. The journey over the mountains to the valley where the little town lay would take three days. Rahab and Salmon traveled with Salmon's parents. Rahab's parents were not invited to go, but they couldn't have anyway because of her mother's illness.

As the wagons came out of the entrance they grouped 100 across. Each group of 20,000 soldiers marched at least 500 men across. Salmon's wagon was, of course, with the Judah group and, as always, it was the first of the 12 tribes in the order of march.

Up the mountain slopes they zigzagged until the wagons reached the peak of the mountain range 3,000 feet above the plains of Jericho. Spotters were out front carefully choosing the pathway. Other spotters were constantly running the entire length of the train watching and caring for everyone. One small group of robbers tried to attack the back of the long column but was quickly subdued. One baby was born on the way, and one elderly woman fell and broke her arm, but the journey continued. Boaz was a good boy with lots of attention from Grandpa and Grandma.

As long as the Ark was on the shoulders of the priests, there was singing. Some groups of people were exchanging positions with other groups and at least one group was singing or chanting while the Ark was being moved. *"I will praise you, O Lord, with all my heart. I will sing of all your wonders. I am glad and rejoice in you. I will sing praise to your name, O Most High."* There was never a silent moment until the Ark was rested on its stand and the big drapery was pulled over it. Then it was very, very quiet. Ever so slowly the Ark of the Covenant was taken up the slope to Bethel and gently lowered over the ridge of the Benjamin Mountains, down into the land of Ephraim and on to Shiloh. Just past the town of Shiloh, a small but sturdy tabernacle had been built by craftsmen from the tribe of Ephraim.

The building was a plain, ordinary structure with no trim or glorification. The glory was God's, not the building. It was a simple structure constructed of logs from the nearby trees. It was covered with a mud and thatch roof, typical of the buildings in the area. This was a place secure against the wind and infrequent rains.

There was one large door in the front. The priests positioned the Ark in front of the building near the door, on its stand and covered with the travel drapery. The remainder of the day allowed the wagons to come in place at the site. That evening Joshua called all of the elders, and leaders to his command wagon and there they completed the inheritance assignments.

The next morning everyone moved to the front of the tabernacle and filled the plains in front and the hillsides nearby. Eleazar, stepped inside the tabernacle to inspect it and came out and gave a signal. The Levites picked up the Ark once again and it was slowly moved inside while everyone watched and prayers were chanted by all the people. "Blessed is the Lord. Blessed is the Lord, our God. Blessed is the Holy God, our Creator."

The priests in their brown robes came out and slowly closed the big door and sealed it shut. The men with the rams' horns had formed a big circle around the tabernacle and now one by one they sounded a single note and held it as long as they could. As one was finishing the note the next would pick it up until the single note sounded completely around the tabernacle. The continuous single sound in the circle was a symbol of eternity in honor of the great I AM. Not one person in the huge throng made a sound.

All 40,000 soldiers of God's Army were gathered on the side of one of the hills with a contingent guard around the tabernacle. They came to attention with the stamping of one foot to the ground and then gave a single, mighty shout in salute. Then all the people there made a long whaling noise that broke into the most holy hymn in praise of Jehovah that Rahab had ever heard. "The Lord God is our God. He protects us. He leads us. He saves us. He cares for us. Holy is the God who created us." And then more than one million people bowed to the earth and kissed it. There was a long pause of silence in holy respect for the Ark of the Covenant, and for the Creator who lived there.

No guards were posted at the tabernacle because God did not need protection any longer. God was the protector. God no longer needed to show them the way to the Promised Land because they were there. God would be with everyone who loved and honored Him by the way they lived their lives.

That evening at dinner Boaz asked Salmon, "Are we just going to leave God behind?"

The young father looked at his son, concerned by the question, but then smiled. "No. We don't leave God behind. We take Him with us in our hearts. For wherever we are, there's God. This is His world. He created it as He created us. And as life goes on, God is here. God is everywhere. We're placing in the tabernacle the golden Ark that Moses had built, that's all. God existed long before the Ark was made in the desert. And God will exist long after this building rots and the gold is returned to the earth. As long as we remember to love God, He is with us and our children, and their children's children."

"That's a long time," reasoned young Boaz.

Shechem

The long procession to Shechem began again at sunrise. The 20,000 soldiers' front guard led the way, then the priests with the rams' horns and then the funeral wagon with Joseph's coffin followed by the mourners. Each wagon was now decorated with black wreaths prepared by the children of Israel.

Shechem was north of Shiloh and stood in a narrow sheltered valley between Mt. Ebal on the north and Mt. Gerizim on the south. These mountains at their base were only some 500 yards apart. Rahab remembered being here. Mt Ebal is where they renewed the covenant. This is where they felt the power of God when His commandments were read.

On this visit to Shechem, the advance spotters steered the column of people to fill the sides of the mountains overlooking the Jacob grave site. The hillside was overgrown, but strong soldiers were able to locate the boulders closing the entrance. They worked for more than an hour to open the grave. This was the family grave site purchased by Jacob long ago.

Very quietly, very softly, the entire group sang the single word "Amen" over and over as the word would float out into the air the men would sing it and then the women voices were heard on top. Very solemnly. Very respectfully. The voice collectively expressed, "Amen. So let it be. The promise is completed. Joseph's journey is completed. Israel has kept its promise. So let it be. Amen."

The patriarch Joseph's bones were laid to rest in the family sepulcher on the property inherited by his two sons, Ephraim and Manasseh. Eleazar said a prayer and the priests carried the coffin into the grave site and placed it on the table in the center of the cave; a place of honor. Then the site was sealed with a large stone and the crowd sang another song.

Joshua's Farewell

From a distance everyone could see old Joshua, slowly moving to the front of the throng. Moving so slowly, with his arched back, flowing white hair and beard, he seemed sad today. In front of the throng, he looked out over the hushed audience. He was hesitant and then he summoned the elders, leaders, judges and officials of Israel and they presented themselves before God.

Then Joshua spoke to all the people, "This is what the Lord, the God of Israel, says: Long ago your forefathers, including Terah, the father of Abraham and Nahor, lived beyond the river, and worshiped other gods. But He took your father, Abraham, from the land beyond the river and led him throughout Canaan and gave him many descendants. He gave him Isaac, and to Isaac he gave Jacob and Esau. God assigned the hill country of Seir to Esau, but Jacob and his sons went down to Egypt."

The wind began to blow a little and Joshua cleared his throat. He had more to say. "Then God sent Moses and Aaron and God afflicted the Egyptians, and He brought you out. When He brought your fathers out of Egypt, you came to the sea, and the Egyptians pursued you with chariots and horsemen as far as the Red Sea. But you cried to the Lord for help, and He put darkness between you and the Egyptians. He brought the sea over them and covered them. You saw with your own eyes what He did to the Egyptians. Then you lived in the desert."

Joshua walked to the side of the area and then turned and walked back again as though to clear his thoughts. Then he raised that tired old hand and said, "God brought you to the land of the Amorites, who lived east of the Jordan. They fought against you, but the Lord gave them into your hands. He destroyed them before you, and you took possession of their land. When Balak, the King of Moab, prepared to fight against Israel, he sent for Balaam, to put a curse on you. But God wouldn't listen to Balaam, so He blessed you again and again, and the Lord delivered you out of his hand.

"Then you crossed the Jordan and came to Jericho. The citizens of Jericho fought against you, as did many other peoples, but God gave them into your hands. He sent the hornet ahead of you, which drove them out before you. You didn't do it with your own sword and bow. So the Lord gave you a land on which you didn't toil and cities you didn't build; and you live in them and eat from vineyards and olive groves that you didn't plant."

Joshua raised his voice again and gripped his fist to make his next point very clear: "Now, fear the Lord and serve him with all faithfulness. Throw away the gods your forefathers worshipped beyond the river and in Egypt. Serve the Lord. But if serving the Lord seems undesirable to you, then choose for yourselves this day whom you will serve, whether the gods your forefathers served beyond the river, or the gods of the Amorites, in whose land you are living. But as for me and my household, we will serve the Lord!"

Then all the people began shouting back to Joshua and to God: From the left they shouted, "Far be it from us to forsake the Lord to serve other gods."

From the right they shouted, "It was the Lord our God, himself, who brought us and our fathers out of Egypt, from that land of slavery, and performed those great signs before our eyes."

Down front someone yelled, "The Lord protected us on our entire journey and among all the nations through which we traveled."

A man in a dark robe shouted, "The Lord drove out before us all the nations, including the Amorites, who lived in the land."

The shouts became chants. Over and over they chanted, "We too will serve the Lord. He is our God."

It seemed everyone in the massive throng was standing and shouting their allegiance to God. Then Joshua stretched out those long skinny arms with his robe flowing in the wind and the crowd hushed. There was a determined look in the old man's eyes and he stated flatly and with measured tempo, "You are not able to serve the Lord. He is a holy God, He is a jealous God. He will not forgive your rebellion and your sins. If you forsake the Lord and serve foreign gods, He will turn and bring disaster on you and make an end of you."

But the people yelled to Joshua, "No! We will serve the Lord!"

Then Joshua said, "You are witnesses against yourselves that you have chosen to serve the Lord."

"Yes, we are witnesses," they cried.

"Now, then," said Joshua, "Throw away the foreign gods that are among you and yield your hearts to the Lord, the God of Israel."

And the people repeated to Joshua, "We will serve the Lord our God and obey him." A great applause burst out of the crowd and the people waved their arms in the air and cheered, partly for Joshua and partly for the Lord. And as the thin man with the long flowing white hair disappeared into the crowd, they suddenly realized that Joshua had said his good-bye. His farewell was a call to serve of the Lord whom he had walked with for more than 100 years.

The service was over. Joshua had said good-bye and it was time to go home. There was no formal procession this time. Every family made their own way at their own pace. The servants and others at home had been preparing for the move to the inherited lands, so all would be ready when everyone got home. This would be a different kind of life.

Salmon suggested that while the family was here they should go see the monument set up by Abraham and to visit Jacob's well.

A young man was acting as a guide at the well and its surroundings. He repeated his story as each new group came into hearing range. So Salmon's group heard him say, "Jacob's Well is more than nine feet across and more than 135 feet deep. And, as you can see, it is still in use: watering the sheep and all thirsty people who come by — even though it is more than 450 years old. Please, everyone, come around and taste the water from of our father's well." So they all joined the others in the line to taste the water. They rested for a day and planned to head back in a much more relaxed state.

At dinner time that night a tall, priestly looking man came out of the dusk to their fire and said, "Hey, something smells good."

Recognizing Jonathan's voice, Salmon called back, "The moochers must be out tonight." And with his white teeth shining through his smile, Salmon rose to greet his good friend.

"What's going on over here?" The tall priest asked.

Rahab rose from her little stool and stood up to get her hug. "Just looking for some good company." Jonathan reached over with his strong arms and gave Rahab one of his best hugs.

Jonathan smiled. "Did you leave your boy behind?"

"Oh no, Boaz is over there with Salmon's mother," Rahab said.

Jonathan waved to the parents and Boaz but did not go see them. Instead he asked, "Where do you think you might settle?"

"We are not sure yet. Probably not far from Gilgal. We're not sure if her family will go with us or not. We still have some conferences before we make a big decision. You got any suggestions?"

"You might consider Bethlehem. It's a small town near Jerusalem. It is not far from the Jordan, and not far from the trade routes and there's plenty of grazing grounds nearby. Nice scenery, I understand," Jonathan said.

"And where will you be going?" Salmon and Rahab asked the question together.

"I'm not sure yet. The assignments haven't come down, but I will know by the time we are back in Gilgal. I'm praying to be in the Jerusalem-Bethlehem area. And if you two relocate there, I can come over and heckle you at times."

"You would certainly be welcome. We could use a baby sitter from time to time."

"In that case I may go all the way down to Hebron. They don't have baby sitters down there." And everyone smiled.

They invited Jonathan to join them for dinner, but he declined, saying he had already eaten and was just making the rounds, checking on people. Making sure everyone was all right. He always took his position as priest very seriously.

"But I do hope to see you soon so that I can hold the boy and bless him," and their friend placed his hands on their shoulders. "I wish you well and may God bless you for the rest of your lives and those of your children. I pray that good things will come from not only your lives but those of your children and your children's children. I feel God has a purpose in this marriage and that people will be recalling your names whenever they look back through history to these events. I predict that you will have a very famous and important person born into your lineage. You two are very special. God bless you and keep on blessing you, my friends." And then he kissed his finger and placed it on Salmon's brow and then on Rahab's.

"I trust that God will bring us together again and often," Salmon said as he reached for his friend and hugged him good-bye. Then Rahab hugged him and Jonathan turned and faded into the darkness.

The next morning they rose early, helped the servants pack the wagons again and Rahab and Salmon headed back home to Gilgal to decide on where they would live.

20

The Inheritance

Salmon, Rahab and his family took four days to return to Gilgal. It was good to feel the freedom of the plains and to see the mountains in the distance. Some other people took the opportunity to do some sight-seeing as well. For safety, they traveled with about a dozen other wagons and shared meals and visiting time.

The entire trip was a wonderful experience. The open land, the joy of the people, the happy conversations, and the reverence for the Almighty: everything about the trip made Rahab feel closer to the Lord.

News came that Joshua had his things moved to Tinnan-sera and while he was so close, he went from Shechem directly to his new home and there to rest after such a stressful journey. Salmon asked Rahab where she would like to live and she told him that it was up to him, of course, as head of the household. "I've lived in Jericho all of my life and it would be nice to see some more of the country. I don't want to move too far away from my parents. They are getting old and it would be nice to be close to them," she said.

"Bethlehem wouldn't be too far away. We could get away at times and go up to visit with them." Salmon was thinking as he was talking. Her family would likely stay near Jericho because of their ties to the memories of their homeland. Salmon's parents were getting old, too, and would not be able to travel far.

Choosing Bethlehem

Salmon talked it over with her folks and his parents. He remembered Jonathan's suggestion and told them of a little town to the south called Bethlehem that had good farm land around it. It had not been crowded with so many people as had Gilgal and Jericho area. It had some trees and was also rugged like much of the desert that his family had lived in for the last forty years and all of Salmon's life. It would be a good family place.

All the families in the camp were going through much of the same exercises. Some began to move out, others stayed longer. There was no real hurry. The first major groups to move from the camp in Gilgal were the TransJordans who had provided the bulk of the basic army. They returned in mass to be with their families in the land east of the Jordan. They returned home very rich families. They took their tribe's portions of the plunder and spoils of the captured cities. They had many herds of animals. Their servants drove thousands of wagons packed with a great variety of things. They were a caravan of their own. The Lord had paid them well for their time west of the Jordan.

Since Salmon was no longer in the army, he was looking forward to farming and carpentry work. He had never built a house, but was ready to try. He wanted to build furniture, too. As the camp began to empty, Salmon's family, also, decided it was time to gather their herds and with a few other families head toward Bethlehem. They took 15 servants to help manage their herds of horses, cattle, donkeys, sheep and goats. Rahab's brother, sisters and parents all elected to stay behind and rebuild near Jericho. She was lonely for them, but excited about this new adventure as well. It took several days to make the move because of the herds, but at last they began to see the fields and more and more evidences of people living nearby.

Salmon pitched their tent near the edge of Bethlehem but away from the people already living there. The others in their caravan set up housekeeping nearby, making their own little community. The area was lovely. It was a day of blue sky and soft breezes. The edge of winter had passed by and it was a season of new beginnings.

They must have been quite a sight for those families living in Bethlehem. About a dozen Hebrew families coming down the road to their town with wagons driven by servants and herds of animals driven by herdsmen who enjoyed singing at the top of their voices. They said that it kept the herds from being nervous, but Rahab reasoned it just helped the herdsmen pass the time.

The new neighbors came out to meet the Hebrews when they began to unload the tents and corral the animals. They had heard that the Hebrews were coming and they ran out to reassure them that they were not idol worshipers and they wanted to be friends. So the new arrivals invited the old citizens to a party.

As soon as their tents were set up for the night, the servants began unloading food, tables, wine, and oil lamps. Some of the new neighbors brought gifts of food to contribute to the fare. Soon it was a very festive scene. As the people gathered around the tables Salmon climbed up on a bench and spread his hands as he had seen Joshua and Eleazar do. The crowd became quiet.

"I'm not good at making speeches," Salmon began. "But I know good food and happy times when I see them. I also recognize the blessings from God." Then he bowed his head and clasped his hands in front of him. He said, "Lord, we thank you for a safe journey. We thank you for the riches you have given us. We thank you for the love you show us every day of our lives. As we begin to live in the land you have given us, we ask your continued blessings on us and our friends. We dedicate this community to your honor, power and glory. May we always be close to you. May we always love you as you have loved us. Help us, Lord, to always walk close to you. Bless this food and bless us with your everlasting love. Amen."

Then Rahab's husband clapped his hands together in the fashion that would make Eleazar proud and said, "Let's eat!" Everyone applauded and started filling their plates. The party was noisy well into the night with singing and laughter. Slowly everyone wandered back to their own houses and tents and the night grew still and quiet. Rahab was one of the first to find a pallet and stretch out with Boaz. The sun was already up when her husband brought her a cup of steaming hot tea he had made for them. At last they were home.

Soon Salmon, in cooperation with the others traveling with them, set up an organization to watch after the flocks and graze the animals. It was still early spring and they could get a late crop of barley in and perhaps some oats. The old timers in the town said it was too late, but Salmon replied that there was little to lose — just the seed — and God would bless their efforts, which He did. As the weeks flew by, Salmon had started on their house. He was instrumental in organizing a town square where community business could be conducted and shops could be opened.

Joshua Dies

Soon after the first planting, a runner from Gilgal came riding in just at dusk one day and said he had sad news. Joshua had died. He was 110 years old and was buried quietly in the land of his inheritance, at Timnath-Serah, in the hill country of Ephraim, north of Mount Gaash. All were saddened by the report, but rejoiced at having known him and for being able to absorb a measure of his faith. They all recognized that he had, indeed, walked with God.

They gathered in little huddles to recall the amazing things that Joshua had taught them about God and how God was always working in their lives. "Regardless of how little or how graciously we reflect the glory of God, the Lord is still there in our lives providing amazing things for us," Salmon reflected. He recalled that the number 110 was a perfect number in Hebrew. It was a number dedicated to completion. Joshua had lived a full, completed, life; as had his mentor, Moses.

In late spring the animals gave birth to their new babies. And Salmon presented Boaz with a tiny lamb from the lineage of J.J. Father was teaching son about how to hold the baby, rub its new fuzzy coat and to run after it each time the baby lamb got away. They made a good team and each looked forward to playtime each day.

Soon the lamb was taking naps with Boaz. The little boy often held his four-legged friend in his lap or the lamb would sleep with his head on Boaz's shoulder. They were very close, friends. However, the lamb grew faster than the boy and soon they developed different interests, but they held on to their friendship, and the lamb became the beginning of Boaz's herd of animals. They both lived long productive lives.

With the help of his servants, Salmon began concentrating on building their house. Salmon had spent his entire life living in a big tent, so he was used to one room living. He designed his house much that way: one big room with alcoves off that room for sleeping, cooking, eating and learning. This was typical of the other houses also being erected from the dried mud bricks that were common building material in the area. Rahab was busy with draperies, floor coverings, shelves, vases for flowers and other decorative items. She wanted the most beautiful home in Bethlehem.

At last, Rahab had her walls, draperies and flat roof. She was at home. "Oh, how I enjoy the window out front to see people coming up the roadway," she would often tell visitors. "And the little window in the cooking area that looks toward the barns. But my favorite place is on the roof where we sit in the evening. Sometimes at dusk, if I am there by myself, I find myself looking for the white dove that visited me in my toughest hour at Jericho. The roof is my favorite place," She was very proud of the home Salmon had built. Behind their house, Salmon had houses built for their servants. Many of the other families left their servants in tents, but

Salmon wanted the best for his staff.

While they were busy getting their house in order Boaz continued growing. The months and years ran by as fast as the Jordan raced to the Salt Sea. As more of the Israelites settled nearby, they were able to start a school and Boaz was instructed in the Hebrew ways and laws. Soon he was bringing home little boys and girls to introduce, and then older children. It seems like they always had someone else's children in the house. Boaz had lots of friends. He grew into a strong, tall, handsome teenager with a long twist of hair in the back of his head. He would often go out with the servants to help watch after the animals. And one of the herdsmen had a long twist of hair down his back and Boaz thought that was just the thing. He got the servant to show him how to twist his hair. Salmon and Rahab talked with him several times about how he wore his hair, but his father's stubborn streak was coming out in the boy and they decided to let Boaz's hair be in God's hands.

In his late teens, Boaz began making trips from Bethlehem to Gilgal to visit with his grandparents and Rahab would often go on some of the trips. They had two very good servants who could be trusted to drive the wagon from their house to Gilgal. No one traveled alone on the roads because of thieves and robbers. For the young men, it was not a long journey. Salmon was usually busy with the fields and animals. Their herds kept increasing. God blessed them richly.

Salmon gave Boaz some more animals and helped him start his own field for the time he would want to have his own family. Salmon taught his son the management skills he had learned through his life. So the boy learned about animal husbandry, crop rotation, storage, and kindness towards the less fortunate. "You are growing up rich in the blessings of the Lord," the father would tell the son. "You have many possessions, now. But there may come a time when the Lord will bless you with no possessions. And you need to respect those people who are in need of some of the things you have. Sharing is an act of love." Boaz learned many acts of kindness from his father and mother.

There were some small hills with little caves on their property. As Boaz was growing up, Salmon was thinking of special uses for the hills. One of them he decided should be a sepulcher. So he enlisted several of their servants to dig out the cave to bury their people when the time should come. He called on a mason in the group from Gilgal to carve a large round stone with a track system that could be rolled in front of the opening to seal the graves. Burials were always within hours of death and then a memorial might be held for the person later. Having a place ready was very important in this arid land and Salmon demonstrated great responsibility by taking care of the matter.

Salmon and his servants were also able to enlarge and improve a cave in the side of another hill to store grain, dried fruits and other foods "for a rainy day," he would say. Boaz helped his father and together they established a very successful storage system that could seal up the dark, cool insides of the hill. They fashioned their own heavy doors that could be secured. The weather is uncertain in Canaan and Salmon had remembered the reports of droughts and famines that had plagued the land.

A Death in the Family

The family was on the roof one evening, just after sunset, when a rider came up to the house calling out "Rahab, Rahab." She stepped to the front of the roof and called down to him. "I'll be right down."

Salmon went with her and opened the door to the visitor. It was Joseph, her father's servant. He was shaking in his voice when he said, "Miss Rahab, I have very sad news. Your father sends me to tell you that we all grieve at the death of your mother."

Rahab sank to the floor on her knees gasping for breath. Each time they had seen Mother she seemed to be a little worse in her health, but this was so sudden. Such a surprise! She tried to speak but no complete words would come out of her mouth. Joseph understood, for he loved Mother, too. He had been with them in Jericho. He bent down on his knees and almost whispered, "Your mother loved you all her life. She died peacefully and in full knowledge of the Lord that you lead her to. We buried her this afternoon and your father wanted you to know about it." He hesitated a little and then continued, "Your father sends you a gift. He sends you this." And he held out both hands and reached around Rahab and gave her a hug. No servant would ever show affection to their owners, but Joseph was as close to being a member of the family as any one ever born outside the family. "Your father said for me to hug you for him, and to comfort you."

Salmon helped them both to their feet and insisted Joseph stay in the house with them through the night and until after breakfast and then return to Gilgal. He reluctantly agreed. And he gave them a full report on the families in Gilgal. They sat up late into the night catching up on all the news.

Rahab watched Joseph ride away, carrying her heart back to Gilgal. She decided not to go home just yet. Maybe later when she had overcome her grief for her mother and her father had some time to adjust.

10 Year Drought

The rains stopped and the roads and fields became grounds for dust devils to play. Some of the late grain burned up in the fields and the small ponds began to evaporate, leaving scant mud puddles. And then they disappeared. The lack of water began to affect the herds. Salmon attended the meetings in the town square with the other men of the village. They were seeking ways to water their bountiful herds. But there were more animals than water. The livestock had to be reduced in order to save some of them.

Salmon had heard of a means of preserving meat by rubbing salt into the cuts of meat and storing it in a cool, dry place. Perhaps, where they had been storing fruits and vegetables would also work for meat. So as they slaughtered some of their livestock, Salmon had his herdsmen rub salt into the meat and hang it in the hillside cellar.

At one of the meetings, the men decided they needed reservoirs to hold the rain when it did come. So as the fields burned from the hot, dry sun, and the herds were beginning to die from thirst, the men brought all their servants to bear on building a dam across a small dry creek. The men hauled big rocks by the wagon load into the area where a dam could be built. They placed them into the creek bed and then began to cover the rocks with dirt from the basin of the creek. It was their first pond in the desert. But it did little good when the sun was dry, hot and the sky remained clear.

Long after they had finished with their dam, the sky did cloud up and a small shower wet the thirsty land. It was not much of a rain, but a little water did run down the creek and was caught in the curve of the dam. Months later there was another shower and it added water to the muddy lake.

The drought remained and the people's needs grew more desperate. The meetings in the market square grew longer and more desperate. They tried forming a wagon train to haul water from the Jordan from above Gilgal. But they had no facilities to haul enough water. The Jordan did not have much water in it anyway. Their only other source of water was the Great Salt Sea and that water was not usable. They would just have to rely on God to get them through the drought.

Robbers

Rahab was glad that her husband did take precautions with his storage of food products, because when the rains stopped, the crops did not grow and the hot winds dried up everything. There was no harvest for any of the families. Many of their neighbors had to leave the area and move across the Jordan into Moab in order to survive the famine.

Rahab and Salmon stuck it out, living off their rainy day provisions. Salmon told her it was dangerous to move to Moab because of the people who occupied the land. They were descendants of Lot, Abraham's cousin, who had traveled with him into Canaan so long ago. Now they were idol worshipers and were in a lot of trouble with God. But they did have food and some of the group did go there for several years and married into some of their families.

There was very little food throughout the Bethlehem-Jerusalem area. The caravans stopped coming by because there was nothing to trade and little food for the animals. And if they did have something to trade, few people had gold to pay for the purchases. These were tough times.

One day when most of the men were in the marketplace, there was a knock at Rahab's door. Then suddenly it burst open and two men rushed inside, slamming the door behind them. They had daggers drawn. Visions of old Jericho flashed through her mind again when she was young and frightened, but these men were not from God. She could still read faces and their fear and uncertainty told her this was a new experience for them.

They stood, nervous in their stance and speech. Their tunics were old and torn and dirty. They must not have changed clothes or bathed in weeks, if not months. They were bare footed and their feet had sores and scratches on them from a weary journey. Their hair and beard were matted and tangled. These unkept men had sorrow in their eyes. It was no surprise when one of them said, "Woman, gimme your gold and we won't hurt you."

"What could you possibly do with gold?" She asked. "There is nowhere to spend it."

"We're in a hurry," the other desperate man said. "Stand aside, woman, and I'll find it." So while one man held her at dagger point, the other one went through the house gathering up pieces of gold and placing them in an old leather pouch he carried with him. He quickly chose the golden bowl from the center of the table, some candle sticks, a vase and some other things Rahab did not see.

Then as they turned to leave, the big bell in the center of the village rang out. "What's that?" One of them asked

"It's the alarm. Something bad is happening."

The robbers were more frightened than she was. They quickly opened the door and ran for their wagon, taking the few pieces of gold with them.

Rahab grabbed her shawl and ran after them and saw more men running to the wagon; jumping in it as it began to pull away with running donkeys.

Neighbors gathered in the street watching the robbers drive away. Boaz and Salmon came running up asking what had happened. "Those men took some pieces of gold from our house." She was pointing to the vanishing wagon.

Salmon asked, "Are you all right?"

"Yes, yes," she said. She was crying. "They're such poor men."

Some other men had gotten to their horses and with daggers on their sides rode off to capture the robbers. They soon caught the poor desperate men, six in all, and returned them to the market square.

The robbers were brought before Salmon because he was serving as chief of the council that month. The meeting was in the square, where there was a platform for speaking and conducting business and people could hear what was being said. The robbers were poorly dressed, thin and hungry looking. Their getaway wagon was worn out with holes in the side panels and patched wheels. Their donkeys were undernourished with their ribs showing. It was a sad scene.

"What do you say for yourselves?" Salmon asked.

A tall man with ragged beard and sagging tunic lifted his big hands in desperation and tried to talk. He was embarrassed, humiliated and sorrowful. Very hesitantly, he began to mutter, "We come from a village a little distance from here. We have no crops. No food. Very little water. We have spent everything we have trying to out last the drought. Our women are dying. Our children are dying. We have no work. We are just trying to stay alive. We got word yesterday that a caravan was coming this way. They have food from Moab. They're to be at the crossroads just north of here before sundown today. We wanted to buy food for our families, but we had nothing to buy it with. We had heard how you Hebrews were wealthy; that you had gold. So we decided that in order to save our families, we would come take a little of your gold and buy food with it from the caravan. Now you have us at your mercy and our families are still starving."

A second man in the group lifted up his scrawny hands and said, "This is true. It's all true. We have become robbers in order to buy food to save our families. Our babies go to sleep at night crying because they have nothing in their bellies."

There was silence throughout the square. What would Salmon have to say? How would he render a judgment in this case?

Slowly, he looked each of the six men in the eyes, their very sad eyes, and then he spoke. "If you know that we are Hebrew, then you know that we follow the laws of God Almighty. One of those laws is 'You shall not steal.' We have a custom that the one who steals shall lose everything he owns. By taking from others, everything shall be taken from you. Therefore, as you watch, the men will unload your wagon and return the items to their owners."

Three homes had been robbed and the servants from each of the houses went to the wagon and took the things and returned them to their owners. Then Boaz and two of his friends went to the broken wagon and removed the few provisions that belonged to the hungry men and brought them to the platform. Someone else unhitched the donkeys and led them away. Then Salmon said," I said everything. So now take off your tunics and belts here before the people and prepare for your own funerals." So the men took off their belts and the holsters and little compartments they contained and dropped them to the floor and then pulled their dirty tunics over their heads. They stood before the public in only their loin cloths. They were so thin. So skinny. There were no muscles in their legs. Their ribs replaced the chest muscles. Their little bellies were puffed out from malnourishment. They had scratches over their bodies from trying to get roots from thorny bushes to eat. They were barely more than skeletons.

"Now, so you may understand the seriousness of this matter, you are to be escorted to the houses you stole from and there be washed and dressed for your funeral," Salmon was very stern.

The robbers were lead to the houses they had robbed. Boaz

came with his mother to the house as two guards accompanied the robbers. Their servants washed the bodies of the men and gave them fresh clothes. Then their cook brought out some barley soup with warm bread for sopping. One man began to eat rapidly. He must not have had any real food for days. The other asked if he could somehow have the meal sent to his family. He would give up his meal, if his family could have it. The guards said it was his meal and he should eat it.

So the men were prepared to die. Rahab walked back to the square with the two men who had come to their house. Salmon was still sitting in the judgment seat but a group of men were gathered around him. The robbers' wagon and donkeys were gone. People were milling about. Some had gone to their own homes and now had returned.

While the victims were at their houses attending to the last rites of the robbers, Salmon and the elders of the community were busy deciding the judgment. When all six robbers had been escorted to the platform again, Salmon took his seat and again examined the skinny men with those penetrating eyes of his. Then he asked his questions again.

"You say that you came to our village and robbed three households because your families are starving."

"Lord, our whole village is starving. We buried three people just yesterday who had starved to death. Our animals are dying. Our people are dying. Our village is dying."

"And you say that a caravan carrying food from Moab is coming to the crossroads north of here before sundown today?"

"Yes, master, it is our only hope. It's our village's only hope. Do with us whatever you wish. We belong to you for what we have done, but remember our starving families."

"Just how do you know the caravan is coming and that it truly is from Moab? Perhaps they are just a bunch of robbers like you," Salmon questioned.

"If they are like us, then they are not much of a threat. They are certainly not much robbers. For we are starving. Our village is dying. The news received seems to be true. Only by meeting the caravan will we actually know. If someone went with an army escort then there would be no fear of robbers. If there is food, then it is for sale. Just remember our families, please. Have mercy."

Salmon stood up to pronounce his judgment. "The laws of

God say 'You shall not steal.' You have broken one of the very basic commandments of God. In breaking the law you have lost all of your possessions. Even to your very clothes on your back. According to God's Law you are deserving of death. When and how you die will be determined by God Almighty.

"Now there is fortunately another law. A greater law. God said to love the Lord your God with all of your heart, soul, mind, and spirit. And you shall love your neighbor as yourself. You love yourself by loving and helping those people about you. When they are thirsty you give them a drink. When they are hungry you feed them. When they are naked you clothe them. These are acts that reflect the glory of God. This is the purpose of our living and worshiping the one true God. This is what we have just done for you.

"Now we will go one step further. Your village should not have to suffer from your sinful and desperate act. And because you have also brought us news that can perhaps benefit us as well as your village, we will let you go to the crossroads this afternoon. Further, we will provide the armed escort you may need in case this news you received is not exactly as you think it is. You lost your wagon and donkeys so turn around and look. We are providing you a new wagon and pair of healthy donkeys."

With that statement Salmon raised his hand high in the air and a wagon and two healthy donkeys pulled from a side street into the market plaza. Everyone turned to look. At once Rahab recognized it as one of their wagons and two of their donkeys. While they were tending to the robbers, the men of Bethlehem were busy making decisions. They had already decided to help the six men and their village. While they had very little food to spare, they could provide the means for them to buy and deliver the food.

The poor men were surprised at such generosity: A good wagon and healthy strong donkeys. It was something they had not seen in years. They were jumping up and down, clapping their hands and hugging each other. They ran to hug Salmon, who hugged them back.

"Delivering the food has been taken care of, but you will need some gold to buy it with so under that covering in the back of the wagon is gold enough to buy your food. It comes as a contribution from most of the families in Bethlehem," said Salmon.

As they were watching the wagon, a second one came from around the corner and it too had a covering. "Under the tarp in the second wagon is a little food that we have gathered from many of the people in the city. We have very little food to share, but the Lord provides for us and we are confident that he will replace it ten fold. We give this to you in love from our heart."

"Thank you, thank you, thank you, master," they kept repeating. The six skinny men were overjoyed. They had come with one broken down empty wagon. Now they leave with two sturdy wagons with gold and food.

A third wagon came around the corner. It was filled with Hebrews armed with spears, shields and daggers. In front of them were four horses, mighty steeds, carrying armed soldiers. They would provide the military escort. Then a fourth wagon came around the corner. It too had two more of the neighbors driving it. It contained some gold to buy food for the village in Bethlehem.

Salmon grabbed the skinny men and hugged them and said, "Now be off and take care of your families. May the Lord be with you and spare your lives. Show love and mercy to others as you have received love this day in Bethlehem."

"We will. We will," they were shouting as they jumped from the platform in their clean tunics and freshly trimmed beards and ran for the wagons. And everyone waved to them as they all drove north towards the crossroads.

Salmon remained on the platform and the citizens remained in the square. Somehow the event was not complete. Then someone, somewhere, started singing praises. Everyone picked up the chant and together they praised God. "Thank you, Lord, for loving us. Thank you, Lord, for saving our souls. Thank you, Lord, for all your blessings that we might be able to share with others and bring glory to your name in this small way. Go with the men, Lord, and protect them and feed them Take care of their families and their village. Bless us, Lord, as you bless those who visited us. We praise your name in all the earth. You are our God. And we love you."

Late that evening one of the wagons returned home carrying food from the caravan. It was food from Moab. The news the visitors had brought was indeed true. The next morning the wagon load of escorts came back home, grateful for an uneventful trip. The food was distributed to the poorest of the families in Bethlehem. And everyone gave thanks to God for again blessing them with his bounty. Salmon quietly said, "See, you never know when God sends angels your way. You never know how He will be blessing you."

The days remained hot and dry. The wind was biting into their skins and the fields lay burnt yellow with gaping cracks in the land. Little white clouds sometimes would appear and disappear but the heat seemed to scare them away. Day after day and month after month Bethlehem prayed for relief, but the sun always seemed to have its way. So, no one noticed one mid-morning when little clouds appeared and more of them joined to fill the sky and how they grew darker. But once a cool breeze swept through the town, everyone took notice. Could this be the break?

Everyone gathered into the dusty yards in front of their houses and shouted praises to God Almighty for the dark clouds and the touch of raindrops. At first there were just a few. There was just enough to bring joy to parched faces. All the children were running around with their tongues sticking out trying to catch the next rain drop. The women dropped their shawls from their heads so they could feel the blessings from heaven. The falling raindrops got thicker. Salmon came to hold Rahab. Boaz came and held them both. They danced in the streets with the other people. It was raining! The wind ran through the town and blew the rain into the open doors, but no one seemed to care. The ten-year drought was broken and crops could be planted again. Everyone was soaking wet when they finally went inside. Everyone was ecstatic. They watched the rain all that day. It was still raining when Rahab dropped off to sleep.

Drought Broken

With the planting of crops, there was a harvest and there was food again throughout the land. As word of the harvest spread, the Israelites who had fled the famine to Moab began to come back to Judah, even some families returned to Bethlehem.

There was one family in particular Rahab remembered one family: a husband and wife and their two sons had left in search of food. However, soon after they arrived in Moab, the husband died. Later, their grown sons had married and they too died, leaving the widow with only two daughters-in-law and no income. They were very poor and in a strange land. The widow's name was Naomi.

Everyone loved Naomi and her husband and were sorry to see them leave. Rahab had watched as Naomi's two boys grew into fine young men. But they were like so many others who had to go search for food. Rahab and Salmon heard that Naomi had returned but they had not yet seen her nor knew where she was living in Bethlehem.

Boaz had been busy with his fields. Barley was especially good. It was harvest time and he had hired several men with sickles to cut the grain, working their way across the field. Behind them came the women he hired to gather the straw and grain and tie into sheaves. The sheaves would later be taken to the thrashing floor where the grain was beaten from the straw. Behind the women who gathered the sheaves, sometimes were the very poor who would come to the fields and gather any left over stalks of grain for their own meals. This was a custom of the people and in obedience of the Hebrew law. The first cutting was always given to the Lord in praise of a bountiful harvest. So even though their own granaries were almost depleted, the first cutting was presented to the priests who blessed it, offered a sacrifice to the Lord and then shared much of it with the very poor people.

Ruth and Naomi

Late one afternoon, Boaz went to his field to see how the harvest was going. He saw a few women gleaning the remaining straws of grain. One of them was particularly attractive. He waited for her to finish her work and then met her at the side of the field. He learned her name was Ruth and that she was the daughter-in-law of Naomi. He invited her to come back and glean some more in his field. The next morning Boaz told the cutters to leave more of the grain uncut, so there would be more to glean. Ruth went home the second day with almost twice the normal amount of barley.

Ruth told Naomi about meeting Boaz, the son of Salmon. Naomi remembered that they were in the redeemed-relative line. She instructed Ruth to follow Hebrew customs. She should offer herself in marriage by visiting Boaz at the threshing floor and sleep at his feet. Boaz, of course, seemed delighted. However, there was another person who was first in line to redeem.

At the new dawn, Boaz went to the market square where most of the city's business was conducted and waited for the first redeemer to arrive. There in the presence of several witnesses Boaz dutifully reminded him of his duty to marry Ruth, because her husband had died. Indeed, Naomi's husband was dead, too, and it was his honor and duty to marry Ruth and buy back the lands that Naomi and her husband had owned. Then the property might continue in the original family's name.

The man considered it carefully but said that if he did so, it might place his own holdings in jeopardy. So, he decided not to take Ruth and let the honor pass to Boaz. There in front of the town's witnesses Boaz bought Naomi's original land so it would stay in her family's name and he would marry Ruth.

Boaz ran back to his parents' house like a little boy, shouting and jumping in the air. He was talking so fast his mother had to constantly remind him to slow down. When Salmon came home, Boaz repeated his exciting news by picking up his father and dancing great circles around the room. She had never seen such excitement in one tall boy.

Boaz and Ruth were married and before the first year's anniversary of their wedding, they had a son, whom they named Obed. He was such a beautiful grandson. Such big eyes. Such a sweet smile. He was such a good baby. Rahab soon learned why God blesses older people with the gift of grand parenting: It is the best blessing for the peak of life. Of course, the poor little thing hardly got to eat or sleep because either his father or his grandfather had him off to the market, the blacksmith's, the town in general or just up and down the street showing him off. They were all so proud of Obed. The grandson was taught as carefully as Boaz was on how God blesses those who honor Him, who praise His name and keep His law as best as they can.

One day the family took a trip back to Gilgal and they introduced Ruth and Obed to Rahab's family.

"Daddy, I want you to meet Ruth, Boaz's wife. And this is their son Obed." Rahab's father stood up from his bench and tried to straighten his old frame a little. He was slow now with age and grief. His face and body told of the sorrow and loneliness in the passing of Mother. When he was finally standing, he said little, but only reached out and hugged the young people and touched the baby. After a short visit, the next stop was to visit the tomb where they had laid Mother's body. Salmon held Rahab close as they remembered the good times of Jericho and beyond. Then they all went down to a special place just to the southeast of Gilgal where the memorial of twelve stones was built.

With great pride, Salmon placed his grandson on his knee and said, "Obed, see these rocks? They're very special rocks because they come from the center of that big river over there. They're special because they were chosen by the heads of each of the twelve tribes of Israel. They picked them from the center of the river when God stopped it up."

"How did He do that?"The little boy asked.

"God can stop the river when He wants to.And He did that day and we all crossed over the river on dry ground. I know because I was one of them.

"Did you get wet?"

"No, Obed, we crossed the river without getting wet. This memorial was built of stones from the middle of the Jordan to remind us of the great power of God.To remind us who God is. God has His way because He is the Creator. He is the Master, the ruler and the Father of us all. God does good things for us because we are His children and He loves us, just as we love our children. Do you understand, my boy?" Salmon asked the question, not expecting an answer.

There at the memorial they all gathered in a circle around it, held hands and Salmon offered prayers to God."Thank you again, Almighty God, for the countless blessings you have given us. We are surrounded by your great gifts, even our very lives come from you.Thank you for being so generous.We are grateful for everyone here in your presence.

"Thank you, Lord, for Rahab, the one you chose to save from Jericho and come to enrich the lives of her husband, family and so many friends.Thank you, Lord, for Boaz and his family.They bring us so much joy.Thank you for Rahab's family for they have seen your great power and have come to know your great love. Bless every one of us, Lord. For we give you the honor, power and glory that envelopes our very lives."

21

The Legacy

The days in Jericho seemed a million years ago. The area was slowly being rebuilt. Some of the rubble had been cleared away and a few houses were among the palm trees. There was no city wall. Just open yards with children running in them. Rahab and Salmon tried to find the place where her apartment had stood in the great wall, but they were never sure. Too much time had past. There were too many changes. Those days were gone forever.

The sun was setting and the sky was aglow in orange, crimson, blue, and gold. The family spent the night with her brother. Olmad and Rahab stayed up late that night, as they had often done in Friends Camp, recalling old times including their experiences brought indirectly by Joshua. What a fine man he was. "Remember, that phrase of his to consecrate yourself, for the Lord will do amazing things among you?" Rahab asked Olmad.

"I think of it often."

"Then, tell me what amazing things has God done for you recently?"

Olmad turned to look at the sky and then the horizon, and slowly back to Rahab. "I find it amazing at how fast my children are growing up. I count it amazing how God can form a baby and bring him into the world. How he can produce a little lamb, and a little goat and blades of new grass, without getting things all mixed up." Then he smiled and gently bumped her on the shoulder. "How can God hang all those stars in the sky and keep them in a certain order? How can God make a goat give milk and a sheep grow wool? How is it that God can put love in our hearts for our families and tie us all together with strong heart strings and somehow instill in us that there is more to life than we dream? I think all of that is pretty amazing stuff."

"I agree," she told him quietly. Then slowly she said, "It's amazing at the blessings we have yet to count, dreams yet to be imagined, and powers yet untapped as God feeds us His strength and wisdom."

The two grew still and quiet for several minutes. Then Olmad reminded Rahab that it was time to turn in if they were going to make the trip back to Bethlehem tomorrow.

"Yes, it is getting late. I didn't even realize it. Olmad, I was thinking of something Salmon's dad had told me. When I would ask him for more knowledge about God, he would respond that God sent two spies to give me instructions, an army of 40,000 fighting men to provide the way, and two million friends for support. He said that when the Father chooses to answer prayers in a big way, He has the means to do it. That's pretty amazing, too."

"God works in all of our lives to eventually bring about His good works. God can move mountains, stop rivers, cause it to rain or not rain, bring harvests or no harvests, just to be able to work in the lives of His children who honor Him; who bring Him glory." Rahab was still not ready to say good night. She still had some thoughts to express. "He brings us joy in the faces of our children and grandchildren. He brings us closer to Him in our sickness and troubles — when we recognize how weak we really are without His mighty powers."

"God protects us with good spouses, safe homes, a measure of good health and close friends. God is good to each of us because God is Love." Olmad finished his sister's thoughts and then reached for her hand to help her up. Olmad and Rahab picked up their cups and in the cool evening air, walked slowly back to their families to spend another night, under the stars, between the past and the future.

The Death of Nahshon

When the family arrived back in Bethlehem, sad news was awaiting them. While they were gone, Salmon's father, Nahshon, died and had been buried in the new tomb that Salmon and others had dug in the side of the hill. Just as their wagon was pulling up in front of the house, neighbors began running from their homes to greet them and hug them and tell them how sorry they were that they missed Nahshon's burial.

Rahab just fell back in her seat on the wagon, not believing that her father-in-law was dead. He had not been feeling well, but old people often have good and bad days. While everyone was chattering and talking so fast, her mind slowed to a point of only recalling favorite memories. Suddenly, she was back at his tent in Gilgal, sitting on that bench in front with him at her side. He had been counseling Rahab on why God would love someone like her and she got up to leave. He called to her and said, "Hey, where's my hug? Or don't you hug old men any more?" And she snapped back the caustic remark, "Oh, when I'm in a good mood." And he smiled and said, "I sure hope you are in a good mood." And she reached over and hugged that little knobby back and shoulders and pressed his chest against her shoulders. *Oh, to hug him again. Just one more time.*

People were all around the family. Rahab didn't know what happened to Boaz and his family. She didn't know who took the baby. She just remembers seeing some men helping Salmon from the wagon and into the house and others came to help her. They were half carrying her and half helping her walk. There were so many arms, so many kisses and the din of mixed sounds. Voices were coming at her from everywhere. She must have heard 'I'm sorry' thousands of times.

The neighbors were everywhere. They got them into their home and then started bringing in food and gifts. Rahab remembered looking up to see Salmon's mother in the room trying to serve some drinks to people. She, too, was old and feeble and did not need to be on her feet. Rahab pointed her out to Salmon and he got his mother to sit down beside him and let the others do the serving. He held her for a long time. They just sat silently as an oasis in the middle of a thunderstorm.

Nahshon had served as a leader of the Judah tribe while they were in the desert. When they crossed over the Jordan he passed his role on to others, but remained fairly active in the council meetings. When they all came to Bethlehem and made their little settlement outside of the town proper, they chose to keep their big tent and one servant to tend to their flocks. They had lived in that tent all during the desert years, and the eight years in Gilgal. It was comfortable for them and they did not care much for changes all the time. They lived as they had always lived, happily in love.

Hours later, the neighbors began going home and the wake was over. At last the servants closed the door behind the last guest and Salmon and Rahab went up to the roof for some peace and quiet. They wanted to reflect back on the life of his father and recall his advice, his love, his hugs, and his teachings. That exercise filled the night.

The next week, Salmon spent his days surveying their flocks with the servants and started a new census of the animals. God had richly blessed them with new animals in the spring and early summer. Salmon was working at incorporating his mother's flock into theirs so that she would not have to watch after them. They kept her servant-herdsman working. He was a good man, who had been with them for many, many years.

At the end of the first week back from Gilgal, his mother got sick and in four days she too lay dead. Rahab went over and helped wash her body and dress it for burial. Young men from the village brought a litter and they moved her body onto it and brought her to the central room of Salmon's house so the neighbors could pay their respects. Everyone must have come. Each family brought some food or other gifts and Salmon, tearfully, received each and every one. But before sunset the young men carried her body to the sepulcher. There the men moved Nahshon's body from the center table to one of the shelves on the side. His mother's body was placed on the center table and carefully wrapped in the long strips of white cloth filled with herbs and spices in the Egyptian custom. The face covering was last.

Salmon felt weak with sorrow. The grief for his mother weighted heavy on his heart and soul.

Flooding

The next morning the clouds were dark and heavy and the wind was cool. Before noon, the rain drops began to fall and hard rains set in by mid-afternoon. The rain fell hard and continued as though it would never stop.. The herdsmen had a lot of trouble trying to keep the animals fed and protected from the weather. A little rain did not hurt them, but days of rain, like this downpour, was not good for them. Salmon was out with the herdsmen trying to find shelter for such large herds. They worked day and night erecting tarps and shelters for them. Everyone was soaked and stayed soaked all day. Their wet tunics were stuck to their bodies and dripped when they stood still. Their black hair was stuck to their faces and necks and continuously dripped from the rain. The fields were all muddy, little creeks were rising, and water became a real danger, yet the rain continued. Feverishly, they worked to save the animals.

No one had ever seen so much rain in Bethlehem. The few

people who would venture to the market square did so to discuss how it could rain so much in the arid land. Over in the Gentile section of the town, the conversation was much the same. No explanation except it was the will of God.

The bigger animals were rotated in and out of Salmon's barns. They were brought in long enough to get dry and eat and then turned back into the rain while another group came into the barns. Salmon had more than 300 horses and as many cows and donkeys and many more sheep and goats. The Lord had certainly blessed them with livestock. And they were grateful, but the men worked day and night trying to save the animals.

The smaller animals were a different matter. The mud was so deep that they were getting stuck in the swamps. Salmon collected all the tenting that they had from the barns and his parents' storage. He directed the servants to erect the big sheets of waterproof materials on tall poles. They made a big shelter on the side of a hill for good drainage. But it was not enough. It takes sheep a long time to dry out enough to want to eat and sleep. So Salmon sent Boaz into the Gentile section of Bethlehem to buy all the canvas and poles he could find. In a couple of hours, Boaz came back with a wagon load of canvas and poles and more shelters were erected.

Salmon worked tirelessly through eight days of heavy rain with very little sleep or food. He felt he had to be there with the men and the herds. He was so tired when he came in for a little nap, he would pull off his wet tunic at the door, dry off, and Rahab would give him a fresh one. Then he would fall down on his pallet and instantly be asleep. A short time later he would jerk awake and be up ready to eat something and head back to the herds. He did this day and night. The rains just kept coming. They were hard rains. Many of the other people's animals were drowning and theirs would have too, except for the dedicated work of their servants, Boaz and Salmon.

Finally, there was enough shelter on the side of the hill to keep a very large portion of the animals dry. The men had dug out a trench around the upper side of the protected area to drain the rain around the site so that it would be relatively dry. They gathered hay from the barns, carefully wrapped it in heavy canvas and took it to the shelters and spread it on the wet ground.

The animals were protected, but Salmon wasn't. He was so exhausted from the continuous high stress of the week and his lack of sleep and rest and food, that he began coughing. The cough would not go away. He lost his energy. All he wanted to do was sleep. When the rain did let up and the crisis was over, all Salmon seemed to want to do was go up on the roof and lie in the sun and sleep. Rahab had never seen him so listless. He seemed to lose interest in everything. He would just sit and look over the short wall around the roof, or lie on his back and watch for clouds in the sky. She was really worried about him.

She called on the village healing person. He came over and made some herbal tea. Someone else applied salve to his body for blood circulation and energy. Other people did other things, but nothing seemed to help. In a few more days he completely lost his appetite. His eyes glazed over and Rahab knew in her heart that she was going to lose him.

Boaz and Ruth started spending more and more time at the house. Ruth became the hostess, receiving and making the guests comfortable. They had more and more guests. All the neighbors were dropping in at all hours to see how Salmon was doing. Some had suggestions for making him feel better. Everyone brought food and they had no place to store much of it. Ruth began sending some of it to the poor part of Bethlehem.

Salmon's health continued to decline. His speech became slurred when he did talk. They dressed him in diapers and changed out his sleeping tunic every few hours. Much of the time he slept through the change and didn't realize what was being done for him.

Boaz and Obed took over the management of the flocks and herds. Their herdsmen were also concerned about their master and were very loyal. They had become part of the family, too. In the evening they would stop by for a report on Salmon's health.

One evening well after dark there was a knock at the door: A silent knock, a very patient knock. Rahab opened the door and the lamp-light shone through the doorway spilling into the darkness beyond. The figures of two men stood before her. "Hello, Rahab," they said almost as if one voice. It was Daniel and Jonathan. "May we come in?"

"Yes, yes, of course," she stuttered. "Forgive me, for my impoliteness. I couldn't see you very well."

The two men came in and Jonathan grabbed for Rahab and hugged her so tightly against him she could feel his heart beat. She felt like she was being hugged by God himself. "My heart is with you, my very good friend," he said. "I have come to remind you that

God loves you and provides His glory for you." And he held her longer, not expecting an answer.

Then Daniel, impatient Daniel, said, "Hey, it's my turn. Let me hug one of my favorite girl friends." His smile lit up the room. Those white teeth and happy eyes were radiant beams of hope and reassurance. Jonathan let go of Rahab and stepped aside. Daniel reached for her and in his own very loving way hugged her gently. "You know we love you," he whispered.

"Yes, I know." They were crying.

"We have come to see our very best friend in the whole world."

When they heard that Salmon was seriously ill, Daniel found Jonathan and they had traveled all day to get there. She took them into the alcove off the center room where Salmon lay.

"I'm glad you have come. Your visit will do him good," she told the friends. They lighted another lamp and then she called to her husband, "Honey, open your eyes and see who has come to see you."

"I'll bet he will remember me," said the priest. And he took Salmon's hand and squeezed it and leaned over to place his hand under Salmon's head and touched his cheek to his; a makeshift hug.

Salmon opened his eyes and licked his parched lips. He tried two or three times to say something. Finally, he uttered, "Moocher."

"Hey, that's right. I love you my friend. I have always loved you. I bet I will always love you."

Salmon held on to the priest's hand and whispered, "You bet."

"Look who stole a ride with me and keeps drinking up my tea."

Daniel was very perceptive and could see that his friend lay there with very little life in him. "I see that you held on to that pretty little girl that caught your eye when Jericho fell in."

Salmon squinted trying to focus on the new voice that greeted him. Then he smiled and whispered, "Daniel. What you doing.... with him?" His speech was broken.

"You mean traveling with a betting priest? Oh, that's because he makes good tea. I think maybe that's his best talent." Daniel tried to make a joke and be happy with his wisecracking mannerism, but it fell flat. "We came to tell you we love … we still love you. When we heard that you were sick, we just had to come see you and hold you close one more time, my friend."

Salmon smiled and closed his eyes. He never opened them again.

A fever came over him and his whole body was sweating. They tried to bath his face and arms in cool water, but it did little good. The visitors all moved to the main room. One of them must have gone to tell the neighbors that Salmon was dying. Because soon there were voices throughout the house and in the front yard and up and down the street. Softly, ever so softly, they were singing: "Glory to God who gives us life. Glory to God who controls our time on earth and calls us home."

Everyone left the little alcove where Salmon lay except Boaz, Ruth, Obed and Rahab. They gathered around him and held his hand, watching his frail body breathe. In the other room Jonathan was leading everyone quietly in prayer. He was lifting Salmon's name up before God. He was thanking God for all the many blessings He had sent them, especially Salmon. He was recalling their long friendship, the races they had run, the friends they had met, the teaching of God's word to the younger boys, and how heroic Salmon was in the conquering of the Promised Land.

As Rahab stared into her husband's empty face, she heard someone uttering quiet words of thanksgiving. They were saying, "And remember Rahab. Give her strength to let her love shine through this darkness and reach down into the generations to come. Thank you, Lord, for the Woman with the Scarlet Cord that she has found your mercy and love … and has shared it with so many people. May her teachings be effective for generations to come. May her life continue to reflect your great glory."

Then she recognized the quiet, serious voice as that of Daniel. In all of his fun loving ventures, he had this mellow, serious, relationship with the Almighty and it radiated from him.

She felt a cooling, relaxing, stillness come over her and she shifted her eyes from the beams in the ceiling back to her husband. He lay still. Perfectly still. He was no longer breathing. The moment she realized it, Boaz and Ruth both reached for her and hugged her and kissed her. The waiting was over. Her husband had passed..

The four of them walked back into the room where the others were and everyone knew their news before they spoke. Rahab's knees buckled under her and Boaz and Obed carried her to a bench and let her sit down. Quietly, very quietly the people there filed into the alcove and touched Salmon's hand and then came back by Rahab and said something to the effect, "Bless you, my child." Then they went out into the night.

Some people moved Rahab upstairs to the pallet she kept there, so she would be away from the crowds coming to pay their respects to her husband. Perhaps she could get some rest before tomorrow. She cried all night long. From time to time she was filled with doubts and questions, *Why God have you done this to me?* And at other times she was thanking God for the long time and the good times that He had given her with the man she loved so very much. She understood that Daniel and Jonathan spent the night hosting the many people who came to see Salmon, their good friend.

When the dawn chased away the gloom, death was still present in the house. During the night someone, Rahab didn't know who, had already prepared Salmon for burial. They had bathed him, applied the spices, put fresh clothes on him and wrapped the body in the long white streamers. The special covering for the head lay beside him. Someone made sure that Rahab was dressed, and they made her eat something and drink some hot tea. Someone gave her a new mourning shawl and then they all went out the door.

Daniel and Jonathan formed the procession to the tomb. Boaz, Ruth, Obed and Rahab led the group with Daniel and Jonathan behind them. Then came the body on the litter carried by friends and then the host of people. They walked silently to the tomb in the hillside. The stone had already been rolled away. Two men went in and moved the body of Salmon's mother to a nearby shelf and washed down the center stone table to receive the body of Salmon. They carefully laid the body on the clean table and backed out of the tomb. The stone was rolled over the entrance, sealing it until the next time it would be used. Someone started singing a song and everyone joined in. However, Rahab whispered, "God forgive me for not joining. My heart is too heavy."

Everyone returned to their houses. The children, Jonathan, and Daniel came back to the house with Rahab. Even the servants respected the need for privacy in sorrow and stayed away from the house. Jonathan and Daniel only stayed a few minutes, again expressing their love. In departing, Jonathan came over to hug her one last time and whispered, "Take care of my lambs." And he smiled. Rahab wasn't sure if he meant the sheep he had given her so long ago or of the children that God had given her. In any case, she loved his thought.

As they were leaving, Ruth brought her mother, Naomi, to visit briefly. Rahab had been so busy with Salmon's illness that she had not seen Naomi in a long time. She was as beautiful as ever: so loving, so gentle.

"I just wanted you to know that you are not alone," Naomi said in the quiet voice of hers. "You feel alone, but you're not. The spirits of all your friends are with you — and there must be many, many friends, and God's spirit is with you. He is there to comfort you and to help you. I know how you feel, because I still remember the emptiness when I lost my husband over in Moab and I had to leave him there. You can look out your back window and see where your husband lies, but I can't do that." Naomi paused a moment, wiped her eyes and continued, "I know how awful you feel, how frightened about what will become of you and your household, but you have strong children and loving neighbors.

"And you have me. Whenever you want to talk or to cry, just come down the street and I'll be there for you. Or if you want me to sit with you, even if it's in the middle of the night, just tell Boaz or Ruth and they will come get me. Sometimes it's better to just be able to sit next to someone who has experienced what you're experiencing." She paused a long time. She took Rahab's hand in both of hers. Naomi looked at the wall behind Rahab and then back into her eyes. "I've been there. I know what you're going through. It's not easy, but you can do it. You will come out of this valley of shadows a stronger person. I know. I've been there." And with that quiet statement, she turned and Ruth followed her out of the house. The door closed and Rahab was alone for the first time in weeks. How quiet is loneliness.

Rahab wandered around the house seeing traces of her husband everywhere. His clothes hanging on the rod. His little plant in the window, he could never get to grow satisfactorily. His knife on the table by his bench. His handiwork in the furniture he had made. In the windows he had made, and the back yard — he was everywhere. Her life was filled with his memories, but he was still missing. The entire bottom of her heart and soul had fallen out and he was gone. Her husband was gone. He was dead. *How could he leave me still here? Now, Lord what do I do? Oh God, what do I do now?*

Rahab went upstairs to the roof and threw herself on the pallet and felt the day's sunshine fill her empty soul. As the days past, Ruth and Boaz would come over almost everyday to check on Rahab and make sure that she was eating and looking after her health. They were treating her like she was their child and she told them that. But Ruth is strong and said that she could be her mother if she wanted to, and smiled in that quiet way of hers.

Everything she said was filled with love.

One day when Rahab was complaining about being loved so much, Ruth quietly turned on her and said, "Now remember, if you are going to act like a child, then you will be treated like a child. And if you don't remember what that's like, just ask Obed. He'll tell you that when he starts complaining, sometimes it is a whole day before he can sit down after we have had our little session. I don't think you want to have a session with me." Then she smiled.

And the mother said, "Yes, ma'am." And smiled back.

One day when Naomi came by, she told Rahab that she had heard that she had been staying too much on the roof and Ruth said she needed to be out with people more. They sat in the front room of the house where the big window looks out onto the main road. Rahab told her friend, "I just can't remember how Ruth became my mother. She treats me like a little kid."

Naomi smiled back, "That's the way it is when your children you have taught so well, see the responsibility of taking care of everyone they love. If you think she treats you like a child, you should see what she does to me." Then she slapped her thigh and laughed. The formality of the relationship was broken and they sat down and talked all afternoon. They made tea and had bread dipped in honey, and visited some more. What a delightful afternoon. She was no longer that proper person who came to visit. She came as a friend, thigh slapping, giggling and all.

Naomi helped draw her out of her shell of grief and showed her the outside world again. She insisted that they cross the road to a vacant area where the children came to play. They went over and spent several afternoons there in the shade of one of the palms that Salmon had planted. Rahab started going over there most afternoons for a little while to watch the children and talk with them.

The kids were full of questions and she had few answers for them. They were asking things that Rahab never asked until she was grown. This was a whole new generation with a set of bold questions. One day the boys needed a tall person to get a ball out of a tree and Rahab climbed up in the tree a little ways and retrieved it for them and they thought she was great. Then they wanted to know if she could throw the ball through a hoop they had made and fastened to a pole. So she barely looked and threw the ball and it went into the hoop as though it were being directed by the Almighty himself. The boys around her were all cheering and wanted to know how she learned to do that. Rahab didn't know how to respond. She just didn't want to say that it was all an accident — being her first shot and all. So all she said was, "You boys just need to practice more."

So from then on the gray haired grandmother was accepted on the playing field as some sort of star player. They started coming to her for all kinds of advice and she got a lot more of those questions that only parents should answer, but she did the best she could. Every time there was an opportunity she tried to reassure them that God loves them. Just like Salmon and Daniel and Jonathan had done. Over the months that followed, in between scrapped knees and bruised fingers, Rahab found joy in teaching the children that came to the playground. And she got pretty good about landing the ball through the hoop.

An Old Friend's Visit

The days and nights seem to fade from one to another, summer into fall and then the brisk days of winter. Rahab had good days and bad days. Some days she got up feeling good and was ready to do whatever needed to be done. Other times she opened her eyes and wondered why God had left her here this long. One day was particularly overcast and the whole world was blue and sad. *Oh, how I miss Salmon today.* She would go from room to room in the house, trying to keep herself busy, but she seemed to migrate to the back window and look out past the barns to the hills beyond and see the tomb that held her husband's body. She was so sad and lonely for him, so focused on his love for her and how greatly she missed it, when there was a knock at the front door. She didn't know who it would be because Boaz, Ruth, and Obed always just walked in. There were no children out playing today. So she lifted herself up from the window ledge and made it to the front door. When she opened it, there stood Jonathan. "My, you are a sight for sore eyes," she said as she reached for him and he reached for her with his mighty hug.

"And how are you doing this beautiful day?" Jonathan asked.

"Do you remember that time, in Gilgal when you found me so lonesome for Salmon that you brought me a baby lamb to keep?"

"You want me to go find you another lamb?"

"Oh, no, no. Oh, my no, If there is anything I don't need, its another lamb. I've got more sheep than Boaz can tend to anyway."

"Then what," her guest asked.

"You have a knack of surprising me with a visit when I feel the loneliest. This is that kind of day."

"Then I had better come in and see what I can do about it."

"Oh, I'm sorry, Yes. Please come in. Please come in. I'm just not all here today."

They moved over to the couch in the big room and started their visit. She made tea and they visited some more. He never did explain what he was doing in Bethlehem. What she did remember was when he took her hand in both of his and began talking quietly and deliberately.

"I'll bet you are lonely today and many of your days, because you are recognizing the passing of great love from one person to another. You miss Salmon more than any of us. He was my best friend for so many years. I miss him, and I get lonely for the good times we had and for those good experiences we shared as friends. I am sure you must have those moments a hundred to every one of mine. That's the reason I came by; not as a Levite, not as a priest, but as a friend."

"You always know just what to say. I miss him so much."

"You see I miss him too. This is very natural in the course of events. God has made time to pass from one period to another, and this is a passing. People just don't die suddenly and quickly. They die over months and years. Sometimes over a period of many years. Sure the body is gone, but the spirit can stay with us until we no longer need it and God has replaced it with something else. Once we pass from this life to another, as Salmon has, I believe that the confinement of this life is left behind and our new lives have no earthbound limits. So we can be in heaven with God, and a part of us can still be on earth with those who continue to need our love. That is why we feel our loved ones about us from time to time. And when we are saddest, that loving feeling comes to surround us with that old love."

Rahab stopped him. "That is a beautiful thought. I never reasoned anything like that." Her eyes were aimed out the window but they were not focused. She was thinking too hard.

"When your parents passed from this life," Jonathan continued. "You felt them around you and then they gradually passed from you when you were able to handle their absence. You are probably still feeling at times the love of Salmon's parents. This is natural. God's love is always around us, but it takes on the forms and feelings that we can understand. It takes the night to make the day bright. It takes the valleys to make the mountains tall. It takes loneliness to call in great love."

"And, it takes a tall priest to say just the right words to comfort an old woman." Rahab reached over and patted his shoulder.

"The reason we're dedicated to loving God with all of our being, is because God is love. When we love those about us, we reflect God's glory on them. This is God in action. To love others is a Godly act. So call up your fond memories of those you have lost. Relive those happy and sad moments when you struggled to live and wondered if you would make it. Remember the tough times and the good times. That's why we have memories. Salmon lives on in your memories and is in the process of passing. Just as you and I will be someday. We will be called home by God and we will begin our passing from the confines of this earth to a better place and a new kind of life. Part of you will be here with your children and their children and their children. Part of us will remain with friends and their friends to encourage them to be with God. Do you see what I mean?"

She looked into his big eyes and nodded her head. Then he broke the mood and asked, "How's that for a priestly sermon?"

"Pretty good," Rahab replied still trying to absorb the message. "Pretty good, I would say for one that I haven't seen in so long. Is this where you take up the offering or give away the lamb?" Suddenly, Rahab felt mischievous. His explanation of death made her feel better. It was good to be with an old friend. It was great to hear him sharing his love.

"Neither one. I have already been warned about the lamb And I'm not looking for gold. I was just passing by and was looking for someone to make me some tea," he said with a wink.

The conversation continued while she poured tea. "Yes, I'll bet. I'll bet you were just passing by. I'll bet you made a long journey just to be with me." She squeezed his hands. "You're turning gray."

"It comes from drinking so much tea with pretty girls," he said with a grin. "Careful about all that betting. People frown on it, you know." And the tall man in the brown Levite robe stood up and said, "Well, if that is all the tea you are going to serve me, I guess I'll be leaving." And he winked again.

"That's all the tea you can hold for now. But if you promise to come again, I'll bet I can make some more just for the two of us. Thank you so much for coming by. You have always been such an encouragement for me and for Salmon. You always know just when to come."

He turned and faced her and looked deeply into her eyes. He was communicating love without saying a word. Then with a single finger he traced a route down her cheek as he had done so many years before. Only this time her skin was softer and he temporarily smoothed out a winkle or two. But he didn't notice. He hugged her and very quietly said, "Walk with God."

And she repeated it, "Walk with God, my friend, Jonathan."

He turned and walked out the door and out of her life. She never saw him again.

The Stranger

More seasons rushed by, but the loneliness crawled. Winters and summers past as quickly as the days of the week. Rahab's long hair was turning gray and almost overnight, it seems, it became a beautiful silver. She would sit by the window looking out to the hill where the sepulcher was and remember the good times with all who lay there. Boaz and Ruth continued their almost daily visits. If they couldn't come for some reason, they were sure to send Obed. And every time Obed came, Rahab would comment on how tall he was growing. He was taller than his father and wore bigger sandals. Sometimes they would talk about his hair. She would tell him it was interesting or different, or some other safe description. But Obed knew that she really thought he should have it cut like his father's, and not like the other teenagers. The grandmother would inquire about how many girl friends he had and which ones were the prettiest. Obed would make a guess (a different girl each time) and then hug his grandmother. Obed would also go home with a little cake or candy that she kept ready to give to company.

One day when they were at the kitchen table, a powerful sand storm blew in. It came whirling in suddenly, blowing sand and weeds down the street. It rattled the shutters and the entire house smelled of dust. Just then there was a loud knock at the front door.

"Who could that be out in weather like this?" Rahab asked her grandson, but he only shrugged his shoulders. "Obed, dear, you wait here and I'll go see who is at the door. If it is one of your girl friends, I'll just tell her that you are busy with another girl."

"Grandma!" Obed was exclaiming, but the old lady was up and to the door before Obed could say another word.

"Y-e-s," Rahab said as she opened the door. It was a long drawn out word that asked several questions in one syllable.

"The Lord be with you." The voice was cold and dark; a little gravelly. It came from within a rough looking hood that covered the man's head and masked his face.

"And also with you." Rahab returned the blessing, not sure to whom she spoke or even if she wanted to continue the conversation in the storm.

"Miss Rahab, I presume." He was a tall man, dressed as though he could be a salesman. Trimmed, white beard and heavy eyebrows covering droopy eyelids. He was a little stooped shoulder, as though he had lived many years with heavy burdens.

"That's right. How may I help you?"

"Miss Rahab, my name is Jacob. Our lives crossed many years ago. More than twenty years ago, in fact. When you were living in Gilgal. You said some things that changed my life. I have come to apologize to you, and to also express my appreciation to you. May I come in for a few minutes?"

"Yes, of course." Rahab open the door back further to allow the stranger to enter the room. He walked with a limp and smelled of the dusty road. "I was just visiting with my grandson. Please, come in. Have a seat."

"I don't expect you to remember me. The years have been too many to remember brief encounters more than twenty years ago." Jacob eased himself to a little bench opposite the chair where Rahab sat. She could see both the stranger and her grandson in the kitchen.

"You're right. I'm having trouble recalling our meeting. You will have to tell me more." The stranger had her interest.

"First, let me say that you are hard to find. I've been searching for you, off and on, for the last ten years. And then I heard that you had settled in Bethlehem. So, at my first opportunity, I wanted to come see you."

"That was very nice of you. This trip must be important to you."

"It is. You probably never knew my name. Back in Gilgal, I had a close friend and the two of us pretty well stayed to ourselves. At that time we drank a lot and spent a lot of our time being up to no good. But later some events came about that changed our lives. Mine was changed for the better and my friend's life was changed for the worse."

"What happened to your friend? That sounds so bad." Rahab's eyebrows were pointing down in sorrow.

"The events I have come to tell you about, cost him his life, but they saved mine. I have wanted for years to come tell you about them. First, to apologize for the terrible time we gave you, and then to tell you how much I have been blessed by you saving my life." Jacob straightened up his bowed back as though he was about to cross the finish line in a long race.

"I saved your life? How did I save your life?" Now, Rahab was the one sitting up straight. Obed was leaning forward with his elbows on the table, out of view but quietly catching every word,

"Miss Rahab, let me start from the beginning."

"Of course."

"When I was little, I felt like God wanted me to make a great gift to the world. I went through most of my life never knowing what that gift would be. When I was a young man — in my twenties— I pretty well forgot about it. We were all living in the desert, gradually moving towards Moab, and then finally crossing the Jordan into Canaan. I remember walking the eastern banks of the Jordan and looking over the distance to wonder what was happening in Jericho. It was such a magnificent city. I had forgotten about making a gift. I had pretty much forgotten about God. I was too busy discovering girls, and parties, and getting into trouble. I was ruining my life.

"The miracle of the Jordan River meant nothing to me and my friends. It was just another adventure. Setting up tents in Gilgal was just another stop along the way to nowhere. I didn't even go participate in the worship services that surrounded Jericho for seven days. I was hiding out with several friends who would go steal things while everyone was away. I can look back now and see that I had begun isolating myself from most of the people. I'm not sure why, but I settled on one friend and we moved to the edge of the Judah camp and pretty much kept to ourselves."

Rahab jumped forward, "You and your friend were the ones who came by our campsite late at night!"

"Yes, that's true. We were probably drunk and I'm never sure of what all we said to you and your family, but I'm positive that it was not kindly."

"You were always there after dark, and I never got a good look at you. All I can remember is you had heavy beard and curly hair."

"You're too kind. We had scruffy beard and wild hair," he admitted. He smiled and reached up to check his neat white hair. There had certainly been a change in the man's life.

She smiled and he continued his story. "You know how some people build their relationship with God only when it is convenient for them?"

"I would suspect that would be most of us," said Rahab.

"Well, we had heard that a prostitute had moved in as a result of the capture of Jericho, and we took it upon ourselves to rid the plague before God got a hold of us. At least, that was our motive. And that is when we caused you and your family so much trouble. I have come here to apologize for that. I am sorry for our language, our acts, and our abuse to you and your family. Can you ever forgive me?"

"You were forgiven a long time ago. Twenty years ago— if that is how long it has been. It's easy to misunderstand people from different cultures. We all judge the world by our own viewpoint and not from the culture of other people. I saw Israel as a monstrous army that came to kill everybody so they could and take away our things. I couldn't understand how anyone could believe in an invisible God."

"And we could not understand how people as a group would want to worship idols and allow prostitution."

Rahab picked up the reasoning. "Baal and the Moon God were everyday gods to us, a part of our life for hundreds of years. Prostitution was an honorable profession for women. Men looked up to women who could treat a man professionally. In Jericho it was a good profession."

"Please understand Miss Rahab, Israel is not without its own sins. How many times did each of us, perhaps all of us, would forget about God's laws and turn to other gods, and how frequently did the men seek out prostitutes from the villages that the nation moved past. So, in reality, there was very little difference between Israel and Jericho. Perhaps the difference was that God had blessed Israel and had her under his arm at the time we crossed into Canaan. Looking back now, I can see how God had blessed you and your family by saving you from the destruction of Jericho. You are a chosen person. I wanted you to know that I know that now."

"Thank you for coming this way to tell me that. You seem to be a very kind person. A person of kind thoughts, I should say." Rahab was still studying his face, as though he had come to visit during the days of Jericho. She could see the lines of hardship. "After that time of judgment, I thought of you two a lot. I prayed for you almost every night. I was praying that God would have mercy on you as He had mercy on me, and your lives would be spared. Tell me what happened after they took you away from the camp."

"The soldiers took us way out into the wilderness that night. We were completely lost. We didn't know which way to turn. The soldiers turned us loose and rode away. We were all alone. We decided to wait out the night and take our chances in the daylight. So we lay down and used our travel robes to cover with and saved our rations until the next day. We heard the wolves that night and for many more nights. It was scary."

"I can imagine it would be," said Rahab.

"When the sun came up, it was not much different. There were no landmarks. Any direction was just about as good as any other. So we started walking. It was several days before we came to a village. We were starving, sun burned, and dying of thirst. There were some kind folks who cared for us. We didn't tell them who we were or why we were lost. It didn't seem important to them. They gave us food and water. We stayed with them for several days and then moved on. Several times we would almost die of thirst, but would be rescued by travelers or by a family in some small village. Then one time we were out for several days and we didn't find help. My friend kept saying he needed to drink a whole skin of wine. He wanted to get drunk and he started cursing God because of the trouble we were having. Israelites shouldn't have to live this way, he would say and then he would curse God again.

"I could see that this time we were not likely to be rescued. And I started praying to God to have mercy on us. Nothing was working. We went without food and water for several days. We were so weak that we could no longer walk. A sand storm came up and we found protection behind a big rock and lay down to die. The next morning I saw the sun come up but my friend didn't. He had died during the night from starvation and thirst. Or maybe he died because he cursed God, I don't know."

"You must have been so frightened," said Rahab.

"Yes, I was scared. All that was left of me was to pour out my soul to the Lord. I raked hands full of sand over my dead friend. All the time I was pouring out my soul to God. I asked for His mercy to forgive me of my sins. I promised that if He let me live long enough I would find a priest and get him to offer a sacrifice for me. I recounted every wrong and foolish thing I could remember. I did it just so God would know that I knew all those things were wrong. And then I remembered all the good things that had happened to me through my life. I was so desperate. So hungry. So thirsty. I would have given anything for a small cup of water." The stranger leaned back against the wall and straightened his thin legs out in front of him. He took a deep breath and then continued his story.

"I sat there in the shade of that rock, near my dead friend for two days. With every breath I took I was asking for God's mercy and His grace. I was asking for Him to save me from the desert and from my past life. Nothing seemed to happen, but I kept on asking. Only God could save me, if He would have me.

"Some time during the third day I became so weak that I must have fainted, because when I woke up there was a young couple tending to me. The woman was washing my face. They had poured water into my mouth. They had tried to get me to eat. They told me they had been with me for the whole day. They had been traveling to a nearby city when suddenly their donkey just made a turn off the road of its own accord. The donkey brought them straight for the rock where I lay dying. Our only explanation is that God had sent them to rescue me. God was answering my prayers."

"Of course, He was answering your prayers. God is always listening. God has saved you, just as He has saved me." Rahab leaned forward again. "And they helped you to get back to a town and get you back on your feet again?"

"Yes, they did. All I could think about from that time on was that childhood dream of making a gift to the world. There I was, completely destitute, no possessions, no means of support, no strength to earn a living, body starved so that I have very little muscles. I was so weak — yet I had this driving urge to make a gift to the world about me." The lines in his face began to relax a little. A solution was not far away.

"What did you do?"

"I kept recounting to myself and then to others about how many times God had saved me. I always begin with your speech at the judgment. When you emphasized how important God is in our everyday lives, how He is our protector. I always remember your phrase about how God reached into that little embryo and pulled out my arms and legs, how He decided what color hair and eyes, how He decided if I would be a boy or a girl. I shall always remember the power and the love of those statements. That is what God does: He creates. And He is constantly at work in creating each of us everyday of our lives."

"Those have been important words in my life, as well. A little servant girl brought them to me once when I was desperate for love and reassurance." Rahab looked down at her wrinkled hands and tried to smooth them out a little.

"Next, I remember your plea of forgiveness. I recall how you said that you forgave us of our terrible actions. Then you ask the judge to not have us stoned but turned out of the camp and left to the mercy of the Holy One. That is when you saved our lives. You saved us from stoning and left us to the mercy of God. I shall always be grateful to you for that. Most people would have been out gathering rocks during the judgment, but you were forgiving and looked for a way to show love. That was a major turning point in my life."

"So what did you do about your gift?"

"I felt that the only thing left of me was this story. So my gift is my story. I go from place to place telling this story of my salvation every chance I get. I hope that a personal accounting of how I sinned against God and yet was saved will be received by other people. Perhaps, it will give them hope, that regardless of what they have done in their lives, God can forgive them and love them. We are all children of the great Creator."

"I am so glad you told me your story, Jacob. I would have never known. You have such a noble mission. And you have a very powerful message. I shall pray that the Father will give you many more years in which to tell your story to many more people. Everyone needs deliverance. Everyone needs forgiveness." Rahab paused and looked deeply into the man's tired eyes. "So, how are you doing now? Now that you are making your gift — telling your story?"

"Very well, actually. I still have no home, no family, and very few possessions. I stay on the move from one place to another, telling my story to whoever will listen. Things are not important to me anymore. My family seems to be the people who help me get from one place to another. I'm finding a lot of good people out there. I hope to leave even more good people behind when I leave a town."

"What a beautiful thing to say. What have you found to be your most difficult task so far?"

"You know, I'm often asked that question. In the early years, I would say it was trying to survive in the desert. Starvation is a terrible way to live. But later, I began to rethink that and have decided that the hardest thing is to find a way to forgive yourself. Others can forgive you. God can forgive you. But only you can forgive yourself. That is the most difficult for me."

"That has been true in my life. I'm always haunted by old memories of bad times. I can always remember when I was deficient in something. Then I realize that those are things that I have not forgiven myself. Forgiveness is never easy." Rahab turned away from the old man to look out the window as she reflected on her own life.

"I should be going, Miss Rahab, the wind has died down now. You are very kind to let me spend this time with you."

"Let me get you something to eat to take with you. Obed, honey, will you prepare a lunch sack for this man to take with him?"

"Sure, what should I put in it?"

Rahab looked at the old man across from her. He just shrugged his shoulders. "Obed, just make the lunch sack, like you were going to eat it."

"O.K." Obed could be heard moving about in the cooking alcove, opening and closing doors and filling a cloth bag that Rahab kept for carrying things. Then he brought it into the front room and handed it to the stranger.

"My, how generous you are." The old man was surprised.

"Oh, its just lunch," the teenager said.

"I haven't had a teenager's lunch in 50 years," he said. "But I thank you for it." And the old man was smiling.

"I put in two of her date cakes because Grandma makes them kinda small, but they're real good."

"Then, I may have to start with them," and Jacob's eyes were twinkling.

Rahab stood up and so did her guest. They went to the door and she opened it for him. He turned to her and said very quietly, "The Lord bless you and keep you. May He cause His light to shine upon you and give you peace."

"And also to you," Rahab returned the blessing and watched the old man walk slowly out the door, looking for the next place God would send him.

Rahab grew old and wrinkled, but therein lay her beauty. No one seemed to see her flabby arms, fallen breasts or protruding tummy. The people only saw her beautiful smile, her silver hair, and her warm heart. They felt her little thin arms around them every time she greeted them. Most were amazed at her strength. Everyone loved Rahab because she loved them first and that too was her beauty. They said that in her eyes you could see God.

On her good days, she went over to the area where children came to play. At the edge of the area was a big rock by the palm trees. Sometimes Rahab would sit on the rock to watch the children. On the crisp winter days when the breeze was chilly, she would bring a heavy robe and warp up in it as she enjoyed the refreshing breezes.

One day one of the boys brought over a little statue. He told everyone it was a god to help him win the ball game. But when Rahab saw the idol, she called the boy over and explained that the idol was not a god, but only a hindrance to him. It would not help him win the game; instead it put his whole person in jeopardy. As the others gathered around, she told them how God was offended by fake gods. Having idols could cost them their lives.

The visits became less frequent and through the summer when the children were playing the most, Rahab came less and less. One day, one of the bigger boys was missing her and went to her door to see why. A tired old woman answered the door after a long wait. She opened the door a little and said "Y-e-s?" It was long and drawn out, in the typical Rahab fashion.

"We've been missing you at the playground" the boy said. "Will you come out and play with us? Will you tell us another story?"

Rahab had not been well. Today she was a little stronger, but very weak. They bargained that if the boy helped her and with her walking cane, she would try. Everything seemed dark to her. The boy insisted it was daylight. Early afternoon, in fact. It still seemed dark to Rahab. She leaned heavily on him and they made their way to the rock. Another boy came to help their friend find the way. Rahab told them a story about taking the Ark of the Covenant to Shiloh and the excitement of the journey up the side of the mountains and down into the valley beyond. She relayed how Joshua stabbed the air with his long, crooked finger and told everyone to love God Almighty. The children applauded her account of the old man with long silver hair and sang her a song praising God, as had become their custom.

Rahab shivered from a sudden chill and began to fall limp. One of the bigger boys held her up while another child ran to Boaz's house nearby. "Something is wrong with the old woman."

Boaz rushed out the door to find his mother gasping for breath. He picked up her little, frail body and took her back to her house and sent another child to bring Ruth. Rahab whispered to her son that she loved him. Boaz's face was filled with tears and with tears in his voice he told his mother that he loved her too. *More now than ever.* And the angels took her home.

They placed Rahab in the hillside grave behind her house with the flat roof. It was where Salmon's body lay. All the rest of her generation had preceded her. She had outlived her parents, her brother Olmad and his wife, and even her little sisters. An era was passing.

As they laid her in the grave, some recalled their favorite experiences with Rahab and they all sang a song praising God for their time with her. Boaz and Ruth each took a hand full of dirt and sprinkled it in the doorway of the sepulcher.

Her grandson, Obed, went to the front of the group standing at the entrance and opened a scroll. He said, "These are some writings from my grandmother that I believe are appropriate to share with you at this time." The tall teenager with the big feet was nervous. "I've never imagined my standing here to give tribute to my grandmother. It makes me sad." Then after a little pause, he continued, "These are things she says she has learned through the years." He held up the little scroll and began to read. He read slowly.

• You praise God by the way you live your life.

• You bring glory to God when you love people as He has loved you.

• The greatest joy in life is serving others.

• Tending to a neighbor's wound is a holy act.

• A hug is worth a thousand handshakes.

• Praise God in the morning and feel His love all day.

• God can forgive you, but you must forgive yourself.

• God blesses you with every breath you take.

• Sunrise is God's first gift of the day.

• A person's noblest act is to love an unlovable person, for that is how God loves you."

The young man looked up at the crowd standing in front of the grave site. He shuffled from one foot to the other and then said, "Grandmother also leaves this message behind:

'Carry me to the grave and lay me in the darkness. I do not mind, for I am not afraid.

'Carry me to your grave. I do not need your light for I have God's light to guide me.

'Carry me to the grave and lay me in the dust for I am not here. I have gone on. I have passed on to be with the others in God's natural plan of things. But I am also with you. That is the miracle of the Transition. To be eternal — without time constraints, without distance or physical constraints. Although you can't see me, you will know that I am with you. For this is the land that has been promised from the beginning. This is the life that has been promised from the beginning. This is what life is all about.'"

Obed bowed his head and brushed his eye with the corner of his colorful sash. The sash his grandmother had made him.

A baritone voice softly began singing slowly "Ahhh - men. Ahhhh - men." And a tenor joined in harmony on top of the single word melody. And then a few sopranos joined on top of the men's voices. Finally, just as the phrase was about to begin again, the bases filled in the foundation of the chords and the "Amens" were lifted to heaven all over again.

"Rahab. Rahab. Over here, darling." The familiar voice was filled with love.

"Salmon! It is so good to hear your voice again. Where are we?"

"In a good place, darling. A very good place."

"Welcome, my daughter."

"Father!" And Rahab saw him running towards her with his arms outstretched. She hugged him just as a woman's voice was calling to her.

"Rahab, dear. I didn't know you had come."

"I know, Mother. I just got here."

A receiving line was forming. All of her relatives and old friends were lining up to give her hugs and welcoming kisses. One tall figure reached out quietly and with a single finger drew a pathway down her cheek. "Jonathan."

"Welcome," he said softly. "We've been waiting for you." And he hugged her with mountains of love.

"Ma'am, you are sure some fighter."

"Ari El, oh, give me a hug," Rahab grabbed up the man and cherished the light in his delightful face.

And the line continued to pass in front of her. "Remember when you taught me to read?"

"You shared your recipes and taught us to cook."

"Your kind voice taught us patience and love."

"You taught us forgiveness and mercy by the troubles that came into your own life."

Salmon continued to stand beside her with his arm around her waist. As the line finished passing in front of them, he said, "Let us go home."

"Does it have strong walls, and windows with draperies and a flat roof?" Rahab asked her husband.

"Better than that. Better than that," he whispered to her.

The little group standing outside the tomb in Bethlehem started yet another round of the sevenfold Amen song. Only this time they were joined by a thousand invisible angels, and then by 10 thousand arch angles, and then by the heavenly hosts. The Woman with the Scarlet Cord was gone, but not her legacy. She will always be remembered whenever the story of the Promised Land is told. And because of the teachings she provided to her descendants, she will also be remembered for what was to come. You will find hints of her teachings throughout the Old Testament. Just as God called His people into the Promised Land, so He calls new generations into a new land of promise, where there will be singing and praising all day long; where there will be no sickness, no wars, no armies, and no separations. God's people will be around Him forever and ever.

And so, let it be spoken; let it be written:
When Rahab and Salmon were married they had a son named Boaz.

And Boaz married Ruth and they had a son named Obed.

Obed had a son named Jesse, and Jesse was the father of the great King David.

David had a son named Solomon, who broadened the kingdom of Israel and made it one of the richest kingdoms in the whole world.

And King Solomon had sons and grandsons and heirs that through the centuries led to another man named Jacob, whose son was named Joseph.

And Joseph was engaged to Mary. However, before they could be married, Mary was blessed by God and had a son named Jesus, born in Bethlehem, not far from where Salmon and Rahab had lived 1400 years before.

And to this day, through the lineage of Rahab and Salmon, we celebrate the life and teachings of Jesus, who is called

The Christ,
Lord of Lords,
Prince of Peace,
Emanuel,
King of Kings,
Savior of the World,
and Son of God.

Epilog

Here are some things we learn from this story about Rahab:

1.   God always hears our prayers. There are no requirements or specifications to qualify to talk with God Almighty. He is our Father and our Creator. Therefore, God is always listening for us to call on Him. Holy Scripture often uses unusual people in unusual circumstances to teach a simple truth. Here is a prostitute, surrounded by idols, calling for a God she does not know. And God heard her! And God granted her request. And God hears you.

2.   God always answers when we are ready for His answer. God holds all the strings and can grant anything He pleases. There is biblical evidence that God answers our request when we are capable of receiving His answer. God likely could have sent another spy into the Jericho walls to teach Rahab but instead He chose to make her a part of the overall plan of taking the whole land of Canaan away from the idol worshipers and fulfilling His promise to Abraham. God could have sent a fast reply to rescue Rahab from the small cave, or end the 10-year drought by the weekend, or spared the life of Salmon for more years. He could have done it just as He provided fast replies when He made the sun and moon stand still on the longest day, and opened the Jordan River on cue, and caused the hail stones to fall on the idol worshipers and not Joshua's army. When Rahab first cried out, God did not just save her from Jericho; He was saving her to a place in history - something she could never imagine. God has great blessings for those who are prepared to receive them.

3.   Regardless of our past lives, God is ready to forgive and save us by His grace. Almost every human character in the Bible had some deficiency. Noah got drunk. Moses murdered someone. Jacob was a thief. Rahab, a prostitute. In the New Testament, Paul was a murderer, Peter a liar, etc. But God took all of them and did marvelous things with them when they gave themselves to the mercy of the Creator. God is not nearly as interested in your past as He is in your present and what you can become in His great love and grace. He holds your future in His hands.

4.   God's strength is greater than any situation we may find

ourselves in. We have a tendency to look for solutions in the terms we understand. The flooding Jordan was a natural barrier against the Jericho enemies. But God just removed the waters and His people walked across. For 2000 years all the enemies of Jericho had to deal with the mighty walls and the heavy gate that guarded the city. But they were not important to God. When problems come into our lives, God has a solution that can break any barrier – if we are ready to receive it. First, we must tell God about our problem and then prepare our hearts to receive His response. God can always make a way where there seems to be no way.

5.   You love God by loving people – including yourself. This is the strongest principle in the entire Bible, except for the rule "You shall have no other gods before me." People show their lack of love for others by stealing from them, coveting their possessions, killing them, or otherwise hurting them. However, when people love other people who are difficult to love, then they are expressing the love of God and God blesses both parties. When you recognize that you are a creation of the Almighty and He lives in you, then how you treat yourself as well as the other creations of God, then you are loving God. When you offer the simple gifts of food or a cup of cold water you are expressing godly love.

6.   You are precious in his sight. You are a product of God's love. He flows in your blood stream. He lives in your brain. He holds your soul close to His breast. You are worthy of His challenges in your life, because God loves you.

Resources

The Rahab Chronicles is a retelling of the Book of *Joshua*. It is told from the viewpoint of Rahab. Considerable research has been done in order to make the known facts the foundation of this story. The story of Abraham and Jacob is found in *Genesis* beginning in Chapter 12. The story of Moses is captured in the book of *Exodus*. The story of Ruth and Naomi is in the book of *Ruth*. The statistics of the sizes of armies, cities, and census of the Israelites is found in *Leviticus, Deuteronomy*, and *Numbers*. Additional resources include the *Works of Josephus* and several Bible dictionaries, concordances, commentaries, and histories. However, conversations and certain sequences and events are fictional in order to tie the story together. However, the overall message is genuine.

Breinigsville, PA USA
10 June 2010
239493BV00001B/1/P